Praise for the Novels
of Cheryl Robinson

When I Get Where I'm Going

"A wonderfully entertaining read."

—*New York Times* bestselling author Kimberla Lawson Roby

"The story flowed effortlessly as the author proved once again her ability to get inside the hearts of her characters. . . . Cheryl Robinson brings readers still another winning novel about the things that make us who we are, the things that give us hope and joy in being sisters." —African American Literature Book Club

In Love with a Younger Man

"A thought-provoking and entertaining novel. Robinson puts a very modern spin on May/December relationships. . . . This story is full of humor and some unexpected twists that could possibly lead to a sequel. *In Love with a Younger Man* is a wonderful contemporary story about relationships that can be enjoyed by all."

—Urban Reviews

"Robinson won me over as a fan with *Sweet Georgia Brown*, and, as I anticipated, she didn't disappoint with the stunning Olena. . . . I was snagged from the beginning and gracefully led through a torrid romance riddled with themes of self-discovery and women's empowerment. Robinson's smooth writing style enhanced an emotionally profound tale that will speak to women who battle issues of self-worth. . . . *In Love with a Younger Man* was thought-provoking with a clever mix of romance and suspense." —SistahFriend Book Club

"Emotions will run the gamut, as this is a rocky ride, which does not end on the last page."

—Rawsistaz

"In a straightforward and entertaining tale, Robinson delivers what she promises."

—*Publishers Weekly*

"Fans will appreciate this deep, character-driven contemporary romance, as few protagonists are as developed as Olena is." —*Midwest Book Review*

continued . . .

Sweet Georgia Brown

"Will keep you laughing and cheering for Georgia. It will evoke some teary eyes, but more than anything else, *Sweet Georgia Brown* will win your heart and soul."

—Rawsistaz

"Robinson's writing is filled with humor and the revealing, touching moments of everyday life. Women everywhere will cheer." —*Romantic Times*

"Fabulous . . . readers will appreciate this fine tale of transformation."

—*Midwest Book Review*

"What could have started out as a rags-to-riches story becomes a lot more complex as Robinson shows the other side of the riches, and that true happiness comes from the inside of the heart, not the inside of a bank."

—Rachel Kramer Bussel, author of *Peep Show*

"*Sweet Georgia Brown* is a novel that will make women stand up and cheer."

—Idrissa Ugdah, African American Literature Book Club

And Further Praise for Cheryl Robinson
and Her Novels

"A gifted writer, one of the best among contemporary African American novelists."

—Book Remarks

"A stunning character study." —*Midwest Book Review*

"Laugh-out-loud snappy dialogue, compelling plot twists, and heart-feeling, genuine characters." —Cydney Rax

"Fresh and exciting." —*The Charlotte Post*

"A compelling read." —Rawsistaz

"Had me spellbound." —Nubian Sistas Book Club, Inc.

"Cheryl Robinson . . . writes stories that entertain while giving the reader something to think about. Get lost in this complicated love story. You'll love it!"

—BlackLiterature.com

Also by Cheryl Robinson

When I Get Where I'm Going

In Love with a Younger Man

Sweet Georgia Brown

It's Like That

If It Ain't One Thing

Remember Me

Cheryl Robinson

NAL NEW AMERICAN LIBRARY

NEW AMERICAN LIBRARY
Published by New American Library, a division of Penguin Group (USA) Inc.,
375 Hudson Street, New York, New York 10014, USA
Penguin Group (Canada), 90 Eglinton Avenue East, Suite 700, Toronto,
Ontario M4P 2Y3, Canada (a division of Pearson Penguin Canada Inc.)
Penguin Books Ltd., 80 Strand, London WC2R 0RL, England
Penguin Ireland, 25 St. Stephen's Green, Dublin 2,
Ireland (a division of Penguin Books Ltd.)
Penguin Group (Australia), 250 Camberwell Road, Camberwell, Victoria 3124,
Australia (a division of Pearson Australia Group Pty. Ltd.)
Penguin Books India Pvt. Ltd., 11 Community Centre, Panchsheel Park,
New Delhi - 110 017, India
Penguin Group (NZ), 67 Apollo Drive, Rosedale, Auckland 0632,
New Zealand (a division of Pearson New Zealand Ltd.)
Penguin Books (South Africa) (Pty.) Ltd., 24 Sturdee Avenue, Rosebank,
Johannesburg 2196, South Africa

Penguin Books Ltd., Registered Offices:
80 Strand, London WC2R 0RL, England

First published by New American Library,
a division of Penguin Group (USA) Inc.

First Printing, August 2011
10 9 8 7 6 5 4 3 2 1

LIBRARY OF CONGRESS CATALOGING-IN-PUBLICATION DATA:

Robinson, Cheryl.
Remember me/Cheryl Robinson.
p. cm.
ISBN 978-0-451-23338-7
1. Interracial friendship—Fiction. 2. Female friendship—Fiction. 3. Psychological fiction. I. Title.
PS3618.O323R46 2011
813'.6—dc22 2011009676

Set in Bulmer MT
Designed by Alissa Amell

Printed in the United States of America

To Pepper

A good friend is a connection to life—a tie to the past, a road to the future, the key to sanity in a totally insane world.

—Lois Wyse

Remember Me

Prologue

November 2010

Disheveled and appearing frail, Mia Marks-Glitch rushed through the automatic sliding glass doors of the hospital with a powerfully built man by her side. The worst day of her life had arrived, and came with little advance notice. Her husband, Frank, had been arrested earlier that day—something she and Frank knew would be coming sooner rather than later. But now their daughter was in the hospital. After being involved in a horrific chain-reaction car accident on Interstate 94 on her way back to the University of Michigan the day after Thanksgiving. And Mia couldn't help but blame herself. If she hadn't treated Alexa's company so badly at Thanksgiving dinner, Alexa wouldn't have felt forced to leave early, and none of this would've happened. At least that's how Mia saw things. But there was still the young woman on the interstate that needed to take responsibility for what she'd done. According to the news report, it was believed that the woman had been texting while driving.

In an instant, so many lives had been changed. Six fatalities had been confirmed. But the names of those who perished in the crash hadn't been released to the public yet. And Mia was about to find out if her daughter was among the living or the dead. She felt light-headed, as if blood was draining from her head. The lobby was spinning. She was dizzy as she held on to the man beside her. One more thing when she didn't have the strength to handle all the others. They rushed over to the first person they saw—a young woman sitting behind a desk with a phone pressed against her ear, transferring one call after another to patients' rooms.

"Please, can you help me? I really need to know where my daughter is."

"What's your daughter's name?" the woman asked as she hung up the phone.

"Alexandria Glitch."

As the woman checked her computer, Mia grabbed the lapel of the man standing beside her and buried her head in his chest. He wasn't her husband, but rather the man she had hoped would fill that role.

"I need to have the doctor speak with you."

"Please tell me something. Is she alive?" Mia asked as her eyes welled up with tears.

The woman picked up the receiver and dialed the doctor, signaling for Mia to wait a second.

"Can you just tell me what condition she's listed in?" Mia asked the woman. "Are you talking to the doctor?" The woman nodded. "May I speak to him?"

After the young woman hung up the phone, she said, "The doctor is on his way down to speak with you now."

Mia's head dropped and her eyes closed. She said a silent prayer. After calling her daughter for hours and being sent directly to voice mail, Mia, sensing something was wrong, turned on the news to search for answers. That's when she learned of the terrible accident. When the station showed some footage, she thought she may have recognized one of the cars involved. At the time, no names had been released because authorities were still working on contacting the relatives. She called 911 to find out what hospital the victims had been taken to. Then she had phoned Lamont to ask if he'd drive her there. He arrived shortly after two Michigan state troopers appeared on her doorstep, informing her that her daughter was in the hospital and that her condition was unknown at that time.

"I'll be right back," Lamont said to Mia. "I need to move my car so it won't get towed. Are you going to be okay by yourself for a few minutes?"

"Yes—just hurry back."

Mia dropped her head after he rushed through the sliding glass doors.

"What's taking the doctor so long?" Mia asked the woman.

"He should be down any second, ma'am," the woman said as she turned her head in the direction of the elevators. "Here he is."

Mia focused on the elevator door that had just opened. A doctor exited with a slender blonde by his side. Mia didn't recognize the woman's face at first. Not until she came closer into view and Mia was able to look into her ice-blue eyes. Twenty years had passed, and Danielle King looked like a stranger. At one time, she was more than a friend—she was her best friend. And if not for the fact that Mia had seen her face more than a dozen times on the jackets of hardcover books, she might not have been able to distinguish her from any other blond-haired, middle-aged white woman.

Danielle hadn't looked in Mia's direction yet. So she wasn't aware that the woman she'd never apologized to was staring at her—watching her every move and wondering what had brought her there. As the doctor came closer to Mia, Danielle's focus shifted from his face to Mia's. When their eyes met, Danielle cocked her head to the side the same way her dog Pulitzer used to when he didn't understand something.

"Mia? What are you doing here?"

"My daughter was involved in an accident. Why are you here?"

Danielle's face blanched. "For the same reason."

Part One

Memory Lane

Chapter One

December 1976

Mia Marks snuggled inside her green parka with orange lining and faux fur around the hood. After she reclined back in her velour seat, she closed her eyes as the school bus headed west on Seven Mile Road, passing over Livernois, the "Avenue of Fashion." They were minutes from the dry cleaner's where Mia's mother worked as a seamstress.

She needed to rest so she could get ready for whatever the school day might have in store. She wouldn't have been as tired if she hadn't wasted her entire weekend at that stupid retreat in Holland, Michigan. She could've sworn Holland was the headquarters for the KKK—or maybe that was Howell. It was one of those Hs. And now she was back on the same chartered SEMTA bus heading to Our Lady of Glory High School, and all that hate.

Mia's eyes flashed open as the bus passed the University of Detroit High School. Why couldn't U of D be coed? she wondered. That would've solved a lot of her problems. Not just because it was less than ten minutes away from her home and she wouldn't have to contend with a long bus ride. She probably wouldn't have had to ride the bus at all, since her mother could've easily driven Mia to school on her way to work. Chris and his brother, Mark, and some of the cutest guys she knew went there, while she was forced to attend Our Lady of Glory. And so far, the only good thing about Our Lady of Glory was their school buses. They weren't like the yellow buses with the stiff seats and no air-conditioning that she used to ride to and from Holy Angels Catholic School. Where the windows were so hard to open, she was afraid she might chop off a few of her fingers if she tried. Glory's buses were like the one her church chartered to take the youth group to Cedar Point each summer, and every weekday morning she rode this one 17.8 miles from her northwest Detroit home to Farmington Hills, which was a short distance, but worlds apart.

She had always wanted to attend Cass Technical High School, which was a citywide college-preparatory school. But after Mia's parents were called and had to go up to Holy Angels after Mia had gotten in trouble, Mia's wants no longer mattered. During a trip to the science center in Toronto, Sister Ellen, her seventh-grade science teacher, said she'd seen Mia and Chris sitting in the back of the train with a blanket covering their laps up to their waists, and she couldn't see their hands. Which was true, but only because they were warming them underneath the blanket. But Mia's parents didn't buy that. So they'd made up their minds that she was too "fast" to go to a high school with boys and that she was going to an all-girls high school. After learning that her parents wouldn't allow her to go to her school of choice all because of a misunderstanding, Mia started having recurring dreams. In them, Our Lady of Glory was a maximum-security women's prison that Mia had successfully escaped from. She'd always wake up as she was entering the main entrance to Cass Tech.

One thing Mia was certain of was that if she had gone to Cass, she wouldn't have had to attend that weekend retreat, which was mandatory for all black freshmen and the few whites who were involved in the cafeteria fight. It had been voluntary for everyone else. All total there were 50 girls present and 10 members of the faculty.

Mia's freshman class brought 34 blacks, which seemed like a lot compared with the year before, when there were only 8 in the entire school. But in actuality, it was small in comparison with the 472 white freshmen. At Cass Tech there were a thousand incoming freshmen, the majority of which were black, which meant there would probably never be an incident in the cafeteria where a fight would ensue because a black girl accidently bumped into a white girl, which was exactly what had happened at Glory.

The white girl had called the black girl the N-word, and fists started flying between the two. Their friends immediately jumped in. Mia wasn't raised to be prejudiced, but she wasn't raised to be subservient either. So even though she didn't know the black girl very well, she still came to her aid. To Mia, it was the principle that mattered. A white girl calling a black girl the N-word was the equivalent of calling every black girl at Glory that horrible name. Mia had gone to school with whites from kindergarten through the eighth grade, and they'd all gotten along well enough. There were no interracial sleepovers or anything even remotely close to that, but she never remembered any name-calling either. So she could only assume that city whites and suburban whites were altogether different. Whites who lived in Detroit were used to being around black people. Those from the suburbs weren't, and it was obvious that they didn't want to get used to being around them either.

The bus ride to Glory took thirty minutes. Mia wished it could've taken longer, because she wasn't in any rush to get to the one-story building. For one thing, she hated algebra, her first-period class. And today they had a test. It definitely didn't help matters that Mr. Carter, her math teacher, went to the retreat and admitted that he was prejudiced. The counselors there had set the ground rules before starting. Whatever was said that weekend would not be used against anyone—including faculty, which was why Mia assumed Mr. Carter felt comfortable enough to let his whole truth out.

Mr. Carter was there because of an incident that had occurred a few days before the cafeteria fight in which he'd also called one of his black students the N-word. Several of the black students' parents came to the school to complain about Mr. Carter and demand that he be fired. Instead, he was reprimanded and ordered to attend the students' retreat. And that was the only reason he was there. He'd shared his deep-rooted feelings about blacks and his belief that they were inferior to whites, not as smart, and that most of the black students were there only because their tuition was being subsidized. Mia's tuition wasn't and neither was her friend Bridgette's. She couldn't speak for anyone else, but she wasn't sure why it mattered. He'd also said they were loud and disrespectful, and didn't try as hard as the white students. Even though Mia had gotten an A on every one of her algebra quizzes. But that didn't matter to Mr. Carter either.

"Miss Marks, your time is up," Mr. Carter said as he rested the backs of his legs against the front of his desk and folded his arms and peered at her.

"I have ten more minutes," Mia said, glancing up at the wall clock.

"It's a timed test. And as you can see, everyone else has finished."

She sighed heavily before handing him the test.

"I saw that," he said.

"Saw what?"

"You were rolling your eyes at me."

Mia snickered. "I didn't roll my eyes."

"Are you saying I'm lying?"

"I just know my eyes didn't roll. So you can interpret my words any way you wish. Just like I can interpret what you said at the retreat any way I wish."

"You people are unbelievable," he sputtered before snatching the paper from her hand and walking away. She thought about what her father had said when she'd called her parents on Saturday to ask them to pick her up from the retreat. "The world isn't all black, Mia. And it's about time you learned that. We sent you to that school so you can get used to dealing with those white people. So stop whining and deal with 'em. You got a mouth, and they got feelings just like you. If they say something to hurt you, open your mouth and defend yourself."

But if the white girls at Glory had feelings, Mia sure couldn't tell. And she couldn't deal with what some of them were saying about blacks either. "We don't all love watermelon and fried chicken," Mia had responded angrily after one student at the retreat said that was the only thing she knew about blacks. She wanted to leave the retreat so badly, she considered hitchhiking after her father told her there was no way in hell he was driving all the way to Holland just to get her. And if she wasn't so scared that she was in KKK territory, she might have.

As Mia left the classroom, she spotted a white girl in the hallway looking shyly at her. She had frizzy blond hair pulled into a ponytail, and an odd-looking pair of iridescent brown framed eyeglasses with silver-tone accents. Mia couldn't remember her name, though she recognized her from algebra class and the retreat. But then another white girl passed and called the girl Danny, and Mia remembered that her name was Danielle, and "Danny" must've been a nickname.

They'd never spoken before the retreat. They'd been grouped

into fours and Danielle was in Mia's group with another black girl and white girl. Danielle was nicer than the other white girl. But after what had just transpired with Mr. Carter, the last thing Mia wanted to see was another white face.

"How did you do on the test?" Danielle asked.

"How do you think I did? I was the last to finish, wasn't I?" Mia asked sarcastically.

"Oh, I just thought you were being thorough and double-checking your answers."

"That test seemed more like advanced algebra to me. I probably failed it."

Danielle wrinkled her brow in confusion. "It was like our last two quizzes. Actually, it was exactly like our last two quizzes, except with a few new problems."

Mia stopped walking. "Our last two quizzes? No, it wasn't. I wouldn't complain if that was the case, because I got an A on our last two quizzes."

"I can show you if you have your last quiz with you."

Mia pulled out her algebra folder, took out the last quiz, and looked it over before handing it to Danielle. "None of those questions were on the test."

"Yes, they were."

"No, they weren't. I know what was on there."

"Unless he gave you a different test," Danielle said jokingly.

Mia was quiet for a moment while she considered the possibility. She was the only black girl in his class that period. It was obvious he didn't like her. She thought about what he'd said at the retreat. "It wouldn't surprise me if he did." What surprised Mia was that Danielle agreed, on the spot, to go to the principal's office as a witness for Mia in the complaint she wanted to file against Mr. Carter.

"If what you two are saying is true," Sister Maureen, the principal, said, "it would be grossly negligent on the part of Mr. Carter, and highly unethical." She shook her head. "I take this accusation quite seriously. Why would he even do such a thing?"

"Because he's prejudiced," Mia said.

"Whatever was said at the retreat shouldn't be brought up here," Sister Maureen said sternly when Mia tried to tell her what Mr. Carter had said. "However, I will definitely look into this matter expeditiously. And if Mr. Carter has done this, I will decide my next course of action and inform you ladies within the next day or two."

One week later, after a three-day suspension, Mr. Carter was fired and replaced with Mrs. Stein, Our Lady of Glory's first black teacher. She was strict. You couldn't enter her class a minute late. She expected full participation, which meant she would call most of her students to the board to solve a homework problem. And they had homework every night, and quizzes once a week. Her tests were longer than Mr. Carter's, but for Mia they were easier. Because now she had the same test that everyone else did. None of the students, black or white, liked Mrs. Stein. And of course it was their fault—Mia's and Danielle's. But just because they were united as outcasts didn't mean Mia wanted to be Danielle's best friend. Besides, Mia's friends got over it after a few days and she was back in the cafeteria playing bid whist. Danielle's friends seemed to hold a grudge a whole lot longer, so when she came to the cafeteria, she usually sat alone.

Mia put her out of her mind, but she couldn't help wondering about the peculiar white girl now and then.

June 2010

A woman entered the private room of Ocean Prime restaurant in Troy carrying a box with colorful gift bags sticking out—mostly red, a few light blue, and some green ones. From a distance, the woman looked nothing like her author photo. Mia had propped the woman's latest paperback up on a small plastic stand as part of the table's centerpiece. A book Mia had to force herself to read since she'd invited the local author—mainly through the author's persistence—to her book club meeting to discuss it. This was a busy time for Mia, so the only breaks she took for reading were when she was sitting under the dryer at the hairdresser once a week. But her hair was so short that it dried quickly and didn't leave her with much time to read.

Even then, as the meeting was getting under way, so many things were running through her mind. This was their last book club meeting before the Sophisticated Readers of Oakland County went on their summer hiatus. And Mia's daughter had just graduated two days before. The next day was her daughter's baccalaureate mass.

Her husband had flown to Chicago for another business meeting right after their daughter's graduation. He spent almost as much time there as he did in Detroit.

Now Mia was squeezing in dinner with the fifty-member book club and an author none of them had ever heard of. She felt like she was trying to do too much. But she couldn't cancel. She was the one who'd been corresponding with the author via Facebook, since she was responsible for keeping the book club's Facebook wall updated. She was also left with the daunting task of responding to the overwhelming number of messages they received from authors. Many of which she ignored. Because in truth she knew her book club's tastes. The Sophisticated Readers of Oakland County were extremely picky with their selections. If the author's novel wasn't a *New York Times* bestseller, an Oprah's Book Club selection, or favorably reviewed by a well-known publication, such as the *New York Times*, then chances were slimmer than none that the author's book would make their hardcover-only reading list. And that was beginning to bother Mia. She was the one who had to find a polite way to tell authors, "We're not interested." And so far, the easiest way was to say nothing at all.

"It's not that we're being snobs," Viv, the president of the Sophisticated Readers, had said after Mia suggested they relax their criteria a bit, "but we have to be selective. I can count on one hand the number of self-published authors I've read in the last year and I'd have four fingers left over. And the only reason I read that book was because the author teaches at my school, and he bugged me almost every day wanting to know what I thought."

Now they were sitting with an author who didn't have a clue how unenthused many of the members were about her. Viv put on a big smile after she pushed her large prescription frames farther up her nose and said, "Welcome. We are so honored to have you here with us this evening." But that didn't mean much. Because if there was one thing Viv did well, it was smile when she didn't truly mean it. She would've made a great politician.

Mia had known Viv for twenty-four years, which was longer than she'd known her own husband. Mia and Viv had both taught at Pershing High School in Detroit, where Mia had been teaching for two years when Viv started. They quickly became friends, even though they were complete opposites. Mia made it her hobby to keep abreast of fashion trends, and she was usually the one informing coworkers of sales at high-end retailers. Viv couldn't care less whose name was on the tag. She didn't even shop that much. She didn't go for the trendy attire. She purchased clothes that would last, and some of the clothes she wore she'd been wearing for the past ten years. Viv liked to focus on getting ahead. Her hard work had paid off so far—she was the principal at a charter school in Detroit.

Mia stood and greeted the author with a friendly hug before walking her around the large table and introducing her to twenty-eight of their members. The woman was tall. Mia, who was barely five feet tall but compensated by wearing five-inch heels all day every day, had to tilt her head when looking at the author.

Most of them were cordial. A few barely made eye contact. Two others were talking about how they couldn't wait for Terry McMillan's *Waiting to Exhale* sequel, *Getting to Happy,* which was to be released in September.

"I can't wait for that either," the author said. "She's my favorite author."

The two ladies gave her a halfhearted smile before turning toward each other and continuing their conversation.

Mia had the author sit beside her and tried to make her feel as comfortable as possible.

"I'm so excited," the young woman said. "This is my first time meeting with such a large group to discuss my novel. Thank you so much for this opportunity."

Mia patted her hand and smiled. "It's my pleasure." Mia saw the hope in the author's eyes, and thought of Danielle. She could remember seeing that same gleam in her friend's eyes after she'd told Mia about the manuscript she'd just completed. That was over twenty-three years ago. "I want to leave my mark before I die—something that will live on long after me. I refuse to be an average person," Danielle had said. At the time, Mia felt her friend was being melodramatic, as Danielle often was. But days later, after she'd read the manuscript, Mia had told her she had a bestseller on her hands.

"I hope you remember me after you become famous," Mia had said.

"How could I forget my best friend?" Danielle had said with a broad grin.

But many things had changed since then, and Mia sadly brushed the memory away.

After the book club meeting, Mia called her husband's cell phone from the hands-free unit in her Mercedes. He didn't answer, so she tried again when she was five minutes away from their home. He picked up.

"Sorry I didn't answer the last time. I was in the shower."

"I just want to make sure you're going to be home tomorrow in time for Alexa's mass." The last couple of times he'd gone out of town on business, he'd missed his return flight. Once because he'd overslept, and the other time because the meeting he was in had run long. Mia didn't want anything preventing Frank from attending their daughter's baccalaureate mass.

"Baby, of course, this was just a quick trip. I'll be there. How was your book club meeting?"

"It was okay."

"Just okay?"

"As usual not everyone showed up. And the discussion wasn't all that great either, which happens when people don't read the book. But the food was good. And I like having a monthly outing.

I just wish we had more participation. Maybe I'll join an online book club too. . . ."

"That would be nice for you. If anyone can handle being in two book clubs, it's you. You'll have more free time on your hands after Alexa goes away to college. And since I'm always away on business . . ."

"You're right," Mia said after giving it a moment's thought. "I should do it. Books will keep me busy." She laughed. "Can you believe I'm considering joining an online book club?"

"No, not the woman who wishes it was still 1976 and the computer hadn't been invented."

"Make that 1980 . . . even though the fashions were horrible then. And it's not computers I have a problem with—"

"The Internet."

"No, not even the Internet . . . just the void. I mean, even with as much technology as we have now, people aren't any happier."

"Baby, why would technology make someone happy?"

"There's an app for everything."

He laughed. "That's true."

Just then, a woman sang out in the background, "Look what I found."

Mia froze. "Who was that?"

"What?"

"I heard a woman's voice."

"It was the TV."

"Frank, that didn't sound like the TV, and if it was the TV, why don't I hear it anymore?"

"Because I muted the sound."

"Take it off mute."

"Why?"

"Take it off mute. That didn't sound like a TV to me."

"How does a TV sound when you're talking over a cell phone?"

"That was a woman, Frank, and you know it."

"Yes, it was a woman on the TV."

"No, that was a woman in your hotel room."

"You honestly think I have a woman in my room?"

"Yes, I honestly do."

Frank took a deep sigh. "I don't know how to respond to that. I guess I'll see you tomorrow."

"Why are you rushing me off the phone?"

"I'm not rushing you off the phone."

"You are."

"Mia, we can talk all night if you like. I'll probably fall asleep on you, but if it'll make you feel better . . ."

"No, that's okay, because it won't. I know what I heard," she said before she stabbed the END button on her hands-free unit.

What would make her feel better was if she trusted her husband the way she had in the past. But as infrequently as they had sex, it was becoming harder for her to believe he was remaining faithful. She knew how men were, especially a man like her husband, who'd have sex every day if he could. And if she could, she'd never have sex again. She wasn't sure if it was all she'd gone through over the years, or the fact that she wasn't that attracted to him anymore. Within the last five years, Frank had aged noticeably. His hair had started to thin so badly he'd decided to go completely bald. But not every man had the right head shape for that look. He'd gained so much weight that his head had expanded along with his waistline, and now, without hair, he reminded Mia of Humpty Dumpty. A name she'd mumble whenever he made her mad, like he had that night.

What hadn't changed was his sense of style. He was still dapper. He still dressed better than most men in a custom suit. If there was one look that fit him well, it was the look of wealth, which was something he'd tried on for years before it finally fit. They were rich now, and had been for ten years after Frank had hit the big time with his investment firm. They had the big house and fancy cars, but all she had ever wanted, for as long as she could remember, was a man who'd love her like he meant it.

Alexa Glitch stood at the podium in the auditorium of Our Lady of Glory in her burgundy graduation gown. The first thing people noticed about Alexa was her large eyes, which defined her face. She was a beautiful and shapely young lady who stood almost six feet tall. She wore her dark hair in long layers, the longest of which fell a few inches below her shoulders. Her friends usually found someone to compare her to. She had Diana Ross's eyes; she was tall like

Venus Williams, shapely like Serena; she had Rihanna's fashion sense, and hair like Zoë Saldana.

As the class valedictorian, Alexa—Mia and Frank's only child—was selected to speak at her high school's baccalaureate mass. The four-hour service was intermixed with speeches, musical performances, drama, and worship.

By all accounts, it should've been a happy time. Thankfully, Mia was able to take a page from Viv's book and smile when she didn't mean it. At least while Frank was looking. She hadn't forgotten what she heard. But she was letting it simmer for now. Sooner or later, something would happen to bring it to a boil. She would bide her time.

Mia sat between Frank and her daughter's boyfriend, Chris, gleaming with pride for all her daughter's accomplishments: for being the class valedictorian, for being accepted on a full academic scholarship to the University of Michigan. As Mia listened to her daughter's ten-minute speech, she mouthed the words the two of them had rehearsed often.

"Good evening, faculty, family, and friends. My name is Alexandria Glitch. It was my mother's decision to have me attend Glory and follow in her footsteps. The past four years at Glory have been the best years of my life. I have met so many wonderful friends and teachers. People I plan to keep in touch with for the rest of my life . . ."

It was nice to get her mind off what was troubling her. The night before, during her self-examination, she'd felt a small lump on her left breast. She couldn't believe it. Not again, and not now. Mia had rejoiced after hitting the five-year survival mark, but the threat of recurrence was never far from her mind. She was an eight-year cancer survivor. Diagnosed with stage-one breast cancer not long after she and her family had moved into their custom-built home on the outskirts of Detroit in the tiny village of Bingham Farms. She'd opted for the breast-conserving surgery, a lumpectomy, with chemotherapy and radiation treatment. But now she wondered if she'd made the right decision. Perhaps she should've had a mastectomy instead.

"I like your new look, Mrs. Glitch," Chris whispered to her. "You look like Alexa's sister, not her mother."

"Thank you," Mia said. She'd been letting her hair grow out, but her hairstylist had talked her into going real short again, leaving the front longer with a side part and wispy bangs.

Back when Mia was going through her cancer treatments, she discovered who her true friends were—the people she could consider her family. Viv was definitely one of them, as well as a few of the other book club members who took the time to visit her and send flowers and get-well cards. It was nice to see that people cared. And disappointing that while her mother visited regularly, her father didn't come to see her once. But it was Frank who surprised her most of all. She knew he loved her, but she never thought he'd leave his successful investment firm in the hands of his two business partners for six months while he provided round-the-clock care during Mia's treatments. It was also during that time that she made the heart-wrenching decision to put down her chalk and concentrate on her survival. After seventeen years as an English teacher, she quit her job.

Now Mia was praying that the cancer hadn't returned. On Monday, she was going to talk to her doctor about scheduling a mammogram.

One week later, she was at the radiation center waiting her turn. She'd grown used to the procedure, and never found it painful when the machine compressed her small breasts between two plates.

While she waited, she rummaged through one of the magazine racks attached to the wall behind her chair. She spotted a trade publishing magazine with Danielle on the cover. She was fairly certain that once she settled into reading the article, her name would be called. And sure enough, before she could get past the first paragraph, a technician summoned her back. Mia took the magazine with her, because she knew she'd have another room to wait in before the procedure was performed.

Mia walked into a small fitting room and changed into one of the loose-fitting hospital gowns that was rolled up neatly and placed inside a wicker basket resting on a countertop. After exiting the room, she sat in one of five chairs and waited. There were three other ladies in the room ahead of her. She reopened the magazine and flipped to the page she'd dog-eared. It had been twenty years since she and Danielle had last spoken. And several years since she'd picked up one of her novels and read the acknowledgments. Not that she expected to see her name. It did amaze her that as Danielle's popularity grew, her acknowledgments shrank. What used to be five pages was now barely a page.

Mia stared at Danielle's photo. Her hair was still blond, but much shorter now and styled in a bob. She'd done away with the bifocals. Her face appeared slimmer. She looked younger than forty-eight. Maybe she had gone Hollywood like all the other rich people and had some Botox injections.

Mia was curious about what had become of Danielle's life. Had she married and had kids? Or had she turned out the way Mia had envisioned she would—single with a house full of dogs and bookshelves filled with novels of all genres? She'd checked Danielle's Web site once, years ago, but there was little mention of her personal life.

In the article, Danielle mentioned having a miniature schnauzer named Pulitzer, which reminded Mia of the one she'd given Danielle for her fifteenth birthday, after her neighbor's miniature schnauzer had five puppies.

Mia read on.

There was no mention of Danielle's immediate family or even where she lived. The last city Mia recalled Danielle living in from a bio she'd read several years earlier was Beverly Park, California, so maybe she still lived there. Danielle had always told Mia that if she ever became well-known, she planned on keeping her personal life private. "I want them to be more concerned about my characters than me." *She kept true to her word,* Mia thought. The one thing Danielle seemed to be open about was her commitment to fighting breast cancer. In the article, Danielle mentioned she'd had both of her breasts removed, which prompted Mia to flip back to the cover and check the date. It wasn't a current issue. It was from eight months earlier in October—a special breast cancer awareness issue. The year before, Danielle had elected to have a prophylactic double mastectomy along with reconstructive surgery.

"I decided to go public with this, even though I'm a very private person," Danielle was quoted as saying. "Most people wouldn't understand why someone would opt to remove their breasts before being diagnosed with breast cancer, but for me, given my family history, and watching a dear friend go through the battle and lose her life, I felt it was the best choice."

Danielle's mother had passed away from breast cancer the summer before their freshman year in high school, before Mia and Danielle had met. But Mia was by her side when her grandmother passed right before they'd graduated from college. It did surprise Mia that Danielle would remove her breasts voluntarily. Though she did remember how Danielle had always been self-conscious of how large her breasts were. She hated the way men preferred looking at her from below her neck rather than above it.

"It had gotten to the point where I was tired of waiting to find out that I had breast cancer. I felt like I was living under a cloud of fear, and I wanted my days to be sunny."

Mia tossed the magazine to the side after she heard her name called by the technician who was waiting in the hallway. She followed the woman into the room to have her mammography, and she prayed that she too would have sunny days ahead.

Mia trudged up the long, circular driveway. Four days had passed since she'd had her mammogram. She'd just come from the mailbox in front of her home and had two letters in her hand. One was from the radiologist. Another was addressed to Frank from Blue Cross and Blue Shield, and she assumed that had something to do with her. In the twenty years since they'd been married, she couldn't recall her husband's going to the doctor once. But now that he'd turned fifty, Mia had been urging him to at least have a colonoscopy.

She tore the envelope open as she walked through the eight-foot handcrafted mahogany wood door of their home.

"Frank!" Mia said, marching into the kitchen as she read the letter. He was standing near the coffeemaker pouring coffee into his stainless steel travel mug. "Our insurance was canceled for non-payment."

"That has to be a mistake," Frank said calmly.

"I don't think it is, Frank," she said as she continued reading the letter, "because it clearly states here that our policy has been revoked."

He reached out his hand. "Let me take a look at it."

"Yes, please take a look. "

She quickly handed him the letter, which he skimmed over, and then he said, "This doesn't make any sense. I'll call them when I get downtown."

"Frank, I can't wait that long. Can you please call them right now?"

"I can't call them right now, Mia." He checked his watch. "I need to leave. I'm running late."

"You know how important medical insurance is for me. I know you don't care since you never go to the doctor. Maybe you want me to die so you can move that tramp in."

"Whoa, where did that just come from?"

"I mean, you're taking a real lackadaisical I-can't-do-that-right-now attitude toward this issue."

"I said that I will take care of it as soon as I get to the office. And that's what I'm going to do." He leaned down and kissed her on the lips. "Don't stress over this. It's going to be fine. I promise."

"As soon as you get to the office, you'll call them and then call me and let me know what they said, right?"

"That's exactly what I plan to do, just as soon as I get there."

After Frank left, Mia got up the nerve to open the letter from the radiologist. But not before saying a silent prayer. If it was bad news, her doctor would've called her first. But then she remembered that, the day before, their new digital phone service had been installed by their local cable company, and it had gone out a few times.

She used her nail to rip open the flap, then removed the letter and read the contents twice before doing her happy dance.

"They didn't find anything! They didn't find anything!"

"Who didn't find anything?" Alexa asked, dragging her furry slippers across the sparkling hardwood floors.

"No one."

"Someone, or you wouldn't be dancing saying they didn't find anything. Who's the letter from, Mom?"

"Don't worry about this letter. Worry about the fact that June is almost over and all we'll have before you go away to college is two months. I can't believe that, can you? We'll have to spend every waking moment together."

"Um . . . no."

"What do you mean, 'um, no'?"

"Mom, you act like I'm leaving the state. Ann Arbor isn't even an hour away."

"You might as well be leaving the state; you're living on campus, and I won't get to see you that much unless you let me come up and visit you some weekends."

"Um . . . no."

"I'm tired of hearing that 'um . . . no.' Why not? Just tell people I'm your older sister. Chris said I looked like I was."

"Chris was being nice. Everyone will know you're my mother, so it's not happening."

The ringing phone interrupted them.

"It's the doctor's office," Alexa said after glancing down at the caller ID.

"Okay, okay, I'll get it." Mia snatched the cordless phone. "Hello."

"Hello, Mrs. Glitch, this is Dr. Okoro's office."

"Yes." Mia could hear her own heart beating.

"Dr. Okoro wanted me to call you to let you know that we have received your mammogram results and everything is normal. You should be receiving a letter in the mail from the radiologist any day."

"Thank you so much for the call. I received the letter today."

"Okay, so we'll go ahead and schedule you for another mammogram the same time next year."

"Okay, well, there was something I wanted to discuss with Dr. Okoro," Mia said while she stared across at her daughter. She walked out of the kitchen onto the deck and away from Alexa's attentive ears. "I'm considering having a mastectomy."

"I can let Dr. Okoro know. I know he'll want to have a consult with you before he refers you to a surgeon."

"Okay, just let him know I'm almost a hundred percent positive that that's what I want."

After she ended the call and walked back into the house, her daughter looked down at her with fear in her eyes. "Mom, why do you want to have a mastectomy?"

"You were listening to my conversation."

"Some of it."

"I don't listen to your conversations and I don't want you listening to mine," Mia firmly admonished her.

Alexa's large eyes couldn't stop blinking. Mia could see the terror in them. "Has the cancer come back? Please don't lie to me, Mom."

"No, Alexa, it hasn't."

"Are you sure?" By now, there were tears in Alexa's eyes.

"Don't start crying. Come over here," Mia said as she pulled her daughter closer to her and wiped the tears that had started to fall. "I'm fine. Now, stop that before you make me cry."

"Well, then why would you talk about having a mastectomy?"

"It's only a precaution so I won't have to constantly worry that the cancer will come back one day. That's all."

"Promise me."

"I promise."

"Swear to God."

"I swear to God. Now, I've got to go run to Whole Foods, so let's save the third degree for later."

Alexa shook her head as she wiped her eyes with the back of her hand. "If you're lying to me and swearing to God, that would be real ugly."

"I'm not lying. I'm fine; trust me." Mia gave her daughter a quick kiss on the cheek before jogging up the long spiral staircase and down the hallway leading to the master suite. When she entered her bedroom, she immediately spotted her purse on her desk beside her laptop. As she went to grab her purse, a cell phone began ringing. She dug out her cell phone, but it was turned off. She followed the ring to her husband's closet. Inside the front zipper pocket of his carry-on bag was a cheap cell phone with several missed calls from the same number. She phoned the number back.

"Hey, baby," the woman said.

"This isn't baby. This is baby's wife. Who are you and why are you calling my husband?"

The woman quickly hung up.

When Mia called back, the phone didn't ring. She was immediately sent to a voice mail that wasn't personalized. It was at that moment that she reminded herself that everything happened for a reason. Had she not forgotten her purse in her bedroom and gone back to get it right at that moment, she might never have heard that phone ring. In the nearly twenty years they'd been married, she never once suspected her husband of cheating—until recently. She had to admit that the last eight years had been pretty rough. After her series of cancer treatments were completed, sex was the last thing on her mind, and that continued for years. They had sex on occasion, but not nearly as much as Frank wanted. She had never been a very sexual person. And she did have quite a few hang-ups. The only man she ever enjoyed kissing was Lamont, the man she had dated for years before she met Frank.

Mia wanted to know who the woman on the phone was. She wanted to keep calling the woman back until she answered, but she didn't. Instead, she called Frank on his cell phone from the phone she'd found in his bag.

"Hello? Hello? Who is this?"

"You don't recognize the number."

"Um, not really . . . This isn't your cell phone number."

"No, it's yours, and I'm just trying to figure out why my husband has a secret cell phone and some unknown woman calling it constantly."

"It's not a secret cell phone. It's a business phone, and if a woman was calling, it's business."

"Stop, Frank. You know me better than that. I'm not stupid. This cheap-ass pay-as-you-go phone is not for business. It's so you can cheat."

"Look, Mia," he said, frustration rising in his voice. "I don't have time for this. It's real hectic at the office right now, and I just don't feel like being accused of something I'm not doing."

"You're gonna make time, because you didn't have time to talk about the woman who was in your hotel room either. Now you don't have time to talk about this cell phone—"

"Because neither is what you think. We've been together for twenty years, and have you ever once found me cheating?"

"No, but there's always a first for everything."

"No, Mia. You never found me cheating because I'm not cheating. So please just stop snooping, because you're not going to find anything."

"I wasn't snooping when I found this phone. Next time turn your damn ringer off."

She ended the call and called the woman's number one more time, but it still went directly to voice mail.

It's a duck, Mia thought. If it looked like a duck and quacked like a duck, then that's exactly what it was. And she wasn't going to let Frank's nonchalant attitude change her opinion. He thought all he had to do whenever there was some conflict in their marriage was simply act like nothing was wrong or say he didn't want to discuss it. Move on to another subject. Keep things pleasant. Use his stressful job and the fact that he provides such a lavish lifestyle for his family as an excuse for why she should never question him. For twenty years, she'd spoken to him in a tone that wasn't truly hers. Because that soft-spoken voice was one of the things he loved so much about her. Well, the calm, levelheaded, overly optimistic Mia was gone, and the real one wanted answers now. And sooner or later she would get them.

Chapter Two

January 1977

The swim teacher blew her whistle and told everyone to get in the water. Almost everyone did, except for Mia.

"Is there a problem, Mia?" Miss Cooper asked.

Mia stood frozen with her back to the water and her feet not far from the edge. Danielle was floating in the water, watching the entire scene unfold. She felt sorry for Mia, whose body was shaking. She looked so terrified.

She shook her head. "There's no problem."

"Then get in the water, now!" Miss Cooper shouted. But Mia didn't move, so Miss Cooper walked over to her.

"I don't want to learn how to swim," Mia said.

"You do realize that you need to pass this class in order to graduate."

Mia nodded. "But I'm a freshman, so I have plenty of time."

"And there's no time like the present. So get in." Miss Cooper pushed Mia's chest, and Mia fell into the pool backward with her arms flailing.

Some of the girls laughed. Others yelled, "She's drowning!" but didn't attempt to swim over to help. The only person who sprang into action was Danielle, as she paddled over with a flotation tube that Mia quickly grabbed hold of.

"Do you want me to teach you how to swim?" Danielle asked her.

"No," she said, spitting out water. "Just help get me out of this stupid pool." Her tears of embarrassment mixed with the water. "When I tell my parents what that woman did, they're going to sue this stupid school. I hate this dumb school."

Mia ran into the locker room with laughter trailing behind her.

Half an hour later, as Mia left the locker room, she heard Danielle shout after her, "Mia, wait up!"

"What? Why?" Mia said gruffly.

"I can teach you how to swim. Then you don't have to worry about failing the class, and you'll know how to swim. Believe it or not, it could come in handy."

"I'll think about it. Okay, I thought about it. No, thank you."

"What's wrong with you? You make it so difficult for someone like me to be your friend."

"Someone like you?" Mia shook her head and laughed. "I already have a lot of friends. I don't need someone like you to be one of them."

"What did I do to you? Last semester we had algebra together, and you barely spoke to me, even though I stood up for you against Mr. Carter. This semester we have swim class, and you don't talk to me either. I know you already have a ton of friends, but I don't have any, and at the retreat you seemed like a nice person."

Mia paused, at a loss for what to say. After a moment, she said, "A nice person? I told you I hated my father."

"I know, and I hate mine too. So we have that in common."

"I just don't like it here," Mia said after a heavy sigh. "First it was Mr. Carter picking on me. Now it's Miss Cooper—"

"Or maybe it's you."

"Me? What do you mean, maybe it's me? I'm the reason Mr. Carter gave me a different test from the rest of the class? And I'm the reason Miss Cooper pushed me in the pool? No, it's not me."

"I'm just saying, you're not the only black student that goes here, yet you're the only one who's always complaining that something's happening to her."

"I don't always have something happening to me. That was only two things."

"Exactly, so stop acting like it's every second of every day. Next time you see me in the cafeteria, why don't you invite me to your table and teach me how to play bid whist? And I'll teach you how to swim."

"It'll probably be a lot easier for you to teach me how to swim than it will be for me to teach you how to play bid whist, but we'll see," said Mia right before she huffed off.

* * *

Later that evening, while Danielle was sitting at the dinner table, she mentioned what happened in her swim class. Her father stopped eating, and put his fork down after Danielle said that she was going to teach Mia how to swim.

"All you have to do is throw some fried chicken and watermelon in the water. I bet she'll learn how to swim real fast then," Claire, Danielle's stepsister, said, then fell out in laughter.

"Why should you teach that black monkey anything?" Danielle's father said. "They can't teach us anything that we don't already know."

Danielle felt powerless. On the one hand, she wanted to say something, but on the other hand, it was easier for her to zone them out for as long as she could. Block out every negative thing they said about people. Imagine herself out of her father's house and living on her own away from the racist rants. She was angry. Her mother dying when she needed her the most wasn't fair, nor was living with a bunch of strangers. That included her father.

"That's right," said Danielle's stepmother, Linda. "You need to listen to your dad. They're lazy. And if I had my way, not one of 'em would get a job where I work."

Claire wouldn't stop laughing. It bothered Danielle that Claire could laugh, joke around, and have a good time while Danielle was so miserable. These people didn't deserve to sit at the dining room table Danielle's mother had picked out. Or live in the house her mother had died in. Claire didn't deserve to go to the same high school Danielle went to. Claire was a junior at Glory, but she hadn't started going there until after Linda married Danielle's dad shortly after meeting him in a bar. Linda was a weekend drunk just like Danielle's dad. She couldn't afford the tuition at Glory working retail at a small store in the mall. So Danielle's dad, a master mechanic, was paying for it. He also bought a Gremlin from the auto auction where he worked so Claire and her eighteen-year-old brother could share it. He told Danielle that it would be passed down to her when she turned sixteen. Passed down? *Why should I be getting their hand-me-downs?* she wondered. *I'm his actual daughter.*

"Of course they're lazy," Danielle's father said. "And that affirmative action isn't helping matters. Now all these lazy blacks are taking good jobs away from us hardworking whites."

"Your dad is telling the truth," Linda said. "We got a new one who started last week. Any time a customer walks through the door, she hides behind a clothes rack in the back of the store so she won't have to help anybody. My manager said I need to teach her how to sell. Why? So she can become the assistant manager and take my job because of that affirmative action crap? Besides, how hard is it to say, 'Can I help you find something?' "

"I like Mia. She's nice. And we have a lot of things in common."

"Don't you ever say that you have things in common with blacks," her father said, jabbing his finger in Danielle's face.

"Mia?" Claire asked. "Is that the one you're going to teach to swim? The one who got Mr. Carter fired? I hate that black girl and all her little stuck-up friends. Mom and Dad, I wish you could see how they walk the halls. They act like they own the school."

Danielle's father shook his head and scowled. "And they're more prejudiced than we are. Did you know that?" he asked Danielle. "A few work at my job, and they call me 'honky' all the time. My boss doesn't say anything to them. He's too afraid to, because every time you look around, one of them is filing a lawsuit claiming discrimination. I don't want you teaching her how to swim, and next time let her drown. Do you hear me? The world would be a better place without any of them in it."

"Danielle, your dad's talking to you," Linda said.

Danielle's mind had drifted away from their mean-spirited conversation to a world of fiction. Writing had become therapeutic for her after her mother died, saving her from thoughts of suicide. She didn't want to die, she'd decided. She wanted to live, but a much different life, one that wasn't surrounded by people who hated her for no good reason. But that was going to take time. Until then, she'd create the type of lives for her characters that she wanted. Writing grew into her great escape. She stood from the table and proceeded to walk away. She was going to her room so she could transfer her thoughts into her diary.

"You're just going to leave your plate on this table?" her stepmother asked.

"I guess I'm lazy . . . so what's that make me?" Danielle asked, right before slamming her bedroom door.

July 2010

Danielle King sat stiffly on a bright yellow leather sofa across from a woman perched in a white upholstered chair. They were inside a quaint office located on the second floor of a four-story building on Lenox Avenue in Miami Beach—minutes from Danielle's high-rise condominium on Collins Avenue.

"So you're here because of writer's block?" the heavily made-up woman, who looked more like a supermodel than a therapist, asked.

Danielle nodded, momentarily keeping her blue eyes hidden behind dark sunglasses. Sometimes it was easier for her to open up with her "blinders" on.

"I'm not sure why I'm here. It's definitely not because I'm crazy," Danielle said in her usual brash manner. Her loud voice had given many people acquainted with her a headache, and her husband swore it was the root cause of his migraines. "I'm right here. . . . I can hear you perfectly fine. You don't have to scream," he'd always tell her. But she'd grown up shy in a house full of people who talked loud, cursed, and screamed, so when she finally found her voice, she decided she'd never stop using it. "I was just hoping therapy might help me unleash some book ideas, because my new deadline will be here pretty soon and I'm freaking out."

"Feeling a little overwhelmed, are you?"

"This was a really busy year," Danielle said as she removed her sunglasses and set them on the sofa cushion beside her. "My daughter graduated from high school earlier this month. My book tour is coming up, with more engagements after that. I can't even fly out with my husband and daughter to take her to her first day at the University of Michigan. I have to meet them in Michigan later."

"Have you asked your publisher for an extension?"

"Dr. Garcia, I've been writing professionally for twenty years, and I've missed only one deadline, and that was when my agent died. Besides, they already gave me one."

Danielle sighed heavily. "Writing used to be so therapeutic for me. But now I don't know what's wrong. Maybe it's because my daughter's eighteen and she's going away to college and I feel like I've spent more time writing books than I have with her and my husband. I don't think I'm a selfish person. But I did do some things when I was younger that were pretty selfish." She reached for her sunglasses and put them back on. "I'm forty-eight years old and there are still times where I feel like I can't move past my childhood. How crazy is that?"

"It's pretty common actually. It defines us in many ways. But there comes a point when we do need to allow our minds to move away from that. What was your childhood like?"

"It was hell. I lost my mother right before high school, and I was really upset over that. I was so angry, especially at my dad, who I hated for so long. I felt guilty about it later for years. You're not supposed to hate a parent. I went to Catholic school, and they drill the Ten Commandments into you. I remember the fifth commandment clearly—'Honor thy father and thy mother, that thy days may be long upon the land, which the Lord thy God giveth thee.' "

The more Danielle spoke, the more it became obvious that she was there for more than writer's block.

"The first fourteen years of my life I was happy. At least I thought I was. My life seemed normal. The things my dad used to say about certain people, blacks mainly, never bothered me. I believed everything he said. But right before my mom died, she made me realize that it wasn't good to feel that way. That my father was wrong. That was the first time she'd ever spoken against him. After she died, my dad started drinking a lot, mostly on the weekends." She shook the thought out of her mind. "I don't want to talk about him right now, though."

"And you don't have to. You can talk about whatever it is you want to talk about."

"Outside of my husband and daughter, I've had only two people in my life who've meant something to me. One I owe my entire career to, and that's my first agent, Liza Schwartz, who died of breast cancer. The other was my best friend for fourteen years, Mia. It's been twenty years since I've spoken to her, and I still miss her." Danielle removed a handkerchief from her purse, raised her sunglasses, and wiped away the tears.

"What happened to Mia?"

"She decided she didn't want to be my best friend anymore, and I don't blame her because I was in the wrong. I'm a good person, but for some reason I don't always come across that way. And, as I'm sure you know, perception is reality. That's why I love to write. It's the one place I'm most understood."

Danielle crossed her legs and quickly uncrossed them. Something she'd learned from the one and only cotillion etiquette class she'd attended with Mia. "Never cross your legs unless you want to develop varicose veins," the instructor had told the girls. It was a theory that most doctors would dispute years later, but Danielle would continue to avoid doing it.

Danielle glanced down at her diamond-encrusted watch. "I have only a few minutes left." Her bright idea about seeking therapy as a way to break through to whatever was causing her writer's block didn't seem to be working. She was wasting her time, because she knew what was causing the problem. Her relationship with her husband had been going sour for years now, but every time she thought about approaching him with their problems, she'd pushed them aside and focused on herself. At times she was jealous of the bond Allen and their daughter shared. Something that felt foreign to Danielle, since she harbored so much hatred for her own father.

She sighed. She didn't think she could avoid the issue much longer.

It was the second week of July, the morning of her flight out to begin her book tour. Danielle was the first to wake. Her dog,

Pulitzer, opened his eyes right after her socked feet hit the bedroom floor. But he closed them seconds before she strolled onto the balcony. Twenty stories up made for a picturesque view of the Atlantic Ocean. She truly was living the life. Had the Forbes list been extended to include the top fifteen highest-paid authors, she would've landed in either the twelfth or thirteenth spot, she was certain. Last year, her earnings were just under eight million dollars.

As she stood clutching the banister, she watched the seagulls fly low at sunrise and enjoyed the soothing sounds of the crashing waves. Today was the official start of her book tour—a travel day—but she wasn't excited. For one thing, she kept thinking of the recent bedbug reports, which had risen to such epidemic proportions that the national media were covering it. And according to their reports, even some nicer hotels had become infested. Now, in addition to worrying about getting food poisoning, which she'd gotten nearly every year for the past five, she'd be checking her mattresses and obsessing over bedbugs.

Several hours later, Danielle rolled her carry-on bag into the foyer of her condominium and knelt down as she opened her arms to Pulitzer. "I wish I didn't have to leave you, little man." Three weeks she'd be away from her family. Three weeks without Pulitzer would feel like torture.

Pulitzer rolled over and played dead.

"You know if I could take you, I would, but your doctor says I can't."

Pulitzer sat on the floor and started talking, moving his mouth and letting little sounds escape. Danielle didn't care what that little girl at the pet store had said the other day. Pulitzer was not the funniest-looking dog alive. But it was true that he did resemble the male dog from *Lady and the Tramp*. Still, Danielle interpreted "funny-looking" as ugly. And if she had to name a dog that deserved the title "World's Ugliest," she'd go with the hairless Chinese crested that won the title at the Sonoma-Marin Fair in Petaluma, California, in 2005, the year Danielle, Allen, and their daughter attended. As busy as Allen and she used to be when they lived in California, it seemed like they made more time for family then.

"Pulitzer, don't make this harder than it has to be. I promise that I'll rent a car and drive next year, because I know how much you like riding in cars. I'd do anything for my little baby boy."

He wagged his tail and crawled toward her. She scooped him up and kissed him on his cold wet nose as she walked to the living room. After twenty years of touring, one would think she'd be used to the routine, but the only thing she'd finally gotten the swing of was the post-9/11 airport rules. Packing had become second nature. She never wasted time with checking baggage. She always carried on two items. Her oversized purse, which also held her iPad and detachable keyboard, and a carry-on bag easily fit in the first-class bin. She wore mules so she could slide in and out of her shoes quickly while going through security. And she was convinced that there wasn't anyone who could beat her time for getting her items from her carrier into a plastic security bin and out again.

But the full-body scanners that she'd been hearing about were not something she was looking forward to, and she was hoping she wouldn't be among the unlucky ones selected to go through one. And she definitely didn't want a pat down.

"Seems like the dog gets more love than I do these days," Allen said as he entered the living room.

Danielle sighed. "You know I love you." If only Allen were as nice as his friendly face suggested.

She and Allen met in the spring of 1991. She'd moved to LA shortly after she discovered her first novel was being adapted for the screen. She'd wanted to get away from Michigan since she and Mia were no longer speaking, and her family was still getting on her nerves. It was her opportunity to start over. She was allowed to sit in on a casting call even though she wouldn't have any say in who was selected to play the characters she'd spent what felt like a lifetime creating. Allen was there, hoping to land a supporting role, but was cast in a much smaller one. It was just like a line she'd written in one of her novels—"Once their eyes met, they felt an immediate connection. They were destined to meet, fall in love, and live happily ever after." Six months later, they were married. After making the best of the small role he'd played in the movie adaptation of Danielle's book *Private Lies*, he quickly became an A-list actor's best asset. His superb acting skills made good films better. He starred in more than a dozen films and received two Golden Globe nominations, and eventually began earning millions.

But Allen and Danielle's marriage was far from happily ever after. Eight years ago, Allen had told her he was ready to move out of LA. "I'm not sure I love acting anymore, or that I ever did. If it were up to me, I'd sell fruit on the beach," he'd said. His career was on a downslide after a couple of his recent movies failed miserably at the box office. "You and I both know that our busy schedules are taking a toll on our marriage. If it will help, I'll leave the business." And for a while she thought it might, though it wasn't just their busy schedules that were keeping them apart. His declaration came shortly after their second child was delivered stillborn. The situation had heaped stress on an already strained marriage, and they were having a hard time emerging from their grief. They both attempted to work through their pain separately with their characters. But they soon realized they needed to come together and deal with their heartache in the real world. LA provided too many reminders of the child they had lost, and of the career Allen could never keep as firm of a handle on as Danielle did on hers. Three years later, Danielle had eagerly agreed to move to Florida.

But over the years, she realized that Allen had left a piece of himself behind in California. She didn't know how to help him get it back. Most days, like today, when he was giving her an attitude, she wasn't sure she even wanted to try.

Her daughter strolled in from the balcony with her cell phone pressed against her ear, while Allen was walking into the kitchen.

"Tiffany, I'm leaving you in charge of Pulitzer. Don't feed him any table scraps, only his Blue Buffalo dog food and a few treats."

Tiffany nodded. "Okay, Mom."

"You didn't hear anything I just said, did you?"

"I love you too, Mom."

Tiffany was a smart, chatty teenager who made friends easily and belonged to several clubs at school. She was all the things Danielle wasn't at her age. Including overweight.

"Tiffany, I'm getting ready to leave, so will you please get off the phone for one second so I can go over a few things with you?"

"I'll call you later," Tiffany said before ending her call. She was short and stout, much like her father—a look that served him well as a character actor, but left their daughter with a few self-esteem issues. She felt her hair was too curly, and the Florida sun had tanned her skin. She grew tired of people coming up to her speaking Spanish, assuming she was Cuban.

"I said you're in charge of Pulitzer."

"Mom, I already heard you. You don't want him to have any table scraps and only feed him Blue Buffalo."

"The bag is getting low. But don't go to PetSmart without first writing down the type of food we have. It's the one for small breeds. They have several kinds. Please be sure to read the package and get the chicken and brown rice formula for senior dogs."

Tiffany sighed. "I've been with you a million times when you bought the food, Mom. Pulitzer is going to be fine."

Danielle set Pulitzer down and opened her arms to her daughter. "I'm an overprotective mother, I guess."

"Not when it comes to me."

"You're big enough to take care of yourself."

"Big enough? Gee, thanks."

"Oh, Tiffany, stop. You know what I mean."

"Have fun on your book tour," Tiffany said stiffly as Danielle gave her a big hug.

Danielle kissed her daughter on the cheek. "I'm sure I'll be miserable. I'm going to miss you and Pulitzer so much. Ugh, I don't want to go . . . not this time. I hope the plane doesn't crash."

"I thought you liked flying."

"I didn't mind it before the full-body scans. I don't want anybody seeing my body."

"Not even your husband," Allen said from the kitchen.

"Allen, have some respect for your daughter."

"Mom, please, I can handle his humor."

"Make sure your father doesn't feed Pulitzer any junk," Danielle said loud enough so Allen could hear it. "No popcorn or potato chips, only the Blue Buffalo."

"How many times are you going to tell me that? You have repeatitis."

"It's inherited. And once you become a mother, you'll have it too."

"A mother or a dog owner?"

"Was that some sort of dig?"

"You know I'm just joking around, Mom," Tiffany said as she went to the kitchen, and returned to the living room with a big slice of red velvet cake stuffed inside a paper towel. Tiffany would usually have cake for breakfast and then debate with her mother that it was no different from eating a doughnut, when the point was she should've stuck to yogurt. But then Tiffany would point out that she'd also drink eight or more glasses of water a day as if the H_2O would drown the pounds. She, like her mother, hated to exercise. Even though their high-rise condominium housed a state-of-the-art exercise facility that had recently been remodeled. Danielle wanted her daughter to be slim and have self-confidence, but she didn't know what to say or do to help her. It was all too much for Danielle to deal with sometimes. Whom could she talk to other than her new therapist, who listened and then billed for her hourly ear? That's why Pulitzer was so special. He calmed her . . . loved her . . . understood her.

Danielle scooped her four-legged companion from the floor and hugged and kissed him. "He's mad at me. Look at him frown his bushy eyebrows."

"He'll get over it like he always does," Tiffany said.

"Well, I'm off," Danielle said. "Pray that my plane doesn't crash."

"I will, unless you have an insurance policy and I'm one of the beneficiaries," Tiffany said as she stuffed her mouth with cake.

Danielle rolled her luggage into the hallway and bumped into the large box, which held a wooden bookcase. She'd been nagging Allen to assemble the bookcase for weeks now.

"Remind your father to put that bookcase together while I'm gone. I'm tired of looking at it. It's been in the same spot for six months, and we're using it like furniture now."

"I will, Mom." Tiffany waved at her mother before closing their front door.

As soon as Danielle opened the door to her hotel room at the Brown Palace Hotel and Spa in downtown Denver, she was pleasantly surprised that she wasn't greeted with a blast of ice-cold air-conditioning, as she normally was when she checked into hotels. She leaned her carry-on bag against the wall and kicked off her comfortable leather mules. She was planning on making it an early night, but then a phone call came in. It was Tiffany.

"Mom, I have Josh on the other line."

"Josh?"

Josh was Danielle's nephew, though she was hard-pressed to consider his mother, Claire, a sister, or even a stepsister, for that matter.

"He needs your help."

"He always needs my help. Why doesn't he try asking his mother sometimes?"

"Mom, you know Aunt Claire doesn't have any money. What

good is having all your money if you're not going to help family with it?"

"I'll tell you what good it is. It means you'll be a rich young lady when I die."

"I'm bringing him over."

"Tiffany. I had a rocky flight and I'm not in the mood to talk to him," Danielle said right before Tiffany clicked him over.

"He's on the line. . . . Josh?" Tiffany asked.

"Yeah, I'm here," he said in the unusually deep voice he'd had since he was ten.

"How are you doing, Josh?" Danielle's voice dragged.

"Not too good. I think I might need to hire a lawyer. I just got out of jail."

"What happened?"

"Basically, they arrested me because I fit a description. They said—"

Danielle knew one thing. If someone said he fit the description, then most likely he was the one who did it. Joshua was tall and lanky and had two sleeves of colorful tattoos on his arms, spiky jet-black hair, and gauged earrings after permanently stretching his earlobes to wear large metal rings. It would be hard to confuse him with someone else.

"Who are *they*?" Danielle asked as she grew more agitated.

"Sterling Heights Police and the U.S. Marshals—"

"U.S. Marshals, Joshua? How did all of this happen?"

"I was driving home, and about ten SUVs surrounded me.

They said I robbed some ninety-year-old woman at gunpoint in her home in Sterling Heights. That's not me. I'd never do that—"

"Stop right there, Joshua, and remember who you're speaking to. Your aunt created the character Wyatt Rockwell, and did a five-book series around him."

"Who?"

"Wyatt Rockwell. I know you saw the movie *Red Zone*."

"Mom, please stop talking about your characters and just listen to Joshua," Tiffany interrupted.

"I am listening to him, Tiffany. But I know all there is to know about the U.S. Marshals, and they don't pull people over for armed robbery; they hunt down fugitives."

"I thought that's who they said they were, but I'm not positive. All I know is that I was in jail for almost three days. I had to get in a lineup. Then they said I was free to go and they had the wrong guy, so now I want a lawyer, but that costs money."

"A lawyer, Josh?"

"Yeah, I think I can sue for unlawful arrest. They burst through my mom's apartment and turned over mattresses, and tore up the place. I'm waiting on Geoffrey Fieger to return my call."

"Don't hold your breath while you wait, because it's hard to sue for something like that. I'm assuming they felt they had just cause. Something brought them to your mom's."

"Yeah, they said they got a tip from someone."

"There's your answer. And of course they couldn't tell you from whom, right?"

"Right, they couldn't."

"So what else did you need from me besides the lawyer? Because I'm not helping you with that."

"Well, they impounded my car, and I need money to get that out."

"How much do you need?"

"Right now, two hundred and forty-five dollars, but they charge fifteen dollars a day for storage."

"I'll send you an even three hundred."

"Thanks, Auntie. I'm trying to get my life together, but it's hard."

"I was paying for your education, and you dropped out of school. Do you know what's really hard, Josh? Getting a job without a high school diploma, because nowadays you need way more than that. I went out of my way and asked a friend to hire you, and you quit after your first week. You make your own life difficult, and after this I'm not going to be your enabler. Get your life together." She ended the call, knowing her daughter was going to call her back and ask her why she was so mean to Josh. But sometimes tough love was the best course of action.

Danielle blamed a lot of her nephew's problems on her stepsister's poor parenting skills and the fact that his father was never in his life. And now at twenty it didn't seem as though his life was anywhere near getting on the right track. Hopefully, he was truly innocent of the crime. The first thing Danielle was going to do was turn on her computer and Bing his name to find out what, if any, information she could. Tomorrow, she had a signing, and then she'd be flying off—three weeks and fifteen cities. But tonight she was going to do a little detective work. Being a writer for over twenty years had also turned her into one of the best sleuths in the business.

But being successful had not done what she'd hoped it might. At one time she envisioned making loads of money so she could help her family. She bought her father and stepmother a better home, paid for her nieces' and nephews' education. She was the best gift giver at Christmastime—the best party thrower for birthdays. Money was supposed to make the world a better place for her and those she loved. But whoever said "more money, more problems" certainly knew what he was talking about, because the more money she made, the more problems members of her family had, and it was always her responsibility to bail them out.

"Mom, how could you talk to him like that?" Tiffany asked after calling her mother back.

"He needed that from me more than he needed three hundred dollars."

"But, Mom—"

"Tiffany, while I'm on this tour, you have to promise me that if he or any of our so-called relatives call you to get to me, you'll tell them you don't know how to reach me. It may take you a while to realize that often it's the ones closest to you who are most likely to hurt you."

* * *

"I just landed," Danielle told her daughter as she slogged through the entrance to the airport parking complex after an exhausting three-week tour. "How's Pulitzer?"

"He's been sleeping a lot, and he's been looking for you ever since you left. He really *really* missed you this time."

"I missed him too." Danielle heard beeping on the line, and checked her screen. Her literary attorney, Steve Wisk, was calling on the other line. "Tiffany, I'll be home soon, but I have to take another call. Tell your father to have dinner ready. Tell him to cook some salmon." She clicked over to her other line. "Finally, you've decided to return my call."

"Finally? I've been calling you. We have a slight problem."

"I knew it. What was I misquoted as saying—that the *New York Times* is racist? I started not to answer that writer's question."

"I'm not even sure what you're referring to. But who is Claire Chudwick?"

Danielle paused. "My stepsister. Why?"

"She's suing you."

"Suing me for what?"

"Copyright infringement."

"What?" Danielle shouted as her rubber-soled loafers softly pounded through the airport's parking structure. Her hand trembled as she held on to her BlackBerry. "How can that wench sue me for anything, especially plagiarism? She can't even form a complete sentence. She should be glad that I hired her as my assistant and put up with her computer illiteracy for three horrendous years. This is a joke. Please tell me it is."

"Well, it's not a joke, because she's hired an attorney and we have a mediation hearing scheduled for—"

"What?" Danielle fumbled through her messenger bag for her car keys as she approached her Porsche Panamera. "I don't have time to deal with this right now. I just got off the plane. I simply don't want to deal with Claire and her lies today. People rarely change from who they were as teens, and she's certainly proof of that."

"Well, we're going to need to talk about this before the mediation that's scheduled for the eighth."

Danielle slammed her car door after sliding inside. "Not the eighth of September."

"The eighth of September."

"Two days after Labor Day, and the same day I'm scheduled to fly back from Michigan."

"I can try to reschedule. They'd probably be more open to making it earlier than later."

"Steve. I already have several engagements scheduled from now until I fly to meet my husband and daughter in Michigan. I don't want to do it any earlier. And if I could've rearranged my schedule, don't you think I would've done that so that I could fly out with Allen and Tiffany?"

"I'll try to make it for the ninth. . . . I just don't want this getting out to the media."

"Thank you for stroking my ego, but if it gets out in the media, no one will care, so let it get out."

"Your millions of fans will care, and you don't need that type of negative publicity while you're in the middle of promoting a new book."

"It's all lies anyway. I can't believe this. I can't believe that Claire would do this to me. In a way, it doesn't surprise me, but it definitely disappoints me. After all I've done."

"She claims to have a lot of other things on you as well. Do you have any idea what she's talking about?"

"Other things? She must have me confused with her," Danielle said as her heart skipped a beat. She hated Claire for her lame attempt at extortion.

The next morning, Danielle was looking through her Franklin planner for an available date for mediation when the doorbell rang. It was the concierge with a package UPS had dropped off the day before when no one was home. Allen had mentioned to Danielle that his manager had a script he wanted to take a look at. He'd said he was doing it just to get him off the phone, because he wouldn't take no for an answer, but Danielle had her doubts about that one. She wondered if Allen was ready to go back to Hollywood. Her biggest clue had come months earlier after he started watching some of the movies he'd been in years ago.

She covered her ears for a second after her dog let out a furious bark, and then she quickly grabbed the dog's torso, trying to hold him back. But after a few seconds he managed to wiggle free. He was fiercely protective and didn't like visitors, so he darted from her bedroom, where he'd been resting quietly at Danielle's feet, and headed straight for the front door. In a matter of seconds, she heard Pulitzer let out a shrill yelp. She tossed her planner on the bed and bolted into the living room, where she found Pulitzer lying limp beside the large box in the foyer and looking up at her helplessly as he continued to cry.

"Oh my God, Allen, come help me!"

Allen was in the living room, fumbling with the UPS package. "Pick him up and rub him. He'll be okay."

"I'm afraid to move him. What if he broke something?"

"See if he can walk."

Danielle gently rubbed Pulitzer's side. "It's going to be okay, little man. Are you okay?" she asked in that endearing voice that always made Pulitzer's tail wag. He stood and shook his body.

"See, I told you, nothing to worry about."

Later that night as Danielle sat up in bed with her thoughts racing toward the mediation hearing and the lies her stepsister was telling, Pulitzer walked in with his legs squared and began to pant heavily.

"What's wrong, little man?"

He walked around the large bedroom very slowly from corner to corner. He settled beside Danielle but, after looking up at her, decided to move to the far side of the bedroom to a corner he never went to, and lay down.

"Allen," Danielle shouted as she stood outside her bedroom door. "Something's wrong with Pulitzer."

"He's sore from the hit. That's to be expected."

"No, I need to take him to the emergency room right now. I don't like the way he's acting. He went off in a corner far away from me."

"Danielle, you're being silly."

"No, I'm not being silly. You just don't care."

She turned and looked over at Pulitzer, who was still lying in the far corner. She observed him to make sure he was breathing, and sighed in relief after she saw his stomach expand. Then he sat up. She glanced away for a brief second, and heard a loud thump. He was lying lifeless on the floor.

"Oh my God, he's dead!" Danielle screamed as she ran to the corner, scooped him up, and placed him on the bed. He was still breathing, but barely. White foam was oozing from his nose. "Somebody, please help me!" she shouted. "Tiffany, come help me!"

Tiffany bolted into her mother's bedroom. "What's wrong with Pulitzer?"

"He's dying. Get me some tissue and call emergency."

Tiffany ran into her mother's bathroom and brought back a box of Kleenex. Danielle wiped the white foam from Pulitzer's nostrils and attempted to perform mouth-to-mouth.

"I have the animal hospital on the phone," said Tiffany as she handed her mother her cell phone.

"Ma'am, what is the dog doing?" the young man on the other end asked.

"Please help me," Danielle sobbed. "I think he's dying. Please help me. Tell me what I need to do to save him. Please . . . please, he can't die. I love him so much." Danielle broke down after she noticed Pulitzer's dark eyes roll back. "Don't die on me. . . . Please, Pulitzer . . . don't die. What can I do? I was giving him mouth-to-mouth. Is it okay to do that on a dog?"

"You need to perform CPR on a dog through their nose. Make sure the tongue is inside the mouth and the mouth is closed and his head is tilted back slightly."

Danielle turned the speaker on and set the cell phone on the bed beside Pulitzer as she performed CPR.

"He's breathing," she shouted. "He's breathing. Now tell me what else I need to do."

"Bring him in to us as fast as you can."

"Okay, okay. Write down their address." As soon as she tossed the phone to Tiffany, she saw Pulitzer's chest take a deep heave. Danielle gently wiped away more foam and proceeded with CPR. Her dog took one last breath. She felt a warm sensation on her leg. He had urinated on her bed, and it ran onto her white shorts and down her left leg. Then he had a bowel movement right before his hind legs went limp. Danielle cradled him in her arms like a baby, covered his left ear, and yelled for Allen to call a valet and drive her to the emergency vet. She carried him into their den, where Allen was sitting, still reading the script.

"Get up and take me to emergency!" she shouted.

"What's wrong?"

"Dad, just take her!" Tiffany shouted. "Can't you see something's wrong with Pulitzer?" She used their home phone to dial the valet. "Can you please get my mother's car ready? We have an emergency with our dog. Please hurry."

Allen stood and shoved on his shoes. He walked over to Danielle, who was seated in a paisley wingback chair staring off into space while she rocked Pulitzer.

"He's dead, Danny," Allen said nonchalantly after feeling him for a pulse.

She snarled up at him. "Don't you dare tell me he's dead. I want you to take me to the emergency vet right now!"

A young man appeared from the back offices after vanishing for several minutes. He looked at Danielle and shook his head. Then he walked closer.

"I'm sorry. He was DOA."

She'd known as much, but had prayed for a better outcome. She knew while Allen was driving her there and she looked into her miniature schnauzer's glassy eyes and saw his purple tongue hanging from the side of his mouth. But she just didn't want to accept it. She was still hoping there was something a vet could do. A miracle was what she needed. Pulitzer had been with her for nearly twelve years. She loved him like he was her son. He slept in a dog bed beside her bed. Went on book tours with her and rested near her feet whenever she was seated. He was in tune with her moods. Knew when she was sad and would stare at her with his beautiful dark brown eyes as if to say, "It's going to be okay." She couldn't imagine him not being with her any longer. It couldn't be happening. It just couldn't be.

"How much do I owe you?" Danielle asked. Her eyes were the only things that could move at that moment.

"Nothing, but we do work with a company who can cremate him for you. They charge two hundred and fifty dollars, and they'll pick him up tomorrow. You'll probably get him back on Tuesday or Wednesday. Unless you just want them to dispose of him. They only charge sixty-nine dollars for that."

"Let's do that," Allen said.

"Let's?" They were at some matchbox of a place that probably didn't even attempt to save her dog. The young man had scooped Pulitzer out of her arms and gone off to some back room and probably looked at his watch for a few minutes and came back. Maybe he was DOA, or maybe, just maybe, if they'd had enough skill, they could've brought him back to life. What good was having money if she didn't have enough to save Pulitzer?

"I want to take him home with me."

"I'll put him in a box for you, if you could just fill out this form," the young man said as he handed her a clipboard with a piece of paper attached. She scribbled her name and her PO box.

A few minutes later, the young man came in hauling a white box taped shut.

"I'll take him," Allen said.

"Just get the door," she retorted as she struggled with the box. Pulitzer was five pounds overweight, but the box felt as if it had been weighed down with bricks.

"Are you sure you don't want me to take it?" Allen asked again as he held the door to the entrance open and Danielle teetered through.

"*It?* Pulitzer isn't an 'it.' He was smarter than you."

"I was referring to the box, Danny."

A misstep caused her to get her foot caught in the leather strap of one of her flip-flops and fall to her knees on the graveled lot. Her hands kept a firm grasp on both sides of the box. She felt Pulitzer's body slide forward.

"You killed Pulitzer," she shouted as tears streamed down both cheeks.

"Me?"

"Yes, you! Who else?" She looked up at him with hatred. "If you could've simply done what I asked and moved that damn box away from the door, none of this would've happened. Pulitzer would be alive today. Do you realize that?"

"You bought that bookshelf, not me. It's not like we needed another one. Why didn't you just pay whoever you got it from to assemble it for you?"

"Because I have a husband who isn't doing anything right now, and hasn't been doing anything for years."

"He was old, Danny," Allen said through clenched teeth.

"He was eleven and a half, and mini schnauzers can live to be fifteen."

"If they're healthy, and he was having problems. All kinds of problems, and you know it."

"He was a strong dog, and he would've lived to be twenty if it was left up to me and my care alone."

"You can always get another dog."

"How dare you tell me what I can do? I will never get another dog because Pulitzer can't be replaced."

"Please, let's just go." He held his hand out to her. "It's starting to rain."

"I can get up by myself. I don't need your help."

"Let me take the box," he said as he reached for it.

"Don't come near him." She threw her body over the box. "You never liked him, and he knew it, and that's why he barked at you all the time."

The white box was getting wet. Pulitzer hated rain. It was time for Danielle to get up, even though she wanted to lie on the ground crying. But she owed her dog that much. His death came with little warning, and as she walked toward the car, his last few minutes of life played in her mind all over again.

The next day, Danielle arranged for Pulitzer to be cremated, and two days later, the doorbell rang. She was so used to hearing Pulitzer bark whenever the doorbell rang that not hearing him saddened her. The same representative from All Paws Go to Heaven who'd picked up Pulitzer's remains was at the door with a small box containing a walnut urn that held his ashes. Tiffany answered the door, and accepted the box. Once the representative left, she knocked on her mother's bedroom door.

"Pulitzer's here."

No answer.

She knocked again.

"If Pulitzer was still alive, he would've darted for that door as soon as he heard the doorbell," Danielle mumbled to herself as she slunk out of bed, walked to her door, and unlocked it. She was pale. Hadn't showered, brushed her teeth, or eaten in two days. She was surviving on a warm thirty-two-ounce bottle of water that she'd taken only a few sips from.

"I made you a Cuban sandwich and it sorta tastes like Latin American Grill's," Tiffany said, holding on to the small box of Pulitzer's remains.

"I'm not hungry."

"But you have to eat something. I'll split it with you."

Danielle nodded. "Okay."

"I'll be right back." She set the box down on a table and headed downstairs.

Danielle pried open the box with her bare hands and pulled out Pulitzer's urn, which was covered in Bubble Wrap. She tore through the plastic, hugged his urn, and climbed back into bed with it.

Tiffany returned with the sandwich on a plate and two bottles of Diet Snapple.

"Aww, Mom. I know you miss him," she said when she saw her mother clinging to the urn.

"You have no idea how much."

"Eat some food, Mom, please," Tiffany said as she sat beside her mother and fed her.

Danielle took a small bite of the sandwich Tiffany positioned in front of her mother's mouth.

"I just don't understand why he had to die like that. I should've taken him to the hospital right after he hit that box. What was I thinking?" She hit her forehead with the heel of her hand. "I'm so stupid. My dog had a heart murmur and was a senior citizen. He hit a box at top speed, and I was too stupid to realize he might need medical attention." Tears filled her eyes quickly. "I'll never forgive myself." She balled her body up into the fetal position and rested her head against her pillow.

"In a few months, you should get another dog. One that looks like Pulitzer. That'll probably make you feel better."

"If I die, is that what you'd want your dad to do? Replace me in a few months, just like my dad did when he married my stepmother?"

"No, but that's different. You're my mom and you're a person."

"Well, Pulitzer might as well have been a person to me." She cried into her pillow while Tiffany sat beside her, rubbing her back and periodically telling her things would get better.

Chapter Three

December 1977

It was Saturday evening, just after seven, when Mia's doorbell rang.

"Who the hell is that at our door?" Mia's father shouted to her mother. "You expecting somebody?"

"No, Henry, but I think Mia is."

"Mia, who'd you invite over here with this house as junky as it is? Must be that white girl coming over here again. How come she always coming over here? Why don't you ever go to her house? I'll tell you why. 'Cause her people probably won't let blacks in their house—that's why."

"She can hear you," Mia shouted.

"You think I care if she can hear me? I want her to hear me."

"I hate you," Mia screamed, slamming her bedroom door.

"Just 'cause them white kids' parents let them talk any kind of way, don't think that means you can, 'cause I'll slap your ass into next year."

"Mia," her mother said with a series of forceful knocks to Mia's locked door. Knocks she'd heard many times before and resented each time. Her mother did little to stand up for her daughter. "You're being disrespectful to your father, and I expect you to apologize."

"And what about him? Is he going to apologize for embarrassing me?" Mia asked as she sat on the edge of her bed in tears.

"Apologize so you won't have to keep your friend waiting outside."

What possessed her mother? Mia wondered. What qualities did her mother see in the man Mia felt forced to call "Dad" that would have made her mother want to marry him? Did she just marry him for the sake of having a husband, because that's what women were expected to do? Mia wanted to get married one day too, but to a man who was nothing like her father. She wanted to marry for love. No one ever explained to her how marriage wasn't as simple as that.

She stormed to the front door and snatched it open, mumbling her apology to her father as she breezed past him. Her eyes were filled with tears and her chest heaved with anger.

"Did I get you in trouble?" Danielle asked. She'd come over to spend the night and go to Chris and Mark Meyers's house party—the biggest house party of the year. She and Danielle were now sophomores in high school, and it was two days before their winter holiday break. Mia had been looking forward to the party all day, but she wasn't in the mood anymore.

"Don't speak to him. Just keep on walking straight to my room."

"That's rude."

"So what? He's rude too."

"Hi, Mr. and Mrs. Marks," Danielle called to Mia's parents, who were sitting in the living room watching TV.

"Hello, Danielle," Mia's mother said. Mia's father merely grunted.

"Do you think it's a man thing?" Danielle asked as she made herself comfortable on Mia's bed. "Because my dad's mean like that too. Actually, he's meaner than your dad."

"My dad isn't mean. He's crazy. He needs to be locked up at Northville," Mia said, tossing her pillow on the floor in anger.

"She's not going to no party with the dishes piled in the sink like this," they overheard Mia's father yelling to her mother. "She better get to washing if she's trying to leave this house."

"I'll help you with the dishes," Danielle said.

Mia's nostrils flared as she shook her head. "You don't have to do that."

"We don't have to go to the party if you don't want to."

"Oh, I want to. I definitely want to, and we will go."

Danielle shrugged. "It doesn't matter to me, because I can't dance."

Mia flicked her wrist dismissively. "That doesn't matter. No one will notice. It's going to be wall-to-wall people, so close you'll hardly be able to move."

"You're always talking about Chris Meyers. I can't wait to finally meet him. What does he look like?"

"I don't know. I don't really look at him like that," Mia lied. "I've known him and his brother for so long. They have a nice house. It looks big from the outside. I can't wait to finally see the inside."

Chris Meyers's family lived in a large corner house on Stratford in Sherwood Forest, a subdivision Mia wished she lived in so she wouldn't feel so poor among her peers, many of whom lived there or in Palmer Woods, the adjacent subdivision. Chris was cute and so was his older brother, Mark. But Mark was more Mia's type because he was the taller of the two—six feet one; he towered over her, even when she wore her three-inch platform shoes. Mia had had a crush on both brothers since she and Chris had homeroom together in the fourth grade.

"Am I going to be the only white person there?" Danielle asked.

Mia shrugged. "Probably . . . unless Lisa Merchant comes, but she doesn't count."

"Why doesn't she?"

"I mean she's white, but not like you."

"She's white but not like me? What's that supposed to mean?"

"It just means that she went to Holy Angels with us. I've known her since the first grade. She has a black boyfriend, and she dances better than I do. She's an honorary black girl."

An hour later, they were sitting on Mia's bed, waiting for her mother to drive them to the Meyerses' house after she finished a phone call. Suddenly they heard a scream rip through the house.

"If you think for one minute I'm going to allow you to stay in this house after you got some woman pregnant, you've got another think coming!" Mia's mother shouted.

"I don't have no woman pregnant," Mia's father yelled back. "That crazy woman is lying."

"Oh, you're right, I guess she's not pregnant if she already had the baby. Get out!"

A few moments later, Mia heard the door slam. She looked out the window and saw her father driving away.

The two girls were stunned. Danielle carefully studied Mia's face for her reaction. After a moment, Mia whispered, "I'm glad he's gone. I hope he never comes back."

Danielle didn't know what to say to make the situation better for her friend. But she knew that Mia didn't truly mean what she said about her father not coming back.

Mia sat on the edge of her bed. She shook her head as tears streamed down her cheeks and her lower lip trembled. She was embarrassed that Danielle had overheard her parents arguing. She wondered what Danielle must've thought of her family. It didn't shock Mia that her father had a baby out of wedlock, because her assessment of her father was that he cared only about himself, not their family.

"I guess we won't be going to the par—the par—" Mia stumbled on her words. Before she could finish her sentence, she covered her face with both hands and sobbed. "I'm so embarrassed. All he ever does is embarrass me."

"Don't be embarrassed, Mia. Your dad isn't the only one. My dad gets on my nerves all the time. I hate him."

"Yeah, but he didn't get some woman pregnant while he was married."

"No, but he married a woman right after my mom died. She hadn't even been dead for three months. And before that, he was bringing women who were dressed like prostitutes in and out of the house when he thought I was asleep."

"He brought prostitutes to your house?"

Danielle nodded, a stony look on her face. "Now do you understand why I hate him? Why I never ever want to get married? He treats his new wife better than he treated my mom, and he acts like her kids are his. I don't trust men."

"Please don't tell anybody about my dad getting some woman pregnant," Mia said tearfully, shaking her head in disgust.

"Why would I tell anybody? You're my best friend. I don't want to hurt you. I'd never tell anybody any of your business . . . ever."

"I want to start spending the night at your house. I have to get out of here," Mia said.

Danielle's eyes froze. She was at a loss for words. The thought of how her father and stepmother would react if she ever brought Mia to her house was more than she wanted to imagine. "When can I spend the night?" Mia asked.

"Whenever. Anytime you want," Danielle said to appease her.

"Good. I'll be over next weekend."

Danielle forced a smile. Though it was the last thing she wanted to do, she knew Mia needed her right now.

August 2010

On a late Saturday afternoon Mia and Frank were at the casual yet elegant Rattlesnake Club, owned by Jimmy Schmidt, one of Detroit's most famous chefs. They were sitting on a terrace that overlooked the Detroit River. The riverside restaurant where they were waiting for Viv to join them was nestled on a side street just east of downtown. Most of the waitstaff knew Mia and Frank by name, as did the chef. The Rattlesnake Club was the restaurant Frank had taken Mia to for their first date. She had been impressed that he'd taken her to such a nice restaurant, a sign of good things to come, she'd hoped.

There was a boat in the distance that resembled their old Sea Ray Sundancer. She could still remember when Frank first towed it home on a trailer attached to his business partner's Ford Super Duty truck. At the time, ten years earlier, they were living in a modest brick colonial in the University District of Detroit, minutes from her parents' home and Holy Angels Catholic School. He'd always said when he made his first million, he was going to buy a thirty-seven-foot cruiser, custom build a home, and buy Mia a top-of-the-line Mercedes. And he did all those things and more.

Everything came together when one of his long-shot ideas finally paid off. He'd first started by acquiring a few cheap rental properties, fixing them up, and reselling them. This was years before the real estate market tanked. He dabbled in the subprime real estate market a little. Before long he'd decided he wanted to open an investment firm downtown with a goal of helping budding investors who couldn't obtain capital through banks and more traditional means. His idea eventually yielded real results. The year they'd moved into their Bingham Farms estate, which was three years after he'd started his company—Investment Professional Advisers—he'd netted five million dollars.

"What's on your mind?" he asked as he followed her eyes over to the water and the boat. He looked back to her. "Alexa used to love taking the boat out," he said wistfully. He'd sold it shortly after Mia was diagnosed with breast cancer. His big checks weren't coming in as quickly as her health insurance bills, and those couldn't be avoided. That was the only bad thing about Frank's investment company. When he got a payday, it was big enough to last a year. But sometimes it took a year, or almost two, before one came, which was why Mia continued working for as long as she could.

There wasn't a need for Mia to look at the menu. She knew she was ordering salmon before she took her seat. She felt it was the healthiest choice. Years ago she would have ordered the prime Angus beef short ribs. But with so much talk in the media in recent years about red meat and the possible link to breast cancer, she didn't want to take any chances. Moments like these were when Mia ate most—moments of regret. She couldn't believe she had let nearly two months pass without so much as another mention about the cheap cell phone she found ringing inside his luggage. She told herself she didn't care. But as each day went by, she realized she did, because the last thing she wanted to do was live with a liar.

"You know what I wish?" Frank said as he sipped a glass of wine and gazed into Mia's eyes.

"What do you wish, Frank?"

"I wish that my wife would make love to me tonight. So I can have a smile on my face in the morning when I fly to Chicago."

She threw up her hands. "Please. That's the last thing on my mind right now."

"Do you know how long it's been?"

"Not exactly."

"Three months this Sunday."

Her eyes darted to Viv and her companion, who were walking toward them at that moment. "Here they come, so just drop it."

"Of course," he said, after taking another sip of his drink. "Heaven forbid they find out we're not fucking."

"You got that right. *We're* not."

"What's that supposed to mean?"

"Just what I said. *We* aren't."

"Are you sleeping with someone else?" he asked suspiciously.

"Sorry we're late," Viv said, practically singing the words. She dropped her clutch on the table and took a seat between Mia and Viv's friend Charles, who had sat down seconds before Viv. The new couple was all smiles. It was nice for Mia to see Viv happy. She'd married once when she was in her early twenties, but that marriage had lasted only a little over a year. Charles was a high school gym teacher at Pershing whom Mia knew when she taught English there. He was the man all the female teachers were crazy about. He was well built and tall with great looks—and single. Viv had been married at the time, but miserable. They had kept in touch over the years, and now they were finally together.

They ordered appetizers and entrées in between snippets of conversation. Charles and Frank discussed business, while Mia and Viv chatted about a new hardcover release by one of their favorite authors.

Frank's phone vibrated after the waiter placed their appetizers on the table.

"Excuse me, I need to take this. It's an important business call. I'll be right back, baby," Frank said as he stood from the table and squeezed Mia's shoulder.

"Business before pleasure," Mia said, and then mumbled, "Of course for some of us there's very little difference between the two."

Mia's eyes remained focused on her husband until he exited the terrace and disappeared from her sight. He was away from the table long enough for their guests to finish off their calamari appetizers. And by the time he returned, she'd lost her appetite and asked the waiter to wrap up most of her meal so she could take it home.

* * *

A wheel-back armchair was positioned between two tall white doorless linen cabinets. Each one of the four shelves displayed a crisp bright white towel that was neatly folded and perfectly placed. Mia loved bath towels, especially fluffy white ones of good quality. Something she'd never had as a child. Her parents didn't believe in replacing anything unless it nearly disintegrated. The towels she used growing up were so hard that they felt like sandpaper against her skin. She still had a mark on her right arm from where a washcloth had scratched her.

Roughly a foot above the armchair was a round window with an antique starburst mirror hanging in the center. Mia loved their bathroom, appreciated having her own sink, because Frank let the toothpaste dry up in his, and she was tired of cleaning up after him.

There was a Jacuzzi tub, which Frank would often sink into comfortably while he rested the lower part of his large head against the bath pillow and brag about all his lucrative investment deals. Often while puffing on a Cuban cigar with a glass of red wine by his side. It was a gravy train that, according to Frank, would never run out.

The window above the bathtub overlooked the spacious grounds of their home and their Olympic-sized swimming pool. The homes in their neighborhood were tucked away on wooded lots, and ranged in size from one-level sprawling ranches to three- and four-level humongous estates.

A fifty-five-inch waterproof fogless flat-screen TV was mounted flush to the wall. The two-way fireplace for the master bedroom and master bathroom came in handy during the long Michigan winters.

Better Homes and Gardens would certainly have been proud. But what was Mia Marks-Glitch proud of? What was she thinking of as she leaned in to her bathroom mirror and stared at herself long and steady, zeroing in on a few gray strands and the blackheads on her nose that she'd be swiping off with a deep-cleansing pore strip momentarily?

Internally her emotions flared, her insides kicking and screaming and cursing her out. She had barely made it through dinner with Viv. She needed to confront Frank about her suspicions tonight. It had been tearing her up, and she wanted the truth. Tonight.

She splashed water on her face to mix with her minty organic face wash and allowed her pores to open. After brushing her teeth, she stepped into the shower underneath one of two solid-brass Rainheads, tilting her head back and allowing her tears to be washed away. Frank was in bed naked and waiting for her, but if sex was what he wanted, he had better be prepared to get turned down once again.

While Mia was drying off, she noticed the sound from the television go mute. Seconds later, Frank said, "Baby, what's taking you so long?"

"I'm coming."

"That's what I hope to be saying in about twenty minutes."

She rolled her eyes. Twenty minutes was a generous estimate. Maybe that was how long he lasted with the other women he was sleeping with. With Mia, it was more like five minutes too many.

She changed into a long, plain cotton gown—nothing seductive—and pulled open the bathroom door. He sat on the bed, grinning. "You look so sexy."

Mia sat on the edge of the bed and looked at Frank dead-on. "Are you having an affair?"

Frank shifted uncomfortably. "I don't understand where that question is even coming from. No, I'm not cheating on you."

"So why did you have that extra cell phone?"

"What extra cell phone?"

"The one I found ringing in your carry-on luggage, Frank. With the woman on the other line calling you 'baby.' "

"I don't want to talk about this anymore, okay?"

"No, it's not okay, Frank, because I do," she said, her voice rising uncontrollably. "I'd rather you leave me than cheat on me. I'm not going to be with a cheater."

"What are you talking about, Mia? No one's cheating on you."

"I can't sleep next to a person I don't trust. If this cancer comes back, and I die, I don't want you rushing some woman into this house, because Alexa will never forgive you for that."

"Why do you keep saying that?"

"Because it happens. I can handle the truth. But I won't be with a liar. So tell me the truth. Are you cheating on me?"

His eyes fell downward as long seconds of silence passed by, confirming what Mia already believed.

"Listen, Mia, you have absolutely nothing to worry about."

"What exactly does that mean? Either you are, or you're not. If you don't love me anymore, be a man and say it."

"It's not because I don't love you."

"What's not because you don't love me? Say it. I want to hear you say you're having an affair. I want you to be honest."

"It's just . . ." He trailed off with a shrug.

"It's just what?" she shouted. Her tone shocked him to attention. "Will you please just say it?"

He sighed. "Yes, I cheated. One time, a while back. But I ended it. There was nothing to it, just sex. And I felt bad about doing it. I still do. But I swear to you it didn't mean anything. If we were having sex, I wouldn't have even done it—"

"Oh, so it's my fault you cheated?" Mia said, her temper rising.

"Well, if I was making love to my wife, I wouldn't have gotten weak. What was I supposed to do—masturbate?"

"That would've been the best idea," she said as she headed for the door.

"I was already doing that."

"Then you should've kept doing it."

"Until when? Until you made up your mind that you wanted to give me some?"

"Give you some?" Mia said as she shook her head. "I wish I could take back all the times I did give you some."

"Where are you going?"

"I'm sleeping in one of the guest bedrooms. You didn't think I was going to sleep next to a cheater, did you?" She slammed the door behind her and closed her eyes as she stood still for a second, but she didn't cry. She was too upset to cry. It was okay. At least now she knew the truth. She snatched the door back open and shouted, "And if you didn't have money, none of these women would want you, with your old Humpty Dumpty–looking ass." She slammed the door again, and this time she felt much better.

Mia stood confidently at the checkout counter of the exclusive department store in a long-sleeved, red-pepper-colored, belted contrast jacket with a white pencil skirt. She and Alexa—the dynamic duo—walked around Somerset Collection North shopping for Alexa's college wardrobe. They found nearly everything within an hour inside Saks Fifth Avenue, with the exception of the shoes.

"Every young lady needs a nice pair of pumps. They don't have to be like these," Mia said as she kicked back her four-inch Christian Louboutin heels with the signature red soles. "But please, not another pair of flats."

"I'll wear heels when you wear flats."

"You know what? If I wasn't so short, I probably would wear them." She reconsidered her answer. "Actually, probably not."

"And if I wasn't so tall, I'd wear heels. But probably not," Alexa said, teasing her mother.

"I'm sorry, ma'am, but this card was declined," the young saleswoman said as she handed Mia's credit card back to her.

"Declined? That can't be possible. It's a black card. Can't you see that?" Mia asked a bit arrogantly.

"Mom," Alexa said, looking down at her mother and shaking her head with disapproval.

"I just wanted her to know that there's no limit on that card. So can you please try it again?"

"I've already tried it twice, ma'am. Maybe you should call American Express. Maybe their system is down or something—"

Mia cut her off with a swish of her perfectly manicured hand. The sparkle from her ten-carat Neil Lane diamond should've spoken volumes to the minimum-wage-earning salesperson. Mia Marks-Glitch had money, and more than enough of it.

"I'm sorry for this inconvenience," the salesperson added, her tone more respectful.

"I'm sorry too. I know it's not your fault. Mix-ups happen sometimes. Just use this one." She swapped out her Comerica Bank card for the AmEx.

A few seconds later, the salesperson said, "I'm very sorry, but this one was also declined."

"Oh no. Now something really is wrong," Mia said, aggravated. "Because trust me, there's more than enough money in our bank account. I was just there this morning and withdrew some money, so I know our balance."

"I'm not sure why your cards aren't going through, ma'am, but I did run a sale through right before yours, so I doubt there's anything wrong with our system."

"I'll just pay you in cash," Mia said hurriedly. "I don't know what's going on, but this is getting embarrassing, and it's not my fault." She pulled several crisp hundred-dollar bills from a Comerica Bank envelope. She'd withdrawn twenty-five hundred dollars to put inside a greeting card for Alexa as one of her going-away gifts. The other was a brand-new car that would be arriving from the dealer any day.

"That's so strange," she whispered to her daughter.

"You spend too much money. Dad probably cut you off."

"Trust me, he wouldn't do that right now," she said, still fuming about the other night.

"Thank you, Mrs. Glitch," the salesperson said, smiling through braces, after handing Mia her change and a few shopping bags.

"I'm sorry if I had a little attitude. I just need to get to the bottom of this. But I do realize that it's not your fault." Mia plucked her change from the young woman's hand and took the shopping bags from the counter. Alexa grabbed the other bags and they strolled out of the store.

Mia tipped the valet generously after he pulled her Mercedes S-Class around. She couldn't wait to get into her car so she could pry her feet out of her peep-toe pumps. They were adorable, but felt like a torture chamber to her toes.

Mia's cell phone rang. It was her husband, Frank.

"Where are you?" he asked.

"We just left Saks, and for some reason our credit cards were declined. The black card and our Comerica card." Mia sat behind the steering wheel for a second before pulling off.

"I know," Frank said hurriedly. "The SEC has frozen everything. All of our accounts, business and personal. Everything. We don't have any money right now."

Mia slammed on the brakes. "What? Hold on. Let me turn down the radio, because I don't think I heard you correctly."

"You heard me. But I promise you, this is some kind of misunderstanding, and I'm going to handle it as soon as I get back home. But right now, I'm out here stranded in Chicago. I called the office, but no one's answering. Do you have any money on you or at the house?"

"A little. How much do you need?"

"Eighteen hundred dollars."

"I don't have that much."

"Well, I'm going to need you to borrow some money from your parents and Western Union it to me."

"From *my parents*? You can't be serious." She glanced over at Alexa, who was too busy texting, with her iPod headphones stuck in her ears, to pay attention to Mia's conversation. But Mia still didn't feel as if she could speak freely with her daughter in the car. She circled the parking lot of Saks Fifth Avenue. She knew there was no way her parents would loan her eighteen dollars, let alone eighteen hundred, as tight as they were with money. And they'd wonder how she and Frank could afford to buy a million-dollar home and three expensive cars, yet not have enough money to pay a hotel bill. Mia was wondering the same thing. She could just imagine the conversation with her mother. She would certainly remind her of her suspicions of Frank when they were first dating. How she always had a gut feeling that he was up to no good with his fancy cars, flashy suits, and shiny business cards with a PO box for a mailing address and a business phone number he rented from an answering service in Southfield.

"Why so much?" she asked him as she parked in the first available space she could find.

"I'm staying at the Peninsula, where I always stay when I'm in Chicago, and rates aren't cheap here. Just please get the money. I just need to get this straightened out before it hits the news."

Mia's nose flared wildly. "Frank, why would a misunderstanding make the news? What aren't you telling me?"

"Why haven't you been listening to anything I've just said?"

"I have, and none of it's making any sense."

"The SEC froze our accounts—"

"I understand that, but tell me why, and please don't say it's a misunderstanding. Be a little more specific."

There was a momentary pause.

"They're trying to say that I conspired along with a few others to defraud the city's pension fund. Now the FBI is involved. I didn't bribe any city officials. I didn't steal from any of the pension funds either. It's all one huge misunderstanding." He paused again. "But it's possible one of my business partners might've been involved."

"Oh my God, oh my God," Mia said, feeling a twinge of panic.

Alexa stopped texting and removed the headphones from her ears. "What's wrong, Mom? Why are we still here?"

"We have to return all of this. I'll take you shopping next week."

"Return it for what? What's wrong?"

"Nothing . . . just a big mix-up," she muttered as she avoided her daughter's gaze.

Frank's voice came through clearly on the other end, strong and resolute. "I'm going to get this straightened out as soon as I get home. I don't want you or Alexa to worry. It's going to be fine."

Mia's head shook slowly. She believed him as much as she believed the woman in the background was the TV. As much as she believed that he'd only cheated on her once.

"I should have the Western Union to you in an hour, if not sooner," she said. She ended the call just as he was saying "I love you."

It was amazing how her life had changed so drastically in twenty-four hours.

Chapter Four

July 1978

During the summer before Mia's junior year in high school, she started working as a bus girl at a cafeteria-style restaurant in Northland mall in Southfield, a nearby Detroit suburb. She'd need money if she planned on going to Mexico in April with Glory's Spanish National Honor Society. It cost a sizable sum of money—money her parents didn't have.

Her mom had worked for fifteen years as a seamstress and loved the family who owned the dry cleaner's. But she didn't make that much. As a 1099 employee, she was considered an independent contractor, which meant she was basically self-employed, and therefore wasn't entitled to any benefits. It was also her responsibility to pay the IRS taxes on the money she earned.

Mia's father worked for the City of Detroit's Public Works

Department. He was part of a team responsible for maintaining the city streets, alleys, and sidewalks. He often complained that his pay could've been better if he had a college degree. It was something that seemed to bother both of her parents. So they worked hard and saved as much as they could. Splurged on very little, if anything at all, to ensure their three children—Mia and her two brothers—were provided with a quality education, which meant the family often did without.

But that quality education also meant that Mia went to school with kids who had a lot more than she had. Even though they all wore uniforms, she could still tell who had money and who didn't. All she had to do was look at the shoes they wore, the clothes they wore on free-dress day. Their parents drove nicer cars and lived in better houses. Mia wanted what they had. She never wanted to ask how much something cost before she bought it, like her parents always did. She wanted to buy without worrying about price. She'd often tell herself that when she became an adult, she was going to buy designer clothes for herself and her children instead of making their clothes, like her mother did. She was going to dine at four-star restaurants—something she and her siblings weren't exposed to, even on special occasions. She wanted to live in a gated mansion and have a maid and a chef. She wanted a life that her parents probably never dreamed of. She could do better than they did. All she had to do was marry a man who had a lot more than her father did, which she was sure wouldn't be difficult.

As Mia prepped one of the booths at York Steakhouse, she

reminisced about her floater job at J.L. Hudson's. Working in retail was a lot better than cleaning dirty tables and washing dishes at a restaurant. She loved it when she used to be assigned to the Woodward Shop at Hudson's. That was her chance to see what she considered to be the wealthy women of Detroit, or at least those with the best fashion sense, like Chris's mom, whom she'd helped once.

"I went to school with your sons," Mia had told the woman, who had arched her right eyebrow and said, "I don't recognize you. Do you live in the neighborhood?"

Fortunately for Mia, a woman whom Chris's mom actually recognized tapped her on the shoulder before Mia had a chance to respond. The two women both wore huge rocks on their wedding fingers, which Mia noticed as they embraced. She used that as her opportunity to help another woman, who was waiting at a far register. Anything so she wouldn't have to continue the conversation with Chris's mom. Most likely Mia would've lied and said she lived in Palmer Woods.

Mia decided to quit that job after she spent her first paycheck—what little she made working twenty hours a week for minimum wage—on clothes. She ended up at York, where she'd gone for lunch once with a coworker. York offered more hours, which was what Mia needed if she was going to save up enough money for her Mexico trip.

Mia spotted Danielle as soon as she entered the restaurant. Danielle had said she had something urgent she wanted to talk to her about. Something she couldn't wait until later that evening to share, even though Mia would be at Danielle's house for the weekend.

Mia sat in the booth she was cleaning, with her hairnet and apron on, and Danielle slid in across from her.

"What's wrong?" Mia asked.

Danielle looked at her sheepishly. "Me and my dad got into it—"

"Again?" Mia said with a sigh. She was becoming annoyed. They'd known each other for two years, and Mia couldn't count the number of times Danielle had spent the night at her house to escape her dad. She also couldn't count the number of times she'd slept over at Danielle's house—because she never had.

"What do you mean 'again'? You and your dad always get into it," Danielle retorted. Shortly after the night Mia's dad had left, he returned to the house with proof that the child wasn't his. His mistress grudgingly supported his claim. Mia's mom forgave him for what he claimed was a onetime affair. Mia would never understand why.

"Every time I'm supposed to spend the night, you and your dad get into it. So what's the real reason I can't spend the night? Is it because I'm black?"

"What? No," Danielle said firmly. But Mia wasn't so sure. Mia's other best friend, Bridgette, wasn't allowed to sleep over at Mia's house because of the neighborhood Mia lived in, which hurt—once again making Mia feel like she wasn't good enough. And it would really hurt if Mia couldn't go to her other best friend's house because she was black.

August 2010

They were at the mediator's office in downtown Miami in a large conference room encased in glass. Danielle was sitting beside her attorney, Steve Wisk, and across from her stepsister, Claire, who was sitting beside her own attorney. There were also attorneys present on behalf of Danielle's publisher.

Danielle cast her eyes over her stepsister. Claire was ghostly pale. She'd always been that way. She avoided the sun to the extreme, and Danielle almost thought she was a vampire when they were growing up. She doubted if Claire had an ounce of blood in her body, which explained how she could be so cold. Her dark beady eyes reminded Danielle of marbles as she shifted them nervously. The only sane thing about her stepsister was the outfit she was wearing—a conservative gray pantsuit that Danielle was certain someone had picked out for her, because it wasn't Claire's style at all. She usually dressed like the tramp Danielle felt she was, often exposing her sagging cleavage, her skirts too short and cheap heels too high for her to comfortably walk in.

On her way to the mediation, Danielle had stopped by the post office to check her post office box. It had been a month since she'd last cleaned it out, and it was overflowing with mail. Going to the post office was something her assistant would normally do, but she still hadn't found a replacement for the last one she'd fired, whom she originally hired after she fired Claire.

A small envelope rested on top of her pile of mail. The return address was from "The Doctors and Staff of the Miami-Dade Animal Emergency Hospital." She opened the card as she sat in silence at the conference table while the attorneys reviewed legal documents.

On the front of the card was a picture of two dogs and the words:

> Though the sun sets, it rises yet again. . . .
>
> May fond memories of your beloved pet comfort you during your time of loss.

Inside, on a small separate sheet of paper was the "Rainbow Bridge" poem. The first sentence made Danielle's eyes water: *When a beloved pet dies, it goes to the rainbow bridge. . . .*

She had to pull herself together. She couldn't appear weak at that mediation hearing. Any sign of weakness could mean instant defeat. She tossed the card into her large leather tote bag and turned her cold gaze upon Claire. "You can afford to hire an attorney, but you can't afford to pay for your son to get his car out of the impound? He had to call me for the money. I'd bet my life you're suing me because you're broke. You never even worked before I hired you."

"That's a lie. I've had plenty of jobs," Claire said frostily.

"And you've been fired from every last one of them. You were my assistant for three long and miserable years. I paid you more than I paid any of my other assistants, even though you didn't work nearly as hard. I trusted you. I guess I'm a fool, just like my dad."

"All of your other assistants quit after a couple weeks," Claire scoffed.

"You're such a liar. None of my assistants quit. They were all fired."

"And that's better? You're so high-and-mighty, aren't you? You're just like you were in high school, which is why you had no friends then, and still don't."

"That's a lie. I had friends."

"One . . . and where is she now? You think you're all that just because you're a published author," Claire said with a smirk on her face. "Well, I write books too. And one of the books I wrote you stole from me."

"You can't even write a complete sentence. English was your worst subject. In fact, who did you go to when you needed to write a letter to your boyfriend begging him to take you back? And he took you back too, didn't he?" Danielle could feel herself getting mean-spirited, but she couldn't stop.

"Mrs. Newsome," Claire's attorney said. "Let's try to resolve this peacefully. There's really no need to raise your voice at my client."

"My name is Miss King," Danielle snapped. "And it won't be

resolved peacefully, because she's lying, and I'm not settling. I'm not giving her anything. I'll spend every dime I have just to make sure she doesn't get one cent, which means you won't either. And I definitely mean that."

"Danielle," Steve said as he tapped her shoulder. "Let's just listen to what they have to say."

She drew her arm away from his touch. "I don't want to hear what they have to say. And I'll tell you one thing—if Liza were alive today, we wouldn't even be sitting here, because she would've nipped this in the bud before it even got to this point." Danielle darted her eyes in Steve's direction before she stood.

"Miss King," Claire's lawyer said as Danielle headed for the door. "I'd hate to have to resort to going to the media."

"Do whatever you feel is necessary. Your threat doesn't scare me."

She walked out the conference room and slammed the door. Just as she walked away, she wondered if she had made a huge mistake. *The Keys* was her twentieth novel, and had been favorably reviewed. Steve was in the process of negotiating a movie deal. Negative press could put an end to all of that. She knew it didn't always matter whether a person was guilty or innocent. The accusation itself could destroy her.

In the car on the way home, she quickly dialed her daughter's cell number. "Let's go out to dinner," Danielle said over her hands-free unit. "Just the two of us. I'll take you anywhere you want to go."

"Is Dad going too?"

"No, just the two of us."

"But then Dad would be here all alone—"

"He's been alone before, Tiffany. Plenty of times. Everyone needs their space. Let's allow your father to have his 'me' time."

"But, Mom, I'm going off to college soon. Don't you think it would be nice for us to spend time together as a family?"

"I'd rather it just be the two of us spending time together as mother and daughter. Something we rarely do."

"You're still mad at Dad over Pulitzer, aren't you?"

"I don't want to think about that right now. I'd just rather it be the two of us."

"Mom, he didn't do anything to intentionally hurt Pulitzer."

"I was merely asking for you to go out to dinner with your mother. I didn't realize it was that big of a deal."

"It's not a big deal."

"Yes, it is. You've been a daddy's girl since the day you were born. Do you know what I'd give to spend a few hours with my mother?"

Tiffany let out a loud sigh. "Mom, I didn't say I wouldn't go. I'll go."

"Okay, then be ready when I get home."

Later that evening, Danielle and Tiffany sat at a table for four at Capital Grille. The walls were dark wood paneling, the tables covered in thick white cloths. There was marble at their feet, a chandelier over their heads, and plenty of food on their table.

"Do you think we should bring dinner home for Dad?" Tiffany asked.

"I'm sure your father has already eaten."

"But we're at his favorite restaurant, so maybe we should take something home for him."

"If that's what you want to do." Danielle swirled her wine around her glass, ready to shift the conversation away from Allen. "I can't believe you're leaving for school soon. Why would you want to leave the palm trees and ocean of southern Florida for the ice and snow of Michigan?" She took up a forkful of pan-seared red snapper with asparagus smothered in hollandaise sauce.

"Mom, you're from Michigan."

"And I had sense enough to leave. You could've just as easily gone to the University of Miami, or if you just wanted to get away from Miami, there's always the University of Florida or the University of Central Florida."

"But, Mom, I'm going to be a doctor, and I'm sure you, the Internet research queen, already know that U of M has one of the leading medical schools in the country."

"It's just that you're going so far away and we don't have relatives there."

"Yes, we do. I have cousins—"

"*Step*cousins. I know you still keep in touch with them, though I have no idea why."

"Because I've always wanted a big family. It's tough being an only child, and they're the only cousins I have."

"You don't need cousins. All you need is a really good friend like Anna. Where's she going to school again?" Danielle asked, referring to Tiffany's best friend from high school.

"You already know she's going to Miami."

"Oh, yes, that's right." Danielle glanced down at her daughter's plate; remains of a sirloin steak smothered in a rich cream sauce, a side of lobster macaroni and cheese, and onion rings graced the plate. "Where are your green vegetables?"

Tiffany rolled her eyes. "It's too late for that—I'm nearly done with my food. So what's going on in your life, Mom?" she asked, ready to change the subject.

"Well, your aunt Claire is suing me. Which is another reason why I don't want you visiting her when you're at school."

"She is?" Tiffany asked, swiping a bit of cream sauce from her plate with her finger.

Danielle was just about to launch into a tirade against Claire when the waiter approached their table.

"Would you ladies like some dessert?"

Tiffany looked over at her mother. "Will you split it with me?"

"No, I'll pass. Knock yourself out." She observed Tiffany carefully. She didn't want to ruin the night by continuing to lecture her daughter about her eating habits.

Tiffany perused the menu. "No red velvet, huh?" She glanced over at her mother, and after a moment put the menu down. "That's okay. I changed my mind. Could I just have some more water?"

Danielle grinned. "And I'll have a glass of Chartreuse."

"Why are you smiling at me?" Tiffany asked after the waiter left their table.

"My little girl is growing up."

"Why, because I didn't order dessert? If I was really grown-up, I would've ordered a glass of Chartreuse."

Danielle laughed. She hadn't had one-on-one time with Tiffany for so long. She had forgotten what it was like, just the two of them.

"What's wrong?" she asked as Tiffany studied her.

"Can I ask you a question?"

"Of course you can."

"If you had a friend and she had a boyfriend and he was trying to come on to you, would you tell her?"

"A boy hit on you?" Danielle asked in excitement.

"Why are you getting so excited? Forget I asked." Tiffany picked up her water glass, a hurt look in her eyes.

"I'm sorry, but you never talk about boys."

Tiffany's eyes rolled. "I never talk about boys because you act like this."

"Do you have a boyfriend?"

"No, Mom, I don't. Can you just answer the question?"

"Have you ever had a boyfriend?"

Tiffany sighed. "No, I've never had a boyfriend, because guys don't think I'm cute. And it's not just because I'm overweight, because there were plenty of overweight girls at my high school with boyfriends."

"Guys must think you're cute if Anna's boyfriend hit on you."

"How do you know it was Anna's boyfriend?"

"Please. A mother knows."

Tiffany paused. "Yeah, it's Anna's boyfriend. Should I tell her?"

"Does she like this boy?"

"She says she loves him."

"If you tell Anna, she won't believe you. A beautiful, confident girl like Anna is going to find it impossible that a boy would cheat on her. She'll confront him, and he'll laugh it off and call you jealous. The friendship will be over. Are you prepared for that kind of outcome?"

"How do you know so much about this?" Tiffany asked, narrowing her eyes.

Danielle paused, her wineglass at her lips. "Let's just say I've been through a similar situation before."

"Mom, not to be mean, but I didn't know you ever had a close friend before. I mean I know you have writer friends, and I know you're friends with a couple of your fans, but who are your real friends?"

The comment stung. "What's your definition of a real friend?"

"Someone you can share your innermost thoughts with, who will give you great advice. Someone who won't judge you, won't tell other people your secrets."

Danielle looked away, a bit wistful. "I suppose I did, once. Now you're my only real friend."

"And Dad."

"Yes, and your father," she said without hesitation. Even if she had her doubts, there was no reason to express those to their child. Allen wasn't the best husband, but he was a great father, after all.

Danielle looked up and signaled the passing waiter. "I think we'll have dessert after all," she said, winking at her daughter. "Why shouldn't friends share a little sugar?"

Chapter Five

April 1979

Mia stood in front of baggage claim keeping a watchful eye out for her mother's flowered suitcase, which she'd reluctantly borrowed for her Mexico trip. Her mother's bag was ugly, but it was better than putting her clothes in a black trash bag, she supposed. The one week she'd spent in Mexico with the National Honor Society was an unforgettable experience. Now she was back in the States with a few mementos. There was the sterling silver bracelet with sixteen charms that she and Danielle each bought from a large flea market in Mexico City, using some cash and a box of Bic pens for their purchase. They'd been told before they left the States that Bic pens were a precious commodity in Mexico, so they'd stocked up. Their bracelets were similar, but a couple of the charms were different. Danielle's had two pitchers and Mia's had an Aztec calendar and a sandal.

The day before they were to fly back to the States, Mia checked in with her mother to make sure one of her parents would be at the airport to pick her up on time. If there was one thing Mia hated, it was waiting. Something her parents made her do often. Neither of them could come to the airport. Both of her parents' cars had been in the shop for almost the entire week Mia had been in Mexico. Not surprising, since her mother had settled on a Plymouth Volare that had been plagued with problems from the day she drove it off the lot. Her father was still tooling around in an eight-year-old Chrysler Newport Royal.

She'd asked Danielle for a ride home. And even though Danielle told her no problem, she'd seemed so hesitant that Mia asked her again to make sure it was okay.

"Remember when you were embarrassed when I overheard your parents arguing?" Danielle asked. Mia nodded. "Well, that's how I feel about my dad and his wife. She'll probably be the one to pick me up. You already know I don't like her. But don't worry, I'll make her take you home."

"What if she doesn't want to?"

"It's not about what she wants to do. She wouldn't even have a car to drive if it wasn't for my dad."

"But shouldn't you ask her first?"

"I'm not calling her all the way from Mexico to ask her if she'll take you home. She'll do it," Danielle had told Mia.

"But isn't that kind of rude?"

"Rude is marrying a woman you barely know and forcing her and her obnoxious children on your teenage daughter. That's rude."

After picking up their luggage from baggage claim, the girls headed out to the curb in front of the terminal. Danielle's stepmom was parked with a cigarette stuck between two fingers and her driver's window cracked. The top of her head skimmed the hood of her Granada. From the way she darted her dark eyes as Mia loaded her luggage into the trunk and hopped into the backseat, it was evident that there was a problem.

Mia was surprised at the way Danielle's stepmother looked. She assumed that any woman who could seduce a man into marriage within a couple months of his wife's death with little to offer had to be gorgeous. But she was far from it. Her face was long and her chin pointy. She had pale skin and her dirty blond hair had see-through ends from too much bleaching.

"Will you please take my friend home?" Danielle asked as she slid into the passenger seat.

"Well, it's a fine time to ask me after she's sitting in the car." She flicked the cigarette butt out of the window and rolled it up. "I have some bad news for you, Danielle."

"Did something happen to Zeus?" she asked in a panic. She'd been looking forward to the trip, but she didn't want to leave her beloved dog behind. The whole time she was in Mexico, she had worried about him, and wondered whether her father was taking good care of him.

"Claire was walking him and he got loose and a car hit him. He died," she said dispassionately.

Danielle sat stiff and silent for a moment right before she let it rip. "You-all are determined to ruin my life, aren't you?! I feel like I've been forced into hell and you're my tour guide. You let that bitch walk my dog, and now he's dead?" She started crying uncontrollably. "And I know she did it on purpose, because she hates me, but not as much as I hate her!"

"It wasn't on purpose. What is wrong with you? She loved that dog just as much as you did."

"I wouldn't let her near him, because I knew if I did, something like this would probably happen. I just knew it." Danielle burst into tears again. "Where is he?"

"Your dad buried him in the backyard."

"You couldn't even wait until I got home."

"And have a dead dog in the house for two days?"

"I hate you! You and that bitch are evil. All both of you do is take, take, take."

"Listen here—I will not let you disrespect my child. My Claire feels bad enough, so if all you plan on doing when you get home is making her feel worse, I'll drop you over at that girl's house," she said, staring at Mia through the rearview mirror.

"Can't you understand how Danny feels?" Mia asked from the backseat. "I was the one who gave Zeus to her, and I know how much she loved him."

"Was anyone talking to you? No, so just shut the fuck up," Danielle's stepmother said, spitting out the words.

Mia was stunned.

"I'm getting out," Mia said as she tried to open the locked door while Danielle's stepmother was pulling out of the terminal. "Stop and let me out. I'll call Chris to come get me."

"You want to get out, jump," Danielle's stepmother said as she unlocked the back passenger door, "because I didn't want to go into Detroit anyway."

"Stop the car, you bitch," Danielle shouted. "I'm getting out too."

Danielle's stepmother slammed her foot on the brake, unlocked the trunk, and said, "Get out! Both of you."

"Now how are we getting home?" Mia asked Danielle after they got out of the car.

"I thought you said you were calling Chris."

Mia knew Chris would come all the way out to Metro Airport to pick her up. But she quickly changed her mind about calling him. He'd never seen where she lived, and that was intentional. So instead, they got a ride with a parent of one of the other Spanish Honor Society members, who took both of them home.

August 2010

Mia was in the midst of vacuuming the lower level of her house when she inadvertently knocked the home phone, which had been ringing nonstop, off a table.

She picked it up and heard a voice at the other end. "Hello," she said as she turned off the vacuum cleaner.

"Hi, I was trying to reach Frank. Is he in?" a man asked.

"No, he isn't. Is there a message you'd like to leave, or something I can help you with?"

"Is this his wife?"

"Yes."

"Mrs. Glitch, this is Ed Jordon with Allied Recovery."

"Is there something I can help you with?"

"Actually, yes. We handled the leases on the two Mercedes and your Rolls-Royce Phantom."

"We only have one Mercedes."

"Actually, my records indicate that you have an S600 and a CL65 AMG."

"I have the S600. I wish I did have a CL65 AMG."

"Okay, well, all three of these cars are on the same account. And two of them are almost three months past due."

"Which two?"

"The two Mercedes."

"So the Phantom is paid?"

"Yes."

It was all Mia could do to contain her anger. Where was this other Mercedes? And why were Frank's car payments up-to-date but not hers? "Interesting," she said, biting her lip.

"We received a check today without a payment slip and we have no idea which vehicle to apply the payments to. The memo line has your husband's last name and it says 'for Mercedes.' The check isn't large enough to cover both, so I'm not sure which one you wanted to pay. It can bring your S600 current and paid up one month in advance, or it can pay two months on the CL65."

"You received a check from my husband?"

"No, from a Stephanie Reese."

"Oh, okay, yes, Stephanie," Mia said, playing along. She had no idea who the woman was, but she could make an educated guess. "What was the address on the check? I'm trying to figure out which one of our accounts she's using," Mia said as she reached for a notepad and pen in their home office.

"It appears to be her personal account. But the address is Eighty-two Hundred East Jefferson in Detroit."

"Shoreline East," Mia mumbled as he proceeded to give the apartment number. It was Frank's old condominium. The one he was living in when they started dating. And the one they lived in for the first two years of marriage. They moved after Mia became pregnant. He rented it out for a few years afterward, but he claimed he'd sold it. That was fifteen years ago. "Okay, yes, that's intended for the S600."

"So we'll apply those funds to the S600. Now, as for the CL65 AMG, as I mentioned, it's approaching three months past due. In order to stop the repossession that's scheduled for the end of this month, which, as you know, is just a couple of days away, we'll need at least two payments."

"I understand. And I will work on getting that for you. I need to also give you an updated phone number. My cell is the best number to reach us on."

After she gave the man her number and ended the call, she sat stewing over the information. She always said she could handle the truth. But this was the first time she'd felt like she was finally getting it. She had thought fast on her feet, and she was proud of herself. Now she had the other woman's name, she knew where she lived, and she knew what kind of car she drove. Mia had taken the money the woman intended to pay for her own car and used it to pay Mia's car note, which was a nice little payback. She seriously doubted Frank would say anything to her. He'd have to give himself away.

The phone started ringing again, and Mia snatched it up, eager to see what other lies she could catch Frank in. But this collector wasn't as nice as the last. He was calling about one of their credit cards, which had been maxed out with a balance of just over fifteen thousand dollars. And they wanted the money now.

"Let me have six glazed and six powdered," Mia said as she stood behind the bulletproof glass at Dutch Girl Donuts.

Though she had returned the clothes Alexa had picked out at Saks for school and sent Frank the money by Western Union to pay his hotel bill, they still had to pay off the collectors that were calling night and day. She had every intention of stopping by her parents' home to ask for the cash she so desperately needed. But first, she stopped at the doughnut shop that sat on the corner of their street. It was sad for her to see how much the area had changed, and how many of the existing businesses had either moved or closed.

Sydney Bogg's, the candy shop that had been right next door to Dutch Girl for years, had moved to the suburbs. Backstage Deli, another favorite spot of Mia and Danielle's when they were teenagers, never reopened after it burned down.

After Mia paid the man behind the glass, he quickly boxed up her doughnuts and handed them over to her. Her cash was dwindling, and while it may not have made much sense to waste what little she did have on doughnuts, it was cheaper than alcohol, and for Mia much tastier.

She sat in her car for a few minutes with the white box resting on her lap. Her tears fell on the blue lettering that read SO DELICIOUS! and smeared it. Why should she even bother to ask her parents for money? They didn't have any. And even if they did, they'd say they didn't. And besides, she couldn't admit to being broke. Not after she'd rubbed her husband's success in their face with her extravagant gifts they never wanted to accept.

For years, Mia had held fast to an idea. People admired successful people. They were nicer to those who had versus those who didn't. She'd grown up a have-not and was determined to have much more than she ever did as a child. And she was going to make sure that her daughter did too. When she was younger, she had known her teacher's salary wouldn't be enough to provide the lifestyle she desired, even with a master's degree. So she used what she did have—her good looks—to get what she wanted: money. But now both were slipping away. She certainly didn't look as good as she used to when she was younger. Rarely did a man look in her direction these days. As for the money, well, Frank might have some stashed away, but he wasn't telling her about it.

Mia drove down the one-way street her parents lived on, and stopped in front of their brown brick home. It still had ivy growing between the bricks that covered most of the front and a great deal of the sides. Downstairs was an enclosed patio, and directly above it was a porch that looked as if it might cave in at any minute.

The street Mia had grown up on had never been the best, but it certainly used to look a whole lot better than it did now. There were so many boarded-up homes that the entire street of mostly two-family flats could easily be mistaken for abandoned. Her parents had owned their home outright for thirty-three years. For many years, Mia's entire family lived downstairs, and her parents rented out the upstairs flat. And the money they collected for the upstairs rent was enough to pay her parents' mortgage each month.

Now her mother lived downstairs and her father lived upstairs. It had been that way ever since her mother discovered her father had had an affair. Though she had forgiven him, she altered their living arrangement. And seemed all the happier for it. Mia was ready to follow in her mother's footsteps, and more. She wasn't just moving to another level of the house. She was ready to leave Frank. Let people think what they wanted to think. She wasn't leaving because the money was gone. She was leaving because she wasn't going to sit silently by while her husband fed her lie after lie.

Mia rang the doorbell to her mother's house even though she had a key. The last time she entered without the decency of knocking first, her mother told her she was being inconsiderate. But Mia figured her mother was mad because Mia saw her father downstairs in the kitchen with her mother having breakfast in his pajamas. That was her mother's business, and whatever she wanted to do with Mia's father was also her business. Mia no longer lived there, and she thanked God for that nearly every day.

"You look purdy," Mia said after her mother answered the door with a bottle of dark red nail polish in her hand. "I know you bought that one, didn't you, Mama?" she asked, eyeing her outfit.

"You know I only buy shoes, underwear, and panty hose. Everything else I make myself," she said proudly. Mia's mother had on a scoop-neck royal blue dress that was belted at the waist and a pair of flip-flops with bright yellow spacers between her toes.

"So you're giving yourself a pedicure? Your husband must be taking you out," Mia said.

"He's taking me out to dinner for my birthday."

Mia stopped cold as she walked down a short hallway to the downstairs flat. She had been so wrapped up in her own problems, she had forgotten her own mother's birthday, which was the day before. "Happy birthday, Mom," she said, tentatively.

"Thank you, sweetie." Her mother settled down on the sofa and propped her foot up on the coffee table. "I have to admit, it's a surprise to see you here. Did you just come to wish your mother a happy belated birthday? Your father had himself a field day talking about how you couldn't even pick up the phone and call me yesterday. But I told him you're busy getting Alexa ready for school."

"If you had gotten on Facebook like I told you, I would've gotten a reminder," Mia said, halfheartedly defending herself.

"I told you I'm too old for that space book, and besides, I'm your mother and I've been your mother for forty-eight years. What more of a reminder do you need than that?"

As Mia watched her mother glide that same dark red nail polish that she'd been wearing for years over the nail of the big toe on her left foot, she became too nervous to ask for help. Growing up, she worked and saved up for whatever she wanted as soon as she was old enough to work. Before that, she did without whenever they told her no, which was often. She took a deep breath and then swallowed. "Mom, I'm actually here because I need to ask you a huge favor."

"I'm listening," she said nonchalantly as she continued painting her toes. She didn't even glance over at Mia, who was sitting on a love seat kitty-corner from the sofa her mother was sitting on.

"Frank's business is going through a little rough patch right now, and we just need to borrow some money to sustain ourselves until he gets everything back in order."

"How much money are you talking about?"

"It would just be a loan."

"How much?"

"I'm thinking twenty thousand."

Mia's mother started to chuckle. At first her laugh was so soft that Mia didn't know if it was a laugh or a cough, but the more her mother shook her head, the louder her laughter became. She looked over at Mia. "You must be out of your mind. Do you honestly think I have that kind of money?"

"I was just asking. Believe me, it took a lot for me to come here."

"I definitely believe that, because you hardly ever come over and visit us. I can't even remember the last time. We're always going to your house. It's not like you live in another state like your brothers. They call me more than you do. You act like you're ashamed of us. And you've acted that way for the longest time."

"Why would you say that?"

"Your father has been telling you for years that you and Frank have been spending too much money living high on the hog. I know it must be real bad if you have to ask us for money. Because the one thing I will say about you, you've always worked for what you wanted. The problem must be that husband of yours."

"Mom, I'm not here to discuss Frank. I just wanted . . . I just need help. I thought that's what family was supposed to do. Help each other when they need it."

"I'm not rich. And I never have been. I can't speak for your father. He's upstairs if you want to ask him and see what he says."

Mia crossed her arms. "No, thank you. I already know what he'd say."

"So what happened with his business?"

"It doesn't matter."

"Do you still have your health insurance?"

Mia stood and prepared to leave. "Happy belated birthday again, Mom. Forget I asked you, and please don't mention it to Dad."

"Oh, I won't, because I'm not in the mood to hear all that cursing."

Mia kissed her mother on the cheek, and walked back to her car feeling foolish. There she was, stepping into one of the most expensive Mercedeses ever made, parked outside a house that probably wouldn't sell for the amount of money she was asking to borrow. Times were tough for so many, including her mother. And her dad . . . well, going to him wasn't even a consideration. She glanced down at her Rolex watch. She and Frank had plenty of expensive jewelry they could pawn. And he had parents he could ask for help as well.

When she arrived home, she headed straight for her walk-in closet and the safe with combination lock where she kept all her jewelry. Over the years, she and Frank both managed to accumulate an impressive collection of gold and diamonds. Mostly everything she acquired was gifts from Frank. And she was pawning all of it, including her wedding ring, which had been upgraded for the third time two years earlier. As she was setting aside pieces that she assumed would fetch the most at a pawnshop, she came across the sterling silver charm bracelet that she bought in Mexico. It made her think of Danielle and wonder about the type of life she was living. One thing she knew she wasn't doing right now was struggling to pay bills. Danielle had managed to accumulate a fortune on her own, which was something Mia wished she had done as well. "It's always best to have your own so you won't have to depend on a man for nothing," her mother had told Mia and Danielle when they were fifteen, after she'd kicked Mia's father out the house. Evidently, Danielle took heed of Mia's mother's advice. If only Mia had.

Mia tossed the charm bracelet back in the safe in a tray where she kept her higher-priced costume jewelry.

"Why do you have your jewelry out?" Frank asked as he walked into the room.

"We need money, and this is the answer," she told him. "You need to get yours out too. We need to pawn everything."

Frank shook his head. "No."

"What do you mean, no?"

"I mean no. It may be tight right now, but it's not that tight. Have you ever been to a pawnshop?"

"No."

"A piece like this," he said, holding up a Cartier watch he'd bought Mia for her forty-fifth birthday, "I paid forty-eight thousand dollars for. The pawnshop would probably give us five hundred, if we're lucky."

"Then maybe we should sell it. If the watch cost that much, I'm sure someone will pay ten or fifteen thousand for it. And you have tons of expensive watches."

"Because I collect watches. And I'm not selling any of 'em."

"We don't have any money, Frank. We have to do something. Now is not the time to be materialistic. Do you think I don't like nice things?"

"Oh, trust me, I know you do."

Mia ignored the comment. "But right now we don't have any

money, and we probably have a million dollars' worth of jewelry in this house, and we need to get rid of some of it. Most of it, actually, because we need money. I'm tired of these bill collectors calling and threatening me. I can't handle all of this stress."

"I told you not to answer those calls. Just let them go to voice mail. I'm getting some money from my parents."

"We need a lot of money, Frank."

"I'll get enough money to pay the main bills."

"I'm going to ask Viv for a job, because I can't live this way. I need health care, which means I need a job."

"Okay, well, you know what you need."

"That's right, I do."

Mia had been tempted to let him know what she knew about Stephanie Reese, the other Mercedes, the condo—the truth. But she was so proud of herself for not mentioning the call from the collector. Frank would find out in a couple days after the woman's car was repossessed. But in the meantime, Mia had a secret of her own for once. And she was going to pretend everything was normal until it all came to the forefront.

The next day Mia arranged to meet Viv for lunch. Viv was on time, but Mia had arrived early and anxious. They sat in a booth at the Beverly Hills Grill. Mia was nursing a glass of water with lemon. The restaurant wasn't far from her home, and practically right beside the hair salon she used to go to, when she could afford to pay to be pampered. But now she could barely afford to buy the hair products she needed to do her own hair. *Yet, somehow, Frank manages to keep the car note on his Rolls-Royce current,* she fumed.

A waiter came to their table to take their orders. Mia didn't bother ordering an appetizer, even though she had a taste for fried calamari. But she had only twenty dollars on her, which was barely enough for a Caesar salad with grilled chicken breast.

"So, what's going on, Mia? You're going to be on the holiday planning committee with me, right?" Viv asked. Viv always began planning the annual holiday book club party months in advance. It was often a swanky event.

"I am, but I'm not sure I'm going to have a lot of time this year. I've just got some things going on with me and Frank. We're going through a hard time right now."

Viv brushed past the remark as if she didn't hear it. "I want to go all out this year. I might look into inviting authors and combining it with a couple of other book clubs in the area."

"That would be nice," Mia said distractedly. She stared at Viv, not quite sure how to approach the subject, so she just blurted it out. "Is your school hiring?"

"Actually, yes. Why, do you know someone who needs a job?"

"Me."

Viv looked startled. "You?"

"I'm ready to go back into the classroom."

"You're ready to teach again after eight years?"

"I'm ready. And you know the Detroit board isn't hiring. They're laying off. And just between you and me, I need to work."

"Is everything okay?"

Mia decided to stay mum on the details. She trusted Viv to a certain extent. But like Mia's mother always said, "If you don't want your business to get out on the street, don't tell it." Besides, she'd been burned before by a good friend, and ever since then she'd kept her guard up. "I just want my own money. You know."

Viv didn't push her. "Believe me, I understand. That's the reason I couldn't care less if I get married again. I don't need a man for money. Not saying that you did."

Mia assumed that's exactly what Viv was saying, but she didn't care. All she cared about was finding a job with benefits. "I know this is short notice with school getting ready to start. So I'm sure you can't bring me on this year." She looked down at her napkin in her lap, hoping Viv would tell her she was wrong.

"Actually, I can bring you on at the start of the school year. I got some grant money, and we need to improve our test scores. I need a literature teacher."

Mia beamed. "You know I'd love to teach English."

Viv smiled back. "We go way back, and I know I can trust you. So let me forewarn you. The school is a little run-down. We have a lot of problem students, and many of the parents simply don't care if their kids are learning or not. But you can definitely have the job."

"Gee, thanks," Mia said facetiously.

"I'm just being honest with you. Even charter schools have their fair share of problems."

"I'm still looking forward to it." Mia couldn't believe her luck.

"Oh, and you definitely need to get a little cheap car. Don't drive up to that school in your Benz. I repeat, do not drive up there in your S600 Mercedes-Benz."

"Frank's parents have an old van they'll let me drive. It isn't a minivan, though. It's one of those big passenger vans, but at least it's in good shape."

Viv grabbed her hand. "I hope you and Frank can work it out. I mean, twenty years is a lot of time to invest just to walk away."

Mia shrugged, feigning nonchalance. There was a small mention of Frank's business trouble on the Internet. Mia had Googled Frank's business along with his name and found an article in the *Detroit Free Press* that briefly mentioned the SEC investigation. She doubted if Viv or anyone else she knew saw the article. Most people paid more attention to the big headlines anyway. But Mia had read the article three times and paid special attention to the part that mentioned that federal charges could possibly follow.

"We're going to be okay," she said before tucking in to her Caesar salad.

Their French-style country estate became a fading backdrop as Mia and Alexa trekked down their winding driveway. They wore similar Dri-FIT knit running pants and half-zip mock-neck tops. Mia held on to two bottles of water like they were small arm weights. One of the bottles was for Alexa, whose hands were preoccupied with selecting a song from her iPod's extensive playlist.

After Alexa was better situated, she reached for her water.

"What are you listening to?" asked Mia.

" 'Sweet Sweet Love.' That was back in your day," Alexa said after she removed her earphones. She enjoyed old-school music as much as Mia did.

"That was my jam. I can still remember the video with Vesta riding in that 'Vette. I wanted a 'Vette so bad after that."

"Why didn't you get one?"

"Well, by the time I could afford to, I didn't want one anymore."

"Yeah, I'm not really into 'Vettes either. Still waiting on my car, though."

"About your car," Mia said, her eyes cast downward.

"You and Dad can't afford to buy one, right?"

Mia was startled by her daughter's pronouncement. How much did she know? "Not right now."

"I'm glad you finally came out and told me, because I knew something was up."

"How?"

"Well, Saks was a big clue. I mean, we'd just left there and we had to turn around and go right back to return everything. And so many bill collectors have been calling. It's just pretty obvious. Not to mention you and Dad argue every day like you forget I live there too."

They passed several homes situated a great distance from the road. Alexa shoved the earphones back into her ears.

"I have some money now, so we can go back to Saks for your school clothes."

"Mom, keep that money. Something else might come up. I have more than enough clothes. It's not going to be a fashion show up there. Trust me—I'll be fine."

"Let's talk about you and Chris. How are you-all doing?"

"Fine."

"Do you think he's the one?"

"The one for what?"

"You know, the one that you'll marry."

"Mom, marry? I'm too young to be thinking about that right now. The only things on my mind are going to college and then to med school."

"I know. I was just curious. He bought you that promise ring and he looked me directly in my eyes and told me how serious he was about you."

"That made you happy, didn't it? You love Chris and his family."

"They're nice people."

"I already know that you and his father went to Holy Angels together."

"And his uncle Mark. Chris looks just like his father."

"I actually heard from his dad that you dated once?"

Mia laughed. "It was brief. Very brief. But I do still have a letter he wrote me somewhere. It was so beautifully worded."

Alexa's eyes enlarged as she gasped before covering her mouth.

"I thought he was just joking. Mr. Meyers used to be your boyfriend?"

"Back when we were fifteen."

"I can't wait to tell Chris that his dad wasn't joking."

"No, please don't do that. I don't want his wife to feel uncomfortable."

"She won't think like that. Mr. and Mrs. Meyers have the best relationship. They're not like you and Dad. They're like best friends. She'd think it was ironic."

"What do you mean, they're not like me and Dad?"

"Some of your fights get pretty loud. Dad cheated on you, right?"

Her daughter's question shocked her. Alexa was much more observant than she gave her credit for. "What made you ask me that question?"

"I was just wondering. He did. Didn't he?"

"No, he didn't. Your father would never do something like that. He's a good man."

"Mom, I love you and Dad, and I'm not taking sides, but it's obvious he's done something. Something is going down. Are you and Dad getting a divorce?"

"We have some issues, but hopefully we'll work them out. Don't you want your parents to stay together?"

"I want whatever will make both of you happy, and right now neither of you are. It's written all over your faces." Alexa took off on a sprint, and Mia trailed behind.

Chapter Six

May 1980

Danielle was parked in front of Mia's parents' home.

"I can't believe he stood me up," Mia said as she sat in the passenger seat of Danielle's Gremlin—the one she shared with her stepsister, Claire—in her fuchsia prom dress. "But then again, I can."

"What did your mom say?"

"The usual. 'I'm glad. . . . You didn't need to be going to the prom with him anyway. . . . He's too old . . . already in college. . . . Where did you meet him? . . . Where do you meet half the guys that call this house? . . . You're too fast.' The usual. If I'm so fast, why am I still a virgin?"

"This may not be what you want to hear right now, but your dress is pretty."

"You're right—I don't want to hear that. I've been stood up, and it doesn't matter how pretty my dress is. No one's going to see it."

"I don't usually like to say I told you so, but in this case—"

"Danielle, you know you love saying 'I told you so.' But did you tell me I was going to get stood up?"

"No. I just can't believe you quit Chris for that guy. I told you not to quit Chris."

"I didn't quit Chris for Raymond. I quit Chris for Peter. Then Peter quit me because I wouldn't have sex."

"So who is this guy?"

"This is the one I met at the Pub."

"I don't remember him."

"You weren't with me that night."

"Where was I?"

"I can't remember. That was last year."

"So who went with you?"

"Bridgette."

"Oh, that's why I didn't go. She doesn't like me."

"Everything happens for a reason," Mia said. "Remember that. Maybe the reason I'm not going to the prom is because I hate these shoes." She took one off and held it in her hand. They were pumps covered in silver glitter.

"When I said Bridgette didn't like me, why didn't you say, 'Yes, she does'?" Danielle asked.

Mia shrugged. "Because she probably doesn't, but she doesn't like a lot of people." She looked out the window, her arms crossed over her chest. "Forget him . . . his loss."

"I'm not going to the prom either. Not because I was stood up, but because no one asked. But that's okay. One day I'll be rich and famous and one of those boys who never gave me a second look will wish they'd asked me."

"I really wanted to go to prom. I was so looking forward to walking into the Henry Ford Museum with a college guy on my arm," Mia said angrily. "I never thought I'd be one of those girls who didn't go to their prom. I feel so lame."

"Like me, you mean."

"I'm just saying—"

"Yeah, I know. Anyway, I have a good idea, but this is only if you really want to freak Raymond out. Make him regret he ever stood you up."

"What?" Mia asked as she sat sulking.

"I'll drive you to Eastern in your prom dress. You can knock on his dorm room and start crying and saying, 'I thought you loved me,' and then burn down the dorm."

"Now you're scaring me. You've been reading too much Stephen King. I'm not Carrie."

"How about you just change and we go downtown?"

"On prom night?"

"Yeah, let's go see a movie."

"A movie? On prom night?"

"Got any better ideas?"

"Riding up to Eastern is starting to sound better than going to a movie on prom night."

"Go get changed. I'll show you what it's like to be lame."

So that night, instead of going to prom, they went to the Americana to see *The Empire Strikes Back*. It was as good a time as two dateless girls could expect on the night of their prom.

When Danielle made it home late that night, her stepmother was outside with a bottle of beer in one hand and a gun in the other.

"I'm going to kill that bastard," Linda said as she pointed the gun toward the house. "I don't care if the police are on the way. I'm still gonna kill him."

"Give me the gun, Linda," Danielle said sternly.

"If I give you the gun, I can't kill him. Maybe you'll kill him. You don't like him, and now I understand why." She turned to the darkened house. "I'm going to tell your daughter what you did," she shouted.

"What did he do, Linda?"

"I had to bail your father out of jail tonight. I should've let his ass rot there."

"Why was he in jail, Linda?" Danielle said nonchalantly.

"For trying to pick up a prostitute in *Detroit*," Linda said, spitting out the word. Danielle wasn't surprised, nor did she particularly care. If she had to deal with her father and his prostitutes, why shouldn't Linda have to? "Only she was an undercover cop, and you'll never guess what else she was."

"What else was she, Linda?"

"Black," she said, screaming the word "black."

"How do you know what color she was?"

"Didn't you hear me say he was picked up in Detroit? That's how I know. And besides, I drove around that Six Mile and Woodward area, and that's all I saw were a bunch of black whores like your little friend Mia."

Danielle was annoyed by the comment, but she wasn't going to convert her drunken stepmother from her ignorant ways. "Leave him. You don't have to deal with that," Danielle said, seizing the opportunity to finally get her and her kids out of the house.

"You want me to leave him. You'd love that, wouldn't you? Well, I'm not going to leave him. I'm going to take him to church so he can repent before the Lord."

And what about her stepmother's repentance? Danielle wondered. She was a sinner too. "We're all sinners," Danielle said. "He without sin cast the first stone."

The beer bottle her stepmother was holding fell to the ground and broke. "There's my stone."

"You don't think it's a sin to be prejudiced."

"I'm not prejudiced. I'm just not afraid to speak the truth."

"Like when you told the black girl at your job she wasn't going to ever amount to anything."

"It's the truth—she isn't."

"Just because she couldn't go to the manager's going-away party."

"Adrienne hired her, so the least she could've done was spend a couple of hours saying good-bye. Why was that so hard?"

"I wouldn't have been able to spend a couple hours with you either."

"Oh, just shut up," she said, jabbing the gun in her direction.

"I'm not scared of you, or your toy," Danielle said as she pushed past her stepmother and headed for the front door. "You might not be leaving, but I'm getting out of here soon," she said over her shoulder before letting the door swing shut behind her.

August 2010

Danielle and Allen were seated in the reception area of her therapist's office, where they remained even after Dr. Garcia walked out of her office to greet them.

"I'm back," Danielle said, still seated, regretting coming at all.

"It's good to see you again, Danielle."

"And this time I brought my husband," Danielle said, tipping her head toward Allen.

"Nice to meet you, Mr. King," Dr. Garcia said as she extended her hand toward him.

"Stand up, Allen," Danielle said as she got to her feet.

"My last name is actually Newsome," he said as he shook her

hand firmly. "She didn't take my name. I guess it didn't have enough of a ring to it."

"There you go again, Allen. Will you please get up and go into her office and stop all your complaining?"

"Please, after the two of you," the therapist told them as she waited for Danielle and Allen to enter her office. She followed behind them and closed the door. They each took their seats, and because no one wanted to talk, they sat in silence.

Dr. Garcia spoke up. "Couples therapy is the area I'm most passionate about. I believe that a person can have a soul mate, and when you connect to a person on a deeper level, there is no greater love. But I also believe that it sometimes takes time to build that level of intimacy. It's rarely love at first sight, like some people think it is."

"I know I'm not my wife's soul mate. If I were, I wouldn't be hearing day after day that I killed her dog."

"I asked you a million times to move that box. That's all you had to do, Allen. Move the box, and we wouldn't be sitting here."

"This is what I hear constantly," Allen told Dr. Garcia. "Coming here was not my idea. I'm not against therapy, but in our case, I don't believe it's going to help. My wife believes her money can solve all of our problems. We're here because she can afford to pay for therapy. If she can buy something to fix her problems, she will."

Danielle shot Allen a dirty look. "I'm doing the best I possibly can to get all of the disorder and chaos out of our lives before our daughter leaves for college and we're on our own. So, here we are, straightening things out. That's why we're here."

"Her issues started way before I even came into the picture. Let's talk about the fact that you were more heartbroken over the death of your dog than your own father." He darted his eyes in Dr. Garcia's direction. "Analyze that. Her issues stem from her father. Her dad was a nice man. And I always thought at some point she needed to forgive him, and that she should've done that while he was still alive."

"You didn't even know him," Danielle shot back angrily, hurt that Allen had touched upon such a sore spot. "He'd put his mask on and pretend to be one person in public, but when he came home, he took it off. And boy was he ugly. It wasn't until my mother died that I really learned what kind of man he was."

"In her eyes, I'm her father," Allen said. "So typical."

Danielle turned to the therapist. "The last time I saw him was a couple years before he died. I was in town for a book signing, so I figured I'd stop by, even though I didn't want to. The encounter was so negative that when I left the house, I vowed never to come back." She waved her hands. "It's more complicated than Allen will ever understand."

"Half the time you act like you hate me," Allen told Danielle.

"I don't hate you." Danielle took a long pause. "I just don't like you that much."

"Exactly what did I do to make you stop loving me, or even liking me?"

Danielle sighed heavily. "I don't want to deal with this right now."

"No, we shouldn't deal with this here in therapy. Let's just wait till we get back home."

Danielle sat there, silent. Allen was not without fault; that much she knew for sure.

A few days later, Allen and Tiffany left for the University of Michigan. Danielle stayed behind to do a signing at Books & Books and a reading at the Miami-Dade Main Library. Danielle was going to fly out and meet them two days later. But that afternoon, dark clouds suddenly rolled over the Miami sky. Danielle made sure all the windows in their condo were secured with permanent storm shutters after the National Hurricane Center upgraded the tropical storm to a hurricane warning.

"Are you at U of M?" Danielle asked as she drove northbound on the Florida Turnpike, as she passed the service plaza in West Palm Beach.

"No, Danny," Allen said, sounding rushed. "We just landed. Where are you?"

"Heading to Aunt Martha's."

"So they must've evacuated? So you're not coming?"

"Well, not unless you know of an airline that will fly out during a hurricane. I doubt this will pass quickly."

"I'll just spend more time with my daughter alone, I guess. That's what we're used to anyway."

Danielle held her tongue. Therapy had been a disaster, and

now she and Allen could barely say a civil word to each other. But she wasn't going to take the bait. Not this time. "Allen, listen to me. I want you to remind Tiffany to start taking the Quick Trim I bought her."

"She's not going to take that stuff."

"How do you know?"

"Because I told her not to."

"So you want our daughter to be fat and miserable while she's in college?"

"She's not fat."

"I don't have time to listen to this. Put Tiffany on the phone."

"Hold on," Allen said grudgingly.

"Hey, Mom," Tiffany said.

"Tiffany. I have some bad news—"

"You're not going to be able to make it."

"No, I'm not, but let me tell you why—"

"Because of your book deadline."

Danielle sighed. She didn't need this from both of them. "No, it's not because of that. There's a hurricane coming. I'm on the turnpike right now heading to Aunt Martha's."

"I guess I'll see you when I graduate."

"No, honey, I'll see you on Thanksgiving. Have a wonderful time at—"

"Okay, bye," Tiffany said, cutting her off.

Danielle heard the phone click before she could finish her sentence. She picked up her cell phone, which was resting in the center compartment, and was about to text a quick "I love you!" but her car started to drift into another lane. An eighteen-wheeler blew its horn, startling her.

She threw down the phone and put her hand to her chest, her heart thumping wildly.

"Damn it," she muttered. She was so distraught, she almost caused an accident.

The rest of the trip passed without incident. The drive from Miami to Belleview, a city in Marion County, Florida, with a population of just less than 3,500, where her aunt Martha lived, took Danielle almost four hours. Her aunt was sitting on her screened-in front porch with two of her miniature poodles sitting beside her as Danielle pulled into the driveway. The sight caused Danielle's eyes to water.

"I'm not going to do this to myself today," Danielle said.

Aunt Martha lived in a modest three-bedroom home with a carport attached and two large outdoor sheds out back: one for her mower and other lawn supplies, and the other for her three dogs to roam in and out of. There was a fence around her entire property to keep the dogs from straying. She'd done some recent upgrades to the property. Danielle didn't remember the stucco being a light gold tone, and there was a sign from a concrete company stuck in the front yard, so it was obvious she'd gotten her driveway repaved.

The two caught up as Aunt Martha walked her into the house, and Danielle relaxed on the sofa.

"So how's Allen and Tiffany doing?" Aunt Martha asked, picking up one of her cats.

"They're in Michigan. Just got there a few hours ago. Tiffany is officially away at college."

"The last time I saw her, you-all had just moved here from California."

"Has it really been that long?" Danielle asked.

"Sure has."

She shook her head. "Wow, time flies. I'm sorry it's taken me so long to get out here."

"That's okay. There haven't been too many hurricane evacuations in the last few years," she said wryly.

Danielle shifted uncomfortably. "Aunt Martha, you're making me feel bad."

"Don't feel bad. I know you're a famous author and you don't have time for your little aunt Martha. Lucky for you, I'm always going to be here for you no matter how many books you write. At least you send me a new one every year. I read *The Keys* in one day. When does your next one come out?"

"I'm having trouble with my next one. Writer's block."

"That's because it can't be all that you do."

"It's not all I do." Danielle knew it was a lie. Allen and Tiffany knew better. When she wasn't writing, she was thinking about a character or a scene she was going to write.

"I want to show you something I found not too long ago," Aunt Martha said as she walked in a room down a small hallway and returned with a framed photograph.

"Do you remember this?"

"That's from my high school graduation." Danielle stared at the picture, taking it into her hands. It was of her and Mia in their caps and gowns.

"Whatever happened to Mia?"

"You remember her name? You have a good memory, Aunt Martha. I haven't spoken to her in years."

"That's too bad."

"Yeah, it is, but that's life." She didn't want to get into it. "Will you make me some deviled eggs, Aunt Martha?"

"What is it with you and my deviled eggs?"

"They're so good. Even Mia thought so, remember?"

"I remember. She was such a sweet girl. And she seemed like a genuine friend."

Danielle followed her aunt into the kitchen and sat at the glass dinette table.

"Do you want me to help?" Danielle asked as her aunt pulled a carton of eggs from the refrigerator.

"No, all you need to do is sit back and relax, because you just had a long drive." Aunt Martha put the eight eggs in a large saucepan and filled it with cold water until the eggs were just covered. She set the saucepan on the stove and turned the burner on high to bring them to a boil. After the eggs had simmered for close to ten minutes, she removed the pan from the stove, drained the water, and ran cold water over the eggs to cool. "So what happened between you and Mia?" she asked as she joined her at the table. "I always thought you were the best of friends."

"I don't know, Aunt Martha. It's hard to explain other than to say we drifted apart shortly after my first book was published."

"You don't think she was jealous of your success, do you? Because that can happen."

"I don't think so." Danielle's thoughts flew to Mia screaming at her and telling her how much she hated her the last time they spoke. "No, I don't think it was that at all."

"Well, I guess if she was truly your friend, she would've kept in touch with you. You're a lot easier to find than most. You have your own Web site. I was on it the other day. I like looking at the pictures you put up from all your events. But why aren't you on that Twitter?"

"It's just a bit self-indulgent, if you ask me," Danielle said with a shrug. "I'm all for social networking, but I have to draw the line somewhere, and my line is drawn at tweeting."

Aunt Martha nodded wisely. "I was thinking about your mom the other day."

"You were? What about?"

"Oh, just things we used to do when we were little. Like our Girl Scout troop, and how much she loved to sing. I miss her."

"I miss her so much."

When her aunt stood to finish preparing the deviled eggs, Danielle closed her eyes and rubbed her head.

"Are you tired, honey?"

"I'm not feeling well. I wonder if this is what a migraine feels like."

"Go take a nap. I'll bring the eggs to you when I'm done."

"Thanks," Danielle said as she stood from the table. "You don't have to rush. You know I like to eat them cold anyway."

She dragged herself from her aunt's narrow kitchen into the small guest room. All of a sudden her head had started pounding. She didn't have to guess at the cause. It was her deadline. It was missing her daughter's milestone. It was the mention of Mia. It was a list that went on and on.

Chapter Seven

August 1980

It was the summer before their freshman year in college. They were both set to attend Michigan State, and they wanted to have one last hurrah before plunging into their studies. Mia and Danielle were on the train to Toronto. Mia tried resting, but she couldn't because Danielle was babbling on about all the places she wanted to visit. They had been planning this getaway with each other for so long, but Mia wasn't in the peppiest mood.

"There are tons of restaurants where I want to eat, and of course we have to go shopping at Eaton Centre."

"Who has money for that? I don't know how much money you earned over the last couple of summers, or how much you think I made at York Steakhouse, but it was only enough to pay for the train, half the hotel, and cheap food. That's it. Nothing extra. You know I don't have rich parents."

"I'm not a trust fund baby either," Danielle reminded her. "We can just walk around the mall and look."

"That's what I've been doing all my life, Danielle. Walking around and looking. I'd rather not go if I can't buy."

"Sure, you can. It starts in your mind. If you can imagine it, you can have it. *Think and Grow Rich* by Napoleon Hill. You really need to read that book."

"I don't need to see it in person to imagine it. I know what nice clothes look like. I've seen other people wearing them all my life."

"We can't come all the way to Toronto without going to the Eaton Centre. Ooh, and I want to take a tour of the CN Tower. And ride the trolleybus. Oh, God, we're going to have so much fun. I'm so glad Bridgette didn't come."

Mia nodded. "Yeah, I guess she didn't want to. I wasn't going to beg."

"She's not a real friend. I see it now. Maybe you're right. Maybe she does think she's better than us."

"I never said that."

"Yes, you did."

"No, I didn't."

"Mia, yes, you did."

"I never said that."

"Well, did you say her parents thought that way?"

"I didn't say anything about her parents."

"Mia, why are you denying this? You did. You said she wasn't even allowed to spend the night at your house."

"That's all I said. She wasn't allowed. You're adding in stuff. Besides, if I was going to talk about anybody's parents, it would be your stepmother."

"She's not a parent. Not mine, at least."

"I'm just saying if you're going to go around quoting me, at least get it right."

"Okay, okay." It was clear to Danielle that Mia was in a bad mood.

"And as for all this stuff you want to do in Toronto, we're only going to be there for four days," Mia reminded her before she tossed her head from side to side on the pillow. "Some of that stuff you're going to have to do by yourself."

"I didn't come all the way here to do things by myself. Don't be selfish."

"Selfish? I'm hardly selfish."

"What, are you trying to say that I am?"

"Umm . . . a little bit." Mia hadn't forgotten how Danielle had made a move on a guy she liked at York Steakhouse last summer. She knew Danielle just wanted to make her father mad by having a black boyfriend.

Four hours later, Danielle shook Mia. "Mia, wake up. We're in Toronto."

Mia opened her eyes and smiled. "Maybe we'll meet some cute guys."

"Maybe you will. I don't ever meet cute guys."

"That guy who worked with me was cute."

Danielle didn't take the bait.

They had been there for only three hours before Mia met a man. She and Danielle were sitting in the food court at the Eaton Centre when he walked by. He and Mia briefly made eye contact. When she turned and saw him lingering nearby, he smiled.

"Have you noticed that just about everybody walking by is carrying a Roots bag?"

"Not everybody," Mia said, glancing back at the man.

Danielle followed Mia's eyes. "You think he's cute, don't you?"

"Very. I wonder if he's black."

"What difference does that make?"

"Can't I wonder? He sort of looks black, and I hope he is."

"Well, you know he's not white," Danielle said sarcastically.

"The world isn't just black or white."

"He's way too old for you." Danielle yanked Mia up by the arm. "Let's go find Roots." As they started walking, so did the man Mia had been eyeing. "Is he following us? Do we need to find a cop in this mall?" Danielle asked in annoyance.

"No, let him follow us."

"Mia, he could be a psycho."

"He doesn't look crazy."

They found their way to Roots, and while Danielle tried on a pair of shoes, Mia wandered off so she could find the man who'd been eyeing her. Just as she walked out, he was walking in.

"Are you looking for me?"

Mia smiled. "Sure am."

They settled down on a bench outside the store. His name was Mohammed. He had a foreign accent and wore a suit and a pair of expensive shoes. His hair was black and shiny and cut low. His eyes were clear and his skin was darker than hers. He was handsome, and he told Mia she was beautiful. He was born in Morocco. He worked for the United Nations, and in addition to English, he spoke Arabic, French, Italian, and Spanish fluently.

When Danielle walked out of the store with her purchase in one hand, she tried to pull Mia along with the other hand.

"This is my friend Mohammed. He's going to take us back to our hotel."

"We don't need a ride."

Mia pulled Danielle to the side and said, "Let's get a ride. It's better than taking the bus."

"We can walk. The hotel isn't even that far."

"Look, don't ruin my trip. I'm already in a bad mood. Don't make it go from bad to worse."

Danielle sighed. "Okay, whatever you want, Mia."

"Thank you," she said with a bright smile.

He drove the ladies to the hotel in his compact car, and enthusiastically hummed along to the classical music on the radio.

"Do you know this one?" he asked them, turning up the volume.

Mia shook her head. He turned the volume down. "You ladies don't listen to classical?" Danielle's face remained impassive as she peered out the car window from the backseat and watched the crowds of people milling in the streets.

"Do you, Danielle?" he asked her.

"No, I don't," she answered in an emotionless tone, bothered that the potential psycho had remembered her name.

"I know what you ladies will like," he said with a wide smile right before he started ruffling through his center compartment. He popped in a cassette tape and began singing along to "I Wanna Be Your Lover" by Prince while he drove them to the Sheraton Centre on Queen Street.

"I'll wait for you," he told Mia as she was exiting his car. He blew his horn to get her attention. Mia walked back to his small boxy sedan, a car she'd never seen in Detroit. "Bring a nice dress so I can take you dancing tonight."

"Is he waiting for you?" Danielle asked as they trudged into the hotel and made their way to the elevator. "You don't even know that 'I Wanna Be Your Lover' man."

"So, I can get to know him."

"Mia, he's old and he looks at you real creepy." Danielle shook her head. "I don't like him."

Mia stabbed the up button to the elevator. "He's not for you to like—he's for me to like. Is that what your problem is? Are you jealous because he's interested in me instead of you?"

"Why would I be?"

"Right, why would you be? You tell me."

"Whatever, Mia, we don't even like the same type of guys."

The elevator door opened and the two went inside. There was silence. Mia studied the numbers as they lit up, so she wouldn't have to look at Danielle.

The elevator opened on the fifth floor and they both exited without saying a word. Silence trailed them all the way down the hallway and into their ice-cold room.

Danielle headed straight for the thermostat to turn down the air conditioner.

Mia unzipped her suitcase and removed from her bag a little black dress and a pair of heels higher than the ones she had on. She leaned her suitcase against one of the double beds and headed for the door.

"Are you seriously going to leave me in this hotel all alone?" Danielle asked. "This trip was for us. We're supposed to be here together."

"Just take a nap, and I'll be back before you wake up."

"I slept on the train. I'm hungry, and I don't want to be forced to order room service."

"So just go out and eat in one of the restaurants downstairs or something."

"I don't want to eat in a hotel restaurant."

"Then don't. We're downtown. I'm sure there are plenty of places within walking distance. Go back to the mall."

"Yeah, maybe I can meet a creep like you did," Danielle said frostily.

"Danielle, I'm just spending some time with a friend."

"You don't even know him. Who wears a suit and tie in the summertime?"

"A businessman."

"And so does a con man. I would never do something like this to you."

"I said I'll be back," Mia said as she slammed the door behind her.

Mia hadn't been in Mohammed's home for long before she learned that he'd been married before. His wife left him one day out of the blue right after he'd left for work. He said he'd given her everything, and she'd taken it all when she left. And as Mia looked over his small and sparsely furnished townhome, she believed him.

He cooked fish with rice and green beans for dinner. He offered her a glass of white wine to go along with their meal, but Mia politely refused. The most she'd ever had to drink was a wine cooler, and she didn't even like that.

Later that night, Mia changed into her black dress, and they went to a nightclub on Yonge Street, where they danced to reggae music. It was fun, but she couldn't help but think of Danielle and wonder what she was doing. She knew leaving her alone in the hotel was wrong, but she needed a little break, she told herself. This was her trip too. She was entitled to some fun.

After they left the club, she went back to his town home.

"I want to give you a bath," he said as they sat at the kitchen table staring at each other.

"Do I smell or something?"

He laughed. "No, I just want to give you one." She watched as his dark eyes crawled slowly up and down her body. "Would you like that?"

She shook her head. "Can you just take me back to the hotel?" It was getting late, and the way he was looking at her was making her uncomfortable.

"Right now?"

"Yes, right now."

"I'm not ready to take you to the hotel right now."

"Well, I'm ready to go back to the hotel. So will you please take me?"

He shook his head and looked at her in disappointment. "You young girls are so confused, aren't you? One minute you're throwing yourself at a man, and the next minute you're cold as ice." He reached his hand out for hers, but she drew back. "If it wasn't so late, I'd take you back. You'll have to wait for the morning."

"You don't have to take me—just let me use your phone so I can call a cab."

For a moment Mohammed stared her down, and Mia was afraid she had made the worst mistake of her life. "Of course," he said coolly.

An hour later, Mia walked through the door of the hotel room, accidentally knocking into the room service tray that was in the hallway in front of the door. Mia looked down at the barely eaten food.

Danielle had taken only a few bites from her hamburger, and if she'd eaten any fries at all, it was very few, because there was still a pile of them on the plate.

"Finally made it back, huh?" Danielle said without looking up. It was three in the morning, and Danielle was still wide-awake and watching TV.

When she finally looked at Mia, who hadn't moved from the door, she could see that Mia's face was smeared with tears and runny mascara.

Danielle was silent for a moment, then clicked the TV off. She walked over to Mia's suitcase, pulled out her pajamas, and walked over to her friend. "Let's get you cleaned up."

After Mia changed out of her little black dress, they climbed under the covers of their two double beds.

A few minutes later, Mia's head popped up from beneath her pillow. "I'm sorry. I should've listened to you. Go ahead and tell me you told me so."

Danielle turned to her. "I'm glad to hear you admit that you were wrong, because you really hurt my feelings, Mia."

"I really didn't mean to and I feel bad about it. Are you going to forgive me?" Mia asked.

"You know we can never stay mad at each other for too long. I have a full list of places I want us to go to tomorrow starting at eight in the morning, so you better rest up. You only have a few hours to sleep, and I don't want any excuses."

Mia smiled. "Sounds like a plan."

September 2010

Frank's parents had agreed to help them out with a few of their bills in the short term, including mortgage and utilities. But Mia had overheard Frank's father say they couldn't afford to do any more than that, which meant they were on their own with the car notes. Mia wasn't sure what he'd actually told them. But it wouldn't surprise her if he'd merely said he was waiting on a big check. Frank's parents were so accustomed to him earning lots of money and waiting months to receive payment. They probably just assumed he needed to borrow money in the interim, even though he'd never borrowed money from them before. And seeing how they were always so proud of his success, they'd probably believe any excuse he'd come up with. They'd take out a second mortgage on their home to help any one of their children. But Frank was the only one who'd probably ever need the help. Frank's sister was an ob-gyn who lived in Dallas with her husband, who was also a doctor. Frank's older brother was an economist who lived in Washington, DC, and taught at Georgetown University. Frank was the only one of his siblings who didn't have a college degree. Mia knew he felt like he had something to prove to his parents. That even if he wasn't as smart as his siblings, he could still earn just as much as them.

Mia was convinced that Frank had some money stashed away

somewhere, after she'd called the collection agency at the end of the previous month to find out if they'd repossessed the other Mercedes. That's when she was informed that all three of their accounts were current. Not the outcome she'd been hoping for.

Mia had it all planned, she thought as she relaxed on a leather sofa in their study with her laptop powered on and resting beside her. As soon as she came back from dropping Alexa off at the University of Michigan, she was going to start looking at apartments in person, not just online. She couldn't stand the sight of Frank. To think, when they first married, she'd sit beside him while he was on the toilet just so they could talk. The very thought made her nauseous now. She wouldn't be able to survive five seconds doing that now. Let alone the five minutes that it usually took before he flushed. He always thought it was strange that she would come in when she wanted to tell him something.

But that was then and this was now. And now she didn't want to lie beside him and deal with his sleep apnea. So in the meantime, she toiled around downstairs until the wee hours of the night. She spent most of the time on her laptop, or occasionally she'd watch television—whichever *Real Housewives* franchise was playing as she flipped through. For now, she was online searching apartment rentals, and wondering if Apartment Search still had physical offices.

She recalled that had been Danielle's first employer after college. Having majored in American Thought and Language at the

College of Arts and Letters, she'd had a hard time finding a job. She had told Mia that she definitely wasn't interested in teaching. She'd always known she wanted to be a published author, but she'd had a hard time finding an agent. So she took the first nonstructured, noncorporate type of job she could find.

Danielle always had stories for Mia about her clients. Stories that Danielle said she could write an entire book about. "It's amazing how much you can get out of a person when you're trying to help them find a place to live. It's more than just the number of bedrooms they want," Danielle had told her. She could still remember the story Danielle once told her of a young Indian woman who'd come in looking for an apartment. The woman was a model whose parents had nearly disowned her because she'd refused to study medicine or engineering. For income, she'd checked the more-than-fifty-thousand-dollar box, and when Danielle asked her if she got a lot of modeling jobs in state or if she had to travel out of state, she confided that her source of income was one of the Detroit Pistons. She'd told her she needed to have an apartment with an attached garage and a private entrance, because he was married. Mia and Danielle had gone through the entire starting lineup guessing which one it could be. But that was 1986, two years after college, when they had four hours to burn on gossip and few responsibilities.

Now, if Mia could only remember the name of that apartment complex, she'd look into it for herself. The only thing she remembered was that it was in West Bloomfield on Maple Road. Danielle had driven her past it once, just to show Mia what an apartment that rented for twelve hundred dollars looked like.

Mia heard a sound chirp from her laptop.

`How have you been, stranger?`

Mia read the instant message she received from Lamont on Facebook and debated whether to respond. Lamont was Mia's first love. She'd met him one summer while she was home from college, which eventually led to their seven-year off-and-on relationship. After twenty years without any contact, Mia had received a Facebook friend request six months earlier that seemed entirely out of the blue. She didn't know which was more shocking—the fact that Bridgette, a former best friend from high school, never responded to her friend request, or that Lamont had managed to track her down and send one of his own.

She and Lamont chatted online a few times. They tried catching up on what had been going on in each other's lives. And sometimes, late at night, she'd go through his pictures and learn about his life post-Mia. He had never married and didn't have any children. And he seemed to be quite the world traveler. His most recent uploaded photos were of him at the Forbidden City in Beijing.

After staring at the message for a few moments, she tapped out a quick response.

M: I'm doing great!!!!!

L: Glad to hear it. What have you been doing?

M: Getting ready to take my daughter to school.

L: Empty nester. What are you going to do with all your free time?

M: My book club keeps me busy.

L: You can't just read books. You need to put some excitement back in your life.

M: How do you know I don't already have excitement?

L: Because I'm not in it . . . yet.

M: No comment.

L: Why do you keep ignoring me?

M: Not ignoring you. I just haven't been online all summer.

L: Oh, okay. I see. Well, meet me tomorrow.

M: Sorry, I can't.

L: Why?

M: I'm taking my daughter to Ann Arbor tomorrow.

L: I'll meet you there.

M: And my husband too?

L: Leave him home.

M: Okay, yeah, sure. I'll tell him he can't go with me to take his only child to college for her first year. I'm sure that will go over well.

L: We'll need to do it another time real soon. Okay?

```
M: We'll see. Right now it's time for me to go to
bed. Early morning tomorrow.
L: Dream of me.
```

She shut down her computer without bothering to respond to his last remark.

Mia, Alexa, and Frank pulled in front of Helen Newberry residence hall on State Street.

"Welcome to your home sweet home. Do you know what I love about it?" Mia asked.

"Probably that it's all female."

"That's right," Mia sang as she stepped out of the car and walked toward the entrance of the building with Alexa by her side, leaving Frank behind to handle the luggage.

"Are you nervous?"

Alexa shook her head. "I'm excited. I feel grown-up."

"I hope you like your roommate. I hated my first one."

"Don't say that. I'm trying to stay positive."

"I'm just telling you the girl ran up our phone bill—"

"I don't have to worry about that—we have cell phones now."

"She wore my shoes without asking, and it's not like I had a lot of nice ones."

"If she wears a size ten, she can knock herself out."

"Umm, you're more generous than I was."

"My mom raised me well."

"Listen to you," said Mia as she wrapped her arm around her daughter's shoulders, pulled her closer, and kissed her on the cheek. "I'm going to miss my baby so much. What am I going to do with myself?"

"You'll survive."

Mia put on her sad face right before they entered Alexa's dorm room. Alexa's roommate was already inside, making up their beds with bright floral comforter sets while a man who she assumed was Alexa's roommate's father hung a rod for matching curtains.

"Hi, I'm Tiffany," the girl said after shoving one of the pillows into a pillowcase.

"I'm Alexa, and this is my mom—"

"Mrs. Glitch," Mia said, shaking the young lady's hand.

"That's my dad," Tiffany said.

The man got off the stepladder, put down his power tool, and stuck out his hand. "Allen Newsome. I hope you don't mind that we took the liberty of decorating the room a little bit. Well, a lot. We were here a couple of days early and did a little shopping. But if it's too much or not enough, just let us know. We can always take some stuff back."

"Oh, no, I think it's lovely," Mia said. "Don't you, Alexa?"

Alexa nodded with a genuine smile. "I like it."

"How much do we owe you?" Mia asked, praying he'd say something reasonable like fifty dollars, because that was as much as she had on her at the time.

"Nothing," Allen said.

"Nothing? We must owe you something."

"No, you don't owe us anything," Allen said.

Frank used his foot to knock on the door.

"That must be Dad," Alexa said as she opened the door for him and saw him standing there with his hands full. As soon as he entered and set the luggage down, Mia said, "This is Alexa's new roommate, Tiffany, and her father, Allen."

"Why does your face look so familiar?" Frank asked.

Allen chuckled. "I used to be in movies, but that was a long time ago."

Mia tilted her head. "I'm sorry, I don't recognize you. I can't say that I get to the movies very often. I'm more of a books person."

"You'd get along well with my mom," Tiffany chimed in.

"Look, Dad, they bought all of this for our room," Alexa said as she smoothed her hand over the comforter on her bed. "Isn't it beautiful?"

"It's very nice," Frank said. "How much do we owe you?"

"Your wife already asked me the same question. You don't owe us anything."

"Nothing? Well, at least let us take you to dinner."

"Dinner sounds great," Allen said amiably.

"Dinner?" Mia asked as she stood in the bathroom inside their hotel room. She tossed a makeup sponge in the wastebasket. "That color is too light for me. It makes me look sick. But then again, when you can only afford to buy the drugstore brand, these things can happen. And yet, as broke as we are, my husband still decides to invite people out to dinner."

"I can afford dinner."

"I bet you can. But how? That's what I want to know."

"You make everything seem like it's the end of the world."

"How should I make it seem? Any suggestions? Because I feel like it's the end of my world. I'm a cancer survivor without health insurance, and my husband is being investigated by the SEC. How would you feel if you were in my shoes?"

"Have confidence in your husband. I'll make things right."

"The same husband who cheated on me—"

"Here we go again."

"Right, Frank, here we go again. I know a lot. More than you think." Mia instantly regretted the remark. She'd been tight-lipped up until now, and she wanted to keep it that way until the time was right. Luckily, Frank didn't seem to think anything of the comment.

"Are you ready?"

"No, I'm not, because I'm not going. It'll be one less mouth for you to feed."

"You can't be serious."

"Look at me. Don't I look serious?"

"You are a completely different person now. I don't know this woman you've turned into."

"Why? Because I'm not saying, 'Yes, dear . . . whatever you want, dear . . . You're the greatest. . . . You're so smart. . . . You're so handsome,'" Mia said in a mimicky, high-pitched tone.

"So how am I going to explain Alexa's mother's absence at dinner?"

"Where's Tiffany's mom? She didn't even come to see her daughter off to college. At least I'm here. Just tell them I don't feel well. You won't be lying, because I don't."

He left their hotel room without saying good-bye. If they could've afforded separate hotel rooms, she would've gotten her own. Instead, she settled for double beds. She took a sigh of relief. She'd have a few hours by herself, and she wouldn't have to be around Frank while he played Mr. Big Shot.

Chapter Eight

June 1981

It was Thursday. Mia was fresh out of her freshman year for the summer and hanging out with Les, a guy she liked from Michigan State. He had a preppy style of dress with Roots shoes that laced on the side, blue jeans, and a long-sleeved Izod shirt. He had deep-set waves in his hair. Mia couldn't tell whether his waves were natural or manufactured with a stocking cap. Either way, they suited him well.

"Let's go out to a club," Les said.

"Tonight?" Mia asked.

"Yeah . . . why not?"

"All right," Mia said with a shrug. "Which one?"

"This one place where I like to hang out."

Mia had met Les, whose full name was Leslie Starks, on her

very first night of college. After Mia's parents had dropped her off, she'd roamed the floors of Holmes Hall until she came to an open door. He was singing "Rock with You." She stood outside his dorm room and listened. When he finished, she walked into the open doorway and started clapping. They became fast friends after that. By the second semester of her freshman year, she was spending a lot of her free time with the music major. They were always laughing and talking. He was like a best friend and a boyfriend rolled into one, though she hadn't been able to confess her feelings to him yet.

He stopped on Six Mile Road and Hamilton in Highland Park, a city that was completely surrounded by Detroit, except for one small part where it abutted Hamtramck. Les parked in a church parking lot and they walked the rest of the way. There were lines of cars and men walking along the street. Some were holding hands.

"There are a lot of gay guys out tonight," Mia remarked.

"Yeah, there are," he said as they approached the club. "Well, here it is."

"Here what is?" Mia asked, as she stopped in front of the entrance to Menjo's nightclub, a well-known gay bar in the city.

"This is where I'm taking you."

"Here? But it's a gay bar."

He nodded. "I know. I come here all the time."

"You're gay?" she whispered.

"Yes," he whispered back.

Mia took a deep breath. Her heart disintegrated. "You didn't have to bring me here to let me know you're gay. You could've just told me."

"I didn't know how to just come out and tell you. I don't know how to come out and tell anybody."

Mia's eyes started to water. And then tears fell. She moved away from the entrance and stood at the side of the building.

"What's wrong?" he asked, walking over to her and taking her by the hand.

She shook her head. "I liked you."

Les squeezed her hand. "Oh, Mia, you're a beautiful girl, and if I was straight, I'd definitely date you."

"That would make me feel a lot better . . . if you were straight."

"What do you want me to say?"

"Are you sure you're gay?"

"I'm positive."

"Have you ever had sex with a woman?"

"No."

"Then how do you know you're gay?"

"Have you ever had sex with a man?"

"I told you I was a virgin," she whispered.

"Then how do you know you're not gay?"

She sighed and shook her head. She didn't want to believe that Les liked men. Not when she'd really thought she'd found her future husband.

"Let's go in there and party and have a good time. If there's one thing gay people know how to do, it's have a good time."

Mia nodded.

As soon as he pulled the door open for her, she was immediately greeted with Blondie's "Call Me." Her eyes enlarged at a scene she'd never witnessed before—men dancing with other men, some in corners making out, and several eyeing and winking at Les. By the time the DJ played Queen's "Another One Bites the Dust," Mia had loosened up and was out on the dance floor.

Les was another one who had bitten the dust. And Mia wondered when and if she'd ever meet Mr. Right.

Mia had just pulled up at Folland's in Southfield, a store mostly known for its jewelry, but which sold other items such as kitchen appliances and TVs. She was fifteen minutes early for the start of her shift. But for her, it was better to be early than late, because if she was late, her boss, Clyde, would embarrass her in front of not only the other employees but the customers. It had happened before.

"Mia!" Danielle said, knocking on the driver's-side window. As in high school, they still did almost everything together, including working at the same store and attending the same college. Mia rolled down the window to her mother's car. "I was calling you all night and this morning. Where did you go last night?" Danielle asked.

"Les and I went out," Mia said.

Danielle smiled. "Did any sparks fly?"

"Oh yeah . . . a whole lot," Mia mumbled.

"Really . . . so you finally told him that you like him?"

"Yeah, I finally told him."

"What did he say?"

"He's gay."

Danielle's face turned beet red. "Aww, I'm sorry."

Mia shrugged. "He's a good dancer, though."

"So you guys went dancing?"

"Yeah, we hung out," she said as she got out of her mother's car and started walking with Danielle to the store's entrance.

"Where?"

"A gay club, and, Danielle, please don't tell anybody, because he's in the closet."

"I won't tell. You know that. Just cheer up."

"Yeah, I know," she said glumly.

"I need both of you on registers right now!" Clyde said as he whizzed past them on his way to the storage area. "Don't you see all these customers in here?" Mia's boss said as he passed her.

"Our shift hasn't even started yet," Danielle said, "so why is he yelling?"

"Because he probably forgot to take his medication."

"Don't forget that we need to go up to East Lansing to look at that apartment," Danielle said as Mia stood beside her and they both prepared to open up registers. "We get paid next weekend, so we can head over there on Friday right after work. We need to hurry up and put a deposit down—"

"Mia, please do me a favor?" a saleswoman called her, interrupting Danielle's chatter. "I have to run to the bathroom—can you watch my section? It'll only be a second."

"Clyde asked me to open a register."

"It'll only take a second, I promise. That guy wants to look at a watch."

"Okay, please hurry up. You know how Clyde gets." Mia headed toward the saleswoman's section, where a young man was waiting.

"Which watch would you like to see, sir?"

"That one right there," he said as he pointed to a digital watch with a metal band and a calculator by Casio.

As soon as Mia went to grab the key for the case, Clyde grabbed her by the arm. "Did I send you over there?"

"No, but—"

"No buts, get back to the register."

"I was just helping this customer."

Clyde's head swiveled. "I could've sworn Trish was over there before I went to the back. I can't even leave the floor for five minutes before chaos happens. Get back to the register, and I'll take care of it."

Trish hurried back to the jewelry counter as Mia returned to the register beside Danielle. The man with the Casio watched Mia, then hurried after Clyde.

"Hey," the young man said. "Why were you just yelling at this young lady?"

"Excuse me?" Clyde said.

"Why were you just yelling at her?"

"Because I'm her boss and I told her to do something and she should've done it."

"She was trying to help me, and you didn't have to yell at her. So why don't you let me speak to your boss?"

"He's not in today."

"Of course he isn't. What's his name? I'll come back tomorrow."

"He won't be in tomorrow either. He won't be in until next week."

"Just let me have his name. I'll take care of the rest."

After Clyde grudgingly gave the young man his boss's name, the customer walked over to Mia and said, "I'm sorry helping me caused you so much grief. Why don't you let me make it up to you?"

"You don't have to do that. It wasn't your fault."

"Let me cook for you."

"You can cook?"

"I'm one of the chefs at the Summit."

Mia's jaw dropped. She'd never been to the Summit restaurant, which rotated to allow for a 360-degree view from the top of the Renaissance Center. She could never afford to go, and none of the young men she dated could afford to take her.

His name was Lamont Smith, and he was tall and slender. But not too tall and too slender—which was exactly Mia's type, as Danielle often noted. He wore dress slacks and Stacy Adams wing-tip shoes, along with a bow tie and suspenders. The only negative was that his Calvin by Calvin Klein cologne was a little too strong. She could smell him before she saw him. Everything else was pure perfection. He was a couple of years older. He'd attended Michigan State for a year before deciding to drop out and enroll in a culinary arts school. Mia was still a junior in high school at that point.

Later that night, she and Danielle arrived at the Summit. He was working and would have only ten minutes or so to pop by their table and say hello.

"For him to be so young and work at a restaurant like this says a lot about him," Danielle said as her eyes surveyed the large revolving restaurant. "He's obviously good at what he does. And he's kind of cute. Don't you think?"

"He reminds me of Chris in a way," Mia admitted.

While they waited for their meal to come out, Danielle started talking about the apartment again. "So like I've been trying to tell you, I know we can find an apartment where both of the bedrooms are the same size so we don't have to fight over who gets the larger one. It also needs to have two bathrooms."

Mia avoided Danielle's gaze. "I already found an apartment."

"Oh, good! Where is it? Close to campus?"

Mia hesitated. "I'm rooming with Bridgette. Her roommate decided to move in with her boyfriend and backed out on her at the last minute. She said if I moved in with her, I didn't have to worry about paying the security deposit or my portion of first month's rent, because her other roommate had already paid. It was just too good to pass up. . . ."

Danielle's eyes bugged out. "I can't believe you. Who's your best friend, me or Bridgette?"

"You both are."

"You can't have two best friends, hence the word 'best.' "

"I have two best friends."

"No, you don't. She didn't go to Toronto with us—"

"Just because she didn't go to Toronto with us doesn't mean she's not my best friend."

"Well, I sure wish I had two. Then I wouldn't have to worry about what I was going to do about a roommate." Danielle slumped into her seat, a dejected look on her face.

"You have other friends. Ask one of them."

"I can't believe you're really going to room with Bridgette."

"Why can't you?" Mia said, getting defensive.

Danielle shook her head. "Don't worry about it. I'll keep my opinions to myself for now."

"Say what you feel."

"I will when I feel like it," Danielle said flatly.

Lamont arrived at their table with a tray of food he'd prepared for them. He had on a big smile, while the ladies frowned.

"You don't like the dishes I prepared?"

Mia tried to smile, but it didn't come off in a genuine way. "They look great. I'm sure they taste good too."

"If working for that guy at Folland's makes you ladies this miserable, you should quit."

"It's just for the summer," Mia said, dragging out the words and twirling the straw in her water glass.

"In the fall we'll be back at Michigan State, and at least one of us will have a place to stay," Danielle said.

"So I wasn't supposed to room with her?" Mia asked.

"No, not when you told me you were going to be my roommate."

"I never said I was going to be your roommate. I said I didn't want to live in a dorm again this year. You said we should take a look at some apartments."

"That's the same thing."

"No, it isn't. Is it?" Mia asked Lamont.

He shrugged. "I think I'll stay out of it, because I honestly don't know what this is about anyway."

"I'm going to the bathroom so you can talk to your new friend," Danielle said as she tossed her white cloth napkin from her lap to the table and huffed away.

"Sorry your friend's upset, but I'm glad you could come out. I was really looking forward to seeing you again," Lamont said, his eyes settling on Mia.

"I was looking forward to seeing you too," Mia said with a smile.

"I hope you enjoy the food I prepared. I tried to give you a little sampling of a few of my specialties."

Mia smiled. "I appreciate it."

"And maybe next time it can be just the two of us," he said, singing the words like the Bill Withers song.

"That would be really nice."

He left after Danielle returned to the table. She and Mia ate in silence. For the next week at work, Danielle didn't have two words to say to Mia, which was fine with her. It wasn't the first time they'd fallen out and it wouldn't be the last.

Danielle will get over this, Mia thought.

September 2010

There were metal detectors at the Clayborne High School's entrance as Mia cautiously strolled through.

Not a good sign. Charter schools were supposed to be safer. That's what Mia had always heard. Security guards were stationed inside the school, patting down students as they entered. A police car patrolled the perimeter before and after school. The security officers had the right to perform random body searches, according to the large sign that was posted near the entrance.

BE PREPARED

WHEN ASKED TO:
OPEN YOUR BOOK BAGS AND/OR PURSES
REMOVE YOUR COAT OR JACKET, GLOVES, HATS, AND SHOES

EMPTY ALL POCKETS

ALL STUDENTS AND VISITORS MAY BE SUBJECTED TO RANDOM BODY SEARCH BY USE OF A METAL DETECTOR.

YOUR COOPERATION IS APPRECIATED

SINCERELY,
THE ADMINISTRATIVE STAFF OF
CLAYBORNE HIGH SCHOOL

One of the security guards even asked to check Mia's leather briefcase.

"I'm a teacher," she told him.

"ID, please."

She didn't have her school ID yet, but that was only because she was new, she explained. "I'm supposed to report to Viv."

"Viv?" he asked skeptically.

"The principal."

"You mean Dr. Davis?"

Mia nodded quickly, biting down on her bottom lip. "Yes, Dr. Davis."

"Okay, sorry about this, Mrs. Glitch," the officer said after looking at her driver's license. "We've had problems in the past with visitors, mainly parents, trying to bypass the office and go directly to the classroom, so we have to follow procedure. And if we don't know you, you will get stopped."

He directed Mia to the principal's office and sent her on her way.

"Viv, I'm here," Mia said with a big smile as soon as she entered the office and saw Viv standing near the secretary.

"*Dr.* Davis," Viv sternly corrected her.

"Yes, excuse me, Dr. Davis." Mia clenched her jaw. That second slip of the tongue had to be her last. She truly meant no disrespect. It was hard for Mia to refer to her longtime friend with such formality. But she definitely remembered Viv explicitly warning her that no one at Clayborne could have even the slightest intimation that they were friends. Especially not after some charter school principals had come under fire recently by local media after an investigation uncovered several incidents of nepotism. Viv didn't want them digging into her records and uncovering the $150,000 building-maintenance contract she'd awarded to her cousin's company. Even though she'd technically done nothing wrong. As principal, she was allowed to hire whomever she pleased. But some still might take issue with it.

"I'm reporting for my first day. I didn't have any ID, so the security guard wanted me to stop by the office first."

"That's the correct protocol. You can follow me into my office."

Mia followed quietly behind Viv, who closed her glass office door as soon as Mia walked in.

"Viv? I already know what you're going to say, and I am so sorry," Mia said.

"It just can't happen again."

"It won't, I swear."

Viv sat at her desk and took out Mia's ID card from her top desk drawer. Mia knew Viv was upset from the expression on her face. Her right eyebrow wouldn't stop twitching. Viv darted her eyes at Mia over the rim of her reading glasses as she handed Mia the ID. "I'm trying to be a good friend, but if I have to choose between being a good friend or keeping a good job, you already know which one it's gonna be."

"I know." Mia really did feel bad. She wanted to protect Viv's job as much as her own. "I really appreciate what you've done for me. I guess I'm still thinking back to when we used to work together at Pershing and it was always Viv, Viv, Viv. But I'll get it together. I promise."

Mia focused on the students milling into the school, whom she could see through Viv's glass door. Some huddled in groups. Most of them looked despondent, and many were wearing the same T-shirt with a picture on the front.

"What does their shirt say?" Mia asked as she squinted to try to bring the print into focus. "'Rest in Peace' who?"

"Fenton Phillips. He would've been in your first period if he hadn't been savagely beaten at a house party over the weekend. I'm surprised you haven't heard about it. It's been on all the local news networks the last couple of days."

"We took Alexa to college this weekend. I must've missed it."

"It's so sad and senseless."

"I hate to hear about anybody losing their life, but especially a young person. My thoughts immediately go to their parents. I can't imagine burying my child."

"A lot of his closest friends are in your first-period class, so be prepared. Encourage them to open up and share their feelings about what happened. Let them know that grief counselors will be in a little later this morning to counsel everyone who needs it."

"I'll definitely do that."

"The most important thing you can do for them right now is simply let them get whatever they're thinking out."

Viv looked through the glass door as a middle-aged black man with long dreads who was short in stature walked into the main office. "Here comes Mr. Ross with one of his books. I swear that man reminds me of a gnat. You just can't get away from him, and he's always pushing his book."

"You might not remember, but he's the author I told you about. Please don't slip up and mention you're in a book club when he tries to peddle his book, because he already knows I'm the president of one, and knowing him, he'll put two and two together. Just tell him you're not a reader."

"I'm teaching literature," Mia said with a laugh.

Viv paused. "Well, have your twenty dollars ready, because he can be a pain."

As soon as Mia walked out of Viv's office, Mr. Ross was there to greet her.

"I'm Byron Ross," he said as he extended his right hand to shake hers. "Are you one of the new teachers?"

"Yes, I'm Mia Marks-Glitch," she said as she hurried out of the office with Mr. Ross on her heels.

She was trying to hold back her laughter from what Viv had said. But as he buzzed around her just like a gnat, she couldn't help but smile—until she spotted more students with their "R.I.P." shirts and sad faces, which melted her smile.

"I like your shoes," Mr. Ross said.

She stopped in her tracks. "These?" she said, glancing down at her nude-colored, patent leather, four-and-a-half-inch pointy-toe platform pumps.

"Very nice. And very expensive too. Aren't those Christian Louboutins?"

Mia didn't know whether to be turned on by his keen fashion sense or suspicious.

"Yes. How did you know?"

"I worked in the ladies' shoe department at Saks over the summer," he replied. A teacher, writer, and shoe salesman. Now she didn't know whether to be turned on because he was hardworking or turned off because he needed to work so hard. Maybe he didn't need to. Maybe he just wanted to. "I always wondered what women do so they can afford to pay six hundred dollars for a pair of pumps. But now I know," he said, flashing Mia a broad smile. "Teach at a charter school. What subject do you teach?"

"Literature."

"Literature," he said with a nod of his head. "Great subject. Did you ever teach in the public school system?"

"Yes, about eight years ago."

"Welcome back."

"Thank you. How long have you been in the system?"

"I taught biology at Cass Tech for thirty years before coming here."

"I can still remember how badly I wanted to go there as a teenager. You don't look like you could've worked there for thirty years, though."

"I'm fifty-six. I try to take good care of myself," he said. Mia was charmed by his easy and open manner. "I don't just teach, though. I'm also a writer. I just self-published a book, actually."

Mia had been wondering when he was going to broach the subject. For a moment, she'd thought Viv had judged him too harshly, and she still did. He seemed nice enough.

"I'll buy a copy. How much is it?" she asked, reaching for her wallet.

"Actually I was going to give it to you for free."

"Wow . . . really. That's so nice of you."

"Just read it and let me know what you think."

"I'll definitely do that."

She overheard a few students discussing Fenton as they walked into her classroom. Mr. Ross shook his head and sighed while they stood in the hallway near Mia's classroom. "What happened this past weekend shouldn't have happened. Idle minds can lead to destruction."

"Viv . . . I mean Dr. Davis was telling me about that. That was terrible what happened."

"Fenton was such a great kid. He was one of the nicest, most respectful young men you'd ever meet. I get choked up just thinking about how he died. He came from a good family . . . has a great mother and father. They really took an active role in his life. It's just a damn shame. In our day, I went to plenty of house parties, and I never encountered something like that. We went to parties to dance and have fun, not to fight."

"I totally agree with you. I can't imagine how his parents are feeling, and it's so sad. I feel for these kids, who must be terrified, because you hear about this happening so much now. When is the madness ever going to stop? Do they even know who did it?"

"Yeah, they got the little punks in custody."

"Did they go to this school?"

"No . . . nobody from this school would hurt Fenton. He got along with everyone here, from the roughest to the toughest. He was a small kid, but really mature and funny, like an Eddie Murphy type. I just hope no one retaliates. We don't need that either."

"No, we definitely don't need that," she said as she stood in front of her classroom trying to figure out what to say next. "Well, thanks for the book. This is my room."

"Right next to mine," he said with a broad smile, "so I'll be seeing you."

Mia stood in front of the class after all her students took their seats.

"My name is Mrs. Marks-Glitch, and I will be your new literature teacher." She looked around at the empty faces. "Before I start, I just want to send out my deepest condolences. I heard about what happened over the weekend, and I want you to know there will be grief counselors at the school in a few hours to talk to anyone who needs it. And today, I want to do whatever I can to help." She sat at her desk.

A young girl in the front row introduced herself as Chantel. "This makes me so mad," she said. "I wasn't there or anything, but I know a lot of people who were, and I don't understand why nobody helped him. They stood around with their phones out making sure they got a video they could post on YouTube, but nobody tried to pull those guys off of him."

"Like you said, you weren't there," said one of the male students, who was large in stature and sat in the back row, "and I wasn't either, because trust me, if I had been, Fenton would be here today. Maybe not me, but he would. They beat my man for no reason."

"They beat him because they were jealous," Chantel said. "They were a bunch of ugly-looking goons, and Fenton was fine. He knew how to dress, and he always looked good, and they were just jealous. He didn't deserve that. And I'm sick of my friends getting hurt and killed. All I keep thinking about are his parents and his little sister, because he loved them so much and they were so close."

Mia noticed a student in the first row with tears in her eyes. "What's your name, young lady?"

"Tanya."

"Do you feel like talking about what happened?"

Tears started to rush down her face. She wiped them away with her hands. "He sent me a text that night. I still have it." She handed her cell phone to Mia.

"Do you want me to read it?" Mia asked. Tanya nodded quickly.

Sorry you couldn't make it to the party, it's pretty live. I'm going to come over tomorrow so we can hang out. It's time to get you out of your shell.

`Life's too short. And you're too young to stop living. Peace and Love, Fen.`

"Look at the time stamp. It was just minutes before the police said he was attacked." Tanya buried her face in her hands and sobbed uncontrollably. She ran out of the room seconds later.

"Should I go get her?" the girl who was sitting next to Tanya asked.

"Yes, if you don't mind, could you go see about her?" Mia answered.

That student ran out after Tanya. Several of Mia's other students had blank stares, and Mia could feel their rage.

"Fenton was a good young man. Obviously, I didn't know him personally, but I've heard a lot about him," Mia interjected. "Take this terrible experience and ask yourself what you can do to continue Fenton's legacy so that your friend did not lose his life in vain. What can you do to help stop this cycle of violence?"

The first young man nodded while his eyes welled with tears. "I just wish I had been there. . . . That's all. I just wish I'd been there to protect him, because if I would've lost my life, I wouldn't have lost much."

It tugged at Mia's heart to know that someone so young felt that life wasn't worth living. "What's your name?"

"Nathan."

"Right now you feel like you have nothing to live for because he was your good friend—"

"He was my best friend. I was like his bodyguard. I should've been there. And some dudes at this school just stood back like Chantel said, and did nothing, and they're gonna need to answer to me about that."

"Okay, listen to me, the worst thing that any of you can do right now is fight violence with violence," Mia said, worried about the direction of the conversation. "From my understanding, Fenton was well liked at this school. So anyone who didn't step in to help may have been paralyzed by their own fear."

Nathan quickly took to his feet in a fit of rage, turning over his desk. The classroom took a collective gasp. "I don't want to hear that. Those fools didn't have guns! They beat him to death. Stomped on him. He was a small guy, and somebody should've helped him."

"Nathan," Mia said calmly. "Please settle down."

"You didn't know him and you don't know me."

"I know you," said Mr. Ross as he entered Mia's classroom, walking over to Nathan and turning his desk right side up. "And I heard you all the way in my room. You need to calm down and sit back down. I know you're hurt. And I understand your pain. We're all hurt. What happened to Fenton didn't make sense, but the main ones at fault are all in custody right now. Justice will be served, Nathan. God rights wrongs—remember that."

Nathan's eyes quickly scanned the frightened faces of his classmates before he begrudgingly took his seat.

"Are you okay?" Mr. Ross asked Mia. Mia nodded even though she was still a little shaken up from Nathan's outburst. "If you need me, I'm right next door," he whispered. Mia nodded gratefully. Things had certainly changed since her days at Pershing.

Mia's eyes shifted to the clock in her van. She'd been standing idle in the same spot—at the end of the long street where the school was located—for nearly ten minutes. She hated standing still, wasting time and gas. Her first day at work had been stressful. She was debating whether she should even return to the classroom. The last thing she needed was more stress, but she definitely needed the health insurance. She was ready to go home, kick off her heels, and take a long, hot bubble bath to help relieve some of the stress she was feeling.

As her patience dwindled, she balled her fist and hammered the horn.

What was going on? she wondered. The sizable crowd jamming the streets grew larger.

"What in the hell? I know this isn't a fight. Not today. I know they are not fighting right after that young man was killed." Mia shoved her gearshift into park, opened her door, and stood with one foot resting inside the van. In the near distance she spotted a mob of students, fists flying. One of Mia's students, Chantel, ran up to her.

"Nathan's in a fight."

"Who is he fighting?"

"The guy who went to the party with Fenton."

"What . . . ? Why?"

"Because he drove off while Fenton was getting beat up."

"Call 911," Mia said when she noticed Chantel pull her cell phone out.

"That's what I'm doing."

Mia made her way through the sizable crowd, not sure what, if anything, she could do other than shout at Nathan to stop. She was nervous and wondering what she'd gotten herself into, when she noticed police officers converging on the scene. She spotted Mr. Ross and a few other male teachers trying to break it up.

The large group of spectators quickly dispersed.

Please let everyone be okay, she thought. *Don't let another young person lose his life over some more foolishness.* She locked eyes with Mr. Ross, who nodded and made a shooing motion with his hand, as if to say that he had the situation under control. She nodded and headed back to the van.

A few hours later, Mia pulled her in-laws' van into her garage and noticed the Rolls-Royce was missing. She'd stopped at Kroger on the way home and bought several cans of tuna fish for her lunch and a few other items.

"How was your first day?" Frank asked as soon as Mia walked into the house.

"Trust me, you don't want to know." Mia's head was pounding. She had never had a headache that severe.

"I would like to know."

"Frank, I just don't feel like talking about my day. It was a day. Hopefully it won't be like all my other days." She looked across the island in their kitchen. He looked like a broken man. His eyes were distant. It was in that moment that she knew their situation together wouldn't improve. That whatever they used to hold together their marriage, his business, and all the material possessions they managed to accumulate would never be the same. "Did your Rolls-Royce get repossessed?"

"I gave it back."

"You gave it back?" she asked skeptically, rolling her eyes. "Yeah, right." She was showing him a side of herself she knew he didn't like. The attitude. The eye rolling. The back talk. Occasional profanity. All these were traits he found unappealing in a woman. Mia hated being dragged down to what felt like her lowest point, but she couldn't help herself. As bad as her first day at Clayborne was, entering their home felt worse.

"We have the van now. So I can drive the Mercedes when you're not. That's one less bill for me to pay."

"Don't you mean for your parents to pay?"

"I can always count on you for the clarification. But if you recall, they weren't paying our car notes."

She set the plastic grocery bags on the kitchen counter and walked out.

"So, what, you're not even going to put the groceries away now?"

"Is something wrong with your hands?"

Mia waited for his response, but after a few seconds of silence she trudged upstairs.

Later that evening, Mia was in the guest bedroom on her computer. She was watching a video of Fenton's parents on the local news when she received a pop-up message from Lamont on Facebook.

Hello, stranger . . .

She started to ignore his message. She wanted everything she did to have a purpose. She couldn't figure out the purpose of keeping in touch with an ex-boyfriend. And yet, she couldn't help herself.

M: Hi . . . how are you?

L: I started to send a search party out to look for you. When can I see you? I want to see you.

M: I don't think that's a good idea given our history.

L: That's why it is a good idea. I haven't forgotten our connection. How about tomorrow? We can just go for coffee. Meet me at Avalon Bakery.

M: Where is that?

L: You've been living in the suburbs too long. It's in Midtown on West Willis. Meet me there tomorrow.

M: I'm busy working.

L: Working? I thought you gave that up.

M: I did but . . .

L: What about after work?

M: I go straight home after.

```
L: Make a detour.

M: I can't.

L: Let's make a date for Saturday, and don't tell

me no.

M: We'll see.

L: For the record, I am talking about this Saturday.

M: We'll see.
```

As part of Mia's daily routine, she turned to CNN, which was running local news footage, soon after she entered the master bathroom. She listened to the early-morning news while she prepared for work. She and Frank still shared the same bathroom, because it was easier to leave behind her clothes and shoes in her walk-in closet, which was attached to their master bathroom.

She was sitting on her vanity stool with four pairs of conservative designer shoes circling her legs. Trying to decide which one would look best with her outfit. Why was she spending so much extra time getting ready for work this morning? she wondered. Could it be she was trying to look cute for Mr. Ross? No. She quickly shook the thought out of her mind. He was short, which she didn't usually like, but he did have a handsome face, and knew about women's designer shoes, even if his compliment seemed rather backhanded. She glanced up at the television.

"Fenton Phillips was my only son. He was my best friend," the woman standing at the podium said.

Mia's feet slid out of the pair of shoes she had just slipped on.

She focused on the TV screen. Fenton Phillips would be eighteen years old in a matter of weeks, the same age as Mia's daughter. Mia's heart grew weak once again thinking about that mother's loss. She couldn't imagine it. Didn't want to. And yet just like that, a tragedy had occurred to that young man and his family. A picture flashed across the screen, allowing Mia to put his face with his name, which only deepened her pain. He was a handsome young man with a look of such innocence.

More details quickly unfolded and Mia gasped at the senselessness of it all. At least five young men beat Fenton for no reason—because Fenton looked at one of them in what one of the suspects perceived to be the wrong way. Mia's eyes watered. Her insides filled with rage. "Stupid kids. Now their lives are ruined too."

"What's wrong? What happened?" Frank asked as he dragged his leather house shoes into the bathroom. His eyes barely opened as his hand reached for his frayed toothbrush.

Looking in his direction took too much effort. More than she felt he was worth, especially in the morning, when she didn't feel like being bothered. If she were ever a morning person, it was so long ago she'd forgotten. She'd given up caffeine over eight years ago, and the only extra boost she got was from whatever music she listened to on her ride to work.

Mia's nose began twitching involuntarily. She felt like Samantha from *Bewitched*. If she were really a witch, the first spell she'd cast would be making Frank disappear. She was hurt—betrayed—by her husband, the man she'd been sleeping beside for twenty years. The father of her child. Everything about him was in question now.

"Mia, did you hear me? What was on the news? Whose lives are ruined?"

"The kids who killed Fenton Phillips."

"Who?"

"That young man that was murdered over the weekend. He would've been one of my students."

"Fenton Phillips? I don't think I've heard about him. Teen violence happens so much these days, I can't keep up."

"He was beaten to death at a house party over Labor Day weekend. Back in our day we never had to worry about losing our lives at a house party. It just makes me so mad," she said as the tears streaked her foundation. "I feel for his parents."

"You get yourself too worked up over these types of things."

"A child the same age as ours losing his life? Yeah, I do."

"We have our own problems right now."

"The problems we have, *you* caused. Fenton Phillips was an innocent victim."

"I didn't cause those problems, Mia. I don't know how many times I have to tell you that it was my partner's doing and not mine."

"As many lies as you've told me, why should I believe anything you say?"

"I don't lie to you. That's just the way it is."

"Really? Just the way it is, huh . . . like your cheating is just the way it is? You have the nerve to say I've changed. Like I was the one who had an affair. *You've* changed, you selfish bastard."

"Selfish bastard . . . wow. I didn't expect that one from you, after everything I've given you." He slowly spread the toothpaste over his toothbrush bristles. "But I'd be wrong if I called you a bitch."

"You'd be right, because right now I am one, and for good reason."

"But I'd never call you that," he said as he started brushing his teeth.

"You just did. I'm not happy, and sometimes I just want to end this."

He removed his toothbrush from his mouth and spit the toothpaste into the sink.

"I won't stand in your way. You're not the only one who's miserable. I can't even make love to you when I want, but you're upset that I cheated. You don't know how many times I wanted to cheat, but didn't—"

"Do you think knowing that makes me feel better?" Mia said furiously.

"I'm not trying to make you feel better, Mia. I'm tired of fighting. And you sure don't care about how I feel."

"You aren't even concerned about me, and I'm your wife. All Frank cares about is Frank," she said, covering her eyes and huffing, "We're on the verge of losing everything, and I have to go back to work at almost fifty years old. Making half of what I did when I stopped teaching. I feel like I'm starting completely over. Thank

God we only have one child to support. Well, I have one child. Who knows how many you have—"

"Bring it right back around to me as always," he said while he continued brushing his teeth.

"That's right, right back around to you . . . the one who cheated and lied, and cheated and lied some more."

"Okay, Mia, you want to keep going there over and over and over again. I don't even think you care that I cheated—I think you're just mad that I lied about it." He spit his toothpaste into the sink.

She looked up at him, her nose still twitching with disgust. "If you don't mind, could you please for once clean your sink?" she said bitterly before she exited.

Later that same day, she walked into the teachers' lounge. It was a small room—smaller than Mia's master bedroom suite. There was a TV mounted to the wall. It wasn't a flat screen, and she didn't want to sit too close to it, because the mounting didn't look too secure. The room itself wasn't so bad. The seats were comfortable enough.

Mia planned to brown-bag her lunch every day with a tuna fish sandwich, a cup of yogurt, a bottle of water, and a small bag of baked Lay's potato chips. She wasn't on a diet. But the money they'd accumulated from the several trips they'd made to the pawnshop was dwindling. And Frank's parents didn't give them any cash, or so he claimed. They called the creditors directly and paid the bills each month. She couldn't complain about that, because it was a lot more than her parents were willing to do.

"How was your first day?" Mr. Ross asked.

"Challenging. I'm having a hard time wrapping my mind around the fact that a fight broke out on the first day of school, even though that young man was murdered over the weekend."

"In the words of Bishop T. D. Jakes, 'Get ready, get ready, get ready.' Nothing surprises me around here anymore."

"When their parents show up for parent-teacher conferences, that surprises me," Rochelle Banks, one of the female teachers, said. "When their child gets suspended, and they come up to the school out of genuine concern, not just to curse out the faculty, that's surprising too."

"Is it really that bad?" Mia asked. She shook her head. "I always thought charter schools were a little better, didn't have as many problems."

"Some of them are," Mr. Ross said. "And this one used to be. A part of me doesn't want to blame the parents, but you can't really blame a kid either, because they're kids."

"I disagree," Rochelle said. "Kids know right from wrong—"

"If they're taught. If not, a bad student grows up to become a worse parent," Mr. Ross said.

Mia's eyes bounced between Byron and Rochelle like a Ping-Pong ball.

"Don't get me wrong. Not all the kids at this school are bad, but the bad ones leave a lasting impression," Rochelle said. "And the good ones sort of fade into the background, trying to survive long enough to graduate."

"I can feel what you're thinking," Mr. Ross said to Mia. "'What have I gotten myself into?'"

"You're a mind reader."

"Welcome to Clayborne," Mr. Ross said. "A lot has changed, Mia. Back when you were teaching, the economy was still healthy, and so was Detroit. But look at Detroit now. We've fallen so hard and fast as a city. *Dateline* just did a special that puts us in a very bad light."

"Detroit will rebuild," Mia said as she pounded her fist on the table.

"You're a glass-is-half-full type of person, I see," Mr. Ross said with a smile, showing off his beautiful white teeth. One more thing she found attractive about him on a list that continued to grow.

"My husband would disagree with you. But after twenty years, things can get a little rocky."

"After a year, things can get rocky, which is what happened to me. I said I'd never do marriage again, and guess what, I didn't."

"Byron, you gave up on your marriage after one year?" Mia asked.

"After my wife wouldn't give up on the clubs, or her other man. Would you rather me stay in it for nineteen more and waste even more of my time?"

Mia thought about his question. She didn't regret being married to Frank for twenty years. They'd raised an amazing child together and they had wonderful memories. Obviously, she regretted what the last few months had uncovered. "I don't know," she said with a shrug. "I like married life. When it's good, it's great."

"But when it's bad, it's ugly," Mr. Ross said. "And very overrated."

"But what about kids?"

"You don't need marriage to have kids."

Mia shook her head. "I'm a traditional Catholic-school girl."

"I went to Catholic school too."

"Do you have any kids?"

"I have a son from my marriage, and I raised him."

"What Catholic school did you go to?"

"Ah, see, if you read my book, you'd already know," he said teasingly.

"Read your book? You just gave it to me yesterday. Just tell me."

"Just read my book."

"I'm going to read it, but in the meantime can't you tell me?"

"No, sorry, I can't," he said, laughing. Seconds later, the bell rang. "But I can walk you to your class. Now, that's something I can do."

Chapter Nine

October 1981

"I want to meet him," Mia said as Danielle primped in front of a full-length mirror with a curling iron in hand. They were at Danielle's house near campus, which she shared with three other girls. Danielle didn't like the house, and one of the girls she roomed with, but she was trying to make the best of it. She'd forgiven Mia for not being her roommate, even though Mia had never asked to be forgiven.

"Why?"

"I'm just curious," Mia said as Danielle wrapped a section of hair around the iron and held it there. "I mean, you just met him randomly. You don't have a class with him. You don't know much about him. I feel like you need a second opinion. What's his name, at least?"

"Neil."

"Neil, who?"

"I didn't ask him his last name."

"How do you not ask a guy his last name if you're going out with him? How do you even know he's a student?"

"He's a student," Danielle said, her patience wearing thin.

"You didn't ask for his last name? What if something happens to you? How will I know what to tell the police?"

"The same thing I would've told the police if something had happened to you in Toronto. Nothing, I guess."

Mia ignored the comment. "You can at least describe him to me."

Danielle frowned. "I think I'm a pretty good judge of character. He's a nice guy. Attractive. Just be happy for me. I want to have a nice boyfriend like you do. You met Lamont randomly at work, and it's working out fine for you."

"That's different."

"How is it any different?"

"What's the guy look like? Is he white, black—what?"

"He's white."

"Those white boys like to drink and get wild."

"Don't say things like that—"

"Things like what?"

"Racist stuff. I grew up with that, and I just don't want to hear it anymore. Besides, everyone in college likes to drink and get wild. White and black."

"White boys love to drink. It's the truth and you know it. Don't be so sensitive about race."

"Your boyfriend is half white."

Mia's eyes rolled. "There's no such thing as half, and I'd expect you to know that, since it was your people who made that rule."

"My people," Danielle said with a loud sigh. "You're obnoxious tonight."

"So where are you-all going?"

"Probably to a club. Or maybe to get something to eat. Is that okay with you, Mother?"

"What club? What's the name of it?"

"I didn't ask him the name."

"You don't even like clubs. You can't even dance. Let me go with you."

"Mia," Danielle said as she grabbed hold of both of Mia's arms, "I'm going to be fine. Don't get all clingy because Lamont couldn't drive up from Detroit and Bridgette is off with her boyfriend."

Mia rolled her eyes. "You're my best friend. That's why I'm clingy. Call me as soon as you get back home. And it better be by midnight."

"I will, Mother."

"You better."

It was long past midnight, and Danielle's head was spinning. The numbers on the elevator were blurred. She could still hear the pulsating disco music from the club they'd just left.

"What's your name?" she asked him.

"What?"

"Your last name. My friend said I should know your last name. What is it?" she asked, slurring her words. She'd only had one drink, but she was staggering and slurring her words like she'd been drinking all night. Something didn't feel right.

"University."

"Neil University?" she asked as she stumbled off the elevator once it reached the tenth floor of the apartment building. "Where are we? Is this my house?"

"Yeah, it's your house. Just follow me," Neil said with a smile.

She staggered behind him, squinting as she looked at each door she passed. "Wait a minute, this isn't my house. You're tricking me, Neil University. I bet University isn't even your last name," she said, falling to the floor.

He yanked her up from the floor, and Danielle turned to head back to the elevator.

"It's this way, not that way. . . . We're almost here."

A door at the end of the hallway opened and three guys chugging beers stood in the doorway, the sound of loud music playing in the background.

One of the guys looked Danielle over. "I thought you were bringing back girls, not one girl." He took another swig. "But I guess we can make it work."

"Shh!" Neil said as he dragged Danielle down the hallway after she'd passed out. "Just help me bring her inside."

* * *

A few days later, Danielle and Mia trudged out of Danielle's house. Both were carrying large boxes in their hands, which they loaded into the U-Haul trailer that was hitched to Danielle's friend's car. They barely talked throughout the process. After half an hour of Danielle's silent treatment, Mia decided to break the ice.

"It was nice of Rob to loan you his car, but why couldn't he help us? This is going to take all day. We need a man's help. Besides, isn't he your boyfriend?"

"No, he's just a friend," Danielle said shortly.

They went in and out of the house carrying boxes to the trailer.

"Well, I just thought since you were moving in with him—"

"A man and a woman can live together without being boyfriend and girlfriend. Just like a boyfriend and girlfriend can stay in a relationship without having sex. I mean, you would know all about that," Danielle muttered.

Mia was shocked by Danielle's rude remark. Not that they hadn't had little tiffs before, but this one seemed to be coming out of left field.

"You know I'm saving myself for marriage. Lamont will just have to wait."

"He's not going to wait, Mia. Don't be so naive. He's a good-looking guy. He lives all the way in Detroit. You don't even see him that much, just once or twice a month. Whatever happened to the girl who left me in that hotel room to go off with her lover man? She would've slept with Lamont by now."

Mia was stunned. "What's wrong with you today? I came over to help you move, and this is how you treat me? Where are your other friends? Let those white girls help you."

"I'm just saying, Lamont is going to find out that you're not a virgin."

"I am a virgin, okay, not that it's even your business, so don't worry about what I am or not."

"I know you're a bitch," Danielle remarked coolly.

Mia was stunned. "I'm a bitch? Why am I a bitch, Danielle?"

"My first clue was when you left me in that hotel room all frickin' day in Toronto. Then you promised to room with me but moved in with Bridgette, of all people. Bridgette didn't even have the time of day for you when we were at Glory."

"I've known Bridgette since third grade. We were friends then, and we're still friends. You're just jealous of her."

"I'm not jealous of her. I just don't like her. I don't like the way she looks at me like she thinks she's better than me, like I'm poor white trash."

"She doesn't think you're poor white trash. She thinks you're prejudiced, and that I'm your little science project to see if you can get along with a black girl from the inner city," Mia snapped. She was livid, but the look on Danielle's face made her realize she'd gone too far.

Anger flashed in Danielle's eyes. "I thought you were my friend. But now you're just a stuck-up black sorority bitch with a hot boyfriend who thinks she's all that."

"What's wrong with you? I ask about Rob and you start going off on me."

"I'm not like you. I don't think it's the greatest thing in the world to be a virgin," Danielle said. "You wear it like it's a damn badge, and it's sickening."

"I'm guessing someone never heard back from Neil. A classic hit-it-and-run," Mia retorted, aiming to sting.

Danielle took the box she herself had been holding and slammed it down into the trailer. "You think you know everything."

"No, actually, Danielle, I don't. Why don't you tell me what to think?"

Danielle's eyes filled with tears. "I never heard from him again because he raped me," she shouted. "He and his buddies. He must've slipped something into my drink. He took me to somebody's apartment, and they raped me. I don't even know how many guys were there. I couldn't fight back. . . . I couldn't fight back." The tears fell faster and faster, and a moment later, she was in Mia's open arms.

November 2010

"I'm not going through arbitration. We already tried mediation. And that was a waste of time," Danielle told her attorney, Steve Wisk, over the phone. She was relaxing on the private beach outside her condominium. "I'm done. This matter is going to be resolved. I refuse to worry about lies. The truth is all that matters. God will not let this go through. Trust me. She'll run out of money before I will. She doesn't have any, which is why I'm getting sued in the first place."

"I really think we should do the arbitration," Steve responded calmly.

"Did you talk to my editor about extending my deadline?"

"That's something that you can do, but keep in mind you extended it several times."

"Several? I think you're exaggerating. Twice."

"Is something wrong? I've seen you have an attitude, but not like this."

"Why should anything be wrong? My stepsister is suing me, which is the least of my worries. I can't think of anything to write, and that's what I do for a living. I miss Pulitzer. I didn't get the chance to see my daughter off to college, because of the hurricane, and now that I want to fly out to see her, she says she's busy. Everything is just fine," she said sourly.

"This too shall pass."

"Yes, it shall, just as soon as you fix everything I need fixed."

She ended the call and leaned her head against her portable lounge chair and closed her eyes behind her shades to rest her mind. *Deep down I'm a very nice person,* she thought. Only most people didn't get to see that side of her. Nice people get hurt. And she'd had plenty of pain in her past. She and Claire had never gotten along when they were growing up under the same roof, but Danielle tried to be the bigger person, given the circumstances. She'd been blessed, so she'd decided to help others, including her stepsister, which was why she'd first put her into rehab for her alcoholism and then hired her as an assistant after she'd completed the program. Claire had cried to her on the phone one evening about how hard her life was after her husband left her and their teenage son. She'd bailed Claire out after she'd been arrested for writing thousands of dollars' worth of bad checks. She even paid back all the retailers Claire had stiffed. That little voice in her head so many speak of had screamed not to, but she followed her heart instead. And now she was being slandered by the very person she'd helped and defended.

She thought of Tiffany, opened her eyes, and phoned her, but as usual there was no answer. When Danielle went off to school, she couldn't wait to get out of her house. She always said once she left, she was never going back, and she almost never did. Not even for holidays. She spent those mostly with her grandmother and her aunt Martha, who shared a home together at that time. Now she wondered if her daughter felt the same way. Tiffany could do anything she wanted, and she didn't have to worry about her mother trying to dictate everything from how she styled her hair to how large a slice of red velvet cake she was cutting.

"God, I bet the next time I see her, she's going to be big as a house," she murmured to herself. The very thought made her head pound. She closed her eyes again, and her thoughts drifted to Mia.

Ever since Pulitzer's death, she'd been thinking of her a lot. How she had hurt her. Even now, she thought the entire ordeal was just one big misunderstanding.

"Surprise," Allen said as soon as Danielle walked through the front door to their condominium. He was holding up a black and silver puppy.

"What is that?"

"What does it look like? It's a miniature schnauzer puppy."

"I know what it is, but what is it doing here?"

"She's for you."

"She? No," Danielle said, shaking her head. "I'm the only bitch allowed in this house."

"Hold her, Danny."

"I don't want to hold her. Where did you get her from, some backyard breeder? She's awfully small."

"The parents were small."

"I prefer owning dogs that are of show quality. Pulitzer was of show quality. He had championship blood on both sides."

"She does too," Allen said, growing impatient.

"Not if her parents were small, she doesn't. And look at those big ears sticking straight up. She looks more like a bat than a schnauzer."

"We can get her ears cropped. Look at her face. She's so cute. Why don't you hold her, Danny?"

"I don't want to hold her. Take her back. I'm just not ready for another dog. I can't replace the twelve years that I had with Pulitzer just like that. I need time," she said, wiping away the frustrated tears that had just started to fall. "I don't mean to take it out on her, but I'm not over Pulitzer."

"God didn't intend for dogs to live as long as humans," Allen said as calmly as he could. "But Pulitzer had a long life for a dog. It was a full life, and a fun one. You two bonded like I've never seen before, but he's gone. You treated him well."

"And it was all negated by the way he died. He suffered," Danielle said as she buried her face in her hands. "Please, take the dog back," she said as she hurried to her bedroom. As she closed the bedroom door and slumped against it, she worried that one day Allen would grow tired of dealing with her and leave, especially now that their daughter was away at college. The woman who grew up never wanting marriage or children was terrified of ending up alone.

"You can contact my attorney, Steven Wisk. Aside from that, I don't have a comment." Danielle had been fielding calls from reporters all day. Word had finally gotten out about the lawsuit. "I said no comment. No, I don't. . . . Okay, here's my comment: There are good people in this world, and there are evil people. Can you guess which one Claire Chudwick is?"

"Which one do you feel she is?" the reporter asked.

"You're a reporter. Why don't you simply check into her background, and I do mean her criminal background. I'm sure you'll get your answer."

"So you have no idea why she's doing this to you?"

"I have every idea. Some people in this world believe they're entitled to the things other people work hard to earn. That's my stepsister's mentality. If she wants money, she needs to pull herself together and earn it," Danielle snapped right before ending the call. She knew she would regret that comment later, but the lawsuit had her blood boiling.

She was sitting in her den, rewinding her most recent *Today* show appearance on her DVR. It was from October, breast cancer awareness month, and she usually made the rounds on national TV. It was the one thing she was as genuinely passionate about as writing.

She watched herself closely. She had some of the same traits she disliked most in her father, and no matter how hard she tried to break away from them, she couldn't. She didn't understand why. She talked too loudly, which was why she hated to do televised interviews. When she watched them, she had to turn the volume down because her voice was so shrill. She had an opinion about everything, and she felt hers was the only one that mattered, unless of course you agreed with her. And when she was right, she loved to rub it in that she'd told the person so. She cut people off, sometimes in midsentence. And all these bad habits persisted despite media training, and her *Today* show appearance was no exception. She was more than a little embarrassed.

While she was mentally critiquing herself, her daughter returned her call. She muted the television before she answered.

"Mom, you called me."

"Yes, I want you to start thinking about what you want to eat for Thanksgiving."

"That's several weeks away, Mom."

"I'm aware of that, but you can still start thinking about it now. You know your mother likes to go all out for family."

"Okay, Mom, I'll think about it. I love you."

"I love you too. Where's Alexa?"

"With her boyfriend. Her new boyfriend."

"You say that like you don't like him."

"He's okay, but I did like her other boyfriend better."

"What about you?"

"Huh? What about me?"

"Are you dating anyone? Have you met any nice guys?"

"I have friends. They're just friends."

"Friends are good, but don't go anywhere with them alone unless you truly know them, Tiffany. Don't go off meeting any strange men."

"Don't worry, Mom. I don't talk to strangers. You've drilled that in my head since I was four years old."

"So what's on your agenda for the rest of the night?" Danielle asked.

"Do some studying and then probably go over to a friend's dorm and watch *Community* and *30 Rock*."

"Who is the friend?"

"A girl who lives in the dorm two doors down."

"And how's the weight loss coming?" Danielle asked tentatively.

Tiffany paused. "I'll talk to you later."

"Don't get off the phone. Am I pestering you?"

"No, Mom, you're not, but I have to go. I love you."

"I love you more, Tiffany."

Her daughter giggled. "I know, Mom."

After the call ended, she thought about her daughter and how content she seemed without a boyfriend. If only Danielle would've been the same way when she was in college, she never would've gone out with Neil University. She'd wanted him and the others to be punished, and she'd filed a police report, providing a rather detailed description of him down to the Pac-Man tattoo he had on the left side of his neck. The other men who'd raped her she couldn't describe at all, or the apartment building she was taken to. During the violence, she'd drifted in and out of consciousness.

Tears clouded Danielle's eyes. Maybe she had a strange way of showing it, but she truly loved her daughter, and only wanted her to be happy and healthy. She knew she was a distant mother, something that had been passed down to her from her father. But there was nothing Tiffany could ever want that Danielle wouldn't provide. She couldn't say that much for her father.

Forgive him, a voice in the back of her mind kept saying. Danielle had wronged one person, and at one time, she would've done anything for her forgiveness. But she just couldn't bring herself to do that for her father.

A few minutes later, her attorney called.

"I have bad news, and slightly better news. Which would you like first?" Steve asked.

"I would've preferred you left out the intro and simply said what you had to."

"The bad news is your publisher is not going for another delay of your book. They want it at the end of this month, or they're going to cancel, and I would assume sue for their advance."

"Why would they sue me, Steve?" He was no Liza. "Twenty years and you assume they'd sue me? I'd give it back, but don't you worry, I'll have the book finished. I always come through," Danielle snapped.

"Maybe I should call you back," Steve shot back unexpectedly. "I've got things on my own plate and the attitude—"

Danielle forced herself to calm down. "I'm sorry, Steve. I'm ready to listen. What's the other news?"

"Claire's team is about to drop the lawsuit."

Danielle leaped up to her feet. She was ecstatic. "Finally! That's the best thing I've heard in weeks. Maybe her conscience finally got the best of her."

"I think the attorney fees got the best of her."

"Didn't I tell you she was going to drop the case because she didn't have money?"

"Yes, Danielle. You told me. I knew you'd be happy. Well, I don't want to disturb you because I know you have a lot of writing to do. . . ."

"Don't worry," Danielle reassured him, her spirits lifting. "I work best under pressure."

"What do you mean, you're not coming home for Thanksgiving? You were supposed to meet us in Key West," Danielle asked her daughter a few weeks later. "Turn on your FaceTime. I want you to look into my eyes while you rip my heart out."

"Mom, stop. You're saying something one of your characters would say."

"How would you know what one my characters would say? Neither you nor your father have read any of my books."

"I read your books, Mom," Tiffany said with a sigh.

"Well, it would mean more to me if you came home for Thanksgiving."

"I'm just not coming this year. We go to Key West every year. It's no big deal. One year without me isn't going to kill you."

"The big deal is that you'd rather spend time with your roommate's parents than your own, which I feel is extremely disrespectful."

"Disrespectful, Mom? That's a pretty strong word."

"And it fits," Danielle said in a huff.

"Have fun in Key West."

"I doubt I will now. But enjoy Thanksgiving with your new family."

"Love you, Mom."

"I love you too," Danielle said grudgingly.

Danielle ended the call. She was upset, but not with her daughter. Maybe it was the PMS that was getting to her. The older she got, the worse it was, and she couldn't wait until her periods stopped once and for all. Or maybe it was the book review from a national publication that her editor had e-mailed her.

> Danielle King, the highly successful author known for her near cultlike fan base and philanthropy, has lost her fire. In *The Keys*, her twentieth novel, King promises a lot and delivers on none of it. . . . Unfortunately, in King's latest offering, she writes as if she's still trying to find her voice. The passionate characters she was once known for have been replaced with flat dialogue and meaningless story lines. One must suffer through 484 pages with an unlikable protagonist who I often wished would jump off the boat he lived on. It looks like King has run out of steam.

The drive from South Beach to Key West one week before Thanksgiving seemed unusually long to Danielle this year. She and Allen left their condo just before eleven that morning, and it was almost three in the afternoon before they approached the Overseas Highway. Allen drove, his eyes adrenalized from the two shots of Cuban espresso he had right before they set out on their adventure. Danielle had her iPad out, trying her best to write and forget that Tiffany wasn't with them. But Allen constantly broke her concentration by fiddling with the radio, switching between country music, jazz standards, and that annoying rock 'n' roll he loved and she hated. But she didn't quite know how to tell him to turn it off, so instead of asking, she simply pushed the off button herself to put an end to her misery.

"Hey, I was listening to that," he said, raking his fingers through his recently colored hair. He'd gone from mostly gray to ash brown right before the trip, and Danielle was trying to adjust to the change.

"I'm writing," she said flatly.

"I thought this was supposed to be a vacation—a bonding experience," he said, a detectable strain in his voice.

"A writer never vacations. We simply change scenery." She paused and looked over at Allen. His face was red with anger.

"What?" she asked.

"I was just thinking how I pledged to love you for better or worse. Lately, it seems like our marriage keeps falling into the latter category."

Danielle started to bite her tongue, but then she wouldn't be herself if she held back her thoughts. "I think we have an amazing life, despite your lack of ambition."

"Lack of ambition? I like to think I came a long way from the small two-bedroom frame house on Yemans I grew up in."

"Yes, you did come a long way. But then you stopped dead in your tracks, and you've been resenting me ever since."

"You'd like to think that. You'd like to dismiss my feelings as mere jealousy. One day, Danny, you're going to realize that you're wasting a lot of your energy defending yourself," Allen snapped back.

After driving in silence for several minutes, Allen announced he needed a cigarette. He pulled off the road in Windley Key at mile marker 84.5—the entrance to the popular tourist attraction Theater of the Sea—a place they'd taken Tiffany to years ago.

Allen puffed away on one cigarette, then another. "How much longer before we can get back on the road?" Danielle asked him through the small crack in the car's window. She wished he would quit smoking. "Not that I'm rushing you. I'm just teetering on a decent idea and I don't want to go all in only to have my concentration broken."

"No problem. This is your world. I'm not even a squirrel," Allen said coolly.

Danielle observed him quietly as he forcefully used the heel of his Mephisto slip-ons to extinguish the butt of his cigarette that he'd just flicked to the ground, and walked back to the driver's side. The slamming of the car door jolted Danielle back into reality. She waited a beat, drew in a deep breath, and continued writing. She knew she was being difficult, but as usual didn't know how to stop.

The rest of the ride passed in stony silence. A couple of hours later, they stopped at Blond Giraffe Key Lime Pie Factory, which had won the vote for Best Key Lime Pie for seven years straight in *Florida Monthly* magazine. They purchased some snacks, and sat on opposite ends of a yellow bench outside.

"Where should we go for dinner?" Danielle asked as she chomped on a frozen Key lime pie stick dipped in chocolate.

"Wherever you want, dear," he said in a falsely cheery tone. "We can even go back to Blue Heaven, if you like."

One of the traits Danielle admired most in her husband was how quickly he recovered from her insults. He rarely held on to a grudge. But this time felt different. She'd insulted his choice to end his career. She knew he'd done it for her, to save the family, and yet she'd thrown the decision back in his face. Though she felt the first stirrings of guilt, she also knew she was right in some ways. She was successful and independent, and lately, Allen had been making it clear that he wasn't always comfortable with that. She didn't want to emasculate her husband, but she didn't want to apologize for her success either.

"Maybe Conch Republic. I love their fresh grouper with Juju sauce."

"If that's what you want. It's whatever you want, as usual."

Danielle ate the rest of her treat, then flicked the Popsicle stick into a nearby garbage bin. Never had she felt so far from Allen. Never had she felt so alone.

Chapter Ten

July 1983

Mia and Danielle had returned home for the summer after their junior year in college. Danielle had pushed the violence that had been inflicted upon her someplace deep inside her. There'd be no justice. The best thing for her to do was move on. She began "living in the now," twenty-five years before the catchphrase was coined. Instead of focusing on the fact that she'd been a victim, she turned her thoughts toward creating characters. She needed something to control. Her fictional worlds became her sanctuary. She was determined that summer to start writing her first novel.

Mia was living with her parents, but spending most of her time with Lamont, whom Mia's parents didn't approve of. "Why buy the cow if you can get the milk for free?" her mother would say whenever Mia came back from one of her overnight stays with Lamont.

But Mia was twenty-one, which meant she was old enough to decide whom she could sleep with. If she hadn't been one hundred percent certain that she and Lamont were going to marry one day, she never would've given up her virginity to him. But he'd waited patiently to make love to her, and she knew in her heart that he was her husband.

Until she received a call from Bridgette that changed her world.

"Are you sure you want to do this?" Danielle asked Mia as she pulled beside a white Audi 100 parked in front of a gold brick apartment building. They were on Six Mile Road near Log Cabin Street, directly across from a line of gated homes in the affluent Detroit Golf Club Estates subdivision where Bridgette's parents lived.

"Yes, because I want to know the truth."

"Well, that's his car, right? Just like Bridgette said, soooo . . . you kind of already do know the truth, right?"

"No, Danielle, I don't. And can you turn off Anita Baker? She's the last person I want to hear right now." Mia stared out the window at the Audi. "Maybe Bridgette is lying."

"Why would she lie?"

"Why did she have to rush to tell me she thinks Lamont is cheating on me? Just because she and her boyfriend broke up doesn't mean she has to go ruining other people's relationships . . . ," Mia mumbled to herself.

"Mia, you know I'm not a fan of Bridgette, but her parents do live right across the street from this girl. If she says she saw Lamont with another woman, I'd believe her."

"Can you please turn off the music? That woman's voice is bothering me right now."

"You love Anita Baker."

"When I'm in love, I do. Not when I'm pretty sure my boyfriend is cheating." Mia took a deep sigh. Danielle turned down the volume to the cassette tape.

"Off, not down!"

"I'm sorry, but I really love this song. . . ."

"You have the tape. Listen to it when I'm not in the car."

Danielle grudgingly obeyed. "So what do you want to do?"

Mia took a deep breath and looked over at the building. "I guess go in."

Danielle drove farther up the street and pulled into an empty space. She turned to look at Mia. "Do you want me to go in with you?"

"No. I want to do this alone."

"How are you going to figure out which apartment the woman lives in?"

"I'll figure it out," Mia said as she huffed out of Danielle's car and slammed the door.

Mia walked up to the building and started hitting each buzzer until someone buzzed her in. Once inside the large building, she had no idea which way to go. So she started on the first floor, knocking on doors one by one.

She knocked on one door, and a woman with a scarf tied around her head with bright pink foam rollers underneath it answered.

"Yes?"

"I'm looking for my boyfriend, Lamont. Is he in there?"

"Who? I don't know no Lamont," the woman said, and then slammed the door.

Mia walked to the next apartment and banged on the door. The woman from the apartment she'd just left opened the door, walked into the hallway, and said, "Are you going to go door to door just to find your cheating man?" Mia nodded and tears filled her eyes. "Honey, don't do that to yourself. First of all, there are over two hundred apartments in this building. Granted, most of the people are at work right now, but you never know who might be behind one of these doors." She gave Mia a sympathetic look. "What's he look like? Maybe I've seen him."

"He's tall. Light skinned—"

"How tall?"

"Six-three . . . kind of slim, but not really . . . more like a muscular slim. Wavy, jet-black hair—"

"Good hair with light eyes? Looks like he might be mixed?"

Mia nodded.

The woman nodded back wisely. "He's here all the time with a girl who lives upstairs. It would be easier for you to try to catch him on the way out rather than going around to each apartment until you find the one he's in. And you know they won't answer the door anyway once they see you in the peephole."

"I saw his car parked out front. What should I do?"

"Wait him out. I would just wait in my car for a couple of hours.

It's just eight thirty in the morning. Obviously, he spent the night, and he's going to be leaving soon."

Mia thanked the woman, bolted out of the apartment building, and marched over to Danielle's car, which was blasting Anita Baker again. Mia's fist hammered the glass. Danielle leaned over and unlocked the door, and Mia got in.

"What happened?"

"We have to wait for him to come out."

Danielle turned the volume to the tape down.

"What did you do that for?"

"You said you didn't want to listen to Anita Baker."

"I can listen to 'No More Tears.'"

Danielle turned the volume back up. Mia turned to look back at the apartment building. "I feel like we're too far away from the building. He could leave without me seeing him."

"I can drive around the corner and come back and park closer. Do you want me to do that?"

"But if you go around the corner, he might come out while we're around the corner."

"It'll be too hard for me to try to make a U-turn on this street. There's too much traffic coming and going. What do you want me to do?"

"We'll just wait here. Turn that music off. . . . She's back to singing about love. Don't you have the *Thriller* tape?"

Danielle replaced her Anita Baker tape with Michael Jackson's

Thriller, and "Wanna Be Startin' Somethin'" was the first song to play.

They waited in the car for three hours.

"I hate seeing you like this. Let's just drive up to East Lansing like we were going to do and start looking at apartments. You really are going to room with me this time, right?"

"I said I was. But that's the last thing I'm thinking about right now." She stopped short as she caught a glimpse of something. "Ooh, that's him!" Mia said as she jumped out of the car. She ran back toward the building where he stood hugging a very tall, shapely woman. He was six-three and the woman wasn't much shorter. Was she a model? Mia wondered. She looked like one. But a model would live in a better apartment, or so Mia assumed. It's not like the woman lived in a large colonial like the ones across the street in the Detroit Golf Club Estates. Mia thought the woman's apartment complex seemed out of place in the neighborhood. Maybe that's why the subdivision was gated.

"You liar, I'm so sick of you. What were you going to tell me when you finally talked to me? What lie were you going to tell me to explain where you were all night? I'm so tired of you. I loved you, and you said you loved me too," Mia said, kicking his leg.

Lamont was visibly shocked, and struggled to retain his cool. "Calm down."

"Who is this?" the other woman asked with a slight frown as she looked down at Mia and swatted her hand in Mia's direction.

"I'm his girlfriend. Who are you?" Mia spit.

"She's your girlfriend, Lamont?"

Mia stared at the woman, then back at Lamont. "That's right. Now, who are you?"

"I thought I was his girlfriend," she said as she shook her head. "Don't worry about it, honey. The one thing I'll never do is fight over a man, especially one like him. He can go right along being your boyfriend," the woman said as she turned and walked away.

"Karina," Lamont said as he turned away from Mia.

"What are you calling her for?"

"Mia, how long have you been out here?"

"Why? What if I've been out here all night?"

"I know you haven't been out here all night. I know you're not that desperate. And I know you didn't bring Danielle with you."

"Yeah, as a matter of fact I did. I've been out here long enough to know you've been with her all night, and this isn't the first time." She kicked him in the leg again. "I hate you!"

"Are you done?" Lamont said quietly.

"I thought Bridgette was lying. I actually thought she was lying."

"Look, it's not even what you're thinking. She works at the restaurant with me—"

Mia waved him off. "I don't want to hear any more of your lies. I know what it is. How can you deny her words? But I don't care anymore. I wanted to see it with my own eyes, and now I have. Good-bye."

"She's just a friend, Mia," Lamont shouted as Mia walked away.

As if on cue, a window flew up on a third-floor apartment, and Mia caught a glimpse of Karina's head as she tossed underwear, pants, shoes, and toiletries out the window. A pair of shoes fell near where Mia stood in the street. She picked up a shoe and flung it at Lamont, aiming for his head and just barely missing.

She ran back to Danielle's car and jumped inside. "Let's go. I'm done with him. I hate him."

"Do you want me to take you home?" Danielle asked as she pulled off.

"No, because he'll probably go there, and I don't want to talk to him. Do you mind if we just drive around for a while?"

Danielle squeezed Mia's hand. "Let's go eat at Backstage. We can get a Reuben."

"I'm not really hungry, but take me anywhere as long as it's away from here."

"It's going to be okay, Mia. He didn't deserve your love, but one day you'll meet a man who does."

"He'll have to buy the cow before he gets the milk. That's for sure," Mia said, tossing her hair.

November 2010

"They're putting us through all of this pressure to improve the MEAP scores," Rochelle Banks complained. Mia was sitting at a table in the teachers' lounge with Mr. Ross, Ms. Banks, and Mrs. Stein. "Every year I try to prepare my students to the very best of their abilities, but the majority of them are going to achieve either not proficient or partially proficient scores, especially in math and science. No matter what I do. It has absolutely nothing to do with the way I teach. I blame the parents before anyone else. But I've said it before and I'll say it again: These parents just don't care."

"Nathan's mother cared," said Mia, recalling the student who had gotten in a fight on her first day. Mia had thought he was the one who had started the fight, but she'd later discovered from Mr. Ross that he'd been defending himself against another boy. "She took him out of this school, and put him in a private school after that fight."

"Not every parent can afford to do that—," Ms. Banks interrupted.

"Nathan's mother couldn't afford it either," Mia said. "She told me she was going to get a second job if she had to. Sometimes you have to do what you have to do, because the kids didn't ask to be here. And as parents, it's our responsibility to try to give them the best life they can have."

"But if every parent did that, we wouldn't have anything to do, and we'd all be out of a job," Ms. Banks said. "I know you've heard the expression 'You can run, but you can't hide.' "

"I've heard it," Mia said, "but I also believe if you can run fast enough, there's no need to hide. That young man was practically beaten to death, and Fenton was killed. As a mother, I would've done the same thing."

"Everyone wants to fault the teacher," Ms. Banks said, "but you just wait and see who comes to parent-teacher conference tonight. I guarantee that you'll be able to count on one hand the number of parents who show. Tell her, Byron," she said to Mr. Ross. "Most of these parents don't care."

"Most?" Mia questioned. "Really? I hope not."

"Some of these parents are younger than me, and I'm only thirty-five," Ms. Banks continued. "More than half of them are single parents who are too busy shaking their asses at some club to raise their kids. Is it that hard to make sure your child is studying, turn off the television, and tell them to read a book? I'm a divorced mother of two boys. I work a full-time job, and I'm a licensed Realtor. If I can do it, anybody can do it."

"That's why we're here, I guess," said Mr. Ross. "To be the parent and the teacher. Why don't we just have a conference with ourselves?" He looked over at Mia. "You'll probably have about one or two parents show up per class. So you'll probably see about twelve parents."

"Yeah, right," scoffed Ms. Banks. "I called a parent the other day and she cursed me out so badly I got scared. I'm not used to all that. Cursing out a teacher who's trying to inform a parent about her child instigating fights? Her response was, 'All my sons are fine, so I'm not surprised if girls fight over him.' That's what she said, like she was proud of him. And then she called me a bitch, told me never to call her house, and hung up."

Mia shook her head. "I'm not saying that when I taught at

Pershing life was perfect, and all my students did what I asked, and every parent was wonderful, but all of this sounds so extreme."

"It is a bit extreme, but true," said Mr. Ross. "Still I'm here for all these kids, even if I can only reach the ones like Fenton who sit at the front of the classroom and truly want to learn. I'm here for the parents who do care, and even if some of them are teenage parents in a one-parent household, that doesn't mean that they don't care."

"I know I come across like the bitter teacher," Ms. Banks said, "but teachers are under fire and I'm sick of it. Should bad teachers get fired? Absolutely. But students have to want to learn, and parents need to help them. I can only control what goes on inside my classroom. Not what happens when they go home. If these kids aren't eating, if they're being abused, if the parents could care less if they do their homework and they spend all night watching TV and playing video games, it shows in their test scores. And teachers have to pay the price for that. How is that fair? I'm looking at the four years I spent in college and asking myself, did I pick the right major? The right career path? I used to love being a teacher. Now we have kids in school texting in the classroom, updating their Facebook pages."

"It's a new day, but not necessarily a better one," Mr. Ross said.

"They can easily figure out mechanical gadgets. But when you ask them to name the forty-four presidents of the United States, they can only name two or three," Ms. Banks said.

Mia's head shook slowly as she let out an exasperated sigh while she bit into her soggy tuna fish sandwich. She'd been so busy fussing at Frank about their ongoing financial woes while she was making her lunch that she used too much mayonnaise. "So we know the problem. Now we need to figure out a solution, because we can complain all day."

Ms. Banks stabbed a fork through the bed of lettuce in her salad. "The only time you can get some of these parents to come to the school is when they need someone to sign off on paperwork to prove their child is a full-time student and get their welfare checks."

"Enough," Mia said, "you have my head spinning. You must be miserable every time you step in your classroom, and I bet your students can tell."

"I'm not making any of this up. Don't you watch the news, or read the paper?"

"I'm not saying you're making anything up, but kids can pick up on things. You think your students don't know how you feel?" Mia knew for a fact that they did. "Instead of focusing on why they're not learning, focus on teaching."

"Excuse me?" Ms. Banks said as she frowned at Mia.

"Okay, we're getting a little overheated here," Mr. Ross quickly interjected. Ms. Banks glared in his direction. "Not just you, Rochelle. We should all calm down a bit."

Ms. Banks pursed her lips with attitude. She shoved her chair back forcefully and stood. "Let me go back to my classroom early so I can spend more time focusing on teaching," she spit.

Mia rubbed her forehead after Ms. Banks left. "Every time I leave this school, I have a severe headache."

"I have some Tylenol if you need it," said Mr. Ross.

"No, thank you. I try not to take anything for pain."

"So you're a strong woman. Is that what you're telling me?"

"She obviously is, because she was the first one with enough nerve to tell Rochelle what we've been thinking for years," said Mrs. Stein, "which is to shut the hell up, stop complaining, and teach. I tip my piece of chalk to you."

Mia smiled. "I really didn't mean it that way."

"Maybe you didn't, but I'm glad that's the way she took it," said Mrs. Stein. "So maybe now when we come to the teachers' lounge for our lunch break, we can really take a break."

The bell rang. The students had been given a half day for parent-teacher conferences, and while Mia was hopeful that more than a dozen parents would show, her headache would allow her to get over her disappointment quickly.

It was Saturday morning, the weekend before Thanksgiving, just before nine o'clock. She was tired, even though she'd had more than enough sleep. It had been a long week, just like every other week since she'd returned to teaching. But she wasn't tired enough not to be nervous about seeing Lamont. She had butterflies in her stomach as she headed south on Woodward Avenue on her way to meet him for coffee at a cute local bakery. She'd been putting him off for months now, but she'd finally agreed to see him.

She was certain she'd recognize him, especially since he had placed current pictures of himself on Facebook. But whether he'd recognize her was another question. When they had dated, she had long hair, which was a preference of his. Now her hair was barely an inch long. And she'd gained fifty pounds and four dress sizes, which was a considerable amount of weight from what he was used to seeing on her. She looked like a well-built woman now. At forty-eight, she was no longer concerned if heads turned, but she'd love to make Lamont's head turn.

The closer she came to the bakery, the more nervous she became. Her palms were sweaty. The last time she'd seen him was days after she'd married Frank. Lamont had just purchased a black 1990 BMW 5 Series that looked exactly like the one parked a few cars away from hers. But would he really be driving the same car from twenty years ago? she wondered.

When she pulled open the door to the bakery, the strong aroma of freshly roasted coffee was enough to wake up all her senses. But it didn't calm her nerves, nor did seeing Lamont, who was seated at a small table near the entrance. He had to have seen her enter, since he had a window seat close to the door. But he obviously didn't recognize her. And even after she approached him, it still took him a few seconds to realize it was her. Her personal Facebook page didn't have any pictures. Not even a profile picture. She appeared as an outlined image, and he'd given her flak about that. He'd teasingly told her she either really let herself go or was hiding from the law.

"So, did I let myself go?" Mia asked.

Lamont grinned. "Not at all. You look great." He stood up and hugged her. "The short hair looks great on you." He was still smiling as she pulled away from his long embrace. "Would you like me to get you something?"

"Yes, if you don't mind."

"Coffee and what else?"

"Tea—green tea if they have it."

"Anything else?"

"I've never been here, so whatever else you think I'd like. Do you still remember what I like?"

"Aside from me?" he asked with a smile. "Not really, it's been a while."

As soon as he walked away, a young woman approached her table and said, "Mrs. Glitch? Do you remember me?"

She studied the young woman, whom she didn't recognize at all.

"It's Heaven Jetter . . . from your freshman English class." Heaven and her sister, Hope, were two students Mia had taken a particular interest in at Pershing. Their father had been incarcerated for killing their mother, and they had been raised by their paternal grandmother.

"Aww, Heaven," Mia said, standing to give her a hug. "How have you been?"

"Good."

"How's Hope?"

"She's doing great. She lives in the lofts on the corner."

"So you must be down here visiting her?"

"I'm actually down here taking pictures. I've been taking

pictures in the Cass Corridor for a while now." Heaven glanced over at Lamont, who was waiting at the counter. "I don't think I've ever met your husband."

"Oh, that's not him. He's just a friend of the family."

"Oh, okay. So, did you ever go back to teaching?"

"Yes, as a matter of fact, I went back to school this year. I'm teaching at a charter high school now."

"I don't think I ever told you this, but you were my favorite teacher."

Mia smiled broadly. "Thank you for saying that, Heaven. So tell me what's going on with your life."

"I moved downtown into the Jeffersonian, but I'm thinking about moving to California. I have family there. And I'm also thinking about going back to school so I can get my degree."

"You should, Heaven. That would be so wonderful."

Heaven smiled. "I will, Mrs. Glitch."

Lamont returned to the table with a tray with a coffee and green tea and two pecan sticky buns.

"Those pecan sticky buns are the bomb," Heaven said as she looked at the tray. "Well, it was nice seeing you, Mrs. Glitch."

"It was nice seeing you too, Heaven," said Mia as she stood to hug her.

"Who was she?" asked Lamont after Heaven walked away to join the line.

Mia removed the cup of tea from the tray. "One of my former students," she said as she took a sip of tea and eyed Heaven for a second longer. "I wonder if she ever stopped dating bad boys. She was a wild one, but she looks completely different now."

"And so do you."

"Completely?"

"Completely. I recognize you only by your eyes. Everything else is different. I feel like asking to see your driver's license just so I can make sure it's you."

"You sound disappointed."

Lamont shook his head. "I'm sorry if I sound that way, because I'm not. You were cute before, but you're sexy now. Look at those legs," he said, his eyes moving from her feet to her thighs.

"Stop," Mia said.

"Did they get longer?"

"No, my heels got higher."

A moment later, Mia waved good-bye to her former student as Heaven headed toward the door with a bag in her hand. Mia smiled and watched her walk to her Saturn.

"She can't be doing too badly. She has a new car."

"I see you still have a fascination with cars."

"I never had a car fascination."

"Trust me, you did. You knew more about cars than I did."

"I didn't know anything about cars aside from the make and model. I wanted a new car so badly, which is what happens when you've never had one before. Speaking of which, I know you're not still driving that black BMW."

"I am. Is that a problem?" he teased.

"You certainly got your money's worth."

"Do you ever think about me?" Lamont asked abruptly.

Mia was taken aback. "I wouldn't be here if I never thought of you," she said carefully.

"What are some of the things you think about?"

Mia shrugged. "I used to wonder if you ever settled down and had kids. But as soon as I accepted your Facebook friend request, I had all of my questions answered."

"That's assuming I told the truth on my profile."

"I would hope you'd tell the truth. You're too old to be lying. You did omit your age, I noticed. You should be proud that you're fifty."

"I am proud. I'm very proud. Just as I'm sure you'll be in two more years. And for the record, I never was a liar."

"Excuse me," she said as she patted her chest while clearing her throat. "Your last statement got caught in my throat, because I have a hard time swallowing BS."

Lamont let out a chuckle. "I never lied when we were together."

"Lamont, don't take me back twenty years, because we can settle this in roughly five seconds."

"We may have had a series of misunderstandings—"

"Oh, is that what they were?" she asked with a laugh.

"But I never lied."

"So, anyway, you don't have any kids. . . . You've never been married. . . . Your car's paid for. That's the only stability I see in you," she said, letting out another laugh. "You're still a chef?"

"Of course. It's my passion. The buzzword of the decade. Find your passion."

"I wish I could find mine."

"I thought teaching was."

"It is, but not the way it used to be," she said as she shook her head. "I'm not sure. I've been away for a while, and I feel like a person must feel when they come back from prison after thirty years."

"Didn't you tell me you were gone for eight years?"

"But it feels like thirty." Mia shook her head and stared out the window. "I just don't know. The kids weren't this bad eight years ago. They weren't angels by any means, but they weren't like this." She sighed. "I should shut up. I'm starting to sound like one of the teachers at my school. So, you own a restaurant? I saw the pictures on Facebook."

"I used to own one for four years, but I had to close it two years ago."

"Did you want to close it, or were you forced to close because of the economy?"

"It was a whole lot of things, honestly. My strength is in the kitchen. Well, that's not my only strength, but I get things started there," he said with a wink.

"Oh please, you have not changed one bit after all these years," Mia said with a laugh. "But back to your restaurant. Tell me what happened."

"When I was working for someone else, I told myself that I was the one that made that restaurant. All those people who were coming there came because of me and the menu I created. The owners were rich—two brothers. So one day I went to one of 'em, and I was just straight with him. I said, 'Either you open up a restaurant for me, and invest in my vision, or I'm leaving by the beginning of next year.' He said there was no need for me to wait, I could leave right then. The funny part was I thought I was cool with those guys. The sad part was that their restaurant started doing even better after I left."

"And yours?"

"I hurried up and opened one out of spite. Poured all my savings into it, and refused to close it for years, even once I realized it was failing. I was stubborn as hell. I knew within the first six months that if I didn't get an investor, my restaurant would close within a year." He paused, searching her eyes. "Am I talking too much?"

Mia shook her head. "Not at all."

"Are you sure?" he asked.

"Positive."

"Because I don't have to talk about the restaurant. I can talk about us," he said with a sly grin.

"Us?" She shook her head and rolled her eyes. "Talk about the restaurant."

"I never got an investor, but my father unwittingly became one, since I was calling him every other week for thousands of dollars. And one day he passed away. I felt like I killed him."

"Why did you feel like that?" Mia asked, scrunching her face.

"I was his only child. And he wanted the best for me. He'd always wanted the best for me. He knew losing my mother when I was young had affected me, and he always tried to do all he could to make me feel like it was okay. That we were going to be okay. He was in his eighties. I was forty-four. And instead of me being in a position where I could take care of him, he was still taking care of me. He'd left me with a decent inheritance, but at that point I'd had enough. I couldn't put another dime in."

"I'm sorry to hear about your dad. I know how much you loved him."

"I'm an orphan now."

"Don't say that. That makes me sad to hear."

"It's the truth. I look back over my life sometimes and I feel like I made a wrong turn a long time ago, and I'm just now finding my way back home. And part of that was reconnecting with you."

"With me?"

"Baby, I made a mistake, and I want you back. I'm ready to settle down."

"At fifty."

"Hey . . . better late than never."

"That's what they say."

"What do you say?" he asked as he stared deeply into her eyes and reached for her hand.

"I'm married. That's what I say," she said, pulling her hand away.

"But are you happy?"

"Twenty years will definitely come with some ups and downs."

"Answer the question. Are you happy?"

She paused, debating whether to be honest or not. "No, I'm not happy. I want a divorce."

"I miss you."

Mia knew she should get up and leave. Go home and read their next book club selection, a Kimberla Lawson Roby book she'd recently downloaded onto her Kindle. Get lost in the drama of Reverend Curtis Black, instead of creating drama for herself. But she picked up her sticky bun, took a small bite from it, and said, "Go on."

Mia had made a mistake. That's how she felt as she was sneaking out of bed hours later while Lamont went on snoring. They hadn't had sex. They kissed and cuddled, which was more than she should've done given their history.

Whatever Mia had hoped to accomplish by seeing him, she didn't. The attraction was there and it was obviously mutual, but his lifestyle left much to be desired. After all, Lamont was living in his parents' house, which was exactly as she remembered it. And there were other things she also remembered. Even though those other things happened so long ago, it felt like it could easily belong to someone else's life instead of hers.

"I'm leaving," she told him after a light nudge to his bare shoulder.

"Why? I don't want you to leave. I want to make love to you," he said as he sat up in bed.

"I've got to go home."

"It's only two thirty in the afternoon," he said, after he picked his cell phone off his nightstand. "You don't have to go home yet." He sat on the edge of the bed and pulled Mia closer to him by her waist.

She wondered if the bed they'd been resting in was one he had bought, or if it was his parents' bed. It made her feel strange.

"I've got to go home. Have you forgotten that I'm married?"

"Have you forgotten you're getting a divorce?"

"I didn't say I was getting one. I said I wanted to get one."

"Mia, that makes no sense. If you want to get one, then you should." He raised her blouse and kissed her belly button. "What your soon-to-be ex-husband doesn't know can't hurt him. And from what I gather, he probably wouldn't care."

"Oh, he'd care. And I'd know, and you should know that I'm not like that. Two wrongs don't make a right."

"So he *has* cheated?" Lamont asked. She nodded before she realized what she was doing. "Two wrongs don't make a right, but it does make it even."

"That's okay. I don't have to get even."

"I need someone who can check in on me from time to time and make sure I'm still alive. I'm not trying to make you my girlfriend, but can you at least be my emergency contact?" he asked, a lightness in his tone that made Mia think he was joking, though she thought she detected a hint of desperation in his voice.

She nodded. "I'll be your emergency contact as long as you give them my cell number."

"That's the only number I have."

Lamont walked Mia down the stairs and outside to her car.

"Don't be a stranger."

She turned and faced him, kept her hand on the door handle to the van while he leaned into her and planted a kiss on the top of her head.

"You're too short for me to reach your lips."

"I wasn't going to let you."

She climbed into her van and waved as she pulled off. Though she knew what she'd done was wrong, she couldn't suppress a delicious shiver of happiness. Even if this was the one and only time she and Lamont fooled around, at least she could cherish the moment.

Mia put on a big smile when she heard Alexa's laughter beyond the front door. It was the day before Thanksgiving, and Mia was looking forward to seeing her daughter again.

"Mom, we're here," Alexa said as she used her key to open the door. Alexa had called her a week earlier to make sure she wouldn't mind if she brought her roommate home. They were planning to drive from school together in Tiffany's car. Now wasn't the best time with Frank's legal woes, but Mia was praying they'd at least be able to fake it through the holiday.

She finished tucking in the bedsheets in the guest room and rushed downstairs.

The smile etched across her face fell quickly once she realized her daughter had brought along more than just her roommate. They were coupled with two guys. And Chris was nowhere in the picture. She'd been asking her daughter about Chris for weeks, but her response was always vague. They'd broken up. But were still close friends. She wasn't dating, and she didn't want to talk about it. Now there was this person. And he looked too old for her daughter.

"Hi, Mom," Alexa said as Mia began to walk down each stair, her pace decreasing with each step. "You remember Tiffany?"

"Yes, I remember Tiffany. Who are your other friends?" she asked, trying to plaster a smile back on her face.

"This is Ordell," Alexa said, taking one of the young men by the hand. "And that's Carson."

"My Lord, how tall are you guys?" Mia asked, trying not to look too displeased. But she felt herself frown.

"I'm six-eight," Ordell said with a grin.

"I'm six-six," Carson said.

"You guys look like you're more than three hundred pounds, easily."

"Yes, ma'am," Ordell said.

"And from the South. I know by the 'ma'am.' "

"Well, I am," Ordell said. "From Florida."

"And I'm from Pennsylvania," Carson said.

"Linemen?"

"Yes, ma'am . . . you know a little something about football?"

"Not really, just enough to get through the Super Bowl every year without feeling completely lost. So are you U of M players, or have you been playing for the NFL for about ten years? Because I'm going to be honest with you—you both look to be in your thirties."

Ordell and Carson chuckled. They seemed polite, but she still didn't care for them. It would take a special man to take the place of Chris. And she found nothing attractive about either one of them. Their necks were unusually large, so much so that the thought of steroid use popped into Mia's mind.

"They're star players at U of M, Mom. Both of them play defensive tackle."

"So you greatly contribute to the violence of the sport?"

Ordell shrugged. "We just get the job done."

"Are you just dropping the girls off?" Mia said, a hopeful note in her voice.

"No, Mom. I invited them to have Thanksgiving dinner."

"Well, that would've been nice to know earlier. But that's fine," Mia said, quickly recovering, as she continued down the stairs.

"They'll also be staying until Friday," Alexa said, avoiding her mother's eyes.

"Excuse me? Did you ask me if that would be all right?" Mia asked, struggling to keep the displeasure from her voice.

"Can we talk about this later?" Alexa asked, clearly embarrassed.

"If you mean after you excuse yourself from your friends and follow me into my bedroom so we can talk about it right now, then yes."

Alexa's nose flared. "Guys, just make yourself comfortable—"

"Not too comfortable," Mia said coldly as she walked up the winding staircase with Alexa trailing behind her.

"I thought we were going to your bedroom," said Alexa as she continued to follow behind her mother to one of the guest rooms.

"We are. This is my bedroom now."

"You and Dad don't sleep in the same room anymore?"

"I'll be the one asking all the questions. So how old is he? Because he looks old . . . out-of-college old."

"Mom, can you stop harping on his looks? I told you he plays for U of M. He's twenty-one and he's a junior. Just ask Dad about Ordell Simpson. He's a star athlete. You can Google his name if you don't believe me."

"I don't need to Google him. Star athlete or not, he's not staying here."

"Dad already said it was okay."

Mia had a bemused expression on her face. "Are you telling me that you asked your father about this and he gave you permission? Is that what you're telling me? Because if so, I really need to talk to your father."

"Yes."

Mia was so angry her head felt like it would explode. How dare he make that kind of decision without consulting her first? Regardless of their personal problems, they never had issues discussing what was best for Alexa. "And where are they supposed to sleep? I know they're not staying with you and Tiffany."

"In the guest bedrooms," Alexa said, shifting from foot to foot.

"I'm in one of them. So that leaves two, and there are three people downstairs."

"I'm grown-up," Alexa protested. "Ordell can stay in my room."

"Girl, you have gone off to college and truly lost your mind. Don't make me snap and throw everybody out of this house."

"Mom, what is wrong with you?"

"Chris has been your boyfriend for three years and I've known his father most of my life, and he has never once spent the night here. And if you expect me to allow a man into your bed under my roof, you must be crazy. That won't ever be happening."

"I really hate you sometimes," Alexa huffed, turning to walk away.

Mia shrugged. "I love you. If I didn't, I wouldn't care what you did. And you might hate me now, but you'll thank me later. The guys can share a room and Tiffany can sleep in the other guest room, or they can leave now. And the only reason I'm allowing that is because your father already told you it would be okay."

"Tiffany can do what she wants to do. You're not her mother."

"Okay, give me her mother's number and I'll call her and see if she's okay with her eighteen-year-old daughter sharing a bed with a boy she's probably never met. Give me her number."

"No, I'm not giving you her number so you can get her mother mad at her too. You're too protective. I'm not ten."

"No, you're eighteen, and in my eyes there's very little difference."

"I shouldn't have even come home."

"Yes, you should have. Holidays are the time you spend with family. And they're not your family. I don't like this Ordell person."

"You don't even know him."

"I don't need to know him to know I don't like him. One look into a person's eyes tells me all I need to know, and his eyes tell me he's no good for you."

"Or maybe, just maybe, you've been holding on to this vision of me marrying Chris since you obviously wanted to marry his father," Alexa lashed out.

"I didn't want to marry Chris's father," Mia said, taken aback.

"Well, you must not have wanted to marry mine either. I mean, you have your own bedroom now."

Mia's eyes quickly swept over her daughter in disgust. Was this the same young woman who just wanted both of her parents to be happy? Mia wondered. "You've changed in such a short time, and it's breaking my heart. I have enough stress in my life right now as it is. I don't want to add you on to the list of things to worry about."

"May I leave now?" Alexa huffed.

"Yes, you can leave."

Alexa walked toward the door, then turned toward her mother.

"Tiffany and I will stay in my bedroom, and the guys can each have their own room. They'll only be here two days, so can you just please try to be nice?"

Mia's heart wouldn't stop racing. There was only one thing she could think to do, and that was call Chris. He didn't answer, so she left him a voice mail. Later that evening, after Alexa went out with her friends, Chris returned Mia's call.

"She started acting different once she got up to U of M," Chris said. "I'm not going to say wild, but it was kind of obvious she went to an all-girls school, because she was acting like she hadn't been around guys before."

"Not used to the attention she was getting, probably," Mia said wisely.

"A lot of guys were coming on to her. I'm trying not to speak from the point of view of a jealous ex-boyfriend or anything, because I know she's a beautiful girl. She looks like a supermodel. She wanted space, and I was fine with that. I could give her that. But I couldn't believe she went from me to someone like him just because he's an athlete. If Alexa doesn't want to be with me right now, I guess I'll have to live with that, but I don't want her to be with him. I'm sure she can find another nice guy. And I really hope she hasn't slept with him, because from what I've heard, he may have something."

"Something like what?"

"I just heard his ex was telling people he gave her something. That's all I keep hearing."

Mia's nose flared as a thousand thoughts ran through her mind simultaneously. She had a very strong indication that her daughter had already slept with Ordell, due to the ease with which she suggested they sleep in the same room, but she was praying she was wrong. "Thank you, Chris. I'm going to handle this. She won't be seeing him much longer."

A couple of hours after Mia ended her call with Chris, she decided to check to see if Frank had finally made it home. She stormed out of her bedroom and burst into their master suite, interrupting Frank while he watched pay-per-view porn on television.

"Can you turn that off, please? We have a problem with Alexa that needs to be addressed right now."

He turned off the television.

"What's the problem, Mia?"

"Ordell Simpson is the problem. I can't believe you told our eighteen-year-old daughter that she could bring men to sleep over at this house, and didn't even bother to discuss it with me."

"I told her that it was okay as long as the guys slept in the guest bedrooms."

"Well, you shouldn't have told her that."

"Mia, she's away at college. Whatever you're afraid she might do here she can easily do there."

"I'm not sure I understand your logic. I doubt most fathers think the way you do. I can only hope and pray that Alexa isn't having premarital sex, but if that's the choice she's made, there's nothing I can do. But one thing I can control is what she does under this roof."

"Ordell Simpson is a star defensive tackle."

"Oh, Frank, that's all you care about. For you, people are what they do. But I don't care what he does. I don't like what I'm hearing about him."

"From?"

"Chris."

"Chris? Mia, what do you expect? Chris is her ex-boyfriend. We know how exes can be . . . don't we?" He shook his head. "Can I go back to my movie now?"

Mia slammed the door and headed downstairs. She decided she would camp out in the family room and wait for them to return. She waited until three in the morning, when Tiffany's car finally pulled into the driveway.

"Alexa, I need to speak with you," Mia said from the shadows as soon as Alexa set foot into the foyer.

Alexa placed her hand on her chest. "God, Mom, you scared me. Why are you up this late?"

"Because I need to speak with you."

"Okay . . ."

"Right now."

"Can I show them to their rooms first?" Alexa asked, clearly giving her mother attitude.

"Didn't they see them earlier? Straight up the stairwell to your right."

Alexa walked her friends to the staircase. "Sorry, I'm not sure what's wrong with my mom," she said loudly, as if she didn't care if Mia overheard. She walked back to Mia after they headed upstairs. "Mom, you are acting so crazy," Alexa whispered through gritted teeth. "You're embarrassing me. They probably think you're bipolar."

"Do you think I care what they think? If they have a problem with it, maybe those boys should leave."

"They're not boys."

"They're not men either. Have you slept with him yet?"

"No," Alexa said, twisting her nose.

"Don't lie to me."

"I haven't."

"Don't. He has an STD."

"Where did you get that from?"

"I talked to Chris."

"And Chris said Ordell has an STD?" Alexa said, her voice rising in anger.

"He said that his ex-girlfriend is telling people he gave her something she can't get rid of."

"Right, his ex-girlfriend. A person's ex is likely to say anything, Mom."

"Oh, don't be so naive and gullible. First thing Friday morning, I want them out."

"Why are you acting like this? I've never seen you like this."

"I've never had a reason to act like this."

"I mean, think about it, Mom. You want to kick me out to try to prevent me from doing something I can easily do at school."

"No, no one said anything about kicking you or Tiffany out. Just the guys. But they can stay until Friday, and then first thing in the morning they have to go."

Alexa turned on her heel and headed toward the staircase. "Don't worry. We'll all be going."

"Can someone please say grace?" Mia asked as she sat at her dining room table beside her husband and directly across from Alexa and her friends. It was Thanksgiving, and Mia's parents were there, but Frank's weren't. This wasn't the first holiday they'd skipped either. Mia's father was a holiday drunk. Give him a bottle of Grey Goose vodka and a good excuse to drink it, and he would. Mia's father could be rude without alcohol, so being drunk made him that much worse. She couldn't blame Frank's parents for not showing.

"Bless us, O Lord, and these thy gifts which we are about to receive, amen," Mia's father said, mumbling quickly through the brief passage. It was the same prayer she'd heard him recite at every holiday dinner since she was a child and old enough to remember.

Frank stood at the head of the table over the turkey and began carving it, placing white and dark meat on a large serving tray, which he passed down the table.

"Everyone please help themselves," Frank said.

Mia's father took two pieces of turkey from the tray and placed them on his plate before passing it down. He took a few swallows of his vodka and said, "I remember when I first saw your dining room table. I said to myself, who in the hell needs a table this big? This is some Henry the Eighth–type mess."

Mia rolled her eyes and shook her head. The situation was bad enough. She and Alexa weren't speaking, and Tiffany and the boys looked uncomfortable. Her father's drunkenness only made matters worse.

"Your dressing is really good, Mrs. Glitch," Ordell said.

Mia didn't respond.

"You're not going to say thank you?" Mia's father asked.

"I'm sorry," Mia said to her father.

"What you sorry for? Don't apologize to me. Apologize to him."

"I didn't hear you," she told her father.

"Did you hear Alexa's friend compliment your dressing?"

"I didn't. Thank you," she said to Ordell without looking at him.

Silence fell over the room for almost the entirety of the meal, which gave Mia even more time to reflect on the phone conversation she and Chris had.

"I just now realized who you are," Mia's father told Ordell as he finished the last spoonful of mashed potatoes on his plate. "You're that kid who plays for Michigan." Mia's eyes rolled again. "What's going on with your coach?"

"I'm not sure what you mean, sir."

"Oh, you know what I mean, they trying to get Rich Rod out of there. He might not be so rich after Saturday's game. You think you-all can beat Ohio State?"

"Of course I think we can."

"Well, I don't," Mia's father said. "You ain't beat 'em since 2003, so I got my money on Ohio."

"I don't want to talk about football," Mia said.

"Well, what you want to talk about, Mia? Turn off the music, everybody put down their forks, and let's see what little Miss Mia would like to talk about."

Ordell chuckled.

"I wish I could see some humor in this situation," Mia said tightly.

"Mom, please," Alexa said. "Not now."

Mia arched her right eyebrow and continued to eat in silence. It was times like these that she could appreciate how hardened she was against her father's behavior. For now, she was going to remain calm.

Mia decided to focus her attention on Tiffany, who didn't

appear to be the least bit into Carson. The more she observed her, the clearer it became that she and Carson were probably just friends, if they even knew each other at all. She supposed Alexa brought Carson along because she thought Mia would be understanding if another couple was involved.

"So, Tiffany, how do you like your first year in college?"

"Oh, I love it. It's a nice campus. Nice dorm."

"I understand your favorite dessert is red velvet cake. Is that right?"

"Yes, I love red velvet cake," Tiffany said as her eyes lit up.

"Why don't you follow me into the kitchen so you can cut the first piece?"

Before Tiffany got up from the dining room table, she looked over at Alexa. The two appeared to be communicating telepathically.

"Tiffany, are you ready, dear?"

"Yes, Mrs. Glitch." Tiffany followed quietly behind Mia.

"I love your curly hair."

"Thanks," Tiffany said, as if she wasn't used to compliments.

"So is Carson your boyfriend?"

"No," Tiffany said, fluttering her eyes. "Just a friend."

"Did you know Chris?" Mia asked. Tiffany nodded. "Which one do you like better between Chris and Ordell?"

Tiffany turned back toward the entrance of the spacious kitchen to see if anyone was listening to their conversation. "Don't tell Alexa I said this, but I do prefer Chris."

"It's good to know we're on the same page. Tell me what you know about Ordell."

Tiffany shrugged. "Not much. I'm not one of those girls who are into athletes."

"I didn't think my daughter was either. How did they meet?" Mia asked, edging the cake closer to Tiffany.

"Mrs. Glitch, I'm not sure what Alexa wants to tell you, and I don't want to be in the middle. I have to live with her, and we're very close. I don't want to make her mad."

"I completely understand," Mia said, cutting a large slice of red velvet cake for Tiffany. She set the plate with the slice of cake on it in front of her. "Have a seat?" Tiffany sat at one of the barstools. "What would you like to drink with that?"

"Just water, thank you."

Mia removed a bottle of water from the fridge and set it beside the plate.

"This is so good," Tiffany said as she took the first bite.

"I made it from scratch. I've always enjoyed baking. Now, how did they meet?"

Tiffany smirked, well aware that Mia's red-velvet-cake bribe would break her.

"At a frat party."

"What's your impression of him?"

"Well, honestly, I—"

"Tiffany," Alexa said from the doorway, abruptly interrupting their conversation. "Come on. We're going to the show."

"Sorry, Mrs. Glitch, I hate to eat and run," Tiffany said after taking a couple more large bites.

"No problem. The cake will be waiting for you when you return, and so will I."

Mia looked over at her daughter just as her daughter rolled her eyes. "Is there a problem, Alexa? Because I'm getting tired of those eyes rolling."

"Well, I'm tired of a lot of things too. Mainly, the way you're embarrassing me by acting so crazy."

"Let me tell you what I'm tired of. I'm tired of you calling me crazy, bipolar, and whatever else. It's disrespectful. Do you want to see crazy? I'm about to show you crazy."

Mia marched into the dining room, where everyone seemed to be enjoying themselves with their lighthearted football conversation.

"I don't know who you are," Mia said, pointing first at Ordell and then at Carson, "but I know who my daughter is, and I feel like I know who Tiffany is, and this situation is not a good one."

"Mom, stop!" Alexa said, practically in tears.

"No, I won't stop. I'm your crazy mother, remember?"

"Dad, tell her to shut up."

"Shut up?" Mia said, bugging her eyes at Alexa. "Yeah, Dad, tell me to shut up," she said as she turned toward Frank. "I dare you."

"Let's . . . let's just hear your mother out," he stuttered.

"As for you," Mia said, turning her attention toward Ordell. "I'm not here to expose any of your personal business, but I will say this—I don't want my daughter seeing you. There's more to life than football. My daughter's going to be a doctor. I refuse to let you distract her from her goals."

Alexa burst into tears and ran upstairs.

"I didn't see you drinking any alcohol," Mia's father said to her, "but I hope you're drunk, because you're acting like a fool."

"I learned from the best," Mia huffed before storming out of the dining room and stomping upstairs.

Friday arrived like a devastating one-two punch.

The doorbell rang at exactly seven in the morning.

Men in dark suits stood at Mia's front door.

Mia was dressed and up early. She stepped onto the porch and closed the door behind her.

"Are you here for my husband, Frank Glitch?" she asked the men. She had a feeling this would be the day when their luck ran out, and she was right.

"Yes, we are," one of the men said, and handed her his business card. He was with the Federal Bureau of Investigation.

"Is there any way I could bring him down to your office later today so he can turn himself in, since it's the holiday weekend?"

"No, I'm afraid there isn't. Is he inside?"

"Yes, he's here. Could you please let me get him? I just don't want to disturb our guests."

"We can give you five minutes to get him down here." They waited at the door while Mia ran upstairs.

"Get up, Frank. Hurry up," she whispered loudly as she stood over his bed.

"For what?"

"They're downstairs."

"Who's downstairs?" he asked as he turned from his side over to his back and stared at the ceiling.

"The FBI. Hurry up and get dressed. They're only giving you five minutes. I don't want Alexa and her friends to see any of this, so hurry up."

"What do they want?"

"You know what they want. Now will you please just hurry up? Do you need me to help you?"

He sat on the side of his bed, rubbing his forehead. "Just let me sit here and think for a minute."

"You don't have time to think. It's time. Now get dressed," she said, tossing his underwear and socks that she'd taken from their dresser drawer onto the bed, "and go down there."

"I don't even believe this is happening right now. How is this even happening?"

"I don't know, Frank, but you have to get dressed right now." She walked into his closet and removed one of his suits.

"I'm not wearing a suit to prison. Who am I playing dress-up for?"

"You know you're going to be on the news."

He reached out his hand. "All right, hand it here. Call my

parents and let them know what happened," he said as he stood and dressed. "Mia, I'm scared."

His words jolted her. As much as he'd hurt her, she felt bad for him, and didn't want to be vindictive. She didn't want her daughter's father going to prison. He was a man who'd worked hard for as long as Mia had known him. What exactly had gone wrong to make him commit white-collar crimes, she didn't know for sure. Maybe he'd decided to do things that were against the law to finance the lavish lifestyle they'd both dreamed of. Did that make her just as much to blame?

"It's going to be okay, Frank."

"I failed you," he said. Those were his last words before he walked outside and rode off in the dark sedan. She'd lost her husband long before the Feds rang their doorbell that morning, but she couldn't help but let her heart go out to him. It had been a horrible week. On top of everything, she felt like she was losing her daughter too. She'd let her emotions get the best of her. Even though she meant every word she said the day before, she probably shouldn't have said any of it in front of Alexa's friends. As much as Mia's father had embarrassed her when she was growing up, she should've known better.

She could hear her daughter and her friends preparing to leave, so she knocked on Alexa's door before turning the locked doorknob.

"Alexa, let me in."

"No, we're leaving soon, and I don't have anything to say to you. Ever."

"Why are you leaving now? You don't have to leave this soon."

"Because I want to. I want to get out of here as fast as I can."

"Alexa, open the door."

"No!"

Mia stood at her daughter's bedroom door with her hands over her eyes, shaking her head. Her life as she'd known it was over. Her husband was on his way to prison, and her daughter was going to head back to school without saying two words to her. The tight bond they had always shared felt broken.

"Okay, Alexa, you don't have to open the door if you don't want to."

A few seconds later, Alexa opened the door, but only so she and Tiffany could file out with their luggage. "How would you like it if I went over to someone's house for the holidays and their mother totally went off on me the way you went off on Ordell? You don't know him. He's someone's child too. You judged him based on absolutely nothing."

"I can apologize to him for what I said."

"Don't bother. It's too late. You already said everything you wanted to say," Alexa said as she breezed past Mia, stopping at both guest bedrooms to knock on the doors. "We're ready," she called out to the young men.

Within minutes, Mia's house was completely empty.

Chapter Eleven

November 2010

The temperature was just above freezing, which was typical for late November in Michigan. The wet strips of grass along the median and the highway's embankment sparkled with leftover rain. The midmorning traffic whizzed eastbound along Interstate 94. Just twenty minutes earlier, the sky had opened up and poured over the southeast part of the state. But now the rain had subsided. A woman in an inferno orange metallic Camaro with a black rally stripe down the center of the hood turned off her windshield wipers and reached for one of the buttons to her radio. Ten minutes had passed since she'd dropped her sister off at Metro Airport. She'd been intent on waiting underneath the archway at Departures until it stopped raining. That was until a Michigan state trooper tapped his knuckles against the driver's-side window of her Camaro and used a forceful hand gesture to usher her along.

Now she was on the highway and had just passed the eighty-foot-tall Uniroyal Tire—a Detroit landmark for over forty years—when she changed CDs from Pink to Bruno Mars and reached for her cell phone. She looked down at the incoming text, giggled, and took her hands off the steering wheel momentarily to text back.

A silver Range Rover traveling in the far-right lane was heading westbound on the interstate with Tiffany and Carson in the front seat and Alexa and Ordell in the backseat.

Kanye West erupted through the car speakers.

"Another text," Alexa said through gritted teeth. "My mother just sent me another text. She was so rude. I'm so mad at her. Is it a coincidence that Chris just texted me too? Look," Alexa said, turning her cell phone toward Ordell. "Read it."

But before she could hand it over, her eyes enlarged as she saw an inferno orange Camaro and a burgundy Taurus barreling across the median toward them. "Watch out!" she screamed.

But it was too late. In a matter of seconds, a chain reaction accident was set off in both the east- and westbound lanes of the interstate while several others swerved to avoid a collision. The burgundy Taurus crashed into a gold Mercedes. Both cars burst into flames.

Seconds later, the Camaro, going in excess of eighty miles an hour, rammed into their Range Rover, which Tiffany was driving, forcing them into a shallow ditch of the embankment.

Sirens echoed in the near distance.

Within minutes, a parade of emergency vehicles swarmed the scene. Michigan state troopers quickly shut off the nearby exits. Drivers would be trapped for hours.

It didn't take long for camera crews to emerge as reporters prepared themselves to deliver the devastating news to viewers. One station managed to find an eyewitness with cell phone video that captured the moments just before the crash and immediately after. The reporter with the exclusive footage adjusted his tie and reminded himself not to smile. His tone needed to be somber, he'd told himself. People had died. Some of their friends and relatives would be watching. Even though no names were being released at that time, before long family members would place calls that would go unanswered. Leave messages that would never be heard by the intended party.

Danielle and Allen had made it back from their Key West trip the day before Thanksgiving, cutting their vacation short by a few days. One week in Key West was plenty. Without Tiffany, they both seemed to get bored easily. There were only so many of their favorite restaurants to eat at. And Danielle wasn't in the mood to shop. Going every year meant she'd seen all the sights more than enough times. And besides, she and Allen were struggling to remain civil. He'd told her he was ready to return to work, and she'd responded with, "You can't be serious. After your last few box office flops, who's going to hire you? I know one thing—I'm not moving back to LA." Ever since then, Allen hadn't even bothered to talk to her.

Their unpacked luggage was still in the foyer of their home, where the box used to be.

"I keep calling Tiffany and I'm not getting an answer," Danielle told Allen. "What do you think could've happened?"

"Don't worry yourself. She's fine. You know how girls are when they're with their boyfriends."

"Boyfriend? I thought she was with her roommate."

"She is. And her boyfriend. At least that's what I think he is."

"She doesn't have a boyfriend . . . does she?" Danielle asked, a little hurt that after all her poking and prodding, Tiffany wouldn't share the news with her. "Tiffany is dating someone?"

"Seems like it."

"So who is this boy?"

"He's a football player, and his name is Carson."

"And when were you going to tell me?"

"She says he's just a friend."

"What if she didn't even go to her roommate's parents' home for Thanksgiving?"

"Trust me, she went. Alexa's boyfriend is a football player too, and he went with them as well."

"It would've been nice to have known all of this," she said sourly. "Things happen to girls in college. I talked to her yesterday and she didn't mention any boys. What are Alexa's parents' names again?"

"Glitch," Allen said, an edge to his voice.

"Do they have first names?" she asked, more than a little impatient.

"I don't know, Danny. I can't remember them."

"You can't remember their names? How did you ever memorize all those lines?"

"The father's card is in my wallet, so just relax. I'm going out to get some air."

While Allen was gone, Danielle searched her husband's wallet for the business card. Frank Glitch was the chief financial officer of Investment Professional Advisers, which was located on Griswold in Detroit. She powered on her iPad and started searching his name and company. Within seconds she found the heading GLITCH INDICTED IN DETROIT CORRUPTION PROBE.

Her eyes tried to refocus on the *Detroit News* article. She couldn't believe what she was reading. He'd been arrested at his home in Bingham Farms earlier that morning.

"And I'm being paranoid. I don't think so." She paced the living room floor, waiting for Allen to return. Her daughter had spent Thanksgiving at a criminal's home. Now that she thought about it, Tiffany had sounded distressed. She went back to the Internet, but this time what caught her attention was an article that had just popped onto the *Detroit News* home page one minute earlier.

TWO UNIVERSITY OF MICHIGAN FOOTBALL PLAYERS
INVOLVED IN FATAL CHAIN REACTION CRASH ON I-94

Danielle's blood froze over. All of a sudden, Mr. Glitch's legal woes didn't matter. She quickly read the article.

> Michigan State Police say two University of Michigan football players are among those seriously injured after crashing in a Range Rover on I-94 West in Wayne County shortly before ten a.m. Friday. It is unclear who was driving the Range Rover, but four students from U of M were in the car and have been identified by their student ID. Six fatalities have been reported, but it is uncertain at this time if either of the football players is among the fatalities.

As soon as Allen came through the door, she said in a panic-stricken voice, "Allen, we have to go."

"Go where?"

"We have to go right now," Danielle said, walking around in a circle trying to figure out what to take.

"Where are we going, Danny?"

"To the airport," Danielle shouted. "Tiffany was involved in a fatal accident."

"What? What are you saying? Where did you get this from?"

"From the Internet!" she screamed.

"Danny, listen to me. Did it actually say her name?"

"No, it didn't say her name, but it's her."

"How do you know it's her?"

"It's her. I feel it. I can't explain it, but I just know."

"What did it say on the Internet?"

"Four University of Michigan students in a Range Rover were

in a car accident on I-94. Two were star athletes. It was her! Stop questioning me and come on."

"You have to call and make sure, Danny. We can't just fly there. What if it wasn't? It could be a coincidence."

"What is wrong with you? I am telling you that I know it's her," Danielle said. "I might not always be a great mother, but nothing can beat a mother's intuition. We're taking the first flight out of here, even if I have to pay for a private jet."

Mia hesitated before turning on the evening news. She was afraid to see her husband's face. But instead of seeing coverage about his arrest, she was startled to see that the lead story was a Breaking News Alert. The caption on the screen read: WESTBOUND I-94 REOPENS AFTER DEADLY ACCIDENT. A young female reporter in a white parka coat and black tam hat stood at the scene along the embankment with a Channel 4 microphone in hand.

"This is a story we reported earlier. Two University of Michigan star athletes are among the injured. We will keep you updated on any new developments we have in this case. For up-to-the-minute information on the top news stories visit clickondetroit dot com."

Mia didn't wait to hear any more. She didn't need to. She knew her daughter was involved. She'd seen the glimpse of Tiffany's Range Rover.

Panic raced through her as she dialed 911 and screamed at the operator, "My daughter and her friends were in that Range Rover."

"Ma'am, I can't understand what you're saying. Please calm down and tell me your emergency."

Mia cried out an unintelligible response, hung up the phone, and called Lamont to come pick her up.

A few minutes later, a police car stopped by to check on her, and Mia explained to the officer why she'd called 911. About thirty minutes later, right before Lamont arrived, her doorbell rang. She rushed to answer.

"I'm Trooper Lewis with the Michigan State Police."

"Where is she?"

"Are you Alexa Glitch's mother?"

"Yes, where is she? Please don't let my baby be dead," Mia said as clung to the front door.

"She was taken to Oakwood Hospital. If you like, I can take you there."

Mia stepped on the porch, leaving her door open, just as Lamont pulled up.

"Ma'am, did you want to get your coat and purse? I can wait while you get your things and lock up."

"I need to see my daughter. I don't care about this house. I need my daughter."

"Yes, ma'am, I know. But it's cold. Let's just step inside so you can get your things. The hospital may ask to see your ID, so we want to make sure you have everything now."

Mia rushed inside, grabbed a jacket and her purse, took her

keys from the counter, and locked her front door behind her. "My friend is driving me. I'll have him follow you."

"Where is my daughter?" Danielle demanded as she rushed through the hospital's automatic sliding glass doors. They'd managed to catch a nonstop Delta flight that arrived at Detroit Metro Airport at 4:40 p.m. "She was involved in some kind of accident and I need to know where she is."

"I need to know your daughter's name."

"Tiffany Newsome."

Danielle's hand nervously tapped the countertop as the woman checked her computer system.

"She's in ICU on the third floor."

"I knew it. I knew that was her," Danielle cried, her face crumpling. "Does it say what her condition is?"

"No, ma'am . . . a doctor would have to give you that information."

She didn't wait for Allen, who was parking their rental car. She rushed to the elevators and waited impatiently for one of the doors to open. Seconds passed slower than hours until finally she heard the sound of an elevator door opening. She barreled inside, stabbing the number three button and then the CLOSE button, narrowly missing a woman in a wheelchair as she was being pushed inside.

"I'm so sorry. My daughter was in an accident and I'm just trying to get to her as fast as I can. I didn't even see you there."

The orderly looked at Danielle with a snarl on her lips. The elderly woman's head bobbed.

Danielle watched the numbers climb, stopping first on the second floor so the woman in the wheelchair could exit. The door wasn't closing fast enough, so she hit the CLOSE button again.

"Come on," she shouted to the door. "Close!"

She rushed off after the door opened on the third floor, and approached the first uniformed person she saw. "My daughter, Tiffany Newsome, was brought here. There was some kind of accident. She's one of the four U of M students."

A doctor who was walking past stopped.

"Mrs. Newsome?"

"Yes. Where is my daughter?"

"Can we go somewhere and talk in private?"

"What's wrong? What's happened? Tell me. Is Tiffany okay?"

"I really think we should go somewhere in private."

"Just tell me!" she screamed.

"Mrs. Newsome—"

"Where is Tiffany? I want to see her right now."

The doctor paused, as if deciding whether to tell her or not. "Mrs. Newsome, your daughter suffered severe head trauma. I'm sorry to say, she's currently in a comatose condition."

"A coma?" She felt her heart drop as tears formed in her eyes. "Are you sure?"

"Yes."

"Where is she? I need to see her!"

"She's getting some more tests done. You should be able to see her within the hour."

"Where is my husband?" she asked as she looked around. "He's probably still downstairs. I have to go back," she said, feeling disoriented.

"You should take the elevator," the doctor said gently.

"Where is that? I can't remember," she asked as she rubbed her head.

"I'll go down with you," the doctor said as he walked down the hallway toward the elevator.

"Is she going to be all right?"

"We're going to do everything we can. Absolutely everything." He stopped at the elevators and walked into the one that had just opened.

"What about the other kids who were with her?" Danielle asked as she walked onto the elevator. "How are they? Her roommate and the football players . . ."

"I'm afraid I can't discuss their condition."

"Can you at least tell me if they're alive?"

"Yes, they are alive."

When the elevator door opened, she saw Allen in the distance. "Will you come with me to tell my husband about Tiffany? I know he'll have a lot of questions."

"Of course."

As they walked toward her husband, a woman approached them.

"Are you my daughter's doctor?" the woman asked.

Danielle's and the woman's eyes met. Much had changed. Their hair, their weight, the lines on their faces. But just as Lamont had said of Mia, their eyes were the same.

"Danielle?" the woman said.

What is happening? Danielle wondered. *Why is she here?*

"Mia? What are you doing here?" she asked in shock.

"My daughter was involved in a car accident. Why are you here?"

"For the same reason," Danielle said.

"The U of M students—"

"Yes, she was one of them."

"So was my daughter."

Suddenly, it all fell into place. "Your daughter is Alexa. Your daughter is my daughter's roommate?" Danielle asked as her eyes began to cloud with tears. It was starting to hit her even more. She was crying for her daughter as well as the cruel irony in their reunion. For years, she'd wanted nothing more than to see Mia and make amends. But not like this. Not through their daughters, and this terrible tragedy.

"How is your daughter doing?" Mia asked.

"She's in a coma right now."

"Oh my God." Mia held her stomach and stood doubled over. "How is Alexandria?" Mia asked the doctor. "What is her condition?"

"She's in surgery right now. She sustained a broken leg, but she has no substantial injuries aside from that, only a few cuts and bruises. She's going to be fine."

Mia took a sigh of relief, though Danielle felt it was inconsiderate of her to do so. It was wonderful her daughter was doing well, and Danielle was happy for her, but she was still considerably distressed by her daughter's much graver condition.

Allen approached Danielle, but the man with Mia kept his distance, seeming to linger in the background. Danielle was too busy worrying about her daughter to even notice him. She wouldn't have recognized Lamont anyway. It'd been over twenty years since she'd seen him.

"Our daughter is in a coma. She's in a coma, Allen," she said as she fell onto his chest sobbing. While Danielle was being consoled by her husband and the doctor, Mia and Lamont quietly drifted away to give them space.

Alexa was very restless as she lay in a hospital bed with her left leg elevated. She had been out of surgery for several hours.

"What happened?" Mia asked her daughter. "Did you see the car and the driver who caused this?"

"There was a car . . . a bright orange Camaro coming straight at us. It was going so fast and I was screaming and then Tiffany's car was hit and it started spinning and I just remember somebody helping me, taking me out of the car. I don't know who it was."

"That was me," Ordell said. "I helped get you out, and Carson got Tiffany out." He had just entered the room. Not a scratch or a bruise on him, except he had one bandage across his nose.

"Did you break your nose?" Mia asked.

"No, just scratches."

"Where's Carson and Tiffany?" Alexa asked.

"Carson already checked out."

"What about Tiffany?" Alexa said, suddenly sitting up. "Where is she? What's wrong with Tiffany? She's okay, isn't she?"

"She's in a coma," Mia said, holding her daughter's hand. "We have to pray for her to get well."

"A coma," Alexa said, her voice shaking. "I don't want her to be in a coma." Tears started to spill from Alexa's eyes.

"I know you don't, honey."

"Someone has to call her parents."

"They're already here."

"They are? But they live in Miami."

"Well, they're here. And they must've found out about it before I did, because they were here before I was." She turned to Ordell. "You-all are going to miss the game tomorrow."

"No, we're going to be there. Coach is flying us out tonight."

"You're strong to take a hit like that and be left with just a cut on your nose," Mia said to him, truly meaning it.

"I'm used to taking hits. All kinds," he said with a shy smile.

"Well, I want to thank you for saving my daughter's life."

"You don't have to thank me for that, Mrs. Glitch. Of course I would do that. I would do that for anybody, and especially someone I care about. I know you don't know me. And I'm not Chris, but I'm not a bad guy either. In fact, I think you might like me once you get to know me."

Mia's heart softened. "I need to apologize for being so rude. I feel like this whole accident is my fault."

"Your fault?" Alexa asked. "Mom, it wasn't your fault."

"You were just being protective of your little girl. I don't blame you for that," Ordell said. "You didn't know me."

Mia looked down at her daughter. "I'll always be protective of my girl." She squeezed Alexa's hand, then walked to the window to allow Ordell and her daughter a moment alone. She was overjoyed that Alexa was in a healthy, stable condition.

But she couldn't help thinking about the woman she'd once known better than anyone else, the woman she'd unexpectedly run into in the lobby. She had never expected to see Danielle King again. She wasn't sure she had entirely healed from the terrible betrayal twenty years ago that had ended their friendship. But now that Danielle was back in her life, she wondered where fate might take them.

Part Two

That's What Friends Are For

Chapter Twelve

September 1987

Danielle and Mia had graduated from Michigan State University three years earlier. Danielle had recently completed her manuscript and was persistently shopping for a literary agent with the aid of the most recent edition of the *Writer's Market*, a thousand-page bible for writers featuring thousands of listings of agents and publishers. She'd highlighted the contact information for Liza Schwartz, one of the top New York literary agents.

Danielle's English degree hadn't provided her with as many job options as she'd hoped for. She didn't want to teach like Mia. Didn't have the patience or the personality for the job. After nearly a year of job searching, Danielle had finally landed an entry-level clerk position at a life insurance company in Southfield, Michigan. But she was fired during her three-month probationary period after her manager discovered a floppy disk in Danielle's computer that she'd inadvertently left behind one evening. She'd been using company time to polish up her manuscript, and was in clear violation of corporate policy.

From there, she went to work for Apartment Search, a company that assisted renters in finding apartments by use of a computerized search and the rental consultants' expertise of the marketplace. Initially, she was reluctant, because the salary was a straight commission. But she did quite well after making some important connections with the human resource directors at many of the larger local hospitals. She began by assisting their medical interns in locating suitable housing. Before long, her commission checks were averaging ten thousand dollars. And Danielle got her first real taste of what it felt like to have money after putting nearly half down for the entry-level Mercedes-Benz 190. As comfortable as she was getting with the job and the money, she knew she'd need to make a move soon, because her office manager loudly announced during a staff meeting that he refused to manage someone who drove a better car than he did. "It could at least be American since this is the Motor City."

By this time, Mia was living downtown on East Jefferson at the Garden Court apartments in a spacious one-bedroom with one and a half bathrooms, which meant her company didn't have to traipse through her bedroom and use her bathroom. They could use the one in the hallway near the entrance. Danielle had helped her find the building, and she fell in love with it because of its sparkling hardwood floors and vaulted ceilings. Even if the outside area on the other side of the door in the kitchen looked more like a fire escape than a balcony and she never once stepped foot on it for fear it might collapse.

She worked at Pershing High School and took master's classes in the evening at Wayne State University. And for the first time in six years, she was single. She'd taken Lamont back after the incident outside the apartment with the other woman. And it seemed to work for a while, but he started pulling late hours at the restaurant. Then there were several nights when she couldn't reach him by phone. She was convinced he was cheating on her again, even if this time she didn't have any proof. So instead of putting herself through more heartbreak, she put an end to their relationship. They'd been heading in opposite directions for years anyway, ever since she'd graduated and expressed her desire to get married and start a family. Lamont wanted his own restaurant in New York City.

It was Friday evening, and Danielle and Mia had just caught the seven o'clock showing of *Fatal Attraction* on opening night. It was a movie they had both been highly anticipating. Finally, something that would scare men into being faithful. Now they were ending the night at one of their old high school stomping grounds—Olga's Kitchen.

"I hope every man goes to see this movie and realizes it doesn't pay to cheat," Mia said as she chomped down on her pita sandwich.

"I doubt one movie will change the minds of many men. I honestly believe it's in their DNA," Danielle replied matter-of-factly.

"Sounds like you're not impressed with your new friend anymore."

Danielle's nose twitched. "There's something about Ronald.

I'm not sure what it is. He's weird, though. Honestly," she said, slurping up her Orange Cream Cooler, "I wouldn't be surprised if he was married."

"How did you meet him?"

"I went through a dating service. They say that it's safer to meet a man that way, since they do screenings, but when I went in for my free consultation, all they wanted was my credit card. I have no idea how the woman got my name and number in the first place, but her office was like five minutes from my job, so I went. I wish I wouldn't have."

"Can't you meet a guy the old-fashioned way? You're blond with blue eyes and big boobs. Isn't that supposed to be the ideal for white men? Maybe it's your personality," Mia said teasingly.

"You may be joking, but yes, I think it is me. I'm picky. You know that. My mother just married any old thing."

"That any old thing was your father."

"If I ever get married, he's going to have to be hot with a good job and real potential. The only reason I did the whole dating-service thing was because my commission check was almost fifteen thousand dollars last month, and I figured, why not?"

"Wow, maybe I need to help people find apartments."

"July and August are always my best months. It's when all the medical interns start coming in. But I don't plan on doing this forever. Just until I can get an agent and sell my manuscript."

"So what are you going to do about your boyfriend?"

Danielle took out a key and twirled it between her fingers.

"Whose key is that?" asked Mia.

"His house. I snuck it off his key ring when he was pumping gas. Then I asked him to take me to the mall and I had a duplicate made."

"Where was he when you were doing all this?"

"Sitting in the mall people watching."

"Oh my God, you're like the woman in *Fatal Attraction*."

"I'm not that bad."

"That all depends on what you plan on doing with his key."

"Find out the truth."

A few hours later, Mia and Danielle were parked in Mia's car outside Ronald's house. "Let's think about this for a minute," Mia said. "You're about to go into the house of a man you believe is married, at close to midnight. The way I see it, only two things can come of that. Either you'll get killed or arrested."

"I don't think he's married, but I do think he's cheating, and he should've answered my calls. If he'd picked up the phone, I wouldn't be doing this."

Mia shook her head. "Maybe seeing that movie wasn't such a good idea. Whatever issue that character has, you must have it too. I can't believe I am helping you do this. This makes me an accessory."

"How soon we forget. Weren't you the one who made me sit and wait with you while you staked out Lamont when he was at the chick's apartment?"

Mia fell out in laughter. "I was so far gone then. Don't be like me."

"I just want to see him with the woman, and then I'll believe it. Isn't that what you said?"

"And didn't you say something like, 'But you already know the truth'? He is with a woman, and she's probably his wife. So let's just go home," Mia whined.

"Not yet. Not before I go in there," Danielle said as she tightened the belt to her black trench coat. "I just need to see for myself."

Still, as she tiptoed up the steps and eased open the door that led to a tiny hallway, she prayed that Ronald wasn't cheating on her. He was weird, but she liked him, because for him it wasn't all about sex. They hadn't even been intimate yet. And she liked that. After what had happened to her, she had hang-ups with intimacy. But now that she was ready to share herself with Ronald, he didn't seem the least bit interested.

She was nervous, because his stairs squeaked and she was certain he'd hear her walking up them.

After standing outside his closed bedroom door for a few minutes, she finally heard moans that erupted into grunts. Her heart started beating faster. It was thumping now. She put her hand on the doorknob and turned it slowly until she heard a faint click. She eased the door open and stood in the background of the candlelit room. She saw long, slender legs wrapped around his back. The woman was wearing fishnet stockings and heels, and no matter how fast he pumped or how loud he moaned, she just lay underneath him quietly.

"I'm coming, baby," he said.

Then he rolled off her, but her legs didn't move until he repositioned them and sat her up in the bed beside him to profess his love while he stroked the long blond hair away from her face.

Danielle flicked on the light. "What are you doing?" she said furiously. Then she saw what was really happening, and couldn't help but suppress a laugh. "That's why we don't have sex, because you'd rather do it with a doll!" He smiled at her, but didn't say a word. She shook her head and sighed. She probably would've been more prepared to find out that he had a wife than see him having sex with a lifelike doll. She tossed his key on the dresser and ran down his creaky stairs.

"So, what did you find out?" Mia asked after Danielle hopped in the car. "Is he married?"

"No, he's not married."

"Does he have another woman?"

"Not really."

"So what was he doing when you went in there? Did he see you?"

"He saw me. And I saw him having sex with a blowup doll."

Mia laughed uproariously. "He's a freak!"

"All men are. Let's get out of here," Danielle said in disgust.

"You have to admit, it is pretty funny," Mia said, busting into hysterics again as she sped off.

December 2010

When Allen left the hospital room to get Danielle something to eat for dinner, he returned so quickly that Danielle assumed he'd gone downstairs to the hospital's cafeteria. But he was empty-handed. A few days had passed and there wasn't any change in Tiffany's condition, and Danielle refused to move from her bedside.

He looked stunned. Like something had happened to him in the matter of minutes he was gone. "What's wrong?" she asked him. "Did the doctor tell you anything?"

"No, not the doctor. Marty called." Marty was Allen's longtime manager.

"Was he calling to check on Tiffany?"

"He wanted to make sure we received the flowers . . . and he thinks he has work for me."

"What kind of work?"

"A movie."

"Really?"

"It's a pretty big part. Marty thinks it could be my comeback role. They wanted me to fly out to read for it. But I told him I couldn't." Danielle searched her husband's eyes, and saw a hint of disappointment.

"Why did you tell him that, Allen? You should go." Since she'd been at the hospital, she'd started to feel different, less like her usual self. She was even soft-spoken again, like she was as a child.

"Go? How can I fly to LA when my daughter's in a coma?" Normally, Danielle would agree with him. But this was Allen's opportunity to prove not only to himself but to Danielle that he was a man who could stand on his own, as he had done for years before she'd come along.

Danielle released a deep sigh. "I want you to go. I know how important this is to you. And Tiffany would definitely want you to go too. I know that she would. You've been here every day, all day and night, right by her side for the past week. Go."

"But if I went and it worked out, they'd want to start filming. It's a tight schedule. I probably wouldn't get back until close to Christmas, and then I'd go right back out again."

"What do you mean by 'if'? I said you're going." She knew it was the right thing to say.

Allen left the next day. A part of her felt immediately lonely. She didn't realize it before, but even when they were fighting, she drew comfort from his very presence. He'd been a stay-at-home father and husband for so long now, she'd taken it for granted that he would always be there, available to her. Now it was just her and her daughter, who hadn't spoken or opened her eyes since the accident. She was tired of the false daylight the hospital's bright lights gave off, the hard seats, nurses coming in and out, and a doctor who didn't give her enough hope. The bathroom was large and sterile. The view from the window was of the parking lot. She used to look out and see Allen coming and going, but not anymore. For the first time in years, she missed her husband.

Later on the evening of his departure, Allen called to check in.

"There hasn't been any change," Danielle said.

"Have you been eating?"

"Eating is such an inconvenience for me right now."

"You need your strength so you can help Tiffany get stronger."

"I'll try to eat a little something. Don't worry." Her heart warmed at the show of true concern.

"I'm going to be back as soon as I can, at least to visit a few days, before the week is up."

"I don't want you to rush back. I want you to stay for as long as you need to, but just check in with me. I like hearing your voice."

"Of course I'm going to check in. I'm going to be calling every hour," he said, a rush of emotion in his voice.

"I love you," she said.

He hesitated. It had been a long time since he'd heard her say those three words and sound like she truly meant them.

"I love you too."

Danielle heard a knock at the open door. The curtain was drawn closed, so she couldn't see who was standing beyond it, but she saw the red-soled pumps.

"Come in," Danielle said, still seated at her daughter's bedside.

Mia pulled back the curtain. "Hi, Danielle," she said softly. "We won't stay long. I brought my daughter. She wanted to see Tiffany before she went to her physical therapy."

"Please, tell her to come in. She's welcome."

Alexa came in on a pair of crutches with Mia's assistance.

Danielle didn't want to stare at Mia, but then again, she did. They'd been the best of friends—the absolute best. But now she felt like a total stranger. More distant in fact, because she'd had total strangers come up to her to have their books signed that were warmer toward her than Mia was at the moment. It felt awkward. After the initial discovery that their two daughters were roommates, she didn't know what to say. They hadn't seen each other since then.

"Hello, Mrs. Newsome," Alexa said. Danielle stopped herself from making the usual name correction. "I'm sorry it took me so long to get down here, but I've been having a hard time with my leg."

"She has a metal plate and nine screws," Mia added.

"I understand," Danielle said. She wished it was just her daughter's leg she had to worry about, and not whether she'd ever regain consciousness again.

Alexa edged closer to the bed, her leg with the cast on it swinging back and forth as she stood still. She looked down at Tiffany and tears streamed down her cheeks.

"I've been praying for her," Alexa said.

"I appreciate your prayers. Please continue them."

Danielle had noticed that Mia was taking small steps backward. Was what she had done so horrible? Perhaps it was bad, but she could think of much worse. And besides, it had been twenty years, and wasn't twenty years long enough to forgive someone, especially given the circumstances?

Alexa stood over her for a few more minutes.

"She can't stand too long," Mia said. "But we'll be back. She has to come back for rehab once a week."

"Hopefully Tiffany won't be here too much longer."

"Like Alexa said, we're definitely praying for her." Mia had stopped in her tracks. Danielle wanted to tell her that she could come closer; she wouldn't bite. *It's me, remember?* she wanted to say. *Remember me, Mia. I've known you since I was fourteen years old. Remember me, Mia. Don't forget me. Don't push me aside. Pray for my daughter, pray for me.*

Danielle couldn't get up the courage to say the words. But before Mia left, she said, "Maybe I'll come up the day after tomorrow and have lunch with you."

"That would be nice," Danielle said lightly. "If you can." She didn't want to seem overeager, but now that Allen was gone, what she really needed was a friend.

Mia visited two days later for their lunch date. Danielle figured she needed to gather her courage as well. Now they were sitting in the cafeteria, and Danielle was staring down at a plateful of food she didn't want. She tasted a small chunk of the meat loaf. "Not good." She shoved her fork around the mashed potatoes and gravy. "The cafeteria at Glory was nicer than this one," she said.

"Hospitals aren't usually known for their food," Mia added. "But the bread is decent."

"Oh, honey, if you think this bread is good, where have you been going out to eat?" Danielle asked.

"I didn't say good. I said decent," Mia said tightly. "But I have had better," she said, softening her tone. Regardless of how she might have felt about Danielle in the past, she wouldn't wish her situation on her worst enemy.

There was awkward silence, each of them scanning the room to find anything besides each other to focus on. "Are you still friends with Bridgette?" Danielle asked. She was proud of herself for finding something to talk about.

"We used to talk on occasion. She moved to DC." Mia brightened. "Guess what? You know how she always said she wanted her husband to become the first black president?"

"She's not Michelle Obama. Unless she changed her name and grew about five inches."

"No, but her husband works for the Obama administration. He didn't become the president, but he's working for one at least."

Danielle nodded. "Not quite there, but impressive, nevertheless. How often do you two talk? Once a week, once a month . . ."

"I honestly can't remember the last time," Mia said, taking a bite of food. "We've gone more than a year without talking, actually. We've just naturally drifted apart over the years, but she used to forward me e-mail chains, which I detest with a passion. You don't send people forwards, do you?"

"My daughter and my husband are the only people in my life, really." Danielle lowered her eyes. "And my dog, Pulitzer, but he died." Her heart ached with a dull pain at the memory of her beloved schnauzer.

"I'm sorry to hear that. I know how much you love dogs."

"Yes, you do. You bought me my first one." They were quiet for a moment. "I'm surprised you cut your hair," Danielle said as if she'd just noticed. She'd noticed it the first time she saw her, but the only thing that had been on her mind was her daughter.

"I lost all of it when I was undergoing chemo."

Danielle's eyes widened. "Chemo? You had cancer?"

Mia nodded. "Eight years ago I was diagnosed with breast cancer. I'm in remission now, thankfully."

"Not you too. I feel like I know all there is to know about that disease. I had both of my breasts removed. You may have noticed they're much smaller."

"I read about it," Mia admitted.

"I did get implants, but I told the plastic surgeon I only wanted to be a B-cup."

Mia nodded. "I didn't have to get my breasts removed, but now I wish I had, and I still might. My health insurance won't kick in for another four months at my new job, which is enough time to decide what I want to do." Another moment of silence ensued. "How's your dad?" Mia asked.

"He died almost ten years ago."

"Oh, I'm sorry to hear that." Mia paused, but Danielle didn't say a word. "Did the two of you ever mend your relationship?" Danielle shook her head.

"What about you and your dad?"

Mia shrugged. "Maybe one day. But if not, I guess my life will go on."

"How are your parents doing?"

"Well, they're still together, living in the same two-family. My mom lives downstairs, and my dad lives upstairs. They seem to be doing fine with that arrangement, much better than when they were living together. Do you ever talk to your stepmom?"

"On occasion. She's not so bad. She still isn't my favorite person, but she's no longer my least. Her daughter dethroned her."

Mia laughed. "Are you serious? I never thought I'd ever hear you say something good about your stepmother. You hated that woman."

"Yeah, well, she fell on hard times after Dad died. Blew through his life insurance in no time, lost the house. But instead of getting depressed, she turned to God. She does a lot of missionary work. She's in Tanzania right now. It's like she's a completely different person at seventy-seven years old. And I can appreciate a total transformation like that. She even asked for my forgiveness."

Mia's eyes went wide. "I wish my dad would apologize, but I suppose in order for a person to do that, they have to feel like they've done something wrong. I don't think he feels like he did anything wrong."

Another long silence ensued. Their conversation was moving in awkward spurts, but Danielle thought they were doing a decent job of keeping things going.

"So I've been wondering, why were the kids on the highway so early in the morning?" Danielle asked. "I spoke to Carson, and he said their flight wasn't leaving until two in the afternoon."

Mia shifted in her seat uncomfortably. "I was upset with Alexa for bringing a guy home, and I definitely let my feelings be known to her. Honestly, in some ways, I sort of blame myself for the accident. I'm sure they left early just to get out of the house and away from me."

"Wait a minute," Danielle said as she lowered the small carton of chocolate milk from her lips to the tray. "So you mean to tell me that my daughter is upstairs in a coma because of you? You're the reason my daughter might die?" she said, her voice growing louder.

Mia looked stunned by Danielle's reaction. "I didn't know they were going to get in an accident," she said, her voice also rising a notch. "Obviously, I wouldn't want that to happen. My daughter was injured too, Danny."

Danielle's eyes were blazing. "Don't call me Danny. Only my friends call me that, and you stopped being mine a long time ago."

"Wow, do you really want to drag up the past? You act like *I* hurt *you*."

"You did. Much worse than I hurt you. Your daughter is going to live. Your daughter is already out of the hospital. My child is the only one still here. And she might die. And I'm sitting here eating and talking to you. For what? You still haven't forgiven me."

"Have you ever asked me to?" Mia snapped.

"I didn't do anything wrong," she shouted. And then she stood and took her tray of half-eaten food with her as she rushed back up to her daughter's room.

Chapter Thirteen

May 1988

"Guess what?" Danielle said as she stood inside a phone booth outside a wedding chapel on the Las Vegas Strip. "I just left a wedding chapel. I got married!"

"No, you didn't," Mia said as she walked with her cordless telephone from her living room to her kitchen, tossing her Chinese carryout cartons in the tall white garbage can. "Please tell me that isn't true."

"I did." She waved to a man standing outside the booth who had just winked at her.

"Danny, I know you're crazy, but I also know you're not that crazy. Now, why are you really in Vegas? Did you win a trip at Apartment Search for having the most rentals?"

"I just told you. I eloped, Mia."

"Danielle, please stop playing and tell me the truth. I'm not in the mood. Lamont is pissing me off, and I have a cold. I hate being sick when it's beautiful outside."

"I told you not to take him back. Every time you do, your life turns into a roller-coaster ride. You have your master's degree now. You got a good raise. You don't need him."

"Why are you in Vegas?" Mia asked sternly.

Danielle fell out in laughter. "God, Mia, you take the fun out of everything. Loosen up. I'm in Vegas for a writers' conference. I told you about it, but who knows where your mind was at the time? Probably on Lamont, or should I say on marrying Lamont."

"No, and we're not going to get married or be together much longer." Mia didn't like talking about Lamont. Danielle knew she was crazy about him, but also embarrassed that she kept going back to a cheater. But as Mia always said, there was no accounting for decisions of the heart. "So, just so we have this straight. You're not married, right?"

"No, so don't worry. You'll definitely beat me walking down the aisle."

"I'm not interested in beating you."

"There are so many literary agents here. Hundreds of them, but all I'm trying to do is get a meeting with Liza Schwartz."

"Who is Liza Schwartz?"

"She's a super-high-profile New York literary agent. She's the agent for some of my favorite authors, and they always say the nicest things about her in their acknowledgments."

"Go after her, girl, and just don't take no for an answer. It'll happen for you, Danny. One day you're going to become a famous author just like you always imagined. But promise me you won't let it get to your head. You'll always remember your best friend from Detroit. Won't you?"

"Oh, Mia, you always say that. You know I'm not like that. How could I forget my best friend? And you'll always be my best friend. And when I get rich, I'm going to do something real nice for you. Something you won't expect."

"Just write my name in the acknowledgments. That's all I want. I would love to see that. I'd show it around to everybody."

"That's a given. But I'm going to do something much bigger than that for you when I blow up."

"Well, why are you wasting time talking to me? Go find Liza and talk her into representing you."

Danielle looked at her watch. "I still have fifteen minutes before her workshop starts, and I'm so nervous."

"It's okay to be nervous, but don't be so nervous that you freeze up. And don't be late."

"I won't," Danielle said excitedly before hanging up.

Danielle had never seen Liza Schwartz in person. But based on the way other authors described her personality, she'd developed a mental picture of what she imagined she'd look like. The image she had of her was of a much older woman in her late fifties or early sixties, tall and slender. In reality, she was in her mid-to-late thirties. She wasn't slender and glamorous, and she was shorter than Danielle. In fact, Danielle felt a little awkward when she approached Liza in the hallway after her seminar, because at five-five in her flat heels, Danielle towered over Liza Schwartz.

"Mrs. Schwartz . . . excuse me—"

"It's Miss Schwartz. Why must everyone assume a woman is married? Some of us know better."

"I'm sorry. Miss Schwartz. I know you're a busy woman and you may not have time—"

She released a heavy sigh and said, "So if you know all of this, why are you bothering me?"

"I'm a writer—"

"You don't say. Why am I not surprised? Okay, give it to me," Liza said with a snap of her fingers.

"Give you what?"

"Let me hear it."

"Hear what?"

"Tell me what your book is about in one sentence."

"In one sentence."

"Give me your tagline."

"A tagline?"

"I'm waiting."

Danielle took a deep breath. She was ill prepared, and she felt it best to be honest. "I don't have a tagline."

"I'll tell you what," Liza Schwartz said as she dug out a business card from her purse. "When you figure it out, call me, but not before.

And have your entire manuscript typed in the proper format and ready to go."

Danielle walked into the elevator and pulled out a thick manila envelope from her tote bag. "Actually, I have it with me."

Danielle handed Liza her manuscript. "Is your contact information in here?"

"Yes."

"If I'm interested, I'll call you." Danielle got off the elevator the next time it reopened and smiled. At least she was one step further than she was before she arrived. She tucked Liza's business card inside her purse, and headed for the exit, her head held high.

"I want this so bad," Danielle told Mia over the phone later that day. She was sitting on the hotel bed in her flowered pajamas. "I don't have anything else. And this is exactly what I want. I don't want a husband or kids. I just want to write books. And that's all I've ever wanted to do since my mom passed."

"Keep writing. Don't wait for that agent to respond. Just keep writing. I heard an author say that the more she writes, the better she gets. So she writes twenty-five hundred words a day, and it's just like getting up and brushing her teeth. It's become so much of a habit."

"But you don't understand, Mia. I don't want anything else but this."

"I understand."

"Every man, including my father, has either hurt me or disappointed me. I can't rely on one of them to make me happy. I'm going to make myself happy. And you should too. Don't settle, Mia. Lamont isn't worth it."

Mia didn't respond.

December 2010

Despite the doctor's prognosis of a six- to eight-week recovery period, Alexa was headstrong and determined to return to school, which didn't make sense to Mia. It was one week before classes ended, and two weeks before final exams. Alexa's professors understood her situation, and were willing to allow her to take her finals at a later time during the spring term. But Alexa was the consummate student, and an incomplete, regardless of whether it was temporary, just wouldn't suffice. Her rehab was going well, and she felt she could simply continue it at the University of Michigan's hospital.

"I could've taken you to school," Mia said as she and Alexa stood by the front door. "You didn't have to have Ordell come get you."

"Your car is too small." Mia purchased a Kia Forte after her in-laws' cargo van stopped running. She couldn't really afford it, but she took money out of her one nest egg—her 401(k)—after she'd decided that it would be cheaper to buy a new car with low monthly payments than repair an old van.

"You like him, don't you?" Mia asked Alexa right as his Expedition pulled up.

Alexa nodded. "Yes, Mom, I like him."

"Chris is such a nice young man. What was wrong with him? Why didn't you like him?" Mia said, still unable to help herself, though she had to admit that Ordell was growing on her.

"Mom, I liked Chris, but sometimes you just know when a person isn't right for you."

"Or you think you do."

"Well, I'm pretty sure I do. Will you help me with my bags?" Alexa asked. Mia grabbed her daughter's purse and a bag that contained a comforter Mia had purchased for Alexa while she was in the hospital. Alexa had grown attached to it.

Mia walked behind her daughter and Ordell with the bags she was carrying to his SUV. As Ordell gently took the bags from Alexa's arms and led her to the car, Mia observed the young man. She would never fully understand why her daughter would give up a great catch like Chris, but it was Alexa's life to live, not hers, and she was happy that she'd found young love with another good man. *If only I could've been so lucky at her age,* Mia thought.

Mia stared at the TV and the investigative reporter in the dark suit and loud tie standing in front of their home. She peeked out the window, her eyes canvassing the perimeter. She didn't see a news crew, so it definitely wasn't a live broadcast. Maybe they'd filmed that segment for the noon broadcast and she was watching a rebroadcast.

Had she told any of the teachers her husband's first name? she wondered. She didn't believe she had. Not even Mr. Ross, whom she talked to more than anyone else. None of them knew where she lived either.

"You might recall the story we first reported last week on Frank Glitch—the man accused by federal regulators of fraud in the handling of several Detroit-area public pension funds. The Feds would like to talk to him to see what, if any, information he may have in the long-standing corruption that has plagued the city of Detroit."

Mia switched the channel. ". . . By all accounts Frank Glitch led a seemingly normal, albeit affluent, life. One neighbor described him as personable, another as a family man. But for the past three years, the SEC claims, Frank Glitch has been living off of the pension funds of City of Detroit retirees."

Mia turned off her television, but not before learning that her husband had been under a federal investigation since September of 2008—for just over two years. She held her face in her hands. Two years? By now her home phone and cell phone were both ringing nonstop. And Frank, who'd been released from custody forty-eight hours after he'd been arrested and headed straight to the hospital where his daughter had been staying at the time, was at his parents' home while he awaited trial. Mia didn't want him in her house because his presence drew local media. He'd explained to Alexa what had been going on, and apologized for the embarrassment and hardship he'd caused the family. He'd cried when she said, "I believe in you, Dad. I don't think you knowingly did anything wrong. I know it'll all work out."

Mia walked into the kitchen and sat at the table with her laptop open and Googled her husband's name. Nothing new came up. But after she'd included the names of his two business partners, she found a few articles she hadn't seen, including the Securities and Exchange Commission's twenty-six-page complaint.

Mia's eyes quickly read each word. Line for line:

> The Commission brings this action to stop an ongoing fraud by Frank Glitch ("Glitch"), an investment adviser, and Investment Professional Advisers, LLC ("Pro Advisers"), his private equity firm, against two Detroit-area public pension funds that invested $60 million in a private equity fund known as Investment Pro Advisory Fund I, LP ("Pro Fund"). Glitch and Pro Fund have misappropriated more than $27.15 million from the Pro Fund. . . .

If she hadn't already known that her life was changing, she had all the evidence she needed now.

Three days after Mia's daughter had gone back to school, she decided to meet Lamont after work at his house for dinner. She'd thought about canceling, but he was sending her messages on

Facebook several times a day begging to see her. He asked about Alexa frequently. Mia hadn't forgotten how he had been kind enough to drop everything he was doing to take her to the hospital the day of the accident. It didn't seem right to just ignore him.

"This is pretty good," Mia said as she sampled a little of Lamont's sweet-and-sour chicken. "It's no Hoy Tin or anything, but not bad."

Lamont smiled. "You loved that place, didn't you?"

"I just love the memories."

"Speaking of memories," Lamont said as he got up from the table, "I'll be right back." He walked out of the kitchen into the den and returned with a Polaroid.

"I stumbled on this photograph. It kinda made me laugh. Took me way back . . . back down memory lane," he said in a singsong voice as he handed her the photograph.

Mia took the photo from his hand and glanced down at it. "Look at us," she said with a smile. "We were babies. I was about twenty in this picture, and skinny. Poor thing, you must've felt sorry for me. No wonder you offered to cook for me. And the more I think about it, everybody was cooking for me back then."

"You're not skinny now, baby."

"No, I'm not. I probably need to lose weight."

"No, you don't need to lose weight. You're perfect."

She shook her head and continued to focus on the picture. "Not like I was back then."

He looked deeply into her eyes and said, "Listen, Mia. I know you're going through a hard time, and this might be one of the last things you want to hear, but . . . I made some mistakes, and letting you go was one of them." He leaned toward her, hesitating a moment before he connected with her lips, and the two began to kiss passionately.

"I've never cheated on my husband . . . ever . . . ," Mia murmured.

"He doesn't know what he has, but I do." He unbuttoned her blouse and kissed her neck.

She gasped and pulled back a moment. "Listen to you. Have you forgotten? You didn't appreciate me when you had me either. You cheated on me."

"I was an asshole, I admit it," Lamont whispered as he nibbled her earlobe. "But now I see all the mistakes I've made, and I know I can make it up to you. I want to make love to you, baby. . . ."

She closed her eyes while taking a deep breath. "I do have a husband." Even if they weren't living together and he'd be in prison soon, she wanted to honor her vows, because she always thought of herself as an honorable person.

Lamont pulled back. "Yeah, you do. And he's going to be serving time soon. And you need to figure out what you're going to do. Are you going to wait for him?"

Mia was filled with confusion. For the first time in years, she felt aroused, ready to be loved by someone. She knew it was wrong, and it went against her beliefs, but Frank had betrayed her, she reasoned. She fought to hold back hot tears, then a moment later calmly looked up at Lamont.

He stood, took her by the hand, and led her up the stairs and into his bedroom.

When Mia's eyes opened, she noticed natural light peeking through the sheer curtains. "Oh my God," she whispered. In a panic, she hurried out of bed and rushed to get dressed. "What time is it?" she asked Lamont, fumbling through her purse for her cell phone.

Lamont turned over, mumbling. Mia's eyes flew to her cell phone display. "It's eight thirty. I didn't go home last night, and I'm late for work." She shook Lamont furiously. "Wake up, I'm late for work!"

He sat up and tried to gain composure. "All you have to do is call your school and explain you're running a little late and you'll be there as soon as you can. Tell 'em you had car trouble—"

"I can't show up in the same clothes I had on yesterday."

"Why not?"

"I'm a teacher . . . you know, a professional who works with impressionable children. Do you honestly think they won't notice that?"

"Well, babe, you can't go all the way home to change."

"I know that." At least Frank wouldn't know she didn't make it home last night. She wasn't quite sure why Frank still mattered. He'd been such a big part of her past. She'd loved him once, even if she didn't love him now.

She couldn't bring herself to have sex with Lamont the previous night. It would be pathetic to allow her forty-eight-year-old self to take a trip back to her twenties. She couldn't ride that rocky Lamont roller coaster and brace herself for the big drop. She needed to close the door on that possibility forever. She knew she deserved something better. Something real.

Mia still couldn't believe she'd let an entire night slip past her. "I'm going to have to call in. And I just got back from taking time off for Alexa," she muttered, angry with herself.

"Good, another day we get to spend together," Lamont said, giving her a sexy grin.

"I'm going home," Mia said, smoothing her clothes and hair. She couldn't believe herself. She was being completely irresponsible about her job.

This isn't who I am, she thought.

"Long day at school yesterday?" Frank asked after Mia came through the garage door at a little after nine. He was waiting for her in the kitchen.

"What are you doing here? Why aren't you at your parents' place?" She'd started to ask him for his set of keys. But what right did she have to do that? This was as much her house as it was his, even if it was up for foreclosure.

"Do you know what I refuse to believe?" he asked in a strained tone. "That my wife would be running around on me."

"Frank, I don't feel like fighting today. I'm tired."

"From what?" Mia tried to walk past him, but he yanked her by the arm. "Where were you?"

"Frank, please let go of my arm," Mia said calmly.

"I will after you tell me where you've been," he said, tightening his grip.

"Where I've been is none of your concern any longer."

"Is that right? Since when did my wife stop being my concern?"

"Since your wife found out what you were really doing on your business trip," she spit out, yanking her arm out of his grip. "And since your wife found out you're a fraud."

"So this is about getting even."

She let out a deep sigh. "I'm just tired, Frank, okay? It wasn't about anything."

"You're tired? Didn't you have an opportunity to sleep? Too busy fuckin'?"

"Don't talk to me like that."

"Isn't that what you were doing? At first, I thought something might've been wrong, so I called the police—"

"Why would you call the police?" she said, her voice rising in panic. "All the trouble you're in, and you have the nerve to call the police."

"I'm in trouble with the Feds."

"Still, why would you do that?"

"Because I was worried. Because in the twenty years that I've been married, this is the first time that I didn't know where my wife was, and the first time she'd ever been gone all night, so I thought something had happened."

"What did the police say?"

"You're an adult. I had to wait seventy-two hours before I could file a missing persons report. So this morning I called your job."

"You called my job."

"I sure as hell did."

"And talked to whom?"

"I had to leave a message with Viv."

"Great . . . I called in this morning, and you called my job. I hope I don't get fired." Mia slammed her purse and cell phone down on the counter in frustration. "I'm sure you wouldn't care."

"Why wouldn't I? I know you need health insurance. I know the predicament we're in right now." He grabbed her arm again. "I went to your computer last night."

"My computer?"

"Let me give you some pointers on how to cheat."

"Oh, I'm sure you can—"

"If you don't want your husband to read your e-mails and Facebook messages, don't set up your accounts with automatic log-ins."

"So you went snooping."

"Isn't that what you did when you found the phone?"

"Actually, no, it isn't. Let me give you a few pointers. If you don't want your wife to know you have another cell phone, you should turn the ringer off. And if you don't want her to know you bought another woman a Mercedes that was more expensive than the one you bought her, pay your damn bills! *And* if you don't want the FBI to arrest your ass the day after Thanksgiving, don't embezzle over twenty-seven million dollars from pension funds."

He loosened his grip, allowing her to wiggle free, and she stormed off.

"Mrs. Glitch, please report to the principal's office," the secretary said over the loudspeaker as Mia sat in her classroom the next day.

"Ooh, you're in trouble," Chantel, one of her students, teasingly said. "You should've come to school yesterday instead of faking like you sick."

"All right, Miss Straight A, be careful there," Mia said, feigning a joking tone as she strolled out of her classroom and over to Mr. Ross's class. In reality, panic rose in the pit of her stomach. She knocked on his door. He was writing on the chalkboard, but immediately came to see what she needed.

"Can you keep an eye on my class while I go to the office?"

"Sure. Do you feel better?"

"Huh?"

"You called in sick yesterday, remember?"

"Oh, yes, right. Well, I feel one hundred percent better."

"That's good. I was worried about you. But I'll definitely keep a lookout on your classroom."

"Thank you," she said with a smile. She didn't need to turn around to confirm whether he was watching her walk, because not only did she feel his eyes on her as soon as she left his door, but she also heard one of his students say, "You're supposed to be watching her class, not her ass." She heard the sound of laughter as she walked down the hallway.

"What did you just say?" Mr. Ross said right before closing his door.

As Mia made her way to Viv's office, she wondered if she was in serious trouble. Policy was to call in an hour prior to the start of school so the office could make arrangements for an emergency sub. Mia had phoned in nearly an hour after school had started.

"I was called to the office," Mia said upon entering.

"Dr. Davis would like to speak with you," the secretary said.

Mia walked to Viv's office and knocked on the closed door. She waited until Viv motioned that it was okay for her to enter.

"I heard you were out yesterday. What happened?"

"I'm sorry. I wasn't feeling well, so I called in."

Viv studied her for a moment. "You can be straight with me. Right now I'm Viv from the book club, not Dr. Davis, because I'm worried about you. Frank called and left a long rambling message. He said you didn't come home last night, and he was worried. What happened? I didn't know if something had happened to Alexa or what."

"I already told you we're having marital problems," Mia replied, still not willing to tell Viv too much of her personal business. "It's just a difficult time right now."

"I can't even imagine. First, with the accident, and then with everything that's going on with his federal investigation. I know you must be a wreck. Do you need more time off?"

"No, it's best for me to work. Stay out of the house. After work tonight, I'm going to the hospital to visit Danielle and her daughter."

"How is her daughter doing?"

"Not well. I feel so badly, and I even feel partially responsible, but now is not the time to talk about that. I have to get back to class. I have Mr. Ross keeping an eye on my students."

"I don't know if Mr. Ross is trying to be funny or what. Did you mention to him that you were in a book club?"

"No, why?"

"He's bugging me about joining."

"What did you tell him?"

"He lives in Wayne County, and it's the Sophisticated Readers of Oakland County."

"We have members who don't live in Oakland County. He seems awful anxious to get in," she said suggestively.

"He doesn't know that."

"Speaking of which, how's it looking for the holiday party?"

"You'll be getting your invitation soon. Do you think you'll feel like coming? I know you have a lot to deal with right now."

"I do, but I need some distractions every now and then."

"Good. We're doing something really different this year, but I'm going to let it be a surprise."

"Okay, great. Works for me," Mia said as she stood. She knew

Viv was going to dissect everything she'd said about her marriage and ask her about it later.

Mia peeked inside the hospital room where Danielle's daughter was lying. Danielle sat right beside her. She had her head down, and she looked as if she might be praying. Mia didn't want to disturb her, so she walked around the floor of the hospital. The accident had brought them together for a reason, and Mia believed it was to deal with their past. She marveled at how it seemed to coincide with her entire life falling apart, and her and Lamont reuniting. But why should Danielle's daughter have to suffer? *Everything happens for a reason, but what is the reason behind this?* she wondered.

In the twenty years that they'd been out of each other's lives, there'd been only a few times that she thought of Danielle, which was understandable, given the circumstances of their falling-out. She had to admit, the anger and hurt were still there. She told herself that she was just playing nice by checking up on Tiffany, but deep down, she knew she was curious about Danielle. After their lunch in the cafeteria, she knew there was much more that needed to be said.

After Mia circled the room once, she peeped inside and saw Danielle seated at a table picking over her food.

She tentatively walked into Tiffany's room. "I can take you to get something to eat. I can imagine you're tired of hospital food. We can go to Olga's."

Danielle looked up in surprise. "You're tempting me," she said with a feigned yawn, as if it didn't matter to her that Mia was there or not. "But I really shouldn't leave."

"I can get you something and bring it back."

"You don't have to."

"I know. I don't mind. Do you want me to bring you back what you always ordered?"

"I can't even remember what I used to get."

"An original Olga with three cheeses, a spinach pie, and cream of broccoli soup."

Danielle laughed. "And an Orange Cream Cooler."

"That's right," Mia said with a smile. "How could I forget the Orange Cream Cooler? Well, I can go and come right back. There's one right here in Dearborn. It won't take me long. When are visiting hours over?"

"Either ten or ten thirty. Or maybe that's when the phone is shut off. I'm not sure since none of it matters. I'm here all night anyway." Danielle and Mia focused their attention on Tiffany, who was attached to several machines. "Look at her, Mia. It's not fair."

"Hello," the doctor said as he walked through the door. "Dr. Raji," he said to Mia as he shook her hand. "Miss King. No change in your daughter's condition right now. No movement at all. We're continuing to monitor her closely. The nurse has already bathed her, right?"

"Yes, I was here," Danielle said.

"I think you should go, get some rest, eat, and come back early in the morning," Dr. Raji said.

"I'd like to spend the night." She looked hesitantly at Mia. "But now that you mention it, I do think that getting out of the room for a little bit would really help me out. I guess I could go out to eat with my friend."

"Good. You need to get out for at least a couple of hours a day," Dr. Raji agreed. "So I will see you tomorrow."

After the doctor left the room, Mia said, "Are you ready?"

"Yeah, I'm ready. I just need to get my purse."

"And your coat."

Danielle's face fell. "I don't have a coat. I flew here from Miami, where it's eighty degrees. Dressing for Florida in November is a lot different from dressing for Michigan."

"You're going to need a winter coat, a pair of gloves, and a scarf. You remember what Detroit winters are like. I better take you to Macy's before we go anywhere."

"Oh, maybe I shouldn't even go. That's just too much to do."

They stood awkwardly together, each avoiding the other's eyes. *Why is this so hard?* Mia asked herself. "It's very cold out. I'll just run out to Olga's. I'll be right back." Mia took a sigh of relief as she stood in the elevator. She wasn't ready to sit down with Danielle again. She wasn't ready for any of it.

Chapter Fourteen

December 1988

Mia and Lamont had moved in together a year ago. Mia had justified it as a commonsense decision. Why pay rent for two apartments when they spent most of their time together? So Lamont had moved in with Mia. But her lease would be up soon and Mia was trying to figure out what she should do. Should she stay or should she go?

"Why do we go through this every holiday?" Lamont asked.

"Lamont, either you marry me, or we can stop this right now. This has been going on too long, and I feel like I'm wasting my time."

"Don't give me an ultimatum, babe. What we have is fine the way it is. It works."

"It's fine for you."

"For both of us."

She shook her head. "How can you tell me what's working for me? Lamont, I want to be married. I want to have kids. I'm almost twenty-seven."

"All that talk about marriage and kids makes you sound desperate. You're better than that. So what if you're almost twenty-seven?"

"My parents had been married for four years with a child on the way when they were my age."

"I know you don't want to do things the way your parents did them."

Mia took a heavy sigh. "If I didn't want it, I wouldn't be saying it. Where's my ring, Lamont? Where's the proof that you're serious about me?"

"Mia, marriage doesn't guarantee that two people are going to be together for the rest of their lives. Your parents are divorced."

"No, my parents aren't divorced. They just live separately. My mom lives in the downstairs flat and my dad in the upstairs one. You know that."

"So they're playing divorced like some people play married."

Mia shrugged her right shoulder. "I guess you could say that. But that doesn't mean we would be like them."

"We don't have to say 'I do' to commit to each other. I love you. Don't you believe me?"

Mia sighed and then nodded. "Yes, I believe you. But I still want to get married—"

"I'm not getting married, Mia. I've told you this a million times before."

"You're twenty-eight and you already know that you're not getting married?"

"Yeah, I do."

"But why?" she whined, desperate to change his mind. "What do you have against it?"

"You won't understand."

"Just talk to me. Tell me. Maybe I will."

"Losing my mother changed my entire life. I saw what happened to my father after she died. It was like he was lost, and so was I. I never wanted love to have that kind of hold on me."

"So your solution to avoiding hurt is to not love as hard?"

"I do love you, Mia. I just . . . I just don't love you the way you need me to love you . . . the way you want to be loved . . . and maybe not even the way you deserve to be." He avoided her gaze. "After all this talk, maybe I'm not the one for you."

Mia's eyes blazed in anger. "You're not the one? Is that how you feel?"

"If I'm going to be honest and not selfish, then, yeah, that's exactly how I feel. It's like I want you to be in my life, but I can't give you the things you want."

Mia stared at him, her face a placid mask containing her fury. "I see." She shrugged, feigning casualness. "Well, then, there's nothing left to talk about. I feel like I wasted seven years of my life trusting you and believing you when you said you only wanted to be with me. I forgave you and took you back after you promised you'd never be unfaithful to me again. I took a big risk because I thought you would come around on the marriage issue. I feel like I wasted my virginity on someone who's never going to commit to me fully."

"In marriage, baby . . . only in marriage. But I'm still committed to you."

"But marriage is something that I want."

"It's not something I want, though."

"Then I guess this is it."

He nodded. "I guess so. Besides, Mia, even if I wanted to, I can't get married right now."

"Why not?"

"Because by the end of next year, I'm going to be making that move to New York and I know you won't follow me there."

"You've been talking about New York since we first met, and aside from going to visit your cousins, you haven't moved yet. And you probably aren't going to, so stop making excuses."

"I'm not making excuses."

"You are. First you don't want to marry because of fear. Now it's about New York."

"Why can't it be all of those things?"

"Because it can't, and I'm just going to have to do what I have to do to be happy."

"I guess so."

He moved out by the end of the week.

Danielle called Mia, screaming with excitement, on Friday. "I can't believe it. I'm about to become a published author. Liza sold my book. My publication date is January 1, 1991. How cool is that? A new book for the New Year!"

"That's really cool," Mia said. She was genuinely happy for her, but for some reason she wasn't as happy as she pretended to be. When was it going to be her turn? When was she going to get what she wanted? She didn't want a book deal. She just wanted to be married and have children. Lots of them. Build a big mansion and fill it with nothing but the best of everything.

"That seemed really fast. I mean you just signed with her three months ago."

"She works fast, which is why I wanted her. You know how impatient I am. Liza is the best agent. And my book deal is the best Christmas gift ever. Something good always happens to me around the Christmas holiday."

"That's your mom, your angel looking down on you. It's good to have people in high places looking out for you. You should go to church with me on Sunday. You have to remember to thank God for your blessings."

"You go to church now?" Danielle asked.

"I will starting this Sunday. I've been neglecting God, and I need him to be on my side, especially after everything that has happened with Lamont. Do you want to go?"

"Are you going to a Catholic church?"

"Baptist."

"Why are you going to a Baptist church if you're Catholic?"

"I'm a lapsed Catholic. Anyway, Viv told me about it. It's her church."

"Viv?"

"She teaches with me at Pershing. She said they have a lot of nice-looking single men who are members, and a very active singles ministry. Supposedly a lot of women have met their husbands there."

"Mia, I'm going to need to write a character like you . . . a woman obsessed with getting married."

"I bet it'll be a bestseller, because there are millions more like me."

That Sunday, Mia made it to church. And she was proud of herself for getting up and out of bed in time for the early-morning service, even though she had to drive from downtown to the northwest side of Detroit. And even though she couldn't find her Bible and she was embarrassed to be the only one aside from small children not to have one with her. But the man sitting beside her shared his. And while she was walking to her car, which was parked in the large church parking lot, the man caught up to her.

"Excuse me," he said. Mia stopped and turned to face him. That's when she noticed how tall he was. "Is this your first time here?" He was a big guy. He was attractive in his own way, but not as handsome as Lamont. She was intrigued.

"Yes. Are you a member?"

"No, I'm visiting several churches trying to decide on one. It's time for me to settle down. I need to find a church home and a good woman. Not necessarily in that order either," he said in a light, joking tone.

"What's your definition of settling down?"

The man seemed startled by the pointed question. "Marriage. That's what I want. That's what I'm looking for. What about you? You're not married, are you?"

"No. Have you ever been married? Do you have any kids?"

He smiled. "No to both of those questions. I'd love to take you out to dinner. I've never met someone as direct as you, and I think we'd get along well. Do you think that would be possible?"

"Perhaps, but before we go out, I'll need to get to know you a little bit first. So, we can start by talking on the phone for a while." She wasn't about to make the same mistakes she made with Lamont.

"Of course, let me give you my cell phone number." Mia's eyes rolled, and he saw them. "What's wrong?"

"I don't have the best luck with men who own cell phones. Most of them seem to be trying too hard to be someone they're not. I mean, really, the average person can't afford one."

His broad grin broke as he laughed a hearty laugh. "I'm a businessman, and the only thing I'm trying too hard to do is to get to know the beautiful lady I sat next to at church." He scribbled his number down on a piece of paper torn from the Sunday program, handed it to Mia, and tipped his hat before walking off.

"What's your name?" Mia called after him.

"Frank Glitch," he called back.

December 2010

"I brought you some of my sweaters," Mia said.

"You're just trying to get me out of here, aren't you?" Danielle said, narrowing her eyes at Mia's gift. It was two days after Mia's most recent visit. "But I can't leave her. She's all I have, and I need her to come back."

"Danny, I mean, Danielle—"

"It's okay to call me Danny. I was mad that day."

"I know that Tiffany is going to get better. I believe it, and I also know that you have to rest. Take a break for a few hours."

"I guess I should rent a hotel so when Allen comes back, he can stay there at night if he wants." She sighed. "Why can't life just be perfect? No worries. That's all I want for my loved ones. No worries."

An hour later, Mia sat in the lobby as Danielle did a speedy check-in to the Embassy Suites. The hotel was so close to the hospital that Danielle could see the back of it from the window in the living room. She kicked off her shoes and got comfortable as she relaxed on the sofa bed in the living room of her one-bedroom suite.

"I feel better knowing how close I am to her." Danielle was struggling to keep her eyes open and focus on Mia. "Looks like I'm not going to finish my book in time . . . I've never missed a deadline. . . . I—" A moment later, Danielle was filling the hotel room with her snores.

She opened her eyes a few hours later, and Mia was still sitting in the same chair she was in before Danielle fell asleep.

"I'm glad you were able to get a little sleep," Mia said, sliding down the retractable reading light attached to the steel blue leather case of her Kindle, which she had been reading while Danielle was sleeping.

"My eyelids are so heavy, like they're about to explode." Danielle sat up and took a long yawn. "Were you here the whole time?"

Mia nodded. "I didn't want to wake you and I didn't want to leave just in case you wanted to go back to the hospital, but I honestly think you should rest tonight. You can call and check on Tiffany, give them the phone number to your room, and try to get one good night's rest."

"I'm actually too tired to argue right now. That was the best sleep I think I've had in twenty years. Maybe I will try to get some more of it."

"And you were on the couch. Just imagine what kind of sleep you'll get when you make it to your bed."

Danielle sat up on the sofa. "You're right. Thank you, Mia, for everything you did today. You didn't have to do any of it."

"I didn't do anything. I was just here."

"I know, and you being here meant a lot."

"Well, I'm a firm believer that doing good always comes back. So if you need me, call me."

Danielle took another long yawn. "I don't have your number."

"Oh, that would help," Mia said. She wrote her cell phone

number on a small pad resting on a table. "Hopefully Sprint hasn't cut it off, because I'm sure my husband hasn't paid that bill either," Mia said with strained laughter.

"Are you laughing because you honestly think it's funny?"

"I'm laughing, as my mother always said, to keep from crying. But it's going to be all right, because I have a job. And you don't know how truly thankful I am for it." She waved good-bye and headed out the door as Danielle settled into bed.

The next morning, Danielle took a shuttle bus to the hospital. There had been no change with Tiffany. Three weeks had already passed and she was starting to wonder if she'd ever open her eyes again.

"I decided to change it up a little bit," Mia said as she pranced into the hospital room with a thermal case. "I made us all some gumbo."

"Even Tiffany?"

"Especially Tiffany. My daughter did some research." Mia set down her thermal case. "And starting today, we need to start treating Tiffany like she's already present."

Mia set up the table in the room with her meal and three place settings.

"She went on the Internet, and there was a case of a woman who woke up after being in a coma for eight years. What stuck out is that her family recorded their experiences and let her listen to them."

"I can do that," Danielle said, brightening at the idea.

"Let me get Alexa on the phone so she can explain to you how it works."

Mia took out her cell phone from her purse and dialed her daughter, who answered on the first ring. "Honey, are you busy?"

"No, Mom."

"I'm at the hospital. I want you to tell Mrs. Newsome what you told me," Mia said.

Mia handed Danielle her cell phone.

"Mrs. Newsome, do you have a digital tape recorder?"

"Yes, I have one."

"I found an article about a woman who was in a coma and her family started taping messages to her and letting her listen to them, and eventually she woke up. So I spoke to one of the researchers here for the medical school. The practice is known as guided imagery. It's alternative medicine, but there has been significant evidence suggesting it works."

"I'm listening. Tell me what I need to do."

"I think you should mix in some affirming statements and say her name a lot. Like say, 'Tiffany, your father and I love you so much and we believe in God and know he's going to deliver you from this, and when you wake up, you can have a big slice of red velvet cake, and we can go hiking at Crater Lake—' "

"She told you about Crater Lake?" Danielle asked in surprise. "She was so young then."

"She loved that. She told me all about it. She said it's one of her happiest memories. Talk about things she loved. And sound upbeat. You might want to get some rest, because you sound drained, Mrs. Newsome," Alexa admonished.

"I'll get some rest," Danielle said with a smile.

"I pray for Tiffany every day."

"Keep praying."

They ended the call a few minutes later, and Danielle and Mia sat down to eat their lunch. They included Tiffany in their conversation, and while she couldn't eat the food, they had her plate out as if she were eating with them.

"For once I feel like I don't have to rely completely on the doctors. There's something that I can do," Danielle said.

Later that day, after Mia dropped Danielle off at the hotel, Allen called.

"I'm on my way back, I promise. I just have a few more auditions."

"Whatever you have to take care of, do it, but please be back here before Christmas."

"I'll definitely be back before Christmas."

"That's only a week away."

"I'll definitely be back. What are you up to?"

"I'm about to make a recording for our daughter that I'm going to play for her, letting her know how much we love her and are waiting to see her."

"That's a good idea. The doctor told you to do that?"

"No, Mia's daughter, Alexa."

"I keep forgetting you two knew each other. It's a small world. And she was your best friend?"

"At one time," Danielle said, not wanting to talk about it. "Will you record some messages for her too so she can hear your voice?"

"I'll definitely do that. I'll go out and buy one of those little digital recorders that you have."

After she ended her call, Danielle dug through her purse and found the digital recorder she used to record any book ideas that randomly popped into her mind. She climbed into bed and started recording.

"I don't believe I ever told you how much I love you. There was a time when your father and I didn't think we'd be able to have children. But then you came right along. In fact, you were born eleven weeks early. Our little preemie. I remember I was so scared that you weren't going to make it, but even then you were so strong. All those sleepless nights we spent with you in the special nursery at the hospital were so worth it. There were so many people going in and out—nurses, doctors, specialists, even a chaplain—and in the background the beeping sound of monitors attached to all those precious little souls. You were too premature to eat on your own, so your father and I would take turns feeding you through a little tube that ran through your mouth into your stomach. We'd take turns holding your tiny little hand, and as you got stronger, we were able to have real contact. Your father would unbutton his shirt and lay you on his bare chest, and then close his shirt to keep you warm. We took you home in a couple of months. You were a fighter then, and you're a fighter now. You've always been strong. Come back to us, Tiffany. We have your favorite red velvet cake waiting at home, and I won't nag at you for eating as much as you want."

* * *

The next day at the hospital, Danielle put earphones into her daughter's ears and pressed play on her digital recorder, which was programmed to run continuously. She sat in her usual seat beside her daughter's bed and waited. She didn't expect the guided imagery to work immediately, though maybe in some ways she was hoping it would. Around six in the evening, Mia arrived with leftovers.

"I made enough gumbo to last till the end of the year. Meijer had a sale on shrimp, but I'm out of crab legs. They didn't have a sale on those."

"Didn't you work today?" Danielle asked. Mia nodded. "You went all the way home and then came all the way here?"

"That's no big deal. I'd rather be here than in that big facade of a home."

"Then you should spend the night sometime at the hotel. I have double beds."

"Why did you get a suite with two beds? Do you and Allen sleep in separate beds?"

"God, no. Sex is the only thing we had left, really, but it's getting better now. The accident has brought us closer."

"That's one silver lining."

"Right now it's hard to see it that way, but I guess.

"So, catch me up to date. Are you still teaching at Pershing?"

"Oh, no, that's been years. Right after I found out about my breast cancer, I gave that up. At the time, Frank's business was doing well, and I became a stay-at-home mom. I'm at a charter school now."

"So what are you teaching?"

"Literature. My students read mostly classics."

"Do you love teaching?" Danielle asked as she paid close attention to a nurse who was attending to her daughter. Nurses entered the room frequently, which made Danielle feel good about the times when she wasn't there—knowing they were very attentive to her daughter.

"I love the responsibility of teaching. I feel honored to be among those shaping the minds of our youth, and I want to help them so they can make a difference."

"That sounded like a public service announcement."

"I know. . . . That's the problem. I mean, there's so much talk about teachers and what an honorable job we have. I'm afraid to admit that it's hard and the pay sucks and it's tough for me to remain motivated when I see kids ruining their lives. Some of them just don't get it, and may never. And I don't want to turn into Rochelle, one of the teachers at my school. I don't want to become that negative. But with everything I'm going through in my personal life, I can see it happening."

"Do you like your coworkers at least?"

"For the most part, but I'd be lying if I didn't say that some of them get on my nerves."

"That's not hard to do," Danielle said as she moved over to the table where Mia had set up their food.

Mia stood frozen with a Tupperware dish filled with corn muffins in her hand. "What is that supposed to mean?"

"It was a joke," Danielle said awkwardly. Perhaps they weren't quite there yet, she thought.

"I'm sorry," Mia said before taking a long sigh. "It's been a very long day at work."

They ate and talked for a little while longer, and then after Mia packed up her food containers, she said, "I'm going to go downstairs and pull the car around. I'll be out front waiting for you when you're ready." Mia had agreed to stay the night at Danielle's hotel suite.

After Mia left, Danielle walked over to Tiffany's bed, held her hand, and said, "Tiffany, I promise you I'll be a changed person if you just open your eyes and come back to us. I want nothing more in this world than to have you come back to me. Whatever you think I should do, I'll do—just please open your eyes. Please speak to me. I love you so much," Danielle said as her tears fell from her eyes to Tiffany's arm. She wiped away her tears and leaned over to kiss Tiffany. "Mommy will be back tomorrow, bright and early."

They wanted to be angry. But as Danielle and Mia watched the news report on the pretrial hearing for the driver who caused the "Post-Thanksgiving Crash," they started to feel some sympathy. Nicole Thomas, the driver, had been texting while driving, and while she was admittedly in the wrong, she was a good person from a loving and very close-knit family. She was a third-year student at the University of Chicago. Her mother owned a popular day care center and her father was an officer in the army, and a war hero.

On the one hand, she had been careless. The accident could've been avoided, and was definitely senseless. On the other hand, they could only imagine how scared she and her mother must've been when the crash occurred. And how much guilt they felt now.

"It's a sad day all the way around," a relative told the news reporter. "Six lives were lost in the accident, and this good family is destroyed, no matter what verdict the jury comes to. Nicole isn't a monster. Up until that day, she had been doing everything right. She was an honor student with a bright future. That could've been any of us. All she did was look away for one second to reply to a text. So before we judge this young woman's actions that day, let's remember that. Perhaps we can all learn a lesson."

The reporter held an earpiece to her ear, then looked into the camera. "Thank you for your statement, ma'am. I've just learned the state offered Nicole Thomas a sentence of fifty years in prison. But that plea has been rejected by Thomas. She is facing sixteen counts, including vehicular homicide, hit-and-run, and reckless driving."

Mia shook her head. "What if that had been Alexa driving? She's always texting."

"I've done it," Danielle said. "One time I had to swerve off the road. It's one of those things you think you can do quickly. Sometimes I actually ask myself how we ever survived without cell phones."

"But we did. Somehow we did. Life was so much simpler then. And I miss that simplicity," Mia said wistfully. "Without them, maybe we wouldn't be in this mess now."

Chapter Fifteen

February 1990

"What do you mean, she won't forgive me? She always forgives me," Lamont said as he sat in Danielle's car outside the Whitney restaurant, where he was a chef. In the backseat of Danielle's car was a bouquet of red roses that he'd bought for Mia and arranged for Danielle to pick up on Valentine's Day and present to her, along with a giant greeting card and a box of candy.

"Like I've been telling you, Lamont, she's not going to change her mind about you. It's been over a year since you broke up. I don't think you really have a chance with her," Danielle said. "But at least you know how to celebrate a girl's favorite holiday."

"Why do you say she's done with me?"

"I just know my friend, and I know that she's fed up. Haven't you noticed how she's been ignoring you all this time? It's not like

Mia isn't a beautiful woman and she can't find another man to love her."

"Why, is she looking?"

"If she is, it's not your business."

"Why isn't it my business?"

"You've hurt her a lot. I know that for a fact. You've cheated on her, and she has forgiven you. And she has never strayed."

"She keeps breaking up with me. Not because I'm a player, but because I don't want to get married. I told her that from day one. But you know how you women are. You think you can change a man." He looked over at Danielle. "What about you? Do you think you can change a man?"

"Most of the guys I've dated have been losers. I didn't waste my time trying to change them. I just left."

"Oh, yeah, like the guy with the doll—"

Danielle buried her face in her hands. "Mia told you that. I'm going to kill her."

"You can't tell her I told you. We have to have some things that we don't share with her if we're going to be close friends."

"Close friends?"

"Yeah, I mean, just because Mia and I aren't together right now doesn't mean you and I can't be friends. I've known you for as long as I've known her."

"You want to be my friend so you can keep tabs on Mia, and my loyalty is with Mia."

"But is her loyalty with you, though?"

"Huh?" Danielle asked.

"I'm just saying. I was with her for all those years. Not everything that came out of her mouth about you was positive."

"Lamont, are you really going to stoop that low? Don't try to turn me against Mia just because she's finally moved on."

"You probably don't even like Mia," Lamont said casually.

"What? Why would you say that? I love her."

Lamont arched his right eyebrow. "I just know how you women are. You call us dogs, but some of you-all are bitches." He looked at his watch. "My break is over. And if you really don't think I have a shot with her, why don't you keep the flowers and candy for yourself and just throw out the card?"

"Why would I do that?"

"Maybe I have a shot with you. I'll be over later," he said with a wink.

"That better be a joke."

"We'll see."

She knew Mia wouldn't have appreciated what he'd just said to her, and she wondered if she should mention it. But then she figured she was making a big deal out of nothing. He was the type of guy to flirt.

There was loud banging at Danielle's front door. It sounded like the police were getting ready to knock it down.

"Who is that?" the man beside her asked before he buried his head underneath the pillow.

"I have no idea," Danielle said as she slunk out of bed and into his white dress shirt.

"I have a doorbell," she hollered as she walked to the private entrance of her apartment and peeped out. "Mia," she said as she cracked open the door secured by a chain. Her heart rose into her throat.

"Open the door. It's cold out here. Hurry up. I've got something to tell you," Mia said, flashing an engagement ring.

"You're getting married?" Danielle said, looking over her shoulder nervously.

"Yes. He proposed on Valentine's Day."

"Who?"

"What's wrong with you? Open the door, please."

Danielle hesitated a moment. "Okay, hold on." She closed the door, removed the chain, and opened the door again. "Now, who are you marrying?"

"Oh my God, Danielle, his name is Frank, and he—"

"Wait, hold on. I've never even heard you speak about someone named Frank before. Where did you meet him?"

"I met him at that church I went to. Nice flowers," Mia said as she saw the two dozen red roses in a vase resting on her round glass dining room table. "Who bought those for you?"

"Just a friend."

"Well, it looks like we both found a love connection. Who's your friend?"

"Don't worry about him. Tell me about your engagement. I'm so happy for you. Are you happy?"

"What do you think? I'm ecstatic."

"Wait a minute—if you're already engaged, how long have you been dating him?"

"Almost a year."

"Almost a year? And you kept this from me?"

"I wanted to tell you about him, but after everything that happened with Lamont, I just wanted to be sure before I shared him with the rest of the world."

Danielle looked down. "Yeah, I guess that makes sense."

"I've found someone else who wants to get married, wants to have children, and is willing to wait until marriage for sex."

"So when are you getting married?"

"We haven't set a date yet, but soon. Probably before the year is up," Mia said, trying to walk past Danielle.

"This year?" Danielle asked as she blocked Mia's steps, leading her back toward the entrance.

"Yes, this year, and I want you in the wedding. Why are we standing in this little hallway? I can't come in? What are you doing?"

She fumbled for an excuse. "I was getting ready to do laundry."

"Okay, so since when can't I come in because you're about to wash your clothes?"

"I have company," Danielle whispered.

"Well, you should've said so. That's why you're acting so weird? Who is he?"

"He's just a friend."

"He's more than a friend if he bought you two dozen red roses. That's the kind of thing Lamont used to do for me."

"I'll call you later and tell you all about him."

Mia stared at her a little longer, then at the shirt Danielle was wearing.

"Why do you smell like Lamont?"

"What?"

She grabbed hold of her lapel and sniffed. "That's Cool Water. . . ."

"A lot of men wear Cool Water, Mia."

Mia grabbed Danielle's arm to examine the shirt's cuff.

"But they don't wear monogrammed shirts with the initials LS that I bought him for Christmas, you idiot."

Mia tried to get by Danielle, but she blocked her.

"Move out of the way," Mia said as she pushed her to the ground and headed for her bedroom. When she opened the door, she saw a man with his head underneath a pillow. She rushed over to the bed and snatched the pillow away. "How could you do this?" she screamed. Danielle couldn't tell if the question was aimed at Lamont or her. "How?" she asked, hitting him continuously with the pillow.

Lamont bolted upright in bed, throwing his arms up in self-defense. "Hold up, calm down. We aren't together anymore, remember?"

"So what? We were for seven years! And Danielle is my best friend!"

"Mia, what difference does it make? You're getting married," Danielle said weakly. She had regretted sleeping with Lamont the moment it happened. She had to defend herself somehow.

"Oh, you're getting married?" Lamont asked. "Congratulations."

"Danielle, shut up!" Mia screamed.

"Wow, it seems like we just broke up, and you're already getting married."

"We haven't been together for more than a year. I never ever, *ever* would've thought that my best friend and my first love would do this to me. I never would've thought that," Mia said, slapping at his arms.

He grabbed her arm, and she pulled away so hard that she fell to the floor.

"I hate you. . . . I hate both of you," Mia screamed.

"I really didn't think it would matter to you," Lamont said, trying to help her to her feet.

"Oh, shut up. I always knew you wanted to be with a white girl, a blond-haired, blue-eyed bitch," Mia spit as she ogled Danielle.

"It's not like that," Danielle said, tears spilling from her eyes.

"And you . . . I thought you were my friend!" Mia raised herself from the floor and headed for the front door. She flung open the door and walked out into the parking lot.

"Mia, you're getting married. If I thought you were still going to be with him—I mean, it was just a one-night thing," Danielle called out.

"Why would you want him, Danielle? He was my boyfriend. He was my first love. Why would you even want him?"

Danielle lowered her head. "I don't know. Things just started happening last night, and we got caught up in the moment. . . . I wasn't thinking. . . ."

"You were like a sister to me," Mia said as the tears fell.

"I still am. I love you like my family," Danielle said, pleading with her.

"Well, that explains everything, because I know how you feel about your family. Don't ever, ever, ever call me again!" she screamed so loud she lost her breath. "I hate you, and I mean it. I never want to see your face again, ever! I don't care if you're on your deathbed, don't call me. I believed in you. I was your friend, and would've been till the end," Mia said, sobbing uncontrollably.

"Mia," Danielle said as she grabbed the arm of Mia's coat to try to prevent her from getting in her car. "You're too upset to drive right now. Just calm down—"

Mia gritted her teeth and shook her head. "Don't touch me, you bitch!" She snatched her arm free, and wiped the tears from her eyes with the backs of both of her hands. "For the record," Mia said as she stood at her car with one foot inside, "he was sleeping with you to hurt me. I told him the one thing he could do that would really hurt me would be to sleep with my best friend. But when I said that, I was talking about Bridgette, because I didn't like the way he used to look at her. I never thought you'd do that to me. But I guess I was wrong."

Danielle stood crying in the parking lot of her apartment complex well after Mia had driven away.

December 2010

"Mia," she heard a man's voice say as she perused the fruit section of Whole Foods. She looked up and saw Chris Senior, the father of her daughter's ex-boyfriend, standing over her.

"Chris, how are you?" she asked with an unusually large smile.

"I'm fine. How's Alexa doing? I heard about the accident. I'm glad it wasn't any worse than a broken leg."

"I am too, but her roommate is still in a coma. In fact, I'm here doing a little bit of shopping for her mother, who hasn't been eating much. Do you remember Danielle from Glory?"

"Danielle, the one who was your best friend?"

"Yes, that's right. Her daughter, Tiffany, is Alexa's roommate. We didn't even know. I hadn't spoken to her in years."

"Looks like you gave her the same treatment you gave me," he said, gently ribbing her.

"I've spoken to you," Mia said in mock defense. "Your son dated my daughter for over three years."

"And in that time how often did we speak?"

"Here and there."

"Well, I won't hold it against you," he said, smiling broadly. "I wish Chris Junior and Alexa could've made it."

"I do too, but who knows what the future holds?"

An awkward silence fell over the pair, as they both no doubt thought of their brief relationship. Mia picked up an orange and placed it in her small basket.

"Just one orange?"

"It's for Danielle. I'm not even sure if she's going to eat any of this stuff."

"You're a good friend."

Mia shrugged. She didn't know what to say. Saying she wasn't really her friend would sound a bit insensitive, though true. She wasn't sure what they were.

"Well, I guess I better finish getting these things so I can head to the hospital."

"Don't let me hold you up." He hesitated a moment before saying, "Actually, Mia, I came up to you for a reason. I've just been thinking about you a lot."

"Me?" Mia was shocked. Why would Chris be thinking of her after all these years?

"I'm happily married, so I don't want you to think it's anything like that," he said as he observed the guarded look in her eyes. "I'm not sure if you do this, but sometimes I look back over my life. I'm happy where I am now, but sometimes I wonder, what if I'd done this instead of that?"

"What exactly are you saying?"

"I don't know," he said wistfully. "It's just funny how your entire life passes, and you don't even know it until you wake up, middle-aged and with grown children. I can still remember what it was like to be Chris and Alexa's age."

Mia smiled sadly. "I think about it all the time." A silence fell between them, before Mia closed the space and reached out for a hug, surprising Chris.

"I think the most we can do is look forward," she whispered before letting him go and walking away.

She stayed composed as she gathered up the last of the items she was taking to Danielle. But a part of her felt the sadness she had read in Chris's eyes.

"I can't believe you ran into Chris. No, what I really can't believe is that your daughter and Chris's son dated for three years. Isn't that cute?" Danielle said as she peeled the orange and began to eat it in sections.

"And he looks just like Chris. He isn't quite as tall, but Chris had a growth spurt, so he might too."

"And your daughter looks just like you," Danielle said with a sigh as she put a section of orange to her mouth. "Isn't life funny and sad sometimes? So what else has been going on? You told me about Bridgette. You told me about Chris."

"You haven't told me about Claire."

"And you're surprised? When did I ever talk about her? Long story short, she's the same person she was twenty years ago, perhaps worse. She even tried to sue me."

"For what?"

"Plagiarism. Copyright infringement. Whatever one chooses to call it. She was forced to drop the suit, or her attorney was forced to drop her when he realized she was broke and a liar."

Mia shook her head. "I guess I'm not surprised." Mia was wondering when it would be the right time to bring up what was on her mind. The reason they'd fallen out. She'd never had the opportunity to talk it out, because at the time she'd been so angry. But as she glanced over at Danielle's comatose daughter, she couldn't bring herself to dredge up the past. At least not there.

"Well," Mia said as she stood, "I'm heading over to my parents' house."

"Tell your parents that I said hello," Danielle called after her.

Mia sat in her car with her hands clasped together over the steering wheel. She was praying that God place on her tongue the right words to use, words that her father would receive sensibly. He was eighty-four years old now, but little had changed. In fact, he became meaner as he aged.

"Dad, I want to talk to you," Mia said after her mother had let her in the house and she went upstairs to her father's home.

"Talk to me about what?" he asked after letting her in and

moving back to the living room, where he was preparing for a prime-time football game.

"My childhood."

"Your childhood? The Eagles are about to play the Cowboys, and that's all I want to talk about. Michael Vick. Some people counted him out. But you can't always count a person out. They may be down, but that doesn't mean they're out."

"I wish you hadn't counted me out," she said suddenly. "You turned your back on me."

"All my kids had the same opportunity—"

"You never liked me. You never let me get close to you."

"What did I ever do to you?"

"You and Mom both beat me."

"You gonna sit here in my house and tell a bald-faced lie like that. When did we ever beat you?"

"When the nuns called you up to Holy Angels about Chris and me on the train."

"Okay, we spanked you for that, but we never beat you."

"Your spankings were beatings in my book, and you yelled at me all the time for no reason. You didn't care who was around. It was so embarrassing. And you were always so negative. No one was good enough. Not even your family."

"If I yelled at you, I had a reason."

"The doorbell ringing is a good reason?"

"So you didn't like my parenting skills. Now you've been a

parent for eighteen years and you've had plenty of opportunity to do what you want, so what's the problem?"

"The problem is you owe me an apology."

"Because you didn't like your childhood? I don't hear your brothers complaining. You're an adult now. Hell, I didn't like mine either. But did you ever hear me crying about it? My father didn't love me. But he was there. He worked and provided. And that should be good enough."

"All you've ever cared about was yourself. Not even your own wife."

"Well, I'm glad you married the perfect man who cared more about you than himself. Tell me, why are you moving out of that big fancy house of yours? There's a reason why your ass is driving a Kia instead of that big Mercedes-Benz. Because he cared so damn much. Isn't that right? You're almost fifty, and you're gonna have to start all over again."

"See, that's exactly what I mean. I wish I could forgive you, but right now I just can't."

"What do you need to forgive me for? For going to work every day and coming home every night, doing the best I could to provide for my family?"

"For turning the love I had for you into hate. For showing me that the love you had came with a price when it was supposed to be unconditional. You didn't even come to see me when I was in the hospital with cancer. What kind of father does that?"

"I don't like seeing people when they're sick. I like 'em when they're doing good and looking good. Why would you want a bunch of people around you looking at you and thinking about how bad you look? I don't want anybody feeling sorry for me."

"You've never made any sense to me."

"There's a reason I treated you different from my boys. You had a mother. Girls belong with their mother. And boys with their fathers. I don't have nothing to apologize for. I was a damn good father. There wasn't anything I did that you could come back thirty years later and complain about on a talk show. So I embarrassed you in front of your friends. So damn what?"

It was at that moment, as she walked away from him and back to her car to drive off, that she realized every wrong man she'd been with was because of her father. It was that truth that caused her to shed a few tears as she stopped on the corner at Dutch Girl for a dozen powdered doughnuts. To cry for the Mia she could've been, should've been—Mia Meyers, perhaps. Maybe the real reason she thought of Chris Junior as the son she never had was that she also saw him as the one she could've had if she'd realized she was good enough to be with a man who came from better means.

There was a knock on her closed classroom door. It was Mr. Ross. He pulled open her door and stepped inside, holding up a plastic grocery bag.

"May I join you? We all miss you in the teachers' lounge . . . even Rochelle," he said with a smile.

"Come on in," she said, offering a smile of her own.

He pulled in the chair he'd taken from his room and sat across from her at her desk. "If the kids see this, rumors are going to start flying."

"The kids and the teachers."

"True."

"So how's your book doing?"

"You know what? It did pretty good, I guess. I only printed a thousand copies, so I didn't lose any money. Did you read it yet?"

"I read most of it."

"And what did you think?"

"I was surprised that it was an autobiography. And that you'd gone to Holy Redeemer and Benedictine. Honestly, I only read it to find out the Catholic schools you went to, since you wouldn't tell me. I was thinking you may have gone to Holy Angels since you look a little familiar to me."

"I lived in Sherwood Forest, and I had a lot of friends who went to U of D."

"Did you know Chris and Mark Meyers?" Mia asked.

"I lived three houses down from them. My younger brother hung out with Chris. I was long out of high school when you started."

"It's a small, small world."

"It is." He looked down at Mia's gumbo. "I can't believe you're eating something other than tuna fish."

"I can't believe you've noticed what I eat for lunch."

"Tuna fish has a very distinct smell, and I actually can't stand it, so yes, I have noticed."

"Well, I'll be eating gumbo for a while now."

Mr. Ross looked at her curiously. "I noticed the change to your nameplate on your door. Are you divorced?"

"Separated," Mia said between bites of gumbo. "The divorce is coming soon."

"That's quite the life change. In three months, I'll be a grandfather. It will be a huge milestone for me." He paused, a gleam in his eye. "And if you go out with me, do you know what that would be?"

Mia paused, a slow smile crossing her lips. "What?"

He shook his head. "A great date. That much I can guarantee."

"Technically, I'm still married," she said slowly.

"I'm just asking for one date."

"Date? I'm forty-eight years old, and I'm going out on dates. I never would've thought."

"I was trying to be a gentleman. But we can skip the date and go straight to my house." He grinned, and Mia found his facial expression sexy. "Just kidding."

"I know you were joking. At fifty-six, you need to take a woman to get something to eat, or to a movie, to allow some time for your Viagra to kick in."

Mr. Ross laughed. "I could take you to one of the bathrooms like these kids do and prove your theory wrong." Mia's mouth dropped. "I'm just saying."

"What are you *just* saying, Mr. Ross? You sound like some of these kids."

"Yeah, sometimes I even find myself picking up things they say."

"So, Mr. Ross, if we went out, where would you take me? What sorts of things do you like doing?"

"I'm old-fashioned." He pulled a pen from his pocket. "I want to give you my phone number. The next time you want to go out to a show or something—not necessarily a date, just a movie and a bite to eat—please call me. We'll be two coworkers kicking it," he said as he wrote his number down on a piece of paper Mia had on her desk.

"Two coworkers kicking it. It has a ring to it." Mia took his number and put it in her purse.

The bell rang and interrupted their conversation. *I have to admit, he's fine for a short man,* Mia thought as she watched him walk out of her classroom. She absolutely loved his neat, long dreads that he wore pulled away from his face, and the fact that he was the complete opposite of what she'd always felt was her "type."

It was Saturday, December 18—the night of Viv's holiday party. Just three weeks after the car accident. *Sometimes you have to do things you don't feel like doing,* Mia thought. And tonight was one of those times. Mia slid into her black cocktail dress and studied herself in the full-length mirror inside her spacious closet. She was wearing the dress she'd worn last year to Frank's annual Feed the City charity that she used to chair. Five-hundred-dollars-a-plate tickets that were supposed to go to charity. But an investigative reporter at the *Detroit News* discovered none of it had. Instead, the money was used to fund expensive trips that he took his mistress on, and lavish gifts he gave her.

Even though she had a built-in excuse and was almost set to use it, she decided she would keep her commitment. Of course, Viv would understand that Mia had to spend the weekend supporting a dear friend from the past.

Viv knew their entire complicated history. She probably assumed they'd mended their problems from the past, even if they hadn't yet had time to discuss them. And Mia seriously doubted they ever would. Even though Mia definitely wanted to get everything out in the open. But how did you talk about the past under the present circumstances? Mia had decided to take a break from the hospital visits while Danielle's husband was back in town. She needed time to figure out how their relationship should progress.

She turned her mind to the present moment. She didn't want to go to the holiday gala, but she wanted to support Viv and the book club. She'd received an invitation in the mail that had been professionally printed at Mays, so she knew how serious Viv was about the party. The party was being cohosted with two other local book clubs at the Marriott Hotel in the GM Renaissance Center. They'd be dining separately beforehand, their book club at Forty-two Degrees North, another at the Coach Insignia, and the other at the Volt. The two-day event included a one-night hotel stay and free dinner and breakfast. Now Mia could finally see their fifty-dollar monthly dues being put to use. All she had to do was bring a Secret Santa gift, which she had purchased at Target.

She took one last look at herself in the mirror before heading out, and decided she looked too good to go alone. She fished Mr. Ross's phone number out of her purse and flipped open her cell phone.

"You're a little too rich for my blood," Mr. Ross said as he opened his car door for Mia. She'd driven to his east-side home and he'd convinced her to park her Kia in his garage so he could drive instead. He believed in chivalry. "I hope the PETA folks don't find out about this."

"I'm sure I'm way off their radar. I've owned this coat for years, and it's warm and looks good with my dress, so I wore it."

"Well, it doesn't look good with your Kia. And besides, my car still has the new-car smell."

"The Regal has come a long way. When did you get it?"

"Yesterday after school, which is the only reason I would agree to go to a ball with fifteen minutes' notice—so I have somewhere to drive my car," he said as he pulled out of his driveway.

"Thirty-five."

"Thirty-five what?"

"You said I gave you fifteen-minute notice, but it took me thirty-five minutes to get here."

"Oh, I thought you were trying to change your age from forty-eight to thirty-five," he teased.

Mia rolled her eyes. "Byron, sometimes, I don't know about you."

He winked as he looked over at her. "I just like to laugh and have a good time. Life's short, you know."

Mia nodded as her mind momentarily went to Danielle and her daughter.

When they arrived, they were both stunned. "Wow," was the first thing Mr. Ross said as they entered Forty-two Degrees North. "This has to have the best riverfront view I've ever seen. I've never heard of this place, have you?"

"It must be new."

It was a bright restaurant on the third floor of the Ren Cen that served regional Midwestern cuisine. It was decorated with vibrant colors, but the best part was the 180-degree view of the Detroit River and Windsor.

They took their seats at a table with Viv and her male friend and two other couples from the book club. She set her purse and Secret Santa gift on the cushion beside her, which provided comfortable enough distance between Mr. Ross and her.

She noticed Viv was looking at her strangely, and then it dawned on her that she probably hated the idea that he was there, not only because he was a teacher, but because she imagined him hustling his books at their event. Unbeknownst to Viv, he'd sold out and wasn't sure if he was going to reorder, look for an agent, or concentrate on other things.

"Maybe if you-all changed your book club name from Sophisticated Readers of Oakland County to something else that didn't sound so limiting, you'd have more members," Mr. Ross noted.

"Look around," Viv said. "We have more than enough members."

"Well, members that knew how to have fun. This is a stiff crowd." Mia laughed. She couldn't agree with him more. "I'd join if it was called something like Metro Detroit Readers. The 'Metro' encompasses all counties. Or Sophisticated Ladies and Gents."

"I don't like either name. Things will liven up. After dinner, all three book clubs are going to meet in salon room one for a reading by our featured authors, and then we'll have our dance, and mingle in the Ambassador banquet hall."

A few hours later, after Mia and Mr. Ross had danced a couple of times and he'd had a couple of glasses of wine, it dawned on Mia why she had wanted to drive to the event.

"I left my overnight bag in my car. This is an overnight event."

"I can drive back and get it."

"That's too much driving. I wouldn't want you to drive all the way home to get my bag, come back here, and then drive back to your house."

"You're right. As much as gas costs, I should just get a room here instead of driving back home after I get your bag, and we can have breakfast together in the morning."

"Gas is cheaper than a hotel room," Mia pointed out.

"True, but this is different. I'm paying for the experience."

"Okay . . . but I'd feel better if you let me go back to your house with you to get my bag. It's late, and you've had a couple glasses of wine. You might get sleepy. The last thing I'd want is for someone else I know to get into an accident."

"I'd love for you to accompany me." He looked into Mia's eyes and said, "What?"

"What?" Mia responded.

"You're giving me a look," he said with a smile. "That 'I'm feeling this guy' look."

"I didn't realize you're a mind reader," Mia teased.

As they got into Mr. Ross's car, she realized she was having the best time she'd had in years. For a few hours, her problems had stood still, and she was excited about the possibility of dating again.

Chapter Sixteen

December 1990

Mia followed the one-way road that circled Belle Isle's perimeter to a path not far from the glass-domed Anna Scripps Whitcomb Conservatory. She parked in front of a patch of rare shumard oak trees and waited. Minutes later, Lamont backed his black BMW beside her Chevy Nova, and the two talked from their open windows until the cold Michigan air finally took its toll on Mia.

She parked, and then zipped over from her Nova into his BMW, knocking rapidly on the glass. "Open it. I'm freezing."

He unlocked the passenger door.

"Did you lock me out on purpose?"

"I wouldn't do that," he said with an endearing smile.

She looked over at him. Where did she begin when he was her beginning?

"How could you? You stole my joy."

"How could I do something like that? It wasn't mine to take."

"Well, you did. You and Danielle both did. How could you sleep with her? She was my best friend."

"I don't have an excuse for what I did. Maybe I was hurt and I knew what I could do to hurt you back."

"I got married last week, and she wasn't there. And I always thought she was going to be my maid of honor. She was one of my closest friends. Why did you have to sleep with her?"

"This whole thing has been really difficult for me. You getting married. Why did you have to marry him?"

"Because I wanted to be married. You slept with her before you even knew I was getting married."

"I can't believe you married some man you met at church. A man you barely knew."

"What's wrong with meeting a man at church? It's better than meeting one in a club."

"Men go to church for the same reason they go to clubs. To pick up women."

"You weren't going to marry me."

"Well, who's to say in time I wouldn't have changed my mind?"

He turned up the radio when "Memory Lane," by Minnie Riperton, began to play.

"You wouldn't have." Mia turned away from him as the music played. "I have to go—"

"Go where? Back to your husband at the Westin?"

"How do you know where we're staying?"

"Your father told me."

"Why am I not surprised?"

"You married the wrong man. I would've at least taken you over to Windsor for your honeymoon so you would've felt like we went somewhere."

"I have to go," she said again as she pulled up his automatic lock, which he immediately locked again.

"I'm sorry that I slept with Danielle. I did it to hurt you because you had hurt me, but I have no idea why she would do it."

"Let me out."

"Just like I have no idea why you would do what you did."

"Let me out. It was a mistake to agree to see you." Mia exited the car, slipped into her own car, and pulled away.

December 2010

For the first time in three weeks, Danielle had eaten a full meal. And it was hospital food of all things: steak with mashed potatoes and gravy, string beans, and a fruit cup. Allen had brought it up from the cafeteria. Alexa had called and said it would be good for them to eat in Tiffany's room, that the smell of food could help wake her senses. At this point, they were willing to try anything.

Around ten at night, they left the hospital and headed back to their hotel. After Danielle showered, she sat on the edge of the bed and said, "Mia's being really nice."

"Why wouldn't she be? Didn't you say she used to be your best friend?"

"She was, but that was then and this is now, and now is a different story altogether."

"What is the story to begin with?"

"Have you ever done something you regretted?" She took a deep breath and blurted out, "I slept with her boyfriend. Well, her ex-boyfriend, but still—"

"You slept with her boyfriend?"

"Ex-boyfriend. I didn't mean to hurt her. I can't explain to you why I did, but I know I'm paying for it now."

"What do you mean?" Allen asked, squeezing Danielle's arm.

"I'm a believer in karma, and I really feel that God is trying to tell me something. Why would he bring our two daughters together and have hers walk away from the accident while ours is left in a coma? I'm being punished," she said as tears streamed down her face. "It's like a slow death—first Pulitzer, then the lawsuit, now this. I just feel so worn-out."

"God isn't punishing you," Allen said softly. "This is life. Things like this happen, and they're out of your control. But if you're looking for redemption," he continued, "you might want to talk to Mia about it."

Danielle considered his words. "Thank you for being here for me, Allen."

"Where else would I be but with my family?"

"I just hate to think about you leaving again so soon. When is the movie being filmed again?"

"Next month, but if Tiffany isn't any better, I may have to pass on it."

"We've talked about this. You're sticking with it. You've been there for Tiffany when I was traveling and promoting my books. Now it's my turn to watch over her. And your turn to focus on your career."

"There will be other roles."

"How do you know there will be?"

"I want to be here."

"And you will be in spirit. Promise me."

"I promise you."

"What are you promising?"

"That I won't pass on the role, Danny."

They embraced. What would she do without him? she wondered. He was the first man she'd ever met that she trusted. She'd forgotten over the years what had drawn her to him. Now she remembered. He would do anything for her.

It was Sunday—bright and early—when Dr. Raji entered Tiffany's hospital room. Danielle was awake. Allen was curled up under a blanket with his eyes closed as he sat in an oversized chair near the window. Danielle shook Allen awake as the doctor stood before them, a grave look on his face.

"I'm sorry, but there's no more that we can do. Her brain was so badly injured that she will either be brain-dead or she will pass away slowly."

"How can you say that?" Danielle said, her face turning sheet white. "You're a doctor, so save her. Save her. Please."

"I'm sorry. There's about a one to two percent chance that she could recover and be a functioning adult. Right now, the machines are keeping her alive."

"Don't tell me that you're sorry. Why don't you learn how to save people so you won't have to apologize to their family? I want someone else, another doctor—"

"Mrs. Newsome," Dr. Raji said, "we have done all we could, but I'm afraid the swelling won't stop."

"Just leave. Get out. You don't care. I want someone who cares. One to two percent is better than no chance at all. Tiffany may be in that one to two percent."

The doctor walked out of their daughter's hospital room.

Allen held Danielle in his arms as she cried, gently stroking her back, and kissing the top of her head.

A chaplain entered the room and said, "Danielle, you've had your daughter for eighteen years, and now it's time to give her back to God."

Danielle shook her head. "No disrespect to God, but I'm not ready to give her back, and until I hear God say I have to, I'm keeping her right here with me."

An hour later, Danielle went downstairs to the chapel and knelt inside one of the pews.

"Dear God, I've always been a better written communicator, but this time I'm going to try something different. When my mother died, I was so mad at you and I told you that I hated you, but I didn't mean it. I just didn't want her to go. She was the one bright spot in a house that was so dark. She was good, and I didn't understand why she had to die. She loved all people. When you took my mother, you sent me a friend. I say you sent her because she was everything I was taught to hate. She showed me that everything my father had tried to teach me about people was wrong. I loved her, but I hurt her and expected her to forgive me. And when she wouldn't, I figured it didn't matter because you blessed me in other ways. I could barely stand to lose her. I can't lose my daughter too. I can't lose Tiffany. I will spend the rest of my life in service to others. I can't lose her. Please, I'm begging you. Don't take my daughter away." With that, she burst into tears.

Chapter Seventeen

January 1991

Danielle's smile brightened the bookstore—a smile that fell off quickly once she realized the petite black girl with long hair entering the Farmington Hills bookstore wasn't Mia after all. She was hoping Mia had purchased a copy of Danielle's first novel, *Private Lies*, read all the kind words about her in the acknowledgments and dedication, and decided to show her support by attending Danielle's first book signing. But, unfortunately, that wasn't the case, and Mia never showed.

Next month would be one year. One year since she and Mia stopped communicating. When Mia said she'd never speak to her again, she proved she was a woman of her words. All of Danielle's attempts to reach out to her went unanswered. She didn't have Mia's new telephone number or address, but she assumed, since she'd written her two letters and they weren't returned to her, that they were forwarded to Mia's new address. Danielle had even called Mia's mother trying to get her new phone number. But Mrs. Marks sounded unusually distant when she said, "I'll have to speak to Mia first before I release her personal information." This prompted Danielle to assume that Mia must've told her mother the awful thing Danielle had done. Danielle had rushed off the phone, because she couldn't bear the thought.

Danielle thought back to their blowout. After Mia had left her apartment, she had stormed into her bedroom and told Lamont to leave.

"You used me to get back at Mia, because you wanted to hurt her," Danielle accused him.

"How was I supposed to know she'd come here this morning? You opened the door when you didn't have to. I mean, who opens the door when there's trouble on the other side? If you want to be mad at anyone, be mad at yourself."

And she was, but the show had to go on. She'd quit her job at Apartment Search. Not because she was overly confident that her first book would do well, or because she'd been given a huge advance. In fact, she wasn't really sure how her first book would do, and she hadn't received a staggering advance. It was much less than she earned annually at Apartment Search. But she had to commit all her time and energy into becoming a successful author. She no longer had a best friend. She didn't have a man in her life. Her father wasn't supportive of her, and never had been. All she had was her imagination. The mind she used to craft characters was the same mind she was going to use to concentrate on becoming a successful author.

Halfway into her twelve-city book tour, she received a call from Liza while she was stretched over her queen-sized bed with her heels kicked up enjoying *Oprah*, waiting to leave for her evening signing in downtown Denver.

"I have some great news that I know you're going to be excited about."

"What?"

"I hope you're ready for this."

Danielle's heart started pounding. She didn't know what Liza was calling to say, but she never called with bad news.

"Danielle King is a *New York Times* bestselling author."

Danielle screamed so hard that she was afraid the hotel management might ask her to leave.

"Are you serious?"

"Oh, honey, I wouldn't lie to you about something like that. Congratulations. This changes the playing field, because not only are you a *New York Times* bestselling author, but your book is coming in at number three."

"Is that good?"

"Is that good? Your first book coming in at number three on the *New York Times* bestseller list is great. Not that I need my job to be made easier, but when it is, I'm able to focus on other things for my clients, like movie deals."

"Movie deals? Are you kidding me?"

"No, I'm not kidding you. Do you know who I am? I'm a deal maker. And guess what? I *got* you a movie deal."

When Danielle ended the call, she felt relieved. God wasn't punishing her. Her prayers were being answered. But her heart felt heavy. She had no one to call with her good news.

December 2010

"Mom, do me a favor?" Alexa asked Mia over the phone as she walked into the house.

"I'd do anything for you, my dear."

"Can you take my Rosetta Stone CD to the hospital so Tiffany can listen to it? From what I understand, it would also be useful for her brain to be challenged, and what better way than to learn a new language?"

"No problem, I'll do it."

"Today, right?"

"I'm not sure I can do it today. I literally just walked in from a two-day book club event."

"So you're dressed, which means you can do it now."

"I'll try."

"I'll be home on Saturday for a week and a half. I'm so excited. I get to see you and Dad and visit Tiffany. I just know she's going to pull out of this. I just know she is."

"Do I need to come up there to get you this Saturday?"

"No, Mom, I already told you that your car is too small. I have a ride."

"Don't bring home any company."

"I thought we got past that."

"We did, but I still don't want you bringing home any company."

"What if it's Chris?"

Mia smiled wide. "That would be different."

"You have such a double standard."

"Is it Chris? Don't play with me."

"No, Mom, it's not Chris. Sorry."

"Then don't bring anybody."

"I won't. Now, don't forget to take Rosetta Stone to the hospital today."

"I'm doing it as soon as we get off the phone. Is there anything else?"

"She's really smart, so take level two and three."

"Has she ever taken Spanish before?"

"She took French, and the two languages are similar. She'll be fine."

"Whatever you say, madam . . . Will there be anything else?"

"That should be it for now. If I happen to think of anything else, I will definitely call you."

"You do that."

A few hours later, Mia headed over to the hospital. "I come bearing gifts from Alexa. She ordered me to the hospital with her Rosetta Stone Spanish course. I even bought this old portable Sony CD player and went to Best Buy to get a new set of earphones."

Danielle started crying in Allen's arms at the sight of Mia.

"Did I do something wrong?" she asked, putting down her packages.

"No, of course not. We appreciate it, and we will use it."

"Why is she crying?"

Allen rubbed Danielle's back. "They want us to give up on her."

"What do you mean?"

"They think we should just give up on her," he said in a shaky voice. "They say the swelling won't go down in her brain, and she has a minuscule chance of survival."

"No. Doctors don't know everything. You can't give up on your child. Don't listen to them. Alexa is getting information from a U of M researcher who is top in her field. I say you should try everything, but whatever you do, don't give up on her."

Danielle raised her head. "I'm not, but I wish they hadn't told me that. I was so encouraged the night before. I could've sworn I saw her pupils move, but the doctor said I was probably just imagining it."

Mia handed Danielle the box set of CDs and the CD player. "Try this. Alexa said it will be good for Tiffany's brain to be challenged." Danielle tearfully took the gift, and Mia squeezed her shoulder. "Don't worry, it's going to be fine. Have faith."

It was Christmas Day, and Mia was at the hospital looking out the window at the snow, which was piled so high she knew there was no way she and Alexa would be driving home that night. This was Alexa's bright idea. "Drive me to the hospital. I have some gifts for Tiffany," she'd said. That was hours ago. They'd come bearing a red velvet cake that Alexa had asked Mia to bake with one day's notice and none of the ingredients at home. But Ordell had gone to the store and returned with everything Mia needed, saving the day, and then he left to stay with an older cousin who lived in Detroit, which made things even better for Mia.

Mia hadn't been back to see Danielle since the day she dropped off the Rosetta Stone CDs, and she felt a sense of relief. Mia hated phoniness and she didn't want to pretend everything was perfect between them, but she also wasn't rude enough to bring up the past at a dire time like this. Still, after passing a few hours with Danielle and Allen in Tiffany's room, she was starting to go stir-crazy. It was only a matter of time before she blew her lid.

"I can't get over how sweet you are," Danielle said to Alexa. "Where did you buy this beautiful cake?" she asked as she slid another slice onto her paper plate.

"My mom made it."

"When did you start baking? Is it a box cake?" Danielle asked, chuckling to herself.

"No, it isn't. It's from scratch. I know how to bake," Mia said in a huff.

"Since when?"

"Twenty years is long enough to learn a lot of things I didn't know before," she snapped. "But as a matter of fact, I knew how to bake a red velvet cake when we were friends. Lamont convinced me to take a culinary class. Did you forget about that? I'm sure you haven't forgotten about Lamont? Or have you?"

Everyone went quiet. Allen was the first to speak up. "Hey, Alexa, I think we could use some cocoa to go with this cake. Would you like to help me bring a few cups down from the cafeteria?" Alexa nodded, and the two hurried off.

"You've never once apologized," Mia said, as soon as the door closed behind them.

"But I did, you just didn't want to hear about it," Danielle retorted. "What more do you want?"

"I want to hear you say it and really mean it. I want you to explain to me why you did it."

"I'm sorry," Danielle said. "I'm sorry, I'm sorry, I'm sorry." Her voice rose higher with each repetition of the refrain, becoming hysterical.

"It's not enough! You hurt me, you really—"

"Can I have some red velvet cake?" a small voice whispered, cutting Mia off.

"Did you hear that?" Danielle asked. "Who said that?"

They both turned around and stared at Tiffany.

"Just one piece, I promise."

Danielle broke past Mia and rushed over to Tiffany's bed. She was lying in bed with her eyes open.

"Can you hear me?" Danielle asked Tiffany.

"Yes, I can hear you. I was trying to sleep, but you were yelling so loud you woke me up. I want some red velvet cake, and you said I could eat as much red velvet cake as I wanted."

"You can eat the whole cake if you want to. Mommy doesn't care," Danielle said as tears poured forth and she ran her hands over her daughter's hair and face.

"Where am I? This looks like a hospital. Why am I in the hospital? Is that Mrs. Glitch standing there?"

"Yes, it's me," Mia said as she rushed over to her bedside. "Alexa's here too. She'll be back in a minute."

"And your daddy," Danielle chimed in. "You don't remember what happened?"

Tiffany shook her head slowly.

Mia ran to call the doctor into the room. Minutes later, Allen and Alexa returned with cups of hot chocolate. As soon as he saw Tiffany sitting up, Allen dropped the hot cocoa on the floor, and Danielle threw herself into Allen's arms.

Once Danielle untangled herself from Allen, she turned to Mia, and they knew. They both knew. Suddenly, the past didn't matter. They clung to each other and cried for Tiffany, for the years they had missed together. Everyone cried, and when they couldn't cry anymore, they laughed from sheer happiness. Tiffany was too weak to eat the red velvet cake, but they sat by her bedside as long as they could. They were in awe of the miracle each of them had witnessed, and they wanted to bask in its glow forever.

Chapter Eighteen

January 2011

It was mid-January. A cold breeze dusted Mia's shoulders, and even with a cable-knit throw wrapped snugly over her, she still felt a deep chill. One week earlier, Frank had received a guilty verdict, and today he'd been sentenced to serve three years in federal prison. While Mia didn't attend the trial or the sentencing hearing, she was informed by Frank via phone while she was in the process of moving into a quaint one-bedroom apartment downtown. She'd gone back to her first apartment complex, Garden Court, which she'd loved so much, but discovered it had been converted into condominiums. So instead, Mr. Ross told her about Grayhaven Marina, which had an entrance right off Lenox Street, the same street he lived on. They would carpool. She smiled at the thought.

Tiffany was expected to make a full recovery. Her speech was slightly slurred, but she was undergoing speech therapy. Just as amazing as coming out of her coma was the fact that she was now proficient in Spanish, which they could only assume was a result of the Spanish CDs she'd listened to continuously for a full week.

"What's wrong?" Mia asked. She could always tell when Danielle had something on her mind that was troubling her.

Mia and Danielle had just come back from lunch at Olga's. Danielle had invited her up to her suite to talk, but she wasn't saying anything. They sat on opposite ends of a sofa, mostly silent.

"How do you think you're going to like your new apartment?" Danielle asked.

"I think it's going to feel strange in some ways, but in other ways it's going to be a new start for me. I just have to really budget."

Danielle hesitated a moment before sliding something across the sofa cushion between them. "I want you to have this." Mia saw that it was a check made out to Danielle, which she'd signed on the back.

"Why are you giving this to me?"

"Because I want you to have it."

"This check is for two hundred and fifty-seven thousand nine hundred and sixty-eight dollars."

"And eighty-six cents. It's one of my smaller royalty checks."

"I can't accept this."

"Yes, you can. I won't even miss it. In fact, I just found it last night when I was cleaning out my purse. It's been in there since the day we left on our Key West trip. So for almost two months."

"I can't," Mia said, handing it back to Danielle.

"Why . . . why can't you? I can afford to give it to you. I want to give it to you. You're my friend, you're struggling, and I'm not, so why won't you let me help you?"

Mia held on to the word "friend." Ever since Tiffany had woken up, they'd been trying to put their friendship back together. It wasn't easy. In fact, it was a daily struggle. But they were both willing to try.

"But we . . . you and I . . . we could've been the best of friends," Mia said as her eyes clouded with tears. "You could've been Alexa's godmother. We could've had so many stories to share with our daughters." She stopped once her emotions got the best of her. She sat swiping her tears away with the back of her hand. "I just wondered what would make someone do that to me who was supposed to be my best friend. I want to know why."

Danielle let out a heavy sigh. "I want you to forgive me."

"I forgave you a long time ago. . . . I had to, for myself. I forgave you after I got diagnosed with breast cancer, because I felt like I'd been carrying around this hate for you for so long that it had made me sick. Still . . . I just don't understand, Danielle, why you would do that. I mean, what was your reasoning for it? Even if I had moved on, he still should've been off-limits. I had been in love with him for years, and a real friend doesn't ever cross that line."

Danielle hesitated. "Mia, I'm just going to be honest with you—"

"I want you to be completely honest with me," Mia said in a rush of words.

"You always feared that I would change if I became successful, but every time you were in a relationship, you were the one to change. In high school and college, we were so close, but after college we started drifting apart. You didn't even tell me about Frank until you were engaged. You used to tell me everything. Instead, you shared everything with Lamont, including my business."

"Your business?" Mia said, a genuine look of confusion on her face.

"Yes, you told Lamont all of my business."

"I didn't tell Lamont all of your business."

"You told him a lot of it . . . all of the things I didn't want him to know. I know, because he told me."

"So you slept with Lamont because we weren't as close, and because I may have told him a few things about you? Is that what you're telling me?" Mia said, her temper rising.

"Just hear me out. I don't know why I slept with him. I guess because I wanted to. I was attracted to him. You weren't with him any longer. I didn't want marriage at the time. He didn't either. He was telling me what I wanted to hear. It just happened—"

"No, Danielle, it didn't just happen. He came over to your apartment to sleep with you. You played his game, and he won. We were the ones who lost out. And he hasn't changed. He's still fine, but full of it."

Danielle grimaced while shaking her head. "That's the perfect description for him. And to this day I feel ashamed for what I did to you."

"You let a man come between us. Granted, you and I drifted apart, but not that much. We still talked on the phone almost every day, but you were working. I was working. We weren't kids anymore. Of course things were going to change."

"I have no excuse for what I did. I regretted it from the moment I did it. The only solace I had was that I never intended for it to happen. I was certainly never going to do it again. Mia, I've thought about you and missed you so much over the years. I know it's going to take time, and that I can't buy your love. I don't want you to think that's what I'm trying to do by giving you that check. But I do want us to be friends again. Start taking trips and enjoying life again. Will you at least consider it? I know you've always believed that everything happens for a reason. And after all these years, here we are."

"There's a part of me that wants to give the check back," Mia said as she held it in her hand, "but then there's this larger part that really wants to keep it because, in a weird way, it ties us together. I understand and believe you've changed. And so have I. I used to be obsessed with money. Now I'm not. I just want to be happy."

"Take the check. Don't feel beholden to me either. It makes me feel good that I can help you. I had a lot of things given to me in my adult life, but the one thing I never had was you, my best friend. And you know what else I'd like to do? Plan a trip for this summer," Danielle said brightly.

Mia's face beamed. "Now, that would feel like old times."

"Only now we don't have to spend years saving up for it."

"Where do you want to go?"

Danielle shrugged. "I don't know. We'll just have to take some time and think about where we'd like to. I'll do some research."

"How long are you going to be here?"

"A few more months while Tiffany is rehabilitating. I don't want to rush and fly her back to Miami before she's ready. I want her to get a lot stronger first, so I'll probably take out a short-term lease at an apartment near the hospital."

"You're welcome to stay with me. I mean, after all, you're paying for it."

"Mia, I don't want you to feel like that."

"It's true. I'm grateful to you for this gift. Thank you."

"You're very welcome. That's what friends are for."

"Let's start thinking about our trip. You can bring Allen."

"I would, but I can't. He was offered two movie roles. He's filming one now and he has another one that he'll be filming over the summer. It'll have to be a girls-only trip," Danielle said with a sly grin.

"Nothing wrong with that," Mia said, her heart full of happiness.

When Mia pulled in front of her parents' two-family flat, her dad was outside shoveling the snow. He had his back toward her.

"Don't you think you're a little too old for all that manual labor?" Mia asked after she got out of her car. He completely ignored her. She didn't notice that he was wearing earphones until he yanked them out. They were attached to the iPod she'd bought him a couple of years earlier. The one gift she'd given him that he actually made use of.

"I guess you're back to tell me how much I messed you up. How much you hate me, huh? Well, save your breath, because I heard you the first time."

"No, Daddy, I'm here to say that I forgive you."

"You forgive me?" he asked with a chuckle as he staked the ground with the shovel. "Is that right?"

"I realized that what you did to me back then was the best you knew how to do, and even if I know it wasn't right, I realize that you honestly don't see anything wrong. I can spend the rest of my life angry and bitter and blaming you for every bad decision I've made and every wrong man I was involved with, or I can forgive you, take responsibility for my part in it, and move on. Put the past where it belongs."

"I didn't do anything wrong to you, girl. You were just too sensitive."

"Whatever the case may be, I want you to know I forgive you. And I do love you."

A silence passed between them. "And I accept your apology."

Mia chuckled as she shook her head. "I'm glad I'm forgiven."

"Did you lose weight? You look kind of skinny."

"Ten pounds. I'm almost where I want to be."

"Don't lose too much. You can't get a man being skinny. And since the one you had is in prison, I figure you might be in the market for one, right?"

"Kind of," Mia said as she walked onto the porch and into her parents' house. "Kind of." She thought of Mr. Ross. The two of them had started seeing each other outside of school quite often.

They enjoyed each other's company, and had more in common than their love for the written word. They were both at that age of maturity when they knew exactly what they wanted, and despite being hurt in the past, they still believed in true love. She didn't know for sure, but she was fairly confident that their relationship would blossom into something serious, and soon.

After Mia had already made it into her parents' home, her father said, "You should eat while you're in there."

Mia walked out of the house back onto the porch. "Daddy, guess what?"

"What?"

"This skinny girl loves you. Now eat that."

He smiled, which was something Mia rarely saw him do. "All right, you got me. I'll leave you alone now."

"You don't have to leave me alone. Just love me back, Daddy. . . . Just love me back. Is that so hard?"

"Girl, you know I love you." Mia ran down from the porch into her father's arms. "And I'm sorry if you didn't know I did, but I always did. And you're going to be just fine. The worst is over."

On her ride back to her new apartment, Mia phoned Danielle, who seemed to answer her cell phone before it even rang. She was bored, waiting for Tiffany to return from physical therapy. Her recovery was going well, but she was having a little trouble keeping her balance.

"I know where we can take our vacation," Danielle said excitedly. "I've had nothing but time to think about it. How about

Acapulco? Wouldn't that be fun to go back there? We can sit out on the balcony and eat banana splits while we watch the cliff divers. We can even go shopping at the flea markets. Do you still have your charm bracelet? I still have mine."

"I do still have my bracelet, but we're not going back there. This isn't about reliving our past. It's about creating new experiences. We have to find a place neither one of us has been to."

"In that case, let me take out my iPad and start searching. I'll get back to you."

"Take your time doing the research, because I want to have fun."

"I am the queen of research. It's what I do, after all."

"In that case, I can't wait to see what you come up with."

Before Danielle hung up, she said, "It's really good talking to you again, Mia. This is definitely a new experience, and one I'm truly thankful for."

"I am too, Danny. I am too."

Starting over was working out better than Mia could've imagined. The worst was finally over. She was leaving the past behind, but she would hold on to the memories. She felt more content than she had in years, because she had finally embraced the one thing she had struggled against her entire life: forgiveness. For Danielle. For her father. For herself. It truly was a new day.

Remember Me

Cheryl Robinson

A CONVERSATION WITH CHERYL ROBINSON

Q. What do you feel Remember Me *is about, and what inspired you to write it?*

A. The book is about family, friendship, and forgiveness. The story is one that may have some readers reminiscing over their high school and college days because it spans thirty-four years and several generations. As for what inspired the story, the car accident was the starting point for the novel. I knew the turning point was going to be an accident before I knew the whole story. And I knew the accident was going to be caused by someone texting while driving. Usually, my inspiration is sparked by a character, but this time it was an event. Then it became a matter of deciding how big of a role I wanted the accident to play in the story. In earlier drafts, the accident played a much bigger role, and even included a story line from the point of view of the distracted driver. But the story was losing its focus. An underlying message was how a split-second decision changes lives. There were several incidents of this, from Danielle's decision that ultimately destroyed a friendship, to the boys' decision to beat up Fenton Phillips, and then of course the accident.

Q. Why did you decide to make Danielle a writer and Mia a teacher?

A. Danielle definitely struck me as someone who would become a writer, given her family background and the fact that she internalized a lot of things. I pictured her using writing as her form of expression after the loss of her mother, and as a means to escape her mean-spirited family. It was also very exciting that she was a successful author because it was as if I could live out my own dream through one of my characters. Mia being a teacher grew more out of familiarity. My mother is a retired schoolteacher. My sister's best friend is a teacher, and I went to school with several people who became teachers. Thankfully, the occupation fit with her personality, because if it hadn't, I would've changed it.

Q. Why did you decide to make Danielle's father prejudiced? And why make the friends of different races?

A. When I started talking to my sister about her racially charged high school experiences, I knew that bigotry often starts in the home. So even though Danielle, a white girl, befriended Mia, a black girl, I still wanted to show her going against what she was taught. I think the only reason she wanted to go against that was because her mother wasn't prejudiced, and after her mother's death, she saw her father in a new light. I imagine it would be difficult to think otherwise if both of your parents felt that way and you were raised with hatred toward certain groups. Danielle knew it was wrong, and she wanted to develop her own opinions. Even though race relations have come a long way in this country, with race we still have a lot of improvement to make.

Q. Were any of the characters or events inspired by anyone you knew?

A. While I was writing the novel, my dog, Pepper, also a miniature schnauzer, died, and I was so hurt. He'd been with me for almost twelve years, and he was the best little dog. Writing him loosely into the story really helped give me some sense of closure, but I still miss him greatly.

Also, my sister attended an all-girls Catholic high school in Farmington Hills, Michigan, in the mid-1970s. She was a member of the Spanish National Honor Society, and went to Mexico with that group. The sterling silver charm bracelet was something she bought for me, which I loved so much that I wore it every day. They also had to attend a retreat because racial tension was at a high at that time, and there had been a fight in the cafeteria, so some of that was loosely based on her high school experiences.

Q. Have you ever had a best friend become a perfect stranger? If so, can you share what happened?

A. For my first two years of college, I attended Howard University, and I had a very close friendship with a girl who was from the Maryland area. Most of our spare time was spent together. She tutored me in accounting because I was a creative type, and assets, depreciation, credits, and debits just didn't gel with me at that time. I truly thought we would be friends forever. But then one day, our friendship was over and I didn't understand why. I found out later, by watching the evening news, that something very difficult had happened to her. Though my situation wasn't the same as Mia and Danielle's, I used that experience to shape my portrayal of a friendship gone awry.

Q. Irresponsible text messaging caused the car crash at the heart of the book. Was there a lesson you hoped to convey?

A. I wanted to draw attention to what I see as a real problem in our increasingly fast-paced and hectic lives. A split-second decision can change the course of someone's life, sometimes for the worse, so we should all work harder to avoid those kinds of situations. But though I feel this way, I tried to convey the message with a certain amount of empathy, which is why I chose to have Mia and Danielle forgive the driver.

Q. This is the sixth novel you've published with New American Library, and the seventh novel you've written. How has the writing process evolved for you?

A. The writing process has evolved for me in many ways. I used to write with a page-count goal instead of a word-count goal. Then I listened to a Nicholas Sparks interview, and he talked about how he works with a two-thousand-word-count goal, and that was an aha moment. I can't tell you how much better it became writing toward a word count instead of a page count. For me, I'm always in danger of overwriting. I have the reverse of writer's block. I don't want to stop. But writing to a word count helps me curb that. Writing is hard work. You are the writer, but you still need to establish enough distance that you can look at your work from the point of view of a reader, while allowing yourself to become each one of your characters. With this book, I was able to establish enough distance so that when I received my manuscript back from my editor and she had suggestions for me to cut scenes and revise others, I wasn't resistant to it. I could see exactly what she saw. I'm very thankful to my editor, Jhanteigh Kupihea. Some of her comments are brutally honest, but I always look forward to reading them, because I realize at the end of the process it will make for a better story.

Q. What do you enjoy most about writing?

A. I love being able to use my imagination to create characters that I really want every reader to enjoy. I love when I'm at the start of the process and I get to discover who these characters are and what issues they're going through that I may or may not relate to. And I like learning as I write, because I do research on subject matters. I love when I'm able to discuss the book with book clubs and it's a lively discussion, and I get to experience the characters coming to life in their minds. I get to understand how other people think, and whether or not they view situations the same way that I do. I remember growing up listening to my mother discuss these people and all the drama they were going through. I thought these were real people, but I quickly found out she was talking about people in her soap opera. I wanted to create characters that my mother and others would become just as enamored of. So now my mother reads my books, and she talks about the characters and what they're going through, and I love that.

Q. What are you working on next?

A. Well, I'm always working on something. I just started outlining a new novel that centers on two women who don't know each other, but are both overcoming huge obstacles, and who come together by circumstance. As I'm outlining, it doesn't appear that this book will be set in Detroit, as so many of my other novels have. This one seems more suited to a small Southern town. And there are quite a few unique supporting characters popping up.

QUESTIONS FOR DISCUSSION

1. What is your overall reaction to the novel? Can you relate to the characters and their situation?

2. In the author's words, the novel is about family, friendship, and forgiveness. What do you think about the development of Mia and Danielle's friendship over the course of the novel? How does their past dynamic compare and contrast with their dynamic after the reunion?

3. How do you feel about Mia's and Danielle's past and present relationships with their families? What type of relationship did they seem to have with their daughters?

4. Discuss Danielle's and Mia's husbands. What did you think of them? Would you have been more supportive of Frank? Do you feel he was innocent, as he claimed, or guilty of the charges? How do you feel about the issues that arose in Danielle and Allen's relationship?

5. Growing up, did you have any close interracial friendships? How did they compare with the relationships in the book?

6. Have you ever had a best friend turn into a perfect stranger? Please feel free to share details.

7. Are there times in the novel that the characters behaved in ways that made you dislike them? When did those moments occur? If so, could you understand why they behaved that way?

8. One of the major turning points was the car accident, which was caused by a driver who was distracted by texting. From early on, the novel establishes that there can be life-changing ramifications due to split-second decisions. Have there been any split-second decisions that impacted your life in a real way?

9. Mia and Danielle both had issues with their fathers. What do you think caused the rifts between the women and their fathers, and how did you feel about these relationships? Do you feel their relationships with their fathers affected their feelings about men in general, and their husbands in particular?

10. Discuss the parallels that you may have noticed in the women's adult lives despite the fact that they had been separated for twenty years.

11. Given Danielle's family history with breast cancer and the fact that her first agent, Liza, also died from the disease, Danielle decided to undergo voluntary breast removal. What do you think about the choice she made?

12. Would you have been able to forgive Danielle if you were Mia? Why or why not?

13. Did you feel *Remember Me* was more a story about Mia or Danielle? Why?

14. At the end of the novel, Danielle's daughter, Tiffany, makes a miraculous recovery from a comatose state. How did you feel about that? Do you believe in miracles? Have you, or anyone you know, personally witnessed one?